Book one of the Sundering

MALEKITH

A Tale of the Sundering

Gav Thorpe

A BLACK LIBRARY PUBLICATION

First published in Great Britain in 2009 by
BL Publishing,
Games Workshop Ltd.,
Willow Road, Nottingham,
NG7 2WS, UK

10 9 8 7 6 5 4 3 2 1

Cover illustration by Jon Sullivan.
Map by Nuala Kinrade.

A CIP record for this book is available from the British Library.

ISBN 13: 978 1 84416 610 7
ISBN 10: 1 84416 610 4

Distributed in the US by Simon & Schuster
1230 Avenue of the Americas, New York, NY 10020.

See the Black Library on the Internet at
www.blacklibrary.com

Find out more about Games Workshop
and the world of Warhammer at
www.games-workshop.com

Printed and bound in the US.

WELCOME TO THE
TIME OF LEGENDS

THE WARHAMMER WORLD is founded upon the exploits of brave heroes, and the rise and fall of powerful enemies. Now for the first time the tales of these mythical events is being brought to life in a new series of books. Divided into a collection of trilogies, each will bring you hitherto untold details of the lives and times of the most legendary of all Warhammer heroes and villains. Combined together, they will also begin to reveal some of the hidden connections that underpin all of the history of the Warhammer world.

THE LEGEND OF SIGMAR

Kicking off with *Heldenhammer*, this explosive trilogy brings Sigmar to the foundation of the Empire.

THE RISE OF NAGASH

Nagash the Sorcerer begins the gruesome tale of a priest king's quest for ultimate power over the living and the dead.

THE SUNDERING

The immense, heart-rending tale of the war between the elves and their dark kin commences with *Malekith*.

Keep up to date with the latest information from the **Time of Legends** at *www.blacklibrary.com*

More Time of Legends from the Black Library

· THE LEGEND OF SIGMAR ·
Book 1 – HELDENHAMMER
Graham McNeill

· THE NAGASH TRILOGY ·
Book 1 – NAGASH THE SORCERER
Mike Lee

NO ACT FROM the Time of Legends is so profound, so despicable, as the fall of Malekith. His is a story of great battles, fell magic and a world conquered by sword and spell.

There was once a time when all was order, now so distant that no mortal creature can remember it. Since time immemorial the elves have dwelt upon the isle of Ulthuan. Here they learnt the secrets of magic from their creators, the mysterious Old Ones. Under the rule of the Everqueen they dwelt upon their idyllic island unblemished by woe.

When the coming of Chaos destroyed the civilisation of the Old Ones, the elves were left without defence. Daemons of the Chaos Gods ravaged Ulthuan and terrorised the elves. From the darkness of this torment rose Aenarion, the Defender, the first of the Phoenix Kings.

Aenarion's life was one of war and strife, yet through the sacrifice of Aenarion and his allies, the daemons were defeated and the elves were saved. In his wake the elves prospered for an age, but all their grand endeavours were to be for naught. All that the elves strived for would be laid to ruin by another of Aenarion's legacies – his son, Prince Malekith.

Where once there was harmony, there came discord. Where once peace had prevailed, now came bitter war.

Heed now this tale of the Sundering.

The Isles

The Shifting Isles

race

Tor Achare

Forests of
Cothique

Averlorn
ests of
rlorn

Cothique

Finuval
Plain

Tor
Yvresse

e a

Tower of
Hoeth

Sea of Dreams

Saphery

Yvresse

Eataine

The Shifting Isles

PART ONE

The Passing of Aenarion; the Conquering of Elthin Arvan; the Grand Alliance; Prince Malekith Becomes Aware of his Destiny

— ❮ ONE ❯ —

Broken Legacy

NONE KNEW AT the time that the greatest saviour of the elves would also be their doom. Yet there was one who foresaw the darkness and death to come: Caledor Dragontamer. When Aenarion the Defender, bulwark against the daemons and first of the Phoenix Kings, drew the Sword of Khaine from its black altar, Caledor, greatest mage of Ulthuan, was gifted with a dark prophecy.

Caledor saw that in taking the dire blade forged for the God of Murder, Aenarion awakened the bloodthirsty spirit that had been buried deep within the elves. In Aenarion's line more than any other, the call for war and the thrill of battle was stirred, and across the isle of Ulthuan love of bloodletting was kindled and the innocence of the Everqueen's rule passed forever.

That Aenarion drew the sword at all was born out of grief and anger, and its call haunted him until the day he drove it back into the fell altar of Khaine just before he died. It was that same anguish and loss that drove him to marry the seeress Morathi, whom the Phoenix King had rescued from the grip of Chaos.

Morathi wielded the power of magic without reserve, eager to harness the great energies unleashed upon the world by the coming of Chaos. There were those who saw such practices as obscene and dangerous, and there were whispers that Morathi had bewitched Aenarion. That she craved power was plain for many to see, yet Aenarion was oblivious to their protests and banished them from his presence.

At Anlec, Aenarion and Morathi held court, and in that bleak time their palace was a fortress of war and sorcery. The deadliest warriors came and learnt at Aenarion's hand, while the most gifted spellweavers were taught the deepest secrets known to Morathi. With spell and spear, the warriors of Anlec carved the kingdom of Nagarythe from the grip of the daemons, wielding grave weapons forged in the furnaces of Vaul the Smith God by the servants of Caledor.

IT WAS INTO the midst of destruction and vengeance that Malekith was born, son of Aenarion and Morathi. As was the tradition of those times, a blade was forged for him at the hour of his birth, and he was taught to wield it as soon as his limbs were strong enough to hold it aloft.

From his father, he learnt the skills of rulership and warcraft, and from his mother, Malekith was gifted the power to bind the tempests of magic to his will.

Into Malekith, the Phoenix King poured all of his wisdom and knowledge, but also his thirst for revenge upon the daemons that had taken his first wife and the children borne by her. Into Malekith, Morathi invested her will to achieve anything no matter the cost, and the hunger for glory and greatness.

'Remember that you are the son of Aenarion,' she told Malekith when he was but a child. 'Remember that you are the son of Morathi. In your blood flows the greatest strength of this isle.'

'You are a warrior born,' Aenarion said. 'You shall be fell with blade and bow, and you shall wield armies as lesser elves wield their swords.'

Day after day they told their son this, from before he was old enough to understand their words, to the day Aenarion died.

IT WAS TO the lament of Aenarion that the tide of daemons did not cease, and his constant battles were thus ever in vain. Caledor it was that created the great vortex, which to this day siphons away the power of Chaos and drains it from the world. With the magical energy needed to sustain their material forms now much diminished, the daemons perished, though Caledor and his mages were trapped in stasis within the vortex, cursed to fight against the encroachment of Chaos for eternity. Aenarion gave his life defending Caledor and his mages, and with his last strength returned to the Blighted Isle and restored the Godslayer to the black altar of Khaine.

In the time after the daemons had passed, the great princes of the elves – those warriors and mages who had fought alongside Caledor and Aenarion – came together to decide the path of the future rule of Ulthuan. In the forests of Avelorn, from where the slain Everqueen had ruled, they held the First Council a year after Aenarion's departure.

The princes met in the Glade of Eternity, a great amphitheatre of trees at the centre of which stood a shrine to Isha, the Goddess of Nature, matron of the Everqueen. Grown of twining silver roots and branches, with emerald-green leaves festooned with blooms in every season, the Aein Yshain glowed with mystical power. By the light of the moons and the stars, the First Council convened, bathed in the twilight of the open skies and the aura of the blessed tree.

Morathi and Malekith were there. Dark-haired and coldly beautiful, the seeress wore a dress of black cloth so fine that it appeared as a diaphanous cloud that barely concealed her alabaster skin. Her raven hair was swept back by bands of finely woven silver threads hung with rubies, and her lips were painted to match the glittering gems. Slender and noble of bearing she stood, and bore a staff of black iron in her hands.

Malekith was no less imposing. As tall as his father and of similarly dark eyes, he wore a suit of golden mail, and a breastplate upon which was embossed the coiling form of a dragon. A long sword hung in a gold-threaded scabbard at his waist, its pommel wrought from the same precious metal: a dragon's claw grasping a sapphire the size of a fist.

With them came other princes of Nagarythe who had survived the fighting on the Isle of the Dead. They were dressed in their fine armour, and wore dark cloaks that hung to their ankles, and proudly bore the scars and trophies of their wars with the daemons.

The sinister princes of the north were arrayed with knives, spears, swords, bows, shields and armour wrought with the runes of Vaul, testaments to the power of Nagarythe and Anlec. Banner bearers with black and silver standards stood in attendance, and heralds sounded the trumpets and pipes at their arrival. A cabal of sorcerers accompanied the Naggarothi contingent, clad in robes of black and purple, their faces tattooed and scarred with ritual sigils, their heads shaved.

Another group there was, of princes from the lands founded by Caledor in the south, and from the new realms to the east – Cothique, Eataine, Yvresse and others. At the fore stood the young mage Thyriol, and golden-haired Menieth, son of Caledor Dragontamer.

In contrast to the Naggarothi these elves of the south and east were as day is to night. Though all had played their part in the war against the daemons, these princes had cast off their wargear and instead carried staves and sceptres, and in the place of war helms they wore golden crowns as symbols of their power. They were clad predominantly in white, the colour of mourning, in remembrance of the losses their people had suffered; the Naggarothi eschewed such affectation even though they had lost more than most.

'Aenarion has passed on,' Morathi declared to the council. 'The Godslayer, the Widowmaker, he returned to the altar of Khaine so that we can be free of war. In peace, my son wishes to rule, and in peace we would explore this new world that surrounds us. Yet, I fear peace now is a thing of memory, and perhaps one day to be nothing more than myth. Do not think that the Great Powers that now gaze upon our world with hungry, immortal eyes can be so easily defeated. Though the daemons are banished from our lands, the power of Chaos is not wholly exiled from the world. I have gazed far and wide this past year, and I have seen what changes the fall of the gods has wrought upon us.'

'In war, I would follow no other king,' said Menieth, striding to the centre of the circle formed by the princes. 'In Nagarythe is found the greatest strength of arms upon this isle. The war is over, though, and I am not sure that the strength of Nagarythe lies in tranquillity. There are other realms now, and cities where there were castles.

Civilisation has triumphed over Chaos on Ulthuan, and we shall take that civilisation across the seas and the elves shall reign where the gods have fallen.'

'And such arrogance and blindness shall see us humbled,' said Morathi. 'Far to the north, the lands are blasted wastelands, where creatures corrupted by dark magic crawl and flit. Ignorant savages build altars of skulls in praise of the new gods, and spill the blood of their kin in worship. Monstrous things melded of flesh and magic prowl the darkness beyond our shores. If we are to bring our light to these benighted lands, it shall be upon the glittering tip of spear and arrow.'

'Hardship and bloodshed are the price we pay for our survival,' argued Menieth. 'Nagarythe shall march at the forefront of our hosts and with the valour of the Naggarothi we shall pierce that darkness. However, we cannot be ruled by war as we were when Aenarion strode amongst us. We must reclaim our spirits from the love of bloodshed that consumed us, and seek a more enlightened path towards building a new world. We must allow the boughs of love and friendship to flourish from the roots of hatred and violence sown by the coming of Aenarion. We shall never forget his legacy, but our hearts cannot be ruled by his anger.'

'My son is the heir of Aenarion,' Morathi said quietly, menace in her soft voice. 'That we stand here at all is the prize wrested from defeat by my late husband.'

'But won no less by my father's sacrifice,' Menieth countered. 'For a year we have pondered what course of action to take, since the deaths of Aenarion and Caledor. Nagarythe shall take its place amongst the other realms; great in its glory, yet not greater than any other kingdom.'

'Greatness is earned by deeds, not bestowed by others,' said Morathi, striding forwards to stand in front of

Menieth. She planted her staff in the ground between them and glared at the prince, her grip tight upon the metal rod.

'It is not to fall upon each other that we fought against the daemons and sacrificed so much,' said Thyriol hurriedly. Clad in robes of white and yellow that glimmered with golden thread, the mage laid a hand upon the shoulder of Morathi and upon the arm of Menieth. 'In us has been awakened a new spirit, and we must temper our haste with cool judgement, just as a newly forged blade must be quenched in the calming waters.'

'Who here feels worthy enough to take up the crown of the Phoenix King?' Morathi asked, glaring at the princes with scorn. 'Who here save my son is worthy of being Aenarion's successor?'

There was silence for a while, and none of the dissenters could meet Morathi's gaze, save for Menieth, who returned her cold stare without flinching. Then a voice rang out across the glade from the shadows of the trees encircling the council.

'I have been chosen!' the voice called.

From the trees walked Bel Shanaar, ruling prince of the plains of Tiranoc. Behind him strode a gigantic figure, in shape as of a tree given the power to walk. Oakheart was his name; one of the treemen of Avelorn who had acted as guard to the Everqueen and tended the sacred shrines of the elves' homeland.

'Chosen by whom?' asked Morathi contemptuously.

'By the princes and the Everqueen,' Bel Shanaar replied, standing to one side of the holy tree of Isha.

'Astarielle was slain,' Morathi said. 'The reign of the Everqueen is no more.'

'She lives on,' said a ghostly, feminine voice that drifted around the glade.

'Astarielle was slain by the daemons,' Morathi insisted, casting her gaze about to spy whence the voice had come, her eyes narrowed with suspicion.

The leaves on all of the trees began to quiver, filling the glade with a gentle susurrus as if a wind whispered through the treetops, though the air was still. The long grass of the glade began to sway in the same invisible breeze, bending towards the Aein Yshain at the clearing's centre. The glow of the sacred tree grew stronger, bathing the council in a golden light dappled with sky blues and verdant greens.

In the shimmering brightness, a silhouette of greater light appeared upon the knotted trunk, resolving itself into the form of a young elf maiden. Morathi gasped, for at first it seemed as if Astarielle indeed still lived.

The maiden's golden hair hung to her waist in long plaited tresses woven with flowers of every colour, and she wore the green robes of the Everqueen. Her face was delicate, even by elven standards, and her eyes the startling blue of the clearest summer skies. As the light dimmed, the elf's features became clearer and Morathi saw that this newcomer was not Astarielle. There was a likeness, of that Morathi was aware, but she relaxed as she scrutinised the girl.

'You are not Astarielle,' Morathi declared confidently. 'You are an impostor!'

'Not Astarielle, you are right,' replied the maiden, her voice soft yet carrying easily to the furthest reaches of the glade. 'I am not an impostor, either. I am Yvraine, daughter of Aenarion and Astarielle.'

'More trickery!' shrieked Morathi, rounding on the princes with such an expression of anger that many flinched from her ire. 'Yvraine is also dead! You conspire to keep my son from his rightful inheritance.'

'She is Yvraine,' said Oakheart, his voice a melodic noise like the sighing of a light wind through branches. 'Though Astarielle remained to protect Avelorn against the daemons, she bid us to take her children to safety. To the Gaen Vale I carried them, where no other elf has trod. There my kin and I fought the daemons and kept Yvraine and Morelion safe those many years.'

At this there were gasps from the Naggarothi, none louder than the exclamation of Malekith.

'Then my half-brother also still lives?' the prince demanded. 'Aenarion's first son is alive?'

'Calm yourself, Malekith,' said Thyriol. 'Morelion has taken ship and sailed from Ulthuan. He is a child of Avelorn, as is Yvraine, and he seeks no claim to the rule of Nagarythe. He is blessed of Isha, not a scion of Khaine, and seeks neither dominion nor fealty.'

'You kept this from Aenarion?' Morathi's tone was full of incredulity. 'You allowed him to believe his children were dead, and raised them separated from their father? You have hidden them from–'

'I am the beloved of Isha,' said Yvraine, her voice stern, silencing Morathi. 'In me is reborn the spirit of the Everqueen. Anlec is a place of blood and rage. It could not be my home, I could not live amongst the taint of Khaine, and so Oakheart and his kind raised me in the manner and place fitting for my station.'

'I see now your conspiracy,' said Morathi, stalking across the glade to confront the princes. 'In secrecy you have muttered and whispered, and kept the Naggarothi from your counsels. You seek to supplant the line of Aenarion with one of your own, and wrest the power of Ulthuan from Nagarythe.'

'There is no power to wrest, no line to break,' replied Thyriol. 'Only in pain and death does Nagarythe prevail.

We sent messengers to Anlec and you turned them away. We sought to include you in our deliberations, but you would send no embassy. We gave you every right and opportunity to make the claim for your son and you chose to tread your own path. There is no conspiracy.'

'I am the widow of Aenarion, the queen of Ulthuan,' Morathi snarled. 'When the daemons preyed upon your people, did Aenarion and his lieutenants stand by and discuss matters in council? When Caledor began his spell, did he debate its merits with the peons? To rule is to wield the right to decide for all.'

'You are queen no longer, Morathi,' said Yvraine, ghosting softly across the glade, her steps as light as settling snowflakes. 'The Everqueen has returned and I shall rule with Bel Shanaar, just as Aenarion reigned with my mother.'

'You will wed Bel Shanaar?' asked Morathi, turning on Yvraine.

'As Aenarion wed my mother, so the Everqueen will marry the Phoenix King, and ever shall it be down all of the ages,' Yvraine declared. 'I cannot marry Malekith, my half-brother, no matter what his entitlement or qualities to succeed his father.'

'Usurpers!' shrieked Morathi, raising up her staff. Malekith leapt forwards and snatched the rod from her grip.

'No more!' the prince of Nagarythe cried out. 'I would not have the realm forged by my father torn asunder by this dispute.'

Malekith laid a comforting hand upon the cheek of his mother, and when she was calmed he returned her staff to her. With a last venomous glare at Yvraine and Bel Shanaar, the seeress turned her back upon them and returned to the Naggarothi contingent to glower and sneer.

'I do not seek the throne of Ulthuan to become a tyrant,' said Malekith. 'It is to honour my father and see his legacy fulfilled that I would become Phoenix King. I do not claim this as a right of birth, but surrender myself to the judgement of those here. If it is the decision of this council that Bel Shanaar should wed my half-sister and become king, I will not oppose it. I ask only that you consider my petition this one last time, for it is plain that we have allowed division and misconception to cloud our minds.'

The princes nodded in agreement at these well-spoken words, and gathered together under the eaves of the Avelorn trees. They talked for a long time, until dawn touched her red fingers upon the treetops and the morning mists drifted up from the fertile earth. Back and forth swayed the debate, for some were heartened by Malekith's gentle entreaty and believed that though he was his father's son, he had not wielded the Godslayer and so was not touched by its darkness. Others reminded the council of Caledor's prophecy that Aenarion's line was touched by Khaine, and argued that a child of Anlec could never be freed from its curse.

'We have made our decision,' Thyriol informed the Naggarothi. 'While Malekith is a fine prince, he is yet young and has much to learn about the world, as do we all. Now is a time for wisdom and guidance, not iron rule, and for these reasons we remain committed to the investiture of Bel Shanaar.'

Morathi gave a scream of derision, but Malekith held up a hand to silence her.

'The fate of Ulthuan is not for a single elf to decide, and I accede to the wisdom of this council,' Malekith declared. He crossed the glade and, to the amazement of all, bent to one knee before Bel Shanaar. 'Bel Shanaar shall succeed my father, though he cannot replace him, and with his wisdom we shall herald a new age for our people. May the gods grant our new king the strength to prosper and rule justly, and know that should ever his will falter or his resolve waver, Nagarythe stands ready.'

THOUGH MALEKITH BORE himself with dignity and respect, he was sorely disappointed by the council's decision. He returned to Nagarythe with his mother, and did not attend the ritual wedding of Bel Shanaar and Yvraine. However, he did travel to the Isle of Flame to bear witness to Bel Shanaar's passing through the sacred flames of Asuryan, though the sight stirred within him a kernel of jealousy that he could not wholly quench.

The shrine itself was a high pyramid in form, built above the burning flame of the king of the gods. The flame danced and flickered at the heart of the temple, thrice the height of an elf, burning without noise or heat. Runes of gold were inlaid into the marble tiles of the floor around the central fire, and these blazed with a light that was not wholly reflected from the flame. Upon the white walls were hung braziers wrought in the shape of phoenixes with their wings furled, and more magical fire burned within them, filling the temple with a golden glow.

All the princes of Ulthuan were there, resplendent in their cloaks and gowns, with high helms and tall crowns of silver and gold studded with gemstones from every colour of the rainbow. Only the Naggarothi stood out amongst this feast of colour, taciturn and sombre in their black and purple robes. Morathi stood with Malekith and his followers, the seeress eyeing the proceedings with suspicion.

Astromancers were present too, seven of them, who had determined that this day was the most auspicious to crown the new Phoenix King. They wore robes of deep blues patterned with glistening diamonds in the constellations of the stars, linked by the finest lines of silver and platinum.

The astrologers stood next to the chanting priests of Asuryan, who weaved their prayers around Bel Shanaar so that he might pass through the flames unscathed. Behind the priests sat the oracles of Asuryan; three elven maidens of pale skin and blonde hair, garbed in raiment of silver that shimmered in the dazzling light.

Yvraine and her maiden guard had journeyed from Avelorn to join the ascension of her ceremonial husband. These warrior-women wore skirts of silvered scale edged with green cloth, and carried garlands of flowers in place of their spears and bows, for no weapon was allowed to pass the threshold of Asuryan's temple.

Bel Shanaar stood with the high priest before the flame, and about his shoulders was hung a cloak of white and black feathers, a newly woven symbol of his power and authority.

'As did Aenarion the Defender, so too shall I submit myself to the judgement of the greatest power,' Bel Shanaar solemnly intoned. 'My purity proven by this ordeal, I shall ascend to the throne of the Phoenix King, to rule wisely and justly in the name of the king of gods.'

'Your father needed no spells of protection,' muttered Morathi. 'This is a fraud, of no more legitimacy than the sham wedding to Yvraine.'

Malekith did not hear her words, for his attention and thoughts were bent entirely upon the unfolding ceremony.

As the priests burned incense and made offerings to Asuryan, the oracles began to sing quietly, their verses almost identical but for a few words here and there, which rose into a joyful harmony as Bel Shanaar was ushered towards the flame of Asuryan. The Phoenix King-to-be turned and looked back towards the princes, with no sign of trepidation or exultation.

With a respectful nod Bel Shanaar faced towards the centre of the shrine and walked forwards, slowly ascending the shallow steps that led up to the dais over which the god's cleansing fires gleamed. All present then fell hushed in anticipation as Bel Shanaar stepped within the flame, which turned to a glaring white and forced the onlookers to cast their gazes away lest they be blinded by its intensity.

As their eyes grew accustomed to the bright burning of the flame, they could see the vague shape of Bel Shanaar within, arms upraised as he offered fealty to Asuryan. Then the Phoenix King turned slowly and stepped back out of the flames unharmed. There was a sighing of exhalation as the princes expressed their relief that all went well. The Naggarothi remained silent.

The entourage left, laughing and chattering, save for Malekith, who stayed for a long while gazing at the flame and pondering his fate. The sacred fire had returned to its shifting colours, now seeming dim after its dazzling eruption. To Malekith it seemed as if they had been diminished, tainted by the presence of Bel Shanaar.

Unaware of anything but that burning shrine, Malekith walked slowly forwards, his mind a swirl of conflicting emotions. If he but dared the flame and survived, without the spells of the priests to protect him, then surely it was the will of Asuryan that he succeed his father. Yet what if he was not strong enough? Would the burning of the flames devour him? What then would be left of his hopes and dreams for Nagarythe?

Without realisation Malekith stood directly before the fires, mesmerised by their shifting patterns. The urge to reach out gripped him and he was about to place his hand into the flame when he heard the footsteps of the priests re-entering the temple. Snatching his hand away, Malekith turned from the sacred fire and strode quickly from the shrine, ignoring the priests' inquiring glances.

There were to be many days of feasting and celebration, but Malekith left as soon as the ceremony was complete, his duty having been fulfilled. He felt no urge to linger here, where his father had first thrown himself upon the mercy of the greatest god and been reborn as the saviour of his people. If Bel Shanaar wished to be Phoenix King, then Malekith was satisfied to acquiesce. There were more than enough challenges ahead for him to overcome, Malekith knew, without inciting rivalry and discord. Content for the moment, he journeyed back to Anlec to take up his rule.

TWO

Voyage to Elthin Arvan

WITH DETERMINATION AND resourcefulness, Malekith bent his mind to the rebuilding of Nagarythe, as the other princes looked to their realms. In this time, Ulthuan raised itself from the ashes of war, and the cities grew and prospered. Farmlands pushed back the wilderness of Ulthuan as the elves shaped their isle to their liking.

In the mountains, hunters found strange beasts twisted by dark magic: many-headed hydras, bizarre chimerae, screeching griffons and other creatures of Chaos. Many of these they slew, others they captured and broke to their will to use as mounts. Here also change had been wrought upon the birds, and the elves became friends with the great eagles who soared upon the mountain thermals and were gifted with the power of speech.

Ships were built and fleets despatched to explore the lands beyond the seas, and the power of the elves grew. Tiranoc, the kingdom of Bel Shanaar, profited greatly from this expansion of the elven realms, as did other king-doms whose people took ship to found new colonies on distant shores.

Seeing that the future of his lands lay not just upon Ulthuan but across the globe, Malekith decided to lead the Naggarothi forth on an expedition of conquest and exploration. Though he had laboured long in the reconstruction of Nagarythe, ever he had chafed at domesticity and would seek the adventure of the mountain hunts or train with the legions of Anlec.

Not for him the life of security and comfort enjoyed by the princes of Ulthuan, for his spirit burned brighter than theirs, and ever the words of his mother and father sprang to mind. He felt destined for greater things than the building of walls and the collection of taxes, and he appointed many chancellors and treasurers to oversee these duties for him.

In the two hundred and fifty-fifth year of Bel Shanaar's reign, Malekith quit Nagarythe as part of a mighty fleet bound for the east, to the unconquered wilderness of Elthin Arvan. To Morathi he gave the stewardship of Nagarythe. Though the relationship between mother and son had been strained at times, for Morathi could not accept her son's fate as placidly as did he, the two remained close.

Beneath a spring sky the two parted on the wharfs of Galthyr, Morathi wrapped against the chill with a shawl of black bear fur, Malekith in his golden armour. Behind the prince his flagship rose and fell at anchor, her white sails cracking in the breeze, the high tiers of her gilded hull shining in the morning sun. Further out to sea waited a dozen warships of Nagarythe, their black and gold hulls rising and falling upon the white surf, five hundred warriors and knights aboard each vessel; a bodyguard befitting the son of Aenarion.

'You will earn glory on your travels,' Morathi said with genuine affection. 'I have seen it in my dreams, and I know it in my heart. You will be a hero and a conqueror, and you will return to Ulthuan to be showered with praise.'

'I have nothing to prove,' Malekith answered.

'You do not,' Morathi agreed. 'Not to yourself, nor I, not to your loyal subjects. You will make a fine Phoenix King when you return and the other princes see your true worth.'

'Even if they do not, Bel Shanaar is not immortal,' Malekith said. 'I shall outlive him, and there will come a time when the princes must again choose a successor. Then the crown of Ulthuan will return to its rightful line and I shall do honour to the memory of my father.'

'It is good that you leave, for I could not bear to see you wither away in our halls like a rose hidden from the sun,' Morathi said. 'One day your name will be upon the lips of every elf, and you will usher in a new age for our people. This is written in the stars and thus in your destiny. Morai-heg has granted me the wisdom to see it thus, and so shall it be.'

The seeress looked away for a moment, her gaze turning towards the north. Malekith opened his mouth to speak but Morathi raised a finger to silence him. When she looked at her son, he felt her gaze fall upon him like a lamb stood before a lion, such was the intensity of her stare.

'Great deeds await you, my son, and renown equal to that of your father,' Morathi said, quietly at first, her voice rising in volume as she spoke. 'Let Bel Shanaar sit upon his throne and grow rich and spoilt upon the labours of his people! As you say, his time will pass and his line will be found weak. Care not for the judgement of others, but go forth and do as you see fit, as prince of Nagarythe and leader of the greatest people in the world!'

They embraced for a long while, sharing in silence what could not be said. There were no tears shed at this parting, for the elves of Nagarythe were ever hardened to adversity and loss. For both, this was simply a new chapter in the story of Nagarythe, to be boldly written upon the pages of history with feats of valour and tales of conquest.

SWIFT AND SURE are the ships of the elves, and the fleet of Malekith sailed north and east for forty days, crossing the Great Ocean without trouble. The elves were masters of the seas, the inheritors of the civilisation of the Old Ones that had now fallen, and the world was theirs to claim. Anticipation and excitement filled the sailors and warriors of Nagarythe as they gazed to the east and wondered what spectacles awaited them.

Malekith was filled with energy, and would pace upon the deck of his ship constantly, when not cloistered in his cabin poring over the charts and maps sent back by elven shipmasters who had begun to explore the wide seas and foreign coasts.

He travelled also from ship to ship when he could, to spend time with the other princes and knights who accompanied his expedition. They feasted on fish caught from the seas, and drank toasts to their prince from caskets of wine brought out of Ulthuan. The mood was of a great celebration, as if setting out was in itself a victory. Malekith could not fault them for their optimism, for as they woke each day heading towards the dawn he felt the lure of adventure too. Other ships they saw passing westwards, laden with timber and ores from the new lands. Ever they exchanged news with the captains of these vessels, and each meeting brought fresh excitement at the wealth and opportunities to be had.

The lands of the east were untamed wilderness for the most part. Savage creatures were there, amidst the majestic mountains and dark forests, but also vast untapped resources that could be taken for those with the wit and daring to do so.

Malekith vowed to his followers that they would build a new realm here, and carve for themselves an empire that would dwarf Ulthuan in size and majesty, worthy of the memory of Aenarion. This cheered them even more, for each prince could see himself as a king, and each knight could picture life as a prince. Under Malekith's reign, it seemed as if anything would be possible, and each would have a castle filled with delights set in breathtaking glades and valleys.

Malekith allowed them to forge their fantasies, for who was he to quell their dreams? He had spoken in truth and looked to the wilds of Elthin Arvan as a new beginning; a place where the ghost of his father would not haunt him and the expectations of his mother would not choke him.

As dawn broke on the forty-first day, a commotion ran through Malekith's fleet. Land had been sighted: jutting headlands of white and dark mud flats that stretched for miles. It was not for this that there was much agitation, for the masters of the ships had known they would make landfall that day, but for a great pall of smoke that hung over the northern horizon. A large fire or fires burned somewhere, and Malekith was filled with foreboding. He ordered his captains to turn northwards at once, and up the coast sped the fleet with all sail set, dancing effortlessly across the waves.

Not long after noon they came upon the port of Athel Toralien, one of the first colonies to be founded in these new lands. Her white towers rose up majestically from the sea of trees that grew right up to the coastline, and a great harbour wall curved out into the ocean, surf crashing upon it. As Malekith feared, the city was alight with many fires, and her walls were blackened with soot.

As the Naggarothi fleet tacked into the bay upon which Athel Toralien stood, they found the quays empty of ships. Malekith guessed that their captains had fled whatever disaster had befallen the city, and that Athel Toralien now lay deserted. He was to be proven wrong in part though, for as the ships approached the harbour, a loud cry went up from the lookouts. There was fighting upon the walls of the city!

As the ship of Malekith came alongside a slender pier, he leapt over the side onto the whitewashed planks. In his wake came his soldiers, jumping from the ship in their haste, not waiting for the boarding bridges to be lowered. Calling his warriors to arms, Malekith raced down the pier towards the high warehouses around the edge of the harbour. As he neared the buildings, clusters of elves came out and hurried towards the Naggarothi. Most were women, unkempt and afraid. With them they brought clusters of children with eyes wide in fear, who hung upon their mother's dresses as if they were gripping upon life itself.

'Bless Asuryan!' the womenfolk cried, and hugged Malekith and his warriors with tears streaming down their cheeks.

'Be quiet!' snapped Malekith to quell their effusive thanks and sobbing. 'What evil passes here?'

'Orcs!' they shrieked in reply. 'The city is besieged!'

'Who commands the city?' he demanded.

'No one, my lord,' he was told. 'Prince Aneron left eight days ago, with the fleet and many of the soldiers. There was not enough room aboard the ships for all to flee. Captain Lorhir defends the walls as best he can, but the orcs have war engines that hurl flaming rocks, and have pounded the city for many days.'

The army was assembling on the dockside, and Malekith ordered that the horses be brought from the ships. As the knights readied themselves, he ordered two companies of spears and his best archers to follow him to the walls. As they marched through the city they saw that the destruction was not as widespread as they first thought. The war machines of the orcs were wildly inaccurate and the damaged buildings were scattered across the city. Even as Malekith reached a stairway leading up to the rampart, a ball of flaming rock and tar flew overhead and crashed into a tower, showering dribbles of flame and debris into the street below.

Leaping up the stone steps three at a time, Malekith swiftly reached the top of the wall, which rose some thirty feet above the ground. The curtain wall of Athel Toralien curved around in a semi-circle for more than a mile, enclosing the city against the bay that lay to the south. Beyond lay an immense forest that stretched as far as the eye could see, cut by the straight lines of roads radiating out from the city's three gates.

There were piles of bodies everywhere; of slain elves, and gruesome green-skinned creatures with fanged mouths and slab-like muscles, clad in crude armour. The current attack appeared to be at a gate tower some two hundred yards further along the wall. A motley assortment of elves, some wearing armour, others in robes, beat back with spears and knives against a swarm of the wildly shouting orcs.

More orcs were pouring up from four ramshackle ladders leaning against the wall.

'Form up for advance!' bellowed Malekith, unsheathing his sword, Avanuir.

The spear companies fell into disciplined ranks six abreast, their shields overlapping, a wall of iron points jutting forwards. Malekith waved them to advance and they set off at a steady pace, their booted feet tramping in unison upon the hard stone.

'Clear those ladders,' the prince told his archers before running to the front of the advancing column.

The archers moved to the wall's edge, some standing upon the battlements, and loosed their bows at the savages climbing up the ladders. Their aim was deadly accurate and dozens of the greenskins tumbled to the ground below, black-fletched arrows piercing eyes, necks and chests.

The orcs had gained a foothold upon the wall and more of their number clambered over the rampart, howling and waving brutal cleavers and axes. The Naggarothi advanced relentlessly, as groups of orcs broke from the main body and ran towards them.

When the first orc reached the black-armoured company Malekith despatched it with a simple overhead cut that left its body cleft from shoulder to groin. The next he slew with a straight thrust through the chest, and another with a backhanded flourish that spilled its entrails onto the stones of the wall.

Malekith continued marching forwards, hewing down an orc with every step, his spearmen tight behind him slaying any orc that evaded the prince's deadly attentions. The Naggarothi stepped over the bodies of the fallen savages as they advanced, never once wavering or changing direction as they headed for the knot of greenskins crowding about the ladders. The elves of Athel Toralien took heart with the arrival of their saviours and fought with greater vigour, stopping the orcs from gaining further ground as the Naggarothi closed in.

Wielded by Malekith, Avanuir sheared through shield, armour, flesh and bone with every strike of the prince, and a line of orc bodies trailed him along the wall until he reached the ladders. No clumsy blow from his foes found its mark as he feinted and swayed through the melee.

Signalling his spears to deal with the other ladders, Malekith leapt up to the battlement by the closest, kicking an orc face as it appeared over the wall. The orc reeled from the blow but did not fall. Avanuir swept down and lopped the orc's head from its body, the lifeless corpse tumbling down the ladder, dislodging more orcs so that they fell flailing to the ground.

As he hewed through another attacker, Malekith held up his left hand and a nimbus of power coalesced around his closed fist. With a snarled word of power, Malekith thrust his hand towards the orcs and unleashed his spell. Forks of blue and purple lightning leapt from his outstretched fingertips, earthing through the skulls of the orcs, causing flesh to catch fire and armour to melt. Down the ladder writhed the bolt, jumping from orc to orc, hurling each to the ground trailing smoke. With a thunderous blast, the ladder itself exploded into a hail of splinters that scythed into the orcs waiting at the foot of the wall, cutting them down by the score.

The spearmen had toppled two more ladders, and as Malekith turned from the wall, the fourth and final ladder collapsed, sending the orcs upon it plunging to a bone-cracking death on the hard earth below. The archers turned their shots now onto the orcs who had gathered around the fallen ladders, shooting any that tried to raise up the siege ladders, until the orcs lost heart and began to retreat.

An elf in bloodstained mail emerged from the knot of weary defenders, his helm scored with many blows, and walked slowly towards the Naggarothi company. He pulled off his tall helmet with a grimace, to reveal blood-matted blond hair, and dropped the helm wearily to the stones.

As he approached, Malekith stooped and tore a rag from one of the orcish dead to clean the gore from the blade of Avanuir. The prince raised an inquiring eye to the approaching elf.

'Captain Lorhir?' asked Malekith, sheathing his blade.

The other nodded and extended a hand in greeting. Malekith ignored the gesture and the elf withdrew his hand. Uncertainty played across Lorhir's face for a moment before he recovered his composure.

'Thank you, highness,' Lorhir panted. 'Praise to Asuryan for guiding you to our walls this day, for I feared this morning we had seen our last sunrise.'

'You may have yet,' replied Malekith. 'I have space upon my ships only for my own troops; there is no room for evacuation. I do not think there is escape by land.'

Malekith pointed out over the wall, to where a sea of orcs seethed along the road and beneath the boughs of the trees. Half a dozen huge catapults stood in clearings slashed raggedly from the forest, mighty pyres burning next to them. Scores of trees swayed and crashed down in every direction as the orcs cut timber to build new ladders and more war engines.

'With your aid we can hold the city until the prince returns,' said Lorhir.

'I do not think the prince will be returning soon,' Malekith said. As he spoke, others of the Toralien defenders gathered about to hear his words. 'Why should I and my soldiers shed our blood for this city?'

'With all the favour of the gods, we few could not hold against this horde for another day,' Lorhir said. 'You must protect us!'

'Must?' said Malekith, his voice an angry hiss. 'In Nagarythe, a captain does not tell a prince what he must do.'

'Forgive me, highness,' pleaded Lorhir. 'We are desperate, and there is no one else. We sent messengers to Tor Alessi and Athel Maraya and other cities, but they have not returned. They have been waylaid, or else our calls for aid have fallen upon uncaring ears. I cannot hold the city alone!'

'I cannot throw away the lives of my warriors defending the lands of a prince who would not defend them himself,' Malekith said sharply.

'Are we not all elves here?' asked one of the other citizens, an ageing elf who held a sword with an edge chipped and dinted by much use and little care. 'You would leave us to the tortures and brutalities of these orcs?'

'If this city were mine, I would defend it to my last breath,' Malekith said, appearing to relent. Then his face hardened. 'But Athel Toralien is not my city. We came to the new world to build a new kingdom, not to spill our blood to protect one of a prince who flees for safety at the first hint of menace. Swear loyalty to me, place yourself under the protection of Nagarythe, and I will defend this city.'

'What of our oaths to Prince Aneron?' replied Lorhir. 'I would not be known as a traitor.'

'It is Aneron of Eataine who has broken his word,' Malekith told them. 'Yes, I know him. He stands upon the labours of his father and abandons his people. He is worthy of no oath of fealty. Stand by me, join the Naggarothi, and I will save your city and from here we will conquer this wild and plentiful land.'

The elves huddled together in forlorn conference, occasionally looking out over the walls at the green-skinned army beyond, and at Malekith's stern demeanour.

'Take us with you on your ships, and we will swear our loyalty to Anlec,' Lorhir said finally. 'What can we few hundred do against that tide of hated beasts?'

'Your eyes must be weary,' said Malekith, waving a hand towards the docks. 'Look again.'

The elves gaped in awe as they watched the Naggarothi host disembarking from the warships. In long columns of black and silver they snaked down the piers, banners fluttering above them. At their head came the knights, already mounted upon their black-flanked destriers. Rank upon rank of spears formed up on the dockyard, moving with poise and precision born of a lifetime of training and fighting.

'A thousand knights, four thousand spears and a thousand bows stand at my command,' Malekith declared.

'The enemy is too great for us to hold the city, even with such numbers,' argued Lorhir. 'Prince Aneron had ten thousand spears and he could not hold the walls.'

'His warriors are not Naggarothi,' Malekith said. 'Each soldier in my host is worth five of Eataine. They are led by me. I am the son of Aenarion, and where my blade falls, death follows. Simply swear oaths of fealty to me and I will save your city. I am the prince of Nagarythe, and where I march, the undying will of my kingdom follows. If I so command it, this city will not fall!'

Such was the bearing and greatness of Malekith at that moment that Lorhir and the others fell to their knees, uttering words of loyalty and dedication.

'So be it,' said Malekith. 'The orcs will be dead by nightfall.'

~< THREE >~

Slaughter at Athel Toralien

It was not long before companies of archers lined the outer wall, and after a few shambolic attacks the orcs soon learned that to approach within a hundred paces was to face certain death. The greenskins tried as best they could to redirect the fall of their catapult shots, but scored only one lucky hit against the rampart while the rest of their fire landed well short or flew over the city into the harbour beyond.

Malekith arrayed his spearmen by companies, near the westernmost of the three gates, and commanded his captains to drive forwards into the enemy. With a fanfare of clarions, the gates were opened and the host of Nagary-the marched forth. At the orders of their commanders, the Naggarothi stepped out in unison, filing through the gate five abreast, their spear tips shining in the light of the orcs' fires. A wall of black shields went before them, and against this barrier the wild arrow shots of the orcs never found a mark.

The vanguard halted some fifty paces from the gateway as the orcs began to gather into rude mobs, clamouring about their haggard standards, the largest of their kind bullying, bellowing and punching their underlings into a rough semblance of order. The main part of the elven column parted to the left and right, and took up positions in sloping echelon beside the vanguard, to form an unbroken wall of spear points that ran from the north-east to the south-west, one flank guarded by the wall, the other by the sea.

Behind them, half of the archers ran swiftly down from the walls and took up positions from which they could shoot over the heads of their kinsmen. Malekith watched this from the gatehouse, Lorhir and a few other worthy citizens of the prince's new realm beside him.

'We still have a company or more of warriors, and we would not have it said that we did not fight for the future of our city,' said Lorhir.

'I do not doubt your gallantry,' said Malekith. 'But watch, and you will see why no elf may stand in the line of Nagarythe without first passing a hundred years training upon the fields of Anlec.'

The prince signalled to a hornblower stood with the group, and the herald raised his instrument and played out three rising notes. Almost instantly, the battleline of the elves shifted position.

With seamless precision, the companies on the right, nearest the wall, turned and marched northwards, each angled to protect the flank of the company in front. Through the gap thus created came the archers, who spread out into a long line three deep. The shouted commands of their captains still ringing from the wall, the archers let loose a single storm of arrows that sailed high into the air as a dark cloud. The shots fell steeply into the gathering orcs, slaying and wounding hundreds in a single devastating volley.

No sooner had the first salvo hit its mark than another was in the air, and eight more times this was repeated, an unending stream of arrowheads that pierced armour and green flesh and left piles of orcish dead littering the forest and road.

Many of the orcs fled from this ceaseless death, but the largest and fiercest were goaded into action and ran towards the elven line, chanting and screaming. As they approached, their charge gathered more momentum and those orcs that were fleeing turned back and rejoined the attack, bolstered by the headlong assault of their betters. When the green horde was no more than a hundred paces from the elves, the archers let loose a flurry of shots into their ranks, but the onslaught did not cease or even pause.

Malekith gave another signal to his musician and the hornblower let out a long, pealing blast that dipped in pitch. The orcs were no more than fifty paces away, but the lightly armed archers seemed unperturbed. They split their line, every second archer stepping to his right. Through these channels, the spearmen swiftly advanced and then reformed, scant moments before the orcish attack hit.

With a crash that could be heard upon the walls, the orcs hurled themselves at the Naggarothi. Spear pierced green hide and heavy blade cut through shaft and shield as the orcs tried to batter their way through the line with brute strength and impetus. Here and there, elves fell to the sheer ferocity of the assault, but other elves quickly stepped forwards and closed these gaps, leaving no path through the shield barrier. All along the line, spears were drawn back and thrust forwards in a rhythmic pulse, undulating from south to north in a wave that left hundreds of orcish dead.

Against the weight of the orcs' numbers, the elves slowly began to give ground, steadily and calmly taking steps backwards towards the wall as the fighting slowed and then renewed. It was then that Lorhir realised what was happening.

'You are drawing them closer to the walls,' he said in amazement.

'Now see the true strength of the Naggarothi host,' Malekith told his companions.

Two short horn blasts followed by a long piercing note then rang out and the archers still upon the walls moved to the battlements. From here they could fire directly into the orc mass, their shots passing no more than a hand's breadth from their comrades, yet loosed with such accuracy that the Naggarothi were never in danger of hitting their own warriors.

Between the spearpoints and arrows of the Nagarythe host, the orcs' enthusiasm for fighting began to waver. Their leaders bellowed and beat those that turned away from the melee, and took up great swords and axes and hewed at the elves as a treecutter might hack at a log. Encouraged by the spirit of the orcish chieftains, the green horde kept fighting.

The crews of the catapults now tried to direct their fire upon the spearmen, and scored a few hits that opened up holes in the elvish line. However, the archers poured arrows into these breaches to hold back the orcs, while the spearmen reformed again and again to keep the companies steady. Boulders and flaming balls of tar-covered wood fell more upon the orcs than the elves, to the perverse delight of the war engines' crews. It seemed that they cared not who died beneath the crushing shots of their engines.

Now the greater part of the besieging army had been drawn forwards onto the spears of the elves, and Malekith enacted the final part of his strategy.

Another signal from the horn, and the northern gate opened allowing the knights of Nagarythe to ride forth. Pennants streamed from their lance tips, and silver and black gonfalons fluttered from a dozen standard poles as the thousand knights charged the greenskins. With the war cries of Nagarythe upon their lips and the horn blasts of their musicians ringing around them, the knights of Anlec carved a swathe into the flank of the army pressed up against the elven line.

The orcs were defenceless against this manoeuvre, unable to turn to face this new threat without exposing themselves to the spears of the infantry. Spitted upon lances and trampled beneath the hooves of the knights' steeds, hundreds of orcs died in the first impact of the charge. The momentum of the knights carried them forwards into the midst of the orcish host, and the infantry pressed forwards again to ensure that the noble cavalry were not surrounded.

Lorhir gave a cry of dismay and pointed eastwards. Not all of the orcs had yet joined the fray and a group of several hundred now marched swiftly from the far end of the wall. They sprinted eagerly towards the battle and would come up behind the knights, or could otherwise turn through the open gate of the city.

'We must intercept them!' said Lorhir, turning to run towards the steps, but Malekith grabbed him by the arm and halted him.

'I said that you are not yet part of the Naggarothi army,' the prince said sternly.

'But you have no other reserve!' cried Lorhir. 'Archers alone will not deter them, who else will hold them back?'

'I will,' said Malekith. 'If each of my warriors is worth five of yours, then I am worth at least one hundred!'

With that, Malekith turned and sprinted eastwards along the wall. As he ran, he began to chant quickly under his breath, drawing the winds of magic towards himself. He could feel them churning in the air around him, heaving through the stone beneath his booted feet. Though not as dense as the magic condensed by the vortex in Ulthuan, the strands of mystical energy that swirled across the whole world blew strongly here, in the northern parts. Malekith was filled with exhilaration as his sorcery grew in power, suffusing his body with its boundless energy.

With a shout, Malekith drew his sword and bounded up to the rampart before leaping from the wall. Silver wings of magic sprang shimmering from his shoulders and carried the prince aloft.

As he sped swiftly towards the orc reinforcements, Malekith's sword glowed with magical power, a piercing blue light burning from its blade. The light spread until it enveloped the whole of the prince so that he became a gleaming thunderbolt of energy.

The orcs stumbled and gazed upwards in amazement and awe as Malekith sped down towards them, one fist held in front of him, his sword swept back ready to strike.

Like a meteor, the prince of Nagarythe crashed into the orcs in an explosion of blue flame that sent burning greenskins and steaming earth flying for many yards in every direction. Dozens more were hurled from their feet as magical flames licked at their flesh. Smoke drifted up from the crater, revealing the prince crouched on one knee. With another shout he sprang forwards, sword in front of him like a lance point, and the blade slid through the chest of the nearest greenskin.

More out of instinct and natural savagery than bravery, the closest orcs charged towards the prince, their weapons upraised, guttural shouts tearing the air. The prince moved in a blur of speed and motion, slicing and thrusting with his gleaming blade, felling an orc with every heartbeat. Within a few moments, all but one of the orcs were running from the wrath of Malekith.

The creature that remained was a gigantic beast, almost twice as tall as the elven prince. It was clad from head to toe in thick plates of armour painted with dried blood. It regarded Malekith with small, brutish red eyes and flexed its clawed fingers on the haft of the great double-headed axe it carried.

With a grunt it hefted the axe above its head and swung down the blade with terrifying force. Malekith stepped nimbly aside at the last moment, and the axe bit deep into the ground where a moment before the prince had been stood. His sword held idly by his side, Malekith took a few steps to his right as the orc warlord ripped its axe free from the earth in a shower of bloody clods.

With a bellow of anger, the orc swung its axe two-handed, but Malekith easily ducked the wild blow and cut his sword across the shoulder of the warlord, sending shards of armour spinning away. As the orc recovered its balance, the lord of Nagarythe spun around behind it and slashed at its legs, drawing his blade across both thighs, hamstringing the monstrous greenskin.

Falling to its knees, it gave a roar of rage and lunged wildly towards the prince, who stepped backwards as the orc fell flat upon its face. With a deft thrust, Malekith sheared his blade through the exposed shoulder of the orc, and then brought the edge of the blade down upon the wrist of the other arm. The orc howled as its axe fell to the ground, one fist still gripped around its rough wooden haft.

Malekith paced back and forth, eyeing the orc with a contemptuous smile. Helpless now, the orc could do nothing but shout and froth at the mouth. With a flourish, Malekith whipped his sword around for a final time and the orc's head spun into the air with a fountain of blood. It fell to the hard earth at Malekith's feet in a spatter of gore. The prince dug the point of his gleaming blade into the still-helmeted skull and lifted it from the ground for all to see.

The remnants of the orcs were fleeing through the woods, abandoning their war machines, and a great roar of triumph rose up from the ranks of the Naggarothi. Thrice they shouted the name of their prince, each time lifting up their spears and bows and lances in salute. As the knights made sport of chasing the fleeing greenskins through the forest, Malekith returned to his city.

WHEN NEWS REACHED Ulthuan of Malekith's actions, there was much debate and confusion. Prince Aneron travelled to Tor Anroc with many allies and demanded audience with the Phoenix King. The benches around the throne chamber were thronged with nobles and courtiers, and the air throbbed with heated discussion.

A respectful hush fell upon the entry of the Phoenix King, who paced from the great double doors, his long cloak of feathers sweeping across the marble floor. As soon as Bel Shanaar was seated upon his throne Aneron stepped forwards and gave a perfunctory bow.

'Malekith must be punished!' Aneron rasped.

'Punished for what crime?' Bel Shanaar asked calmly.

'He has seized my lands, sovereign territory of Eataine,' Aneron said. 'The city of Athel Toralien was founded by my father and passed to me. This Naggarothi villain has no rightful claim.'

'If you allow Malekith to keep his stolen prize, you set a terrifying precedent,' added Galdhiran, one of the lesser

Eataine princes. 'If we can seize each other's lands and claim right of conquest, then what is to prevent us all from doing as we please? Only Nagarythe and Caledor, with their large armies, are served in this manner. You must end this before it begins!'

There were boos and scoffing cries from some amongst the court, and cries of encouragement from others. The tumult continued for some time until Bel Shanaar raised his hand and silence once again descended.

'Are there any that speak on behalf of Malekith?' asked the Phoenix King.

There was a gentle cough, and all eyes turned to the uppermost tier of benches to the Phoenix King's left. Morathi sat amidst a small entourage of grim Naggarothi. She stood languidly and paced slowly down the steps to the floor of the audience hall, her gown billowing behind her like golden dawn clouds.

'I speak not for Malekith, nor Nagarythe,' the seeress said, her voice gentle yet strong. 'I speak for the people of Athel Toralien, left to die in their homes at the hands of the savage orcs by Prince Aneron.'

'There was not room–' began Aneron.

'Be silent,' snarled Morathi, and the Eataine prince stuttered into acquiescence. 'It is not your place to interrupt your betters when they are speaking. Prince Aneron, and the realm of Eataine, forfeited all right to Athel Toralien when they abandoned their duties to protect their citizens.'

Morathi had been speaking to Bel Shanaar but now turned to address the chamber as a whole.

'Prince Malekith usurped no throne,' she declared. 'No blade was lifted against the warriors of Eataine, no blood of fellow elf spilt. The lord of Nagarythe conquered an abandoned city in the grip of the orcs. He saved hundreds of elven lives by his action. That those lands had once belonged to Prince Aneron is of no bearing. If we are to argue ownership in that manner, then perhaps we should ask a representative of the orcs to attend, for they lived there long before we arrived!'

Laughter rippled around the hall at Morathi's suggestion, for Ulthuan had been awash for years with tales of the orcs' brutality and stupidity. The former queen of Ulthuan turned her attention back to the Phoenix King.

'No wrong has been done here,' she said. 'Malekith asks not for reward nor praise, but the simple right to keep what he has fought to claim. Would you deny him that right?'

A greater part of the assembled nobles applauded Morathi's argument. Bel Shanaar considered his position. A large number of Ulthuan's citizenry even now lauded the prince and his heroic defence of the colony city. Prince Aneron had never enjoyed much popularity, even amongst the elves of Eataine, and many enjoyed the snub implicit in Malekith's annexation. The Phoenix King had heard jeers from a large crowd of elves outside the palace during the arrival of Aneron in Tor Anroc.

'I have here one other piece of evidence,' Morathi added.

She gestured to her retainers and one strode down from the benches and passed her a rolled-up parchment. Morathi handed this to Bel Shanaar, who did not open it but merely looked inquiringly at the Naggarothi seeress.

'This is a letter from the people of Athel Toralien,' she said. 'It is signed by all four hundred and seventy-six survivors of the orc attack. They swear loyalty unconditionally to Prince Malekith. Further, they invite their kith and kin to join them in the new lands and are confident that under Naggarothi protection the city will prosper greatly. So, do not simply listen to my opinion, but hearken to the views of the city's people.'

At this there were some cheers from the watching courtiers and princes. Aneron scowled as even some of his fellow Eataine joined in the mockery.

'It appears that a precedent is indeed set,' said Bel Shanaar when the clamour had quietened. 'A prince who quits his property and leaves it unprotected abandons all rights to ownership. We were raised to our station for protecting Ulthuan alongside Aenarion, and we must maintain our rule as guardians of her people. Thus, I make this proclamation. Prince Aneron deserted his lands and his subjects. As Phoenix King, I consider Athel Toralien to have been an abandoned land, and thus suitable for reconquest by any prince. Prince Malekith has established his rightful claim and that shall be recognised by this court. Let this be a warning to all who seek the riches and power available for those in the new world. Go forth in the name of Ulthuan, but never forget your duties.'

Thus was Prince Aneron shamed. With little support for his position, the Eataine prince sheepishly quit the shores of Ulthuan and sailed west to the jungle-crowded coasts of Lustria. Malekith was invested as ruler of Athel Toralien and his conquest of the colonies began in earnest.

⫷ FOUR ⫸

Unheralded Allies

ATHEL TORALIEN WAS but the first in a long line of great victories for Malekith and the Naggarothi. They subdued the greenskins of the forests around the city and forged eastwards across the new continent. After almost half a century, Athel Toralien having grown into a teeming port along with other settlements such as Tor Alessi and Tor Kathyr, Malekith looked to found another city further to the east.

Over the years more Naggarothi had made the journey to the colonies, and Malekith's host now numbered over twenty thousand warriors. With this army, he marched along the great river Anurein, which flowed all the way from the mountains to the sea for hundreds of leagues. He put goblin camps to the torch and forced back the beastmen and other vile creatures of the deepest woods.

In the wake of his advance, the Naggarothi cleared the forests and built fortified farms. To the south, other cities were also prospering greatly, and their rulers were eager to seek alliance with the prince of Nagarythe. The forces of other elven lords joined the move eastwards. There were others, too, who were soon to learn about this brilliant general and charismatic leader: the dwarfs.

IT WAS IN the third year of Malekith's great eastward push that he first came across the folk of the mountains.

The forests of Elthin Arvan began to thin as the foothills of the mountains rose up amongst their boughs, and scouts from the Naggarothi host returned to Malekith to report that they had found something unusual in the woods. Large areas of trees had been cut down, not by the crude hacking of beastmen or orcs, but smoothly sawn and felled. They noted that the tracks of booted feet were plentiful, and evidence of large, well-built campfires had been found in the clearings.

Malekith assembled a company of his finest warriors and for several days they marched further eastwards, following the trail as it led towards the mountains.

The elves found the remains of encampments and marvelled at the precision with which tents had been aligned, fire pits dug and the trees hewn to form clearings of almost uniform squares. The ground was trampled by many feet, and there was also evidence that temporary palisades and ditches had also been dug and then removed or filled in. That the strangers were organised was in no doubt, and Malekith ordered his scouts to remain vigilant, day and night.

It was another three days before the elves came upon a path, or rather a road. It began at the largest campsite that they had encountered, and from the tracks that led to the north, west and south, this had been used as some sort of staging area for forays in all directions. The earth was not merely trodden down, but deliberately packed and seeded with stones to make the footing more secure. The road itself was of similar build, stretching away to the southeast, cutting through trees and hills without deviation for as far as the eye could see.

Malekith ordered his warriors to stay off the road, but they followed its course from a little way into the forest, their stealthy advance concealed by the trees. As night fell, the elves saw the glow of bonfires in the distance, several miles away, and plumes of smoke rising across the stars.

Malekith was torn as to what course of action to take. If these unknown woodcutters were hostile, then it would be far better to surround their camp at night. On the other hand, coming upon the strangers in the hours of darkness could possibly lead to surprise and cause the force they were trailing to respond with justified hostility.

In the end, Malekith decided to compromise. He left a few of his swiftest runners near to the road, and ordered them to return with all speed to warn the colonies if he did not return or otherwise send word by daybreak. His most cunning archers Malekith despatched to circumnavigate the camp and wait in ambush should their unknown quarry attempt to fight. They climbed into the branches of the trees and moved above ground from bough to bough, so silent and unnoticed that not even the birds were disturbed at their passing. The others he brought alongside the road and told them to wait a short distance from the camp, ready to provide reinforcements if things went ill.

With two of his lieutenants, Yeasir and Alandrian, Malekith approached along the road, weapons sheathed, their cloaks thrown back across their shoulders so that they concealed nothing that might cause suspicion. As they neared the camp, the elves saw two large braziers burning on either side of the road, casting a wide illumination.

In the light stood a handful of diminutive beings, the head of the tallest no higher than an elf's chest; in build they were stocky, their shoulders and chests broad with muscle, their guts solid and of considerable girth. They were extremely hairy; each sported a beard that reached his waist, and two of them had facial hair hanging almost to the tips of their weighty boots.

Each of them wore a heavy coat of chainmail tied with a thick leather belt with a broad iron buckle. Their arms were bare but for golden torques twisted into intriguing designs, and the noseguards of their helms covered much of their wide faces.

Atop the helms were small crests of leaping boars, or stylised dragons, and three had horns protruding. It was only after careful consideration that Malekith assured himself that these horns were indeed attached to the strangers' headgear and not sprouting from their skulls and passing through holes in their helms. Each held a single-bladed axe, of design unlike anything Malekith had seen before. They each also had a large round shield, rimmed with riveted iron and emblazoned with extraordinary designs of coiling wyrms, anvils and winged hammers.

They were gathered in a group about one of the braziers, talking amongst themselves. The prince's keen hearing caught snatches of a guttural tongue, much like gravel rolling down a slope or the crunch of shingle underfoot. It grated on Malekith's nerves and he just managed to stop his hand straying to the hilt of his sword.

The sentries saw the three elves approaching and turned as one to stare at them. Malekith and his two companions stopped where they were, just inside the circle of firelight, some fifty or sixty paces from the guards. The strange warriors exchanged hurried glances, and then nods from four of them sent the fifth running back into the camp, moving surprisingly swiftly on his short legs.

The two bands stood and simply eyed each other. They remained in this stalemate for some considerable time.

Eventually a party of the dwarfs came marching up the road from the camp, over a dozen of them. One was obviously their leader, his beard braided into four long plaits bound with many golden clasps. Underneath this expanse of bristle Malekith could see a blue jerkin embroidered with gold thread in angular knotwork designs. The others walked deferentially a few paces behind him, their eyes wary, their grips tight on axes and hammers.

Malekith held his hands far out to his sides, to show no hostile intent, though he knew full well that he would still be capable of drawing his blade in the blink of an eye. Yeasir and Alandrian did likewise. A surreptitious glance to the left and right revealed several of the elven scouts hidden amongst the leaves, arrows bent to bows trained on the camp leader as he stomped forwards.

He stopped between the braziers and gestured for the three elves to approach, and then stood with his arms folded solidly across his chest as they walked slowly up the road. Malekith waved his lieutenants to stop about ten paces short of the dwarfs, and took a few more steps. The leader looked at the prince with a frown, though Malekith could not tell if this was an expression of displeasure or the dwarf's natural demeanour – all of them appeared to be scowling.

This close, Malekith could smell the dwarfs as well as see them. He quelled a sneer as an offensive mixture of cave dirt and sweat assaulted his nostrils. The dwarf leader continued to look Malekith up and down, and then turned his head and barked something to his underlings. They relaxed slightly, lowering their weapons a fraction.

The leader proffered a grimy hand and spat something like 'Kurgrik'. Malekith looked down at the grubby paw extended towards him and fought to keep the disdain from his expression.

'Malekith,' the prince said, giving the dirty hand a quick shake before swiftly withdrawing his grip.

'Malkit?' the dwarf said, finally breaking into a thin smile.

'Close enough,' Malekith replied, fixing his face with a pleasant smile learned from many years spent hiding his frustration in the courts of Ulthuan.

'Elf,' Kurgrik said, pointing at Malekith, and the prince could not keep the surprise from his face. The dwarf broke into a wide grin and let out a gruff laugh and then nodded. 'Elf,' he said again.

With a wave, the dwarf leader invited the three into his camp, and as Malekith stepped forwards, the Naggarothi prince gave the most imperceptible nod to the warriors in the trees. Without disturbing a single leaf, they withdrew from sight.

The layout of the camp was as Malekith had surmised from the evidence they had found in the forest. Five rows each of five tents were spread out across a square glade cut into the woods on one side of the road. At the end of each row burned a small and neat fire in deep pits lined with stones.

The dwarfs had all gathered to look at the newcomers, and shamelessly gaped at the tall, slender elves as they walked into the camp, keeping their pace steady so as not to move quicker than their hosts. Dark, inquisitive eyes glared at them from every angle, but Malekith could feel that the looks were of curiosity, not enmity.

For their part, the elves regarded the dwarfs with neutral expressions, nodding politely as they caught the eye of one camp member or another.

The dwarfs led them to the far side of the camp where a large fire was burning, surrounded by low wooden benches. Here the elders sat themselves down, flanking their leader, who gesticulated for Malekith and his comrades to do likewise. Malekith tried to sit down with as much dignity as possible, but on the low dwarfen seat his knees were well above his waist and so he reclined to one side to assume a more comfortable position. For some reason this raised a chortle amongst some of the dwarfs, but it seemed good-natured enough.

Tin tankards were thrust into the elves' hands, and three dwarfs came forwards, two of them carrying a large barrel between them. The third directed them to place it carefully in front of the dwarf leader, and then with great ceremony drove a tap into the keg with a wooden hammer. He poured a small amount of the frothing contents into his hand, sniffed it and then dipped his tongue into the liquid. He thrust a hand towards Malekith with his thumb pointed up and smiled. Malekith smiled in return, but felt it best not to return the gesture lest it was some sign of disrespect.

The chief dwarf than stood up and strutted over to the barrel and filled his golden tankard with the brew. Hesitantly, Yeasir followed suit, sniffing cautiously at his mug's contents. Malekith looked enquiringly at his lieutenant, who replied with a bemused shrug. The other two elves then filled up their tankards and returned to their seats.

Raising his tankard in a way that even the elves recognised as a toast, the dwarf brought his cup up to his lips and downed the contents with three gargantuan gulps. With a satisfied smacking of his lips, he slammed the tankard down onto the bench beside him. Bubbles of foam were stuck upon his beard, and he wiped them away with the back of his hand and winked at Malekith.

Hesitantly, Malekith allowed a dribble of the liquid to pass his lips. It was quite thick, and almost stung his tongue with its bitterness. He could not suppress a quick, choking cough, which elicited more gentle laughter from the dwarfs.

His pride wounded by their good-natured yet mocking humour, Malekith snarled and took a more serious draught of the potion. He fought against the urge to retch as he swallowed, and then gulped down more and more. He felt his eyes watering at its acrid taste, which was as different from the delicate wines of Ulthuan as winter is from summer.

Gulping down the last mouthful, Malekith fought back the bile rising in his throat and playfully tossed the tankard over his shoulder and raised an inquisitive eyebrow. At this the dwarfs erupted into more laughter, but this time it was clearly directed at their leader, who gave a snort, and then a nod of appreciation.

Malekith glanced across to Yeasir and Alandrian, who appeared to be both finishing their drinks. However, out of the corner of his eye, Malekith spied patches of dampness upon the earth close to his companions and suspected that they had used the distraction offered by his performance to pour away most of their drink.

They spent the rest of the night communicating in crude fashion, naming objects in each of their tongues and suchlike. Malekith despatched Yeasir to take word to the others that all was well, keeping Alandrian close by. His lieutenant displayed an unseen gift for language and had already picked up a smattering of dwarfish.

OVER THE NEXT four days, Malekith and Alandrian spent much time with the dwarfs, and invited Kurgrik to the Naggarothi camp. Through Alandrian, it transpired that

Kurgrik was a thane, one of the nobles of a mighty city in the mountains called Karaz-a-Karak. As alien as the elves had been in the dwarf encampment, so too were the dwarfs in the elves'.

As host, Malekith offered the dwarfs golden goblets of the finest Cothique wine he had, which the dwarfs quaffed with enthusiasm as the elves sampled their cups with more refinement. The dwarfs were inquisitive, but not offensively so, always polite to inquire, through Alandrian, whether they could inspect the elves' tents, weapons, water casks and all other manner of items. They ran their rough hands over elegantly etched armour with surprising delicacy, and gave approving grunts when they looked at the keen spearheads and arrows of the elves.

As night fell on the fourth day, Alandrian returned from the dwarf camp as Malekith sat in his tent, watching one of his many servants polish his armour. Alandrian brought Yeasir with him and the two lieutenants bowed as they entered the pavilion. Catching the look in their eyes Malekith dismissed the retainer and waved a hand for them to sit upon the plush rugs that served as a floor.

'You have news?' Malekith said, idly swirling wine around a silver goblet.

'Indeed, highness,' said Alandrian. 'Kurgrik intends to leave on the morrow.'

Malekith digested this without comment and Alandrian continued.

'Kurgrik has extended to you an invitation to accompany him back to the dwarf realms.'

'Has he?' said Malekith. 'How interesting. What do you make of his motives?'

'I am no expert, highness, but he seems sincere enough to me,' said Alandrian. 'He says that you may take an escort of fifty warriors.'

'Careful, highness,' said Yeasir. 'Though fifty Naggarothi would be guard enough against Kurgrik's small force, only the gods know what lies ahead. Even if we take the dwarfs at their word, which I don't, you would be relying upon them to provide you with adequate protection against any number of unknown perils. There are orcs and beasts aplenty still, I would say. If they should attack, who is to say that the dwarfs will stand their ground and not abandon you?'

'I do not think that the dwarfs would have ventured this far from their mountain homes if they were cowardly,' said Alandrian. 'There was no fear in them that I could see when they came to our camp, though they were at our mercy.'

'Bravery and duty are not the same thing,' said Yeasir, standing up and starting to pace. 'It is one thing for them to fight for themselves, but would they do so for our prince?'

He strode to the tent door and threw open the flap.

'Every elf of Nagarythe out there would lay down his life for our lord,' Yeasir said. 'Yet not one of them would risk his blood for Kurgrik unless the prince commanded it. I would expect no more from the dwarfs, and quite a lot less if I am to be honest. What if Kurgrik falls? Would his warriors fight on for Malekith?'

'We can demand oaths that they will,' answered Alandrian. 'They value honour highly and I would say that their word is almost as good as any elf's promise.'

'No matter!' snapped Malekith. 'If I am to go, I shall look to myself as ever and not rely upon the dwarfs for my safety. A more fundamental question is whether it is worth my time to go at all?'

'It would be most informative, I am sure, highness,' said Alandrian. 'We can learn much not only of the dwarfs but of the world further to the east.'

'We can judge the size of their armies and the quality of their fighters,' added Yeasir. 'It would be best that we know our foes.'

'If foes they are,' said Alandrian. 'As a gesture of faith and friendship, such embassy could bring us valuable allies.'

'Allies?' said Malekith. 'Nagarythe prospers upon her own strength and needs not the charity of others.'

'I have not made my point clearly, your highness,' said Alandrian with an apologetic bow. 'Ever will the other princes of Ulthuan be jealous of our power, and in Elthin Arvan there is none that can equal the power of Prince Malekith. Though all are of one heart and spirit for the moment, the loyalties of the other realms may well change. Bel Shanaar cares not for the colonies at the present, for they are distant from Tor Anroc. Yet, should his gaze turn upon these shores, how many of your fellow princes would stand by your side if the Phoenix Throne desired control over these lands?'

'And how would the dwarfs guard against that?' said Malekith, setting down his goblet and turning an intent stare upon his captain.

'They are entirely free of influence from Ulthuan,' Alandrian explained. 'With the dwarfs as your friends, you will be the powerbroker in Elthin Arvan and it is Bel Shanaar who will have to tread carefully in his dealings with you.'

'My mind is not made for politics,' said Yeasir, striding back from the door to stand before his master. 'I leave that to you. However, what I have seen of the dwarfs' wargear, it is durable and well made. At the moment we still rely much upon imports from Nagarythe to keep your warriors armed and armoured. If you could secure a more local source for such things, it improves our security.'

'Ever the practical one, Yeasir,' said Alandrian. 'Prince, envisage a treaty between Ulthuan and the dwarfs, for the betterment of both. Who is more fitting to herald such an age than Malekith of Nagarythe?'

'Your flattery is crude and obvious, Alandrian, but Yeasir's practicalities convince me,' announced Malekith, standing up. 'Alandrian, you shall convey my wishes to the dwarf thane that I shall accompany him back to his lands. Press upon him the honour he is being granted and extract whatever assurances your worries require and prudence expects.'

'Of course, highness,' replied Alandrian with a bow.

'Yeasir, I have another task for you,' said Malekith.

'I am ready to serve, highness,' said Yeasir.

'I shall write two letters this night, and entrust them to you before I depart,' said the prince. 'One is destined for Tor Anroc and the hand of Bel Shanaar. I would not have the Phoenix King accuse me of keeping this news from him.'

'And the other, highness?' said Yeasir.

'The other shall be for my mother,' said Malekith with a wry smile. 'Make sure that you deliver it first. If Morathi were to learn second-hand of what happens here, none of our lives would be worth living.'

THE FOLLOWING DAY, Malekith, Alandrian and fifty Naggarothi warriors accompanied Kurgrik as the dwarf thane headed back to the mountains. For the most part, the elves marched in silence alongside their new-found allies, who were equally taciturn. Malekith strolled alongside Kurgrik with Alandrian to translate, and though ever he appeared at ease the prince's eyes and ears were always alert.

Though the dwarfs had been confident enough in their camp, as they set out eastwards, their party became more wary. There were roughly two hundred dwarfs in the group, along with many wagons pulled by sturdy ponies, laden with felled trees. A vanguard of some fifty dwarfs preceded the march half a mile ahead of the main group, who walked slowly but surely alongside the wagons.

All of the dwarfs were armed and their hands were never far from the hafts of their axes and swords as they marched along the road. Ever the dwarfs were watchful, sending out scouts into the woods to warn of ambush.

The pace was not quick; Malekith and the other elves could have moved far more swiftly had they chosen to do so. However, the dwarfs marched relentlessly, and such was the efficiency with which they set and broke camp that they covered many miles each day, never wavering or tiring.

At night, the dwarfs would quickly dig defensive ditches lined with sharpened logs from the carts, and watchful guards patrolled ceaselessly. Kurgrik continued to entertain his guest with beer and such stories as Alandrian could translate.

Four days into the trek, the forests finally relinquished their weakening grip on the lands and were replaced by rising meadows and windswept hills. The mountains towered ahead, their snowy peaks lost amongst permanent clouds. Even the highest peaks of the Annulii on Ulthuan were diminutive by the standards of these ancient mounts, which stretched across the horizon north and south, seemingly going on forever.

The hills were covered with long grass and bracken, and littered with tumbled boulders swept down from the mountains in ages past. Paths and animal trails led off from the road, but it continued straight on through briar and across moor heading eastwards. As the group came nearer to the mountains, the first of several dwarf-built keeps came into sight.

It was a low, broad structure, only two storeys high, utterly unlike the majestic towers and spires of Ulthuan and quite ugly to Malekith's eye. The fort was crowned with battlements and protected by square towers at each corner. It stood on a hill overlooking the road, with large catapults and bolt-hurling engines upon its walls.

Dwarfs armed with axes and hammers marched out to meet Kurgrik and his curious guests, and as a storm swept down from the mountains, lashing the hills with driving rains and wind, the travellers were quickly ushered inside by the fort's commander.

Within the thick walls, the keep was sparsely furnished, and Malekith found the bare stone depressing. He wondered why the dwarfs did not hide the grey rock with tapestries and paintings. His mood was somewhat mollified as they were brought into a long low hall with a roaring fire pit at the centre. No matter how dreary the dwarfs' aesthetic crudeness, it was preferable to the tempest that was now raging outside.

Kurgrik introduced their host as Grobrimdor, a venerable dwarf of more than four hundred winters whose white beard was half as long again as he was tall. He wore his thick mail coat at all times, and an axe was hung at his belt even as he introduced the more prominent members of the garrison. It was clear to Malekith that despite the storm the dwarfs were still wary of attack.

Grobrimdor and Kurgrik furnished the elves with rough blankets and bowls of thick soup, and then asked politely if Malekith would talk more with them concerning the elves and Ulthuan. With Alandrian to roughly translate, Malekith seated himself upon a low stool by the fire.

'Far to the west, beyond the vast forests, lies the Great Ocean,' the prince began. 'Travel across the high waves for many days and one comes upon the shores of Ulthuan.

Our isle is fertile and green, an emerald set upon a sea of sapphire. White towers rise above the tall trees and verdant pastures, against the backdrop of the glittering peaks of the Annulii Mountains.'

'And you live in these mountains, yes?' said Kurgrik.

'Only to hunt,' replied Malekith. 'Except in Chrace and Caledor, where all is mountains and hills and there are no meadows or grass-filled plains on which to live.'

Kurgrik took this answer with a disappointed grunt, but then his eyes lit up with a new vigour.

'These mountains contain gems and gold?' asked the thane.

'Gold and silver, diamonds and crystals of all kinds,' said Malekith.

'And perhaps your king would trade these with our people?' said Kurgrik, getting quite animated.

'It is not for the Phoenix King alone to decide such matters,' Malekith said. 'We have many princes, and each of the realms of Ulthuan is ruled over by such an elf. It is for each to decide the fate and future of his lands and people. I rule Nagarythe, greatest of the kingdoms of Ulthuan, and reign over the colonies to the west of here.'

'That is good,' said Grobrimdor, gesturing for his retainers to bring mugs of ale. 'It is so with us. Our kings rule our cities, and the High King commands from Karaz-a-Karak. Your king must be a great leader to rule over so many princes.'

Malekith stifled his reply before it was spoken and suppressed the urge to glance towards Alandrian. Instead he took a sip of ale, buying time to compose his response.

'Bel Shanaar, the Phoenix King, is a clever statesman and diplomatic with his words,' said Malekith. 'My father, the first Phoenix King, was a great leader. He was our greatest warrior and our salvation from darkness.'

'If your father was king, then why does his son not succeed him?' asked Kurgrik, his knotty brows furrowed with suspicion.

Malekith was again forced to think his response through carefully, lest he betray some weakness or flaw that would offend the dwarfs.

'I will rule Ulthuan when she is ready for me,' said the prince. 'She needed time to heal from a great war fought against the daemons of the north, and so the princes chose not to follow the line of my father but to elevate one of their own to the Phoenix Throne. In the interests of harmony and peace, I do not challenge their decision.'

Both Grobrimdor and Kurgrik nodded and grunted approvingly, and Malekith relaxed a little. His thoughts were still turbulent though. The dwarfs' questions stirred old ambitions, feelings that Malekith had travelled to Elthin Arvan to leave behind. Alandrian, sensing his prince's unease, filled the silence.

'You spoke of trade,' said the captain. 'Our cities grow ever more swiftly with each year. What can your people offer us in exchange for our riches?'

The conversation turned once again to a subject dear to the dwarfs' hearts, and all talk of rulership and succession was forgotten. Malekith spoke little for the rest of the evening and allowed his mind to drift, knowing that Alandrian could later convey any news of import.

Long before midnight the dwarfs showed the elves to their rough quarters. Malekith slept in a large dormitory with his warriors, all of them upon the floor for the dwarfs' cots were far too short for the tall elves.

HAVING SLEPT POORLY, Malekith woke early in the morning. Many of the dwarfs were already up and about, or had perhaps passed the night without sleeping. The prince swiftly donned a simple robe and cloak and left the dormitory. The dwarfs said gruff welcomes as he passed into the main hall, but did not attempt to stop him. Guided only by whim, Malekith climbed a short staircase and exited out of a squat tower onto the battlements.

The sun was but a dull glow behind the mountains, which reared up into the dark blue skies in an unending line of jagged peaks. A thick mist coiled about the keep, and the breath of the dwarf sentries formed clouds in the air. Droplets of water shone on their beards and iron armour. All was peaceful save for the sound of metallic boots on stone and the jingle of the dwarfs' mail armour.

Malekith stood looking east towards the mountains for some time, until elven voices from below warned him that his companions were stirring. He was about to descend back to the hall when Alandrian hurried from the tower. The lieutenant visibly relaxed upon seeing his prince and his expression turned to sheepish guilt when Malekith raised an inquiring brow.

'I awoke to find you missing,' said Alandrian, striding quickly along the stone wall. 'I thought that perhaps some ill had befallen you.'

'You thought that perhaps I had been taken hostage?' said Malekith. 'That through some sorcery they had spirited me away without a fight?'

'I don't know what I thought, really, highness,' said Alandrian. 'I was suddenly fearful and reminded of Yeasir's warnings.'

Malekith turned back to the majestic view. The fog had all but gone and the mountains were revealed in all of their majesty. The prince took a deep breath and then let it out with feeling.

'I would not swap such sights for the quiet pedantry of the Phoenix Throne,' he declared. 'Who needs to be

Phoenix King when glory and conquest await? Let Bel Shanaar wither away in courts and audiences, while the wider world awaits me.'

Alandrian looked unconvinced.

'What is it?' said Malekith.

'It is Bel Shanaar who chooses to stay in Ulthuan and turn his reign into one of domesticity and politics,' said Alandrian, turning his gaze towards the mountains. 'Were you to be Phoenix King, I have no doubt that you would do so at the head of our armies, not from the comfort of Anlec. In time, the princes will see that their king leads from behind them, not from the front. Then they will see the true worth of Nagarythe, and her prince.'

'Perhaps,' said Malekith. 'Perhaps one day they will.'

The two stood in silence for a short while, gazing at the mountains, each content in his own thoughts concerning what they and their dwarfen rulers might herald for the Naggarothi. The sun now rose above the lowest peaks and golden light spilled down upon the hills.

A gruff cough attracted Malekith's attention and he turned to see a dwarf standing in the tower doorway.

'We should rejoin our hosts, highness,' said Alandrian. 'Kurgrik will wish to leave soon.'

'Go ahead and prepare for our departure,' said Malekith, looking back at the mountains but his thoughts far to the west upon Ulthuan. 'I'll be with you shortly.'

OVER THE FOLLOWING days, the dwarfs and elves stopped at several more of the way-forts. Each was as drab as the first and Malekith's expectations of the dwarfs' cities sank with every new sighting of the small, functional buildings.

The dwarfs took the time to spend a night in each of these way-fortresses, to gather news from the garrisons and show off their intriguing guests. The beer they had been presented with at the first meeting was much in evidence, and out of courtesy Malekith deigned to sample the different brews offered to him by each of the keep commanders. Though far from enamoured of the vulgar ale, Malekith soon learned the art of swallowing his allotted draught swiftly, so as to leave as little taste as possible in his mouth. He thought that perhaps this was why the dwarfs also drank so quickly; that they did not really like the taste of their own brews. However, the regularity with which the dwarfs returned to their barrels in an evening suggested otherwise.

When they came into the mountains proper, the dwarfs warned the elves to remain on their guard. Though the forests were the realm of Chaotic denizens and bloodthirsty beasts, the mountains were also home to many orcs and goblins, and other creatures such as trolls, giants and monstrous birds that frequently came south in search of food.

'Many daemons and monsters once besieged our holds,' said Kurgrik, via Alandrian's improving skills as a translator. The foothills were now rising steeply towards the mountains. The column was winding its way along a rough track, Kurgrik riding on his wagon, Malekith and Alandrian walking beside it.

'The sun hid and endless night darkened the mountains,' the thane continued. 'The valleys echoed to the howls and roars of the creatures of the north. They beat upon our gates and hurled themselves at our walls. Many dwarfs died defending their homes against the horrors.'

'We too suffered under the assault of Chaos,' Malekith said. 'Then Aenarion, my father, led the war against the daemons and brought us through the dark times.'

'Grimnir was the greatest of our warriors,' said Kurgrik with a wistful smile. 'Grungni, master of the runes and wise beyond mortals, forged two great axes for Grimnir. With these he slaughtered an army of the beasts. Valaya wove a cloak for her kin, and with her protective gift Grimnir fought against the largest and most deadly foes. Yet for all his fierce skill, Grimnir could not defeat every daemon, for they came forth in an unending tide.'

'As it was on Ulthuan,' said Malekith. 'Without end came the legions of Chaos. We fought without hope until Aenarion made the final sacrifice. He spilt his blood upon the altar of Khaine in return for victory.'

'Grimnir travelled far into the north with one of his axes and fought to the great gate of the Chaos gods,' Kurgrik said, frowning slightly at the prince's interruption. 'He was never seen again and his axe was lost. He battled into the gates themselves and even now wages war upon the daemons in their own realm, holding back their unending companies.'

'Caledor's vortex closed the gates,' said Malekith. 'It was the magic of the elves that stemmed the daemonic tide.'

Alandrian looked hesitant and did not translate his master's words.

'Why the silence?' demanded Malekith.

'Perhaps it is better that the dwarfs do not know that we trapped their greatest hero within the Realm of Chaos,' Alandrian said with a warning look. 'They may not take kindly to such knowledge.'

'We cannot let them peddle this fallacy,' Malekith insisted. 'It is the strength of the elves, not the dwarfs, that holds back the forces of the Dark Gods.'

'Who is to say that the dwarfen ancestors did not unwittingly aid Caledor's conjuration?' said Alandrian. 'That they suffered under the darkness of Chaos surely gives us more in common with them. Allow them to celebrate their own victories, for they do not tarnish your father's.'

Malekith considered this, not entirely convinced that he could allow the dwarfs to undermine the achievements of Aenarion. A glance at Kurgrik showed the dwarf watching the elves' exchange with friendly bemusement. The prince relented upon seeing the dwarf's ugly, honest face.

'Say that both elves and dwarfs have earned their right to live free upon this world,' said Malekith. 'Tell him that it is my hope that we no longer fight alone, but as allies.'

Alandrian's expression was one of shock.

'What?' demanded Malekith. 'What's wrong with that?'

'Nothing, highness,' said Alandrian. 'Quite the opposite, in fact. That is the most diplomatic thing I have heard pass from your lips in a hundred years!'

The glint of laughter in Alandrian's eyes quelled the angry retort welling up in Malekith's throat, and the prince merely coughed as if clearing his throat.

'Just keep the dwarf happy,' he finally managed to say, suppressing a smug smile.

THEIR JOURNEY TOOK them on for thirteen days before they reached the dwarf city, or hold as it was known to the dwarfs. Karak Kadrin they named it, one of the most northern cities in the mountains.

The location of the city was unmistakable, and as different from the road stations as could be imagined. High ramparts and towers dotted the sides of the pass, overlooking the approaches with sentries and war engines. Immense faces shaped into stylised likenesses of dwarfs were carved into the mountainsides – the Ancestor Gods, the elves were told.

From dark rock were the gatehouses carved, seen for the first time as the road turned to the north edge of the pass and began to wind back and forth up the hillside. They were as two mighty keeps, their foundations made from the mountain itself, thousands of heavy stones painstakingly cut and fitted to form fortifications that rivalled the great sea gates of Lothern. Golden standards glittered in the mountain sun, and banners stitched with angular runes and more of the curious dwarf designs hung from the ramparts.

Between the two immense flanking towers, the gates were closed. Almost as high as the gatehouse, arching far above the pass below, the gate was covered with plates of gold embossed with ancestor faces and symbols of smithying such as anvils, hammers and forges. Warriors clad in chainmail and heavy plates of armour guarded the portal, their expressions hidden behind full-faced helms wrought in the likenesses of fierce dwarf visages.

As the party came within sight of the gate towers, horns began to sound out, filling the valley with long, sonorous peals that rose and fell in harmony with the rebounding echoes. At this signal a much smaller door in the gate opened, though still thrice the height of an elf and broad enough for them to enter ten abreast.

Malekith had been impressed by the outer workings of the hold, but when he passed through the gate he stopped dead in his tracks and looked around in awe. The entrance hall was dug from the bare rock of the mountain, and far from the dreary stone of the way-keeps, it had been fashioned and polished so that it glittered in the light of hundreds of lanterns, every fault and strata a glorious decoration in its own right.

Long and no wider than the main gate, the hallway delved into the mountain, its high ceiling held by great arches carved from the living rock and sheathed in silver. The columns along the walls were cut in the same stylised fashion as the bastions upon the mountainsides; pillars of angular dwarf faces rising into the vaults above.

The lanterns that illuminated this impressive scene hung from thick chains suspended from the high vaults, each lamp larger than a dwarf and glowing with magical light. In the glow of these, the carvings between the arches could clearly be seen, depicting dwarf warriors at war, workers labouring in mines, smiths pounding at the forges and other vignettes of dwarfish endeavour. The floor was covered with regular flags, but each had been painstakingly etched with runes and lines of knotted patterns, the carved channels filled with coloured glass so that the ground was a riot of blues, reds and greens.

More dwarf guards lined the walls, arrayed in a line down each side, garbed in armour chased with gold, their double-headed axes inlaid with precious gems. Messengers had been sent ahead, and the party was greeted with much ceremony.

As they passed through the gigantic gateway the first pair of guards raised their weapons in salute, and so on down the line as the procession made its way along the long hallway. At the far end stood a delegation of dwarfs in brightly patterned jerkins, wearing elaborate helms adorned with horns or wings of gold, and each wore many rings and bracers, necklaces and brooches, so that they sparkled in the lantern light as they moved.

Behind each stood a banner bearer carrying a standard displaying the arms of the dwarf lords, bedecked with golden and silver badges and woven from fine metallic threads of every conceivable hue and shine. As with the other decorations, these were of axes and hammers, anvils and lightning bolts, displayed with such glimmering perfection that Malekith could imagine the royal standard of Nagarythe created in such a way.

Behind the welcoming party stood a door almost as large as the one by which the elves had entered. Cut from a solid piece of wood from some gigantic mountain oak, it was studded with bronze bolts, the head of each identically crafted as a pair of crossed hammers.

The dignitaries bowed low, sweeping their beards to one side with an arm so that they did not brush upon the ground. Malekith nodded his head in return, and the other elves also bowed in welcome. One of the nobles bore a large ornamental mace, and he turned and struck the door three mighty blows, the booms resounding around the hall. A slot opened in the door at about the height of a dwarf's face, and words were exchanged. There seemed to be some kind of argument, but Malekith suspected that this was some form of purposeful exchange whose significance eluded him.

Then the door opened, swinging effortlessly on hinges buried deep within the walls, to reveal the chambers beyond.

The hold was a veritable maze of corridors, halls and galleries, and though he tried to keep track of his path, Malekith soon found he was lost amongst the unending passages and stairwells. They seemed to be progressing up into the mountain, although by a circuitous route that rose and dipped.

The interior of the hold was not quite so grand as the entrance chamber, but still well built and decorated with gems and precious metals. Here and there the route took them past glowing foundries where the heat of furnaces blasted from open archways and the ringing of hammers echoed all around the visitors. There seemed to be little relent from the labour, though occasionally an artisan or forge worker would look up from his endeavours. The impression Malekith was left with was one of constant industry, as dwarfs wearing dirtied smocks and leather aprons busied themselves about the tunnels and rooms.

Eventually they were brought into the audience chamber of King Gazarund. It was a wide, low hall, with shields and banners hung upon the walls. Two long fire pits blazed to each side, the smoke from which disappeared up a cunning series of chimneys and channels to the mountainside far above. A walkway raised slightly above the rest of the chamber ran from the doorway to the throne dais, ascending up nearly twenty feet in a series of stepped rises. Bathed in the flickering red flames, the gold-inlaid tiles of the floor glimmered with ruddy light.

Kurgrik motioned for the elves to halt, and with the other thanes and notable members of the king's council made his way forwards.

King Gazarund sat upon a throne of black granite decorated with more gold tracery. His expression was austere rather than welcoming, and in the firelight his dark eyes shone from under beetling brows. He was bare-armed, save for two intricately wound torques upon each bicep, and he was robed in a simple tabard of blue and white. His beard was thick and black, straggled with stray wisps of grey, and was so long that despite being coiled through loops upon his belt and woven into winding plaits, it still hung almost to the ground. His face was craggy and creased, his skin pocked with the scars of years.

Most distinctively, he wore a golden patch over his right eye, and to Malekith's inner horror it appeared that this covering was riveted into the king's flesh.

The king's crown was set on a table beside the throne, so large and baroque that even this sturdy dwarf would not have been able to bear its weight upon his head. Wings as large as an eagle's splayed from the war-helm, and its cheek guards were studded with dozens of diamonds. In its place, the king wore a simple steel cap, banded with brazen knotwork, a few wisps of unkempt hair escaping from under its fur-lined brim.

The dwarf nobles made petition to the king, or so it seemed to Malekith from his experience of similar ceremonies at the court of Bel Shanaar. The king nodded once and the elves were waved forwards.

With great deliberation, the true ritual of welcoming began, carried out with solemn decorum by the king of Karak Kadrin and his thanes. Malekith and the king exchanged gifts; for the prince a dwarf-wrought brooch of gold, for the king a fine elven bracelet made of silver and decorated with sapphires.

Malekith was presented to the nobles of the hold via a list of unintelligible names that he soon forgot, and then was ushered into the chambers that had been set aside for them to stay.

The bedrooms were accommodating, but far from plush. The furniture was for dwarfs, and so the chairs and beds were distressingly low. Malekith found it easier to kneel before the clay basin upon the wall to wash his face, rather than clean himself at a constant stoop.

There was no fire in the room, but a steady breeze of warm air came from a grated vent upon the wall; Malekith surmised this was somehow redirected from the forges below by some ingenious means. The fabrics upon the bed and chairs were stiff and unyielding, as was the padding in the mattress. Though Malekith would have preferred something a little more kind to lie upon, it was by no means a necessity for him having spent many of his long years on campaign in the wilderness.

After resting for a short while, Malekith then made it known to the dwarf who stood guard outside his door that he was ready to eat, by the simple expedient of miming food to his mouth and rubbing his stomach. The dwarf nodded in understanding and garbled something in return, and then stood back in his place.

Having called for Alandrian, Malekith again asked for something to eat, only to be told that there was a banquet to be held in their honour that night.

It was a fulsome affair, with much quaffing of ale and long speeches that Malekith did not understand. The feasting hall was bedecked with more banners, and great brass seals displaying the emblems of the various clans and guilds of the hold.

Three tables were arranged down its length, each seating a hundred feasters, and Malekith and his company sat at another table that ran across the head of the hall, along with the king and his most trusted companions.

The food was for the most part palatable, consisting mostly of roast meats and boiled vegetables. Thick gravy and heavy dumplings were also served in abundance, along with pitchers of ale of all varieties and strengths. Malekith had become accustomed to delicately flavoured and fragranced meals, using such herbs and spices as grew on Ulthuan and in the islands on the other side of the world. The menu sat heavily on the prince's stomach, and he could see how the dwarfs were so sturdy of build and wide of girth.

Still, the cooking was done with competence if not finesse, though Malekith despaired of his hosts' table manners at times. Each course was served upon gigantic platters, and once the king had helped himself to whatever he desired, it seemed to become a free-for-all where everybody else was concerned. Ales were slopped over the bare wooden boards of the tables, and Malekith kept a suspicious eye on a puddle of gravy that spread dangerously close to him as the evening progressed.

Kurgrik, sitting on Malekith's left, had taken it upon himself to assist the prince with his dining; assuring himself that his guest was plentifully fed by heaping ladle upon ladle of stew into his bowl, and small mountains of potatoes, roast ducks, barley cakes and other simple fare upon his plate.

Something else that took Malekith aback occurred shortly after the fourth course. There was a pause while the tables were cleared of plates and debris, and all of the dwarfs produced small pouches filled with dried ground leaves. The contents of these small bags they stuffed into pipes of all shapes and sizes, which they then lit and puffed on contentedly for quite some time.

The haze of pipe smoke quickly filled the hall and hung in a thick fug above the table, causing many of the elves to cough violently, including Malekith. Misreading their discomfort as subtle prompts, Kurgrik proffered his tobacco to Malekith. The elven prince declined with a smile and a firm shake of the head, and Kurgrik shrugged and placed his leaf pouch back into the recesses of his robe whence it had come, seeming not to take any offence.

Several more platters of steamed potatoes, venison steaks and immense sausages went by, and then a hush descended upon the hall. There followed several more speeches, which Alandrian attempted to translate as best he could. Most of them spoke about family honour, great tragedies and valour in battle, and after a while Malekith stopped listening to his lieutenant and allowed his mind to drift.

It was then he felt a sharp dig in his ribs and looked around to see Alandrian looking at him pointedly. Casting his gaze around the smoky hall, the prince saw that all eyes were turned upon him.

'It is your turn to make a toast, I believe,' whispered Alandrian with a mischievous smile. 'Shall I translate?'

'I would think it better not to,' said Malekith. 'I know that you have learnt well their strange tongue, but I would not have you accidentally call the king a bloated warthog on my behalf. I shall sound so suitably imperious and charismatic, the exact meaning of my words will not be necessary to convey their spirit.'

The prince of Nagarythe stood up, while Kurgrik leaned over and refilled his tankard with a beer that was so thick and black it could have been mistaken for pitch.

'Your good health!' said Malekith, raising the cup to the hall. The dwarfs sat in respectful expectation, hands hovering close to their tankards. They had no idea what the prince had just said.

'What is the matter with them?' Malekith hissed out of the side of his mouth whilst trying to maintain a genteel smile.

'I think they want something a little, well, longer,' said Alandrian. 'You will have to go on a bit, I believe, to make them think they have been given a proper oratory.'

'Very well,' said Malekith, turning his attention towards the king of the hold. 'Your halls here are mighty, and full of great wonders. I have marvelled at the skills of your people, and I know in my heart that an alliance with you shall bring much benefit to my people.'

A glance towards Alandrian received an encouraging nod, and Malekith continued. Seeing the polite but clueless expressions on the sea of faces before him, the prince decided to indulge himself a little.

'You are very fine people, if a little unwashed and short.'

The elves laughed quietly at this, and taking their cue the dwarfs joined in, chortling uncertainly.

'It has been mostly my pleasure to meet you all, though I have not a clue what your names are, and all of you look pretty much the same to me.'

Another sideways glance at Alandrian was received with a pout of disapproval, but Malekith ignored his aide and carried on with his joke.

'That your mouths produce as much smoke as your chimneys is surprising, and if I do not choke to death before the evening is out, I shall thank the gods for protecting me. I understand that we have only just met, but I hope that in time you will understand the great privilege I have granted you all by allowing you into my presence. There are people of my own homeland who have never been granted an audience with me, and yet here I am, sinking cupfuls of your foul broth and treating you like equals. I am assured that you are an honourable people, and you best well be.'

At this point Malekith stood up and raised his foot upon the table to lean forwards, a feat not difficult for the slender elf, for the table barely came above his knees.

'Know this!' the prince proclaimed, his voice ringing clearly across the hall, focussing the attention of even the most drunkard audience member. 'It will go well for you that we should become friends. The Naggarothi do not treat idly with others, even elves of other realms. Should you wrong us, our vengeance will be sure, swift and deadly. We will burn these halls and we will pile your corpses upon pyres so high that they will rival these mountains. We shall be content to let you dwell in these rocky peaks, and we shall take the lowlands and the forests. Should you oppose us, we will have no option but to drive you before us, as we have the orcs and the beasts and the goblins. I look forward to meeting your High King, for he shall hopefully be of an almost equal standing to myself, and of intelligence enough to treat with me. But I warn you, if I am not impressed with him, I may decide simply to slay all of you. In fact, the next one of you that mispronounces my name might just get my blade through his gizzard. While we may deign to learn your crude language, please do not mangle the heritage of my forefathers and the legacy to my descendants with your ugly lips and thick tongues.'

Raising his goblet once again, Malekith grinned broadly.

'Long may Nagarythe prevail over you all!' he declared.

Before the prince could say any more, Alandrian shot to his feet and gave a shout of celebration, his mug upraised. The other elves, some of them clearly shocked, the rest wearing looks of approval, did likewise; the dwarfs then slowly followed their lead until there was a great rousing cheer that filled the hall with a cacophony of shouting and the slamming of cups upon tables.

'Thank you,' said Malekith, holding up a hand for silence. The dwarfs appeared not to understand the gesture for they continued their banging and clapping.

With Alandrian's hand on his arm pulling him down before he could speak further, Malekith sat, a contented smile upon his face.

This seemed to conclude the round of speeches, and servants came forth bearing great bowls of steaming pudding made from boiled grain and honey, with chunks of stodgy cake to dip into the sweet broth. This was followed by platters of hard cheeses that smelt of diseased goats, as far as Malekith could tell, which were served with small biscuits with the texture and taste of thin slices of dried wood.

Under the stone roof of the hall, Malekith lost all sense of passing time and knew not whether it was midnight or if dawn was fast approaching when the elves were finally allowed to retire to their dormitories. Many of the dwarfs still caroused, though a significant proportion of their number had simply slipped into inebriated stupors at the tables.

For the highest-ranking attendees, the servants brought small pillows, which were carefully placed under the snoring faces of the inebriated lords. The lesser peons were allowed to doze away, their faces in spillages and crumbs.

All Malekith knew was that the banquet had been more tiring than the march, but he went to bed invigorated nonetheless for his overly full stomach, both appalled and yet mesmerised by the strange culture of these people.

On the one hand they were loud, careless and ignorant of any form of etiquette, yet he had seen much evidence that they were also studious, observant, dedicated and loyal. Their attention to detail in matters of craftsmanship equalled that of the elves, and in weapon-making and the construction of mechanical devices their knowledge outstripped that of Ulthuan. That they knew of magic was clear from many of the things Malekith had seen in the hold, yet he had not seen any dwarf openly wielding sorcery, and when Alandrian had enquired on the prince's behalf, he had been met with polite but stern denials that the dwarfs had wizards of any kind.

✦ FIVE ✦

The High King

MALEKITH WAS EAGER to continue their journey to the hold of the High King, and was grateful that Kurgrik apparently had a schedule of his own to keep. The thane's shipment of wood was sorely needed for the mines beneath Karaz-a-Karak, and the party, dwarfs and elves, left the city of Karak Kadrin early the next day.

The king came to wave them off, and seemed much more approachable and friendly away from the formality of his court. He shook the hands of each of the elves in turn, and patted Malekith fondly on the arm. He said something in dwarfish, and Malekith smiled and nodded, not bothering to listen to Alandrian's translation.

Malekith and the party did not travel back to the main gates, but were taken by an underground route to another entrance. Though slightly less grand, this portal was no less impressive to the prince, for it led not to the surface but to a vast passageway dug through the bedrock of the mountain. Due south it struck, paved with flags and large enough for many carts and dwarfs to pass each other by with ease.

Lanterns lit the underground highway, and the walls were hewn so smoothly that no shadow darkened them. Great pillars of wood and metal shored up the roof, which was easily four or five times the height of an elf.

For this stage of the journey, they travelled upon the backs of rocking carts. It was not entirely unpleasant, though the lack of night and day began to wear upon Malekith's nerves. After three days, he wondered just how far this tunnel was. After six, he was longing for a sight of sun or stars, or even a storm-filled sky.

Periodically they came across guard stations, not unlike underground versions of the way-forts they had stayed in on the surface. Warriors with strange-looking, mechanical bows patrolled outwards from these subterranean castles.

Branchways and side tunnels broke off from the main road in clustered junctions, and there was always a steady traffic of dwarfs on wagons and on foot. They carried all manner of goods with them: metal ingots, sacks of coal, bushels of crops, mining tools and all manner of other wares.

By the eighth day, Malekith's interest had been restored, for he was now fully realising the extent of the dwarfen realm. They had covered no less than fifteen leagues each day, and so had travelled three hundred and sixty miles or more. The highway went pretty much straight and so he guessed that they were still heading south. If the side passages and other exits each led to other holds and settlements, then the mountains were swarming with dwarfs.

Some of the prince's earlier arrogance dissipated as he pondered the huge implication of an alliance with these people. If the Naggarothi could forge this friendship with speed, then his people would increase the power they already held in the colonies.

Knowing this, he now paid more attention to the dealings the dwarfs had with each other, and tried harder to get a rough grasp of their language from Alandrian. He endeavoured to learn the names of his dwarfish companions: outlandish monikers such as Gundgrin, Borodin, Hagrun and Barrnok. He learned the words for sword, and axe, and that this highway was called the Ungdrin Ankor.

He learned their word for gold, and another, and another, until he was thoroughly confused. During a break, Malekith steered Alandrian into a quiet alcove and confronted his lieutenant on the matter.

'Azgal, churk, bryn, galaz, gnolgen, gorl, konk, thig, ril, skrottiz…' Malekith complained. 'All of these hideous words, and I cannot work out which one means gold! How am I supposed to learn this stupid language?'

'They all mean gold, highness,' Alandrian said patiently.

'Gold's gold!' said Malekith. 'Why do they need so many damned words for it?'

'Gold is, indeed, gold, highness,' said Alandrian, pulling a neck chain from under his robe, upon which hung a small dwarfish amulet he had been gifted by Kurgrik. 'To a dwarf, however, there are lots of types of gold. The gold on the outer edge, with the reddish tinge, is konk. The inner design is made from a slightly softer metal that they call gorl.'

'I understand,' said Malekith, not understanding at all. Alandrian read the doubt on the prince's face.

'We see one metal, which we call gold,' the captain explained slowly, placing the amulet back under his robe. 'The dwarfs see all sorts of different metals and they have a name for each one.'

'So, each word means a different type of gold?' Malekith said. 'Soft gold, hard gold, shinier gold, that sort of thing?'

'That sort of thing, yes, highness,' said Alandrian with a reassuring nod.

'But there can't be that many types of gold, surely?' said Malekith.

'Not physically, no,' Alandrian said. His face screwed up in consternation as he worked out how to explain further. 'To the dwarfs, gold has other qualities, not just physical ones.'

'Such as?' Malekith said.

'Well, there is lucky gold, for a start,' said Alandrian.

'Lucky gold?' Malekith's brows arrowed into a frown.

'Gold that was found by accident, for example,' replied Alandrian.

'Seems strange, but then they are a strange folk,' said Malekith.

'The type of gold also changes depending on where it came from, where it currently is and its own history,' Alandrian continued under the prince's demanding stare. 'There's a word for gold that is an ingot and hasn't yet been made into something. There's a different word for gold that was once made into something else but has been melted down to make something new. There's gold that is for spending, what they call impatient, and gold that is for keeping. That's almost the same word as they use for waiting or patience. Then there's gold that you don't own yet, such as ore or a loan. Of course, that also means there are words for gold that you would like to own, or once owned–'

'Enough!' snapped Malekith. 'So, they have lots of words for gold. I cannot be expected to learn them all.'

'Oh no, highness,' said Alandrian. 'Not even the dwarfs know all the names for gold, apparently. They can make up any name for gold they like and another dwarf will probably understand what they mean.'

Alandrian cast a look over his shoulder at the dwarfs climbing back on the wagons, making ready to leave.

'It's probably best not to mention gold too much, in any case,' Alandrian said. 'Whenever I mention it, they get a queer look in their eyes. Some of them get quite excited. I once mentioned the golden gates of Lothern and Kurgrik almost fainted!'

'So, it is best not to tell them that we have huge treasuries in Athel Toralien?' said Malekith. 'Just in case they come over funny and decide to try to take it?'

'Yes, highness, something like that,' said Alandrian.

Malekith nodded knowingly and glanced over his companion's shoulder to see Kurgrik scowling ever so slightly in the prince's direction. Malekith smiled cheerily and waved, trying to ignore the picture he had of the thane frothing at the mouth and pawing at a coin.

ON THE TENTH day they turned from the main road, heading west as far as Malekith could judge. Here the traffic increased considerably and Malekith surmised that the capital was not far away. Kurgrik was more animated, and from the comparatively few words that the prince had learned and through the translation of Alandrian, it seemed that they would be at their destination the next day.

Malekith became agitated the closer they came to their destination, and constantly harangued Alandrian to find out more about the dwarfs, and in particular, their High King. On this, Kurgrik proved strangely reticent, saying only that his name was Snorri Whitebeard, and that he was the first to rule over all the holds. The following day, Malekith was to meet this dignitary.

As the caravan readied for the march, Malekith took out his finest cloak from his stores; purple embroidered with golden thread in a design of two dragons coiling about each other. The prince scented his hair with perfumes from his pack, and swept it back over his shoulders with a silver band embellished with five rubies and three diamonds, each cut and polished into an oval as large as a fingertip. Feeling suitably regal, he sat on the wagon at the front of the column alongside Kurgrik. His pride was somewhat punctured by the fact that he had to almost tuck his knees under his chin to fit on the seat.

THE GATEWAY FROM the Ungdrin Ankor to the capital of the dwarf realm was a wide set of golden doors mounted upon a series of gears and cogs that allowed them to be opened effortlessly with a single push despite their immense weight. They were inscribed with many vertical lines of runes, each separated by a sparkling diamond.

The gates were flanked by two pillars of black marble, intricately carved with ancestor faces that glowered at all who approached. The tiles of the floor had an endless array of designs upon them. Kurgrik said something to Alandrian.

'Every clan symbol of the hold is carved into these stones,' Alandrian explained.

Malekith accepted this without word and turned his warrior eye to the gates' defences. Side chambers with stout iron doors looked out upon the corridor, with shuttered windows and murder holes so that defenders could pour arrows into any attacker from almost complete safety. A glance up revealed other openings through which oil could be poured.

Malekith noted all this and, combining it with what he had seen of the great gate of Karak Kadrin, decided that the holds were all but impregnable. With the Ungdrin Ankor to link the cities underground, even protracted siege was impossible, for unless one could control the subterranean highway, there was no way to cut off supplies. Despite these formidable defences, Malekith knew that no stronghold was ever totally secure, but such would be the cost of taking such a city, it was far better to broker a friendship with these people than to anger them.

Dismounting from their carts, Kurgrik and his companions were met with slaps on the back and hearty greetings from their fellow dwarfs as the party passed into the hold. There were curious looks from these dwarfs at the elves, but nothing like the amazement and interest they had raised in Karak Kadrin.

As they progressed into Karaz-a-Karak, the feeling grew more pronounced; these dwarfs already seemed familiar with elf-kind. Recalling Kurgrik's first reaction to Malekith, it seemed that in retrospect the thane had not been surprised to see the elves in and of themselves, but rather to find them in that place.

Malekith's fears were confirmed when they were conveyed by an escort of heavily armed warriors to the throne room of the High King. The chamber was even larger and more opulent than that of Karak Kadrin, and was hung with so many shields, banners and gold emblems that barely a patch of rock could be seen between them. The entire floor was tiled with gold and inset with rubies, and the ceiling was awash with lanterns. More than a hundred steps led up to the dais upon which a large throne was set, similarly bedecked with gold and jewels. Dozens of dwarfs of noble dress and bearing were gathered about the hall.

Most notable of all, and to which Malekith's eyes were immediately drawn, were the two elves stood beside the throne in deep conversation with the king.

One, the prince recognised immediately. He was Prince Aernuis of Eataine, a renowned admiral who had led some of the first ships across the ocean. Nothing had been heard from him for over forty years and it had been widely thought that his expedition had been lost. The reason for his long absence suddenly became clearer to Malekith, and he felt his anger rising at the secretive nature of the prince's dealings with the dwarfs.

The other elf was unknown to the ruler of Nagarythe, but by his bearing Malekith assumed him to be one of Aernuis's councillors. Detecting a change in the atmosphere of the chamber, the elves looked up and saw Malekith striding into the throne room. Though it was hard to tell in the fierce light, it seemed to the prince that their pale faces blanched just a little more.

Kurgrik hurried ahead of Malekith to present the prince to the High King, who was sat on his throne with an elbow upon his knee, his chin rested on his clenched fist. He sat up attentively as Kurgrik approached, and listened intently as the thane spoke for a long while. With a nod, the king directed his stern gaze towards Malekith.

'Happy welcome you are to Karaz-a-Karak,' said Snorri Whitebeard, and Malekith flinched at the mangling of his native tongue, even as he was surprised by the High King's use of it.

'Hello, king,' Malekith replied in his finest Dwarfish, regaining his composure as quickly as he was able. He ignored the smirks upon the faces of Aernuis and his retainer, and saw neither amusement nor anger in the expression of Snorri. 'I Malekith.'

At this the king gave a satisfied nod, and gestured for Malekith to approach up the long stair. Malekith glanced over his shoulder towards Alandrian, and gestured for the lieutenant to follow him. His cloak billowing behind him, the prince of Nagarythe strode up the steps two at a time.

'Malekith?' said the elf whose name the prince did not know. 'You are the last person we expected to see here.'

'So it would seem,' replied Malekith. 'You know me, yet I do not know who you are. Please inform my companion, Alandrian, so that I might know the name of the impudent elf I shall soon slay for not using my full title.'

'Sutherai,' the elf stammered quickly, casting a fearful glance at his prince. Malekith raised an eyebrow in displeasure.

'Your highness,' Sutherai added with a visible shudder.

The High King watched this exchange with what appeared to be an expression of interest, having obviously noted the tone in Malekith's voice and that of Sutherai, if not perhaps understanding fully what had passed between them. Snorri then looked intently at Aernuis, who put on his most obsequious smile and said something in Dwarfish.

'Outrageous!' spat Alandrian from behind Malekith, and the prince turned on his lieutenant with an inquisitive glare. There was also a look of shock upon the face of Sutherai, and one of sudden contrition upon Aernuis.

'The prince just described you to the king as a minor noble, as far as I am able to understand,' Alandrian explained quietly, before quickly adding, 'But do not react too harshly before the High King, I feel that Aernuis has closeted himself closely in his court.'

Malekith absorbed these words and fought back his anger.

'Please announce to the High King my full title, rank and line, so that he might better understand with whom he is meeting,' Malekith said evenly, his eyes piercing holes into Aernuis.

Alandrian spoke at some length, and Malekith realised that his companion was indeed relating every title and rank that Malekith held. The king did not seem overly impressed, but cast a sideways glance at Aernuis, before replying to Alandrian.

'King Snorri asks why it is that elves feel the need to have so many titles,' Alandrian said. 'He is known simply as the High King.'

'Because we value prestige and rank more than you cave-dwelling savages,' was Malekith's mental retort, but he curbed his tongue and paused before replying.

'Tell him that such titles are used only rarely,' Malekith said after a moment's thought, 'such as when lesser nobles forget their place and display a lack of respect.'

This Alandrian truly translated as best he could, and the king looked at Aernuis with a deeper frown, his jaw churning as he considered the events unfolding about him. After a pregnant pause that lasted quite some time, Snorri met Malekith's gaze and there was a peculiar twinkle in his eye. The king then broke into a grin, before laughing out loud. Malekith found himself smiling also, for the High King's amusement was genuine, and there was no hint of mockery in his expression.

Snorri pushed himself from his throne and strode up to Malekith, before grasping his hand and vigorously shaking it and slapping him on the arm. As Snorri returned to his chair of office, Malekith could not stop himself directing a sly smile towards Aernuis while the High King's back was turned, which infuriated the rival prince even further.

The king then muttered something in Dwarfish and ushered them all away with a shooing gesture. Malekith paused to bow before he turned, thinking it prudent to cement this small victory while he could. Aernuis walked beside him as they made their way down the steps.

'Three years I have been here,' Aernuis declared. 'In that time I have worked long and hard to build up the High King's trust for me. You cannot simply stroll into Karaz-a-Karak and expect to be given equal rights as me.'

'Remember whom you are addressing, Aernuis,' replied Malekith. 'I know that these folk despise kinslaying even more than our own people, but if I do not get satisfactory answers from you, I will have your throat slit.'

'In these halls, your threats are idle,' said Aernuis with a snort. 'I have the protection of King Snorri; if you try to cause me harm, it would be like an assault upon the High King himself.'

'We shall see how long that favour lasts,' said Malekith. 'You cannot hide beneath his beard forever, prince. You have wronged me here, and that I will not easily forget, nor soon forgive.'

They had reached the bottom of the steps and parted slightly. Malekith turned and laid a hand upon Aernuis's shoulder, seemingly in friendship from where the High King was sat. In reality, the Eataine prince squirmed under Malekith's iron grip as the Naggarothi lord's fingers dug through his robes, deep into the flesh.

'I look forward to feeding your carcass to the crows,' Malekith said pleasantly. 'The only way you will regain my favour is to make yourself utterly indispensable to my cause. Tell me everything you know about these folk, and how you came to be here, and I may reconsider killing you.'

Aernuis looked into Malekith's eyes, hoping to see some hint of mocking or weakness, but there was none; the Naggarothi's eyes were as hard as flint and as utterly devoid of emotion as a shark's hungry gaze. Looking away, Aernuis freed himself from Malekith's painful grip and straightened the creases in his robe. With a disconcerted look, he turned on his heel and skulked away, enduring the sneers of the Naggarothi still stood at the entrance.

LATER THAT NIGHT, Malekith supposed, though he could not tell for sure, Aernuis came to the prince's chambers. Aernuis's manner was one of conciliation and he gave a formal bow as he entered, though its impact was somewhat lessened by the fact that the tall elf had already been forced to stoop by passing through the low doorway.

Malekith sat along the length of his short cot with his back against the wall. He was dressed in a flowing purple robe, his armour piled carefully upon the floor, for there was no stand tall enough to hold it. Other items such as his sword and helm were placed neatly on the low shelves of the small room. In his hands he held the dwarf-made brooch gifted to him in Karak Kadrin, and after glancing up at his visitor he returned his gaze to wonder at its workmanship.

'I fear there has been some misunderstanding between us,' Aernuis said. 'I am more than willing to share the spoils that founding a solid relationship with the dwarfs will bring. I am almost alone here, and life amongst these folk has led me into bad habits. I would be honoured to serve in whatever capacity I can, for the benefit of Ulthuan.'

'Go on,' Malekith said without looking up.

'It has taken me many years to build what I have with the dwarfs,' explained Aernuis. 'Only these last three years have I spent with the High King. Before that, I dwelt within Karak Izril, a city as far south again as you have travelled from Karak Kadrin. When we sailed across the ocean, we looked to find passage eastwards, but storms blew us onto the coast south-west of where we now are. Though most of my crew survived the wreck, the ship could not be saved and we were cast upon this strange shore with little in the way of supplies, and with no knowledge of where we had landed.'

'Sounds dreadful,' muttered Malekith, still entranced by his brooch.

'It was,' said Aernuis, ignoring the prince's irony. 'The lands between the sea and the mountains are infested with orcs, vicious green-skinned beasts intent on slaughter and destruction.'

'Yes, I know them,' said Malekith, still feigning disinterest. 'My sword has met more than a few.'

'Goblins riding upon wolves assailed us, and we were driven ever eastwards, into the heart of the desolate wilderness that lies south of here,' Aernuis continued. 'We fought as best we could, but their attacks were constant and gradually our numbers dwindled. For several months we wandered, ever trying to head towards the mountains, but often finding our route cut off by orc camps or marauding warbands. There was little to hunt, and hunger and thirst stalked us as much as the goblins. When but a handful of my ship's company were left, the others decided to head back towards the coast in the hope that some other ship may have followed our course. I knew this to be folly, for we had been driven here only by chance, but they would not be dissuaded from their course of action, so I let them go. Only loyal Sutherai stayed with me.'

'How heart-warming, I'm sure,' said Malekith, tossing the brooch onto a table beside the bed and swinging his feet to the floor so that he faced the Eataine prince. 'So tell me, good admiral, what have you been doing for the last forty years?'

'Sutherai and I made it to the foothills, travelling at night, hiding in stream beds and marshes to avoid detection during the day,' said Aernuis, and his haunted expression as he recalled those times was a testament to the fear that he had felt. 'We came upon a strange building, and thinking it abandoned, we took shelter. The orcs did not approach it, and so we made camp there for some time. It was, of course, a dwarf fort, and six days after we came there, the dwarfs returned. At first they were going to slay us out of hand, but I expect that so bedraggled and pitiful we looked, they stayed their axes. Curiosity saved us, and they took us back to Karak Izril, where we lived for many years.'

Aernuis looked at Malekith's unconvinced expression and sighed.

'I do not expect you to understand our plight,' Aernuis said. 'We were two strangers very far from our own lands. We did not know if there were other elves within a thousand miles, and even if there were, there was no way that we could contact them. Even when we had learned a little of the dwarfen tongue, and they came to trust us more, we could not leave. Where would we go? Out into the wilderness, boldly striking out for friends that in all likelihood did not exist? I felt as if I had stumbled upon all the riches of the world, but had nobody with whom to share them, nothing on which to spend them.'

'Riches?' asked Malekith, dropping his pretence of indifference.

'You have seen how they decorate their halls, the gold and silver they wear, the artisanship of their weapons,' said Aernuis. 'It is but a fraction of the wealth of these mountains. Every hold has vast vaults filled with gems and precious metals, I have seen them. They covet gold like no other thing, and hoard it as a squirrel keeps nuts for the winter. Seeing you, I realised that much has changed since I left Ulthuan, and I think that now we must hold all the varied riches of the wide world in our hands. If we can but broker trade with the dwarfs, you and I will become pre-eminent amongst all of the princes.'

'I am already pre-eminent,' said Malekith.

'Your soldiers are perhaps not so sure,' said Aernuis.

'What do you mean?' demanded Malekith, angrily rising to his feet.

'Sutherai has spoken with many of them, and learned that Bel Shanaar has grown rich and powerful on the proceeds of his empire,' Aernuis said. 'Though your claims here grow by the year, who can say how the fortunes of Nagarythe fare back on Ulthuan? Yet if you can reach agreement with the dwarfs, and act as arbiter between their kings and the Phoenix Throne, it is you who shall hold Bel Shanaar's fate.'

'Alandrian should learn to control his tongue,' Malekith muttered.

'With me by your side, you have a partner ready and willing to speak to King Snorri on your behalf,' Aernius continued. 'Without me, it will take you twenty years or more to earn his trust, and in that time many things can happen. It was by chance that we both met with these folk, but as our cities grow and more of our people cross the seas, how long before others encounter them also? If you fear me as a rival, you must fear time more, for we have an opportunity here to create something that will seal our places in history, but it will not last forever.'

'Perhaps I misjudged you,' said Malekith, and hope filled Aernuis's face, but it quickly dissipated when he saw the Naggarothi's cruel expression. 'I thought you a coward, but instead you are merely a merchant. I am the prince of Nagarythe, a warrior and general, not a trader to barter deals and haggle with lesser entities.'

'And how glorious might be the armies of Nagarythe with the wealth of the mountains in your coffers?' said Aernuis with a smile. 'Dwarf-forged spears in their hands, and dwarf-made arrows in their quivers? You have seen their buildings, sturdy and strong. Crude in look, but we can learn their techniques and turn them to our advantage, to create beautiful palaces in which to pass away our long days, and soaring castles that will defend our realm for eternity. Much of what they make is rough and functional, but if guided by an elven hand, think what their mastery of stone and metal and wood would bring to our people. It is not just trade that this relationship will herald, but a new era of elven dominion.'

'I do not think that they will give up their secrets lightly,' said Malekith.

'They will not,' replied Aernuis. 'But if they will give them up at all, they will give them up to us!'

Malekith sat down again, deep in thought. He imagined the legions of Nagarythe marching upon roads that cut through hills and over bridges that spanned wide rivers and mountain passes. He had seen the odd mechanical bows that many of the dwarfs carried, and wondered what his finest marksmen could do with such weapons.

Only after a while did he remember that Aernuis was still in the room. He looked up at the prince, who was wracked between expectation and dread as he looked at Malekith pondering the future.

'Very well,' Malekith declared. 'You have proved yourself useful to me, and I shall not slay you yet. You may leave me now.'

Aernuis bowed again with as much dignity as he could muster, and then departed. Malekith picked up the brooch from the table and looked at it again, tracing a finger over its entwined patterns. With a smile, he attached it to his robe and stood, calling for Alandrian.

‑‑◄ SIX ►‑‑

Beasts in the Mountains

WHAT AERNUIS HAD said proved to be true; the dwarfs were reluctant to treat with any outsiders. However, the Eataine prince's long standing in Karak Izril and his exemplary behaviour in the capital had garnered him a measure of respect, and by association this passed also to Malekith.

The Naggarothi ruler despatched some of his company to return to Athel Toralien, so that proper scribes and diplomats could come to Karaz-a-Karak. The dwarfs laboured likewise, assembling embassies from the many holds across the mountains, for these debates concerned not just Karaz-a-Karak but all of the dwarf empire.

It took the whole of the summer for the preparations to be made, and Malekith was always careful to send regular missives back to Ulthuan so that no suspicion was aroused, whilst conveying as little information as possible so that he would personally remain pivotal to the discussions. This position of influence was helped considerably by the fact that the three elves in the world that had some true understanding of dwarfish were allies of Malekith – Aernuis, Alandrian and Sutherai.

In that time, Malekith also went to great lengths to befriend King Snorri, at first seeking political power but later out of an unexpected but growing affection for the High King. As Malekith's grasp of the dwarfs' language improved, he spent more time with Snorri.

'What is best about Nagarythe?' the High King asked one day.

The two were alone in a reception room of the king's chambers. Malekith sat upon a chair the king had personally commissioned for his tall companion, while the king slouched in a deep armchair upholstered in thick elk hide. The servants had left a keg of ale and a large plate of pies on the low table that lay between them.

'The blue skies,' Malekith answered without hesitation. 'The air is cold and crisp and the north wind stirs the senses. Sometimes she sighs through the pine forests, other times she howls over the mountain peaks.'

'And what do you think of my mountains?' said Snorri. 'Do they compare to your homeland?'

'They are mighty,' laughed Malekith. 'Taller than the peaks of Nagarythe and greater of girth. But I travelled beneath them for the most part and have not yet walked upon them.'

'That will not do!' declared Snorri, jumping to his feet. 'What host am I to show you my rooms and keep from you the beauty of my lands? Do you enjoy hunting?'

'Very much,' said Malekith. 'I have tracked and slain many a monstrous beast in the Annulii.'

'Have you ever killed a troll?' asked Snorri enthusiastically. 'A cragwyrm, or a daggerfang?'

Malekith shook his head. Such beasts were unknown to Ulthuan, at least by the names used by Snorri.

'Then we shall have a troll hunt!' declared Snorri with a wide grin splitting his beard.

TWO DAYS LATER Malekith found himself stood upon a windswept shoulder of rock looking over a deep mountain valley. He was several miles to the north of Karaz-a-Karak, accompanied by Alandrian, the High King and several dozen dwarf escorts. Though the year was well into spring, the mountain air was still chill and the hunting party were swathed in capes and furs. Only a few clouds scudded across the skies, and when the sun broke free the prince could feel his skin prickling with warmth.

Snorri pointed across the valley to a thick forest. The trees were immense in girth, though not tall, not unlike the dwarfs. Square clearings had been chopped into the edges of the woods by dwarfen woodcutters.

'Wutruth,' said the king. 'The strongest trees of the mountains. This forest is older than Karaz-a-Karak, and we cut only five trees every year so that its descendants have time to grow. It is also a haunt of strange and dangerous beasts.'

'That is why we are here,' said Malekith with a smile.

'It is indeed,' said Snorri.

The High King was full of energy as he led the party down a winding track that meandered between rocky crags towards the valley floor. He bounded from stone to stone with an agility surprising for his stature, though Malekith had no difficulty keeping pace with his long, graceful strides. As they walked, Snorri gave a running commentary of everything in sight.

'The peak to the west, with the purple cliffs facing us, is Karag Kazor,' the king said. 'It was upon the fires of her belly that Grungni forged the first of Grimnir's axes.'

A huge flock of dark-feathered birds with bright red beaks swooped overhead and disappeared up the valley.

'Bloodcrows!' exclaimed Snorri. 'That is a good omen! They are scavengers. To see them in such numbers means that there is plenty to eat. Something close by has been killing!'

And so it went on, with Snorri expounding on every type of rock and plant, bird and beast that they encountered. As the sun reached her zenith, bathing the valley in warmth, they reached the well-tended treeline. The forest was dark and clear of undergrowth, the wutruth seeming to claw nourishment from the bare rock.

'If you would like to take a small repast, I'll be back shortly,' said Snorri.

With a handful of dwarf warriors, the High King headed into the woods and was quickly lost in the shadows. The dwarfs that remained sat down on rocks and stumps, and brought forth hard bread and pungent cheeses from their carry-sacks.

Malekith was not hungry and instead watched the dwarfs carefully. They seemed at ease, but every now and then they would glance at their charges. Though the prince considered that they might simply be mindful of their protective duties, he decided that they were present more to protect the High King from any perfidy by the elves.

Snorri returned shortly, a satisfied smile written upon his craggy features.

'Clawed tracks, big ones!' said the High King. 'Not too old either, by my reckoning.'

The king gave the order for the party to get ready to move, which was greeted with quiet, good-natured grumbling. Most dwarfs preferred to stay underground whenever possible, and Snorri's companions were no different. However, they were now used to their High King's strange appetites for sky and fresh air, and indulged him with good humour.

They came across the trail a few hundred paces from the edge of the woods. Malekith bent to one knee to examine them. They were indistinct, the soil here being very thin, but the prince could make out a large footprint as long as his arm and exceptionally broad. It was not unlike orc or goblin tracks, though considerably bigger; four-toed with the marks of ragged claws.

'Troll,' said Snorri with smug confidence. 'You are fortunate. Most trolls will have moved further north by this time of year. This one is either exceptionally stupid or brighter than your average troll.'

'How so?' asked Malekith.

'It could be too stupid to realise it will get too hot for it in the summer,' explained the king. 'Or it could be clever enough to realise that the other trolls have left and there will be plenty for it to eat without competition.'

'Does it make any difference?' said Alandrian.

'Yes and no,' said Snorri with a shrug. 'A stupid troll will be easier to catch, but more likely to attack when caught. A smarter troll might realise it is in danger and try to run away.'

They followed the trail north and eastwards, deeper into the woods. Here and there they found the gnawed remains of an animal carcass or a pile of the foulest-smelling dung Malekith had ever encountered. By this spoor Snorri judged that the troll was close at hand, within a few miles.

'It is afternoon now, so it is likely hiding somewhere in a shady spot out of the sun's gaze,' said the High King. 'There are some caves not far from here that we should explore. It would be good to catch it before nightfall, otherwise it might move away and we'll never find it.'

They continued to follow the tracks, which led towards the caves as Snorri had hoped. Quite some time had passed and the sun was now beginning to slide down behind the peaks to the west. Where Malekith spied the sky through a break in the canopy he saw that clouds were gathering again and the light was fading fast.

The short mountain day was nearing its end when Snorri brought them out of the trees onto a high bluff. A white cliff face opposite was dotted with dark caves, and the High King pointed towards numerous troll tracks on the ground.

'He's here all right,' growled the High King.

Snorri gestured to one of his retainers, who brought forth the king's crossbow. It was a remarkable piece of dwarfish craft, inlaid with gems and silver, its crosspiece and firing lever gilded. As the king loaded his weapon with measured precision, Malekith brought forth his bow from the quiver on his back and quickly strung it. He nocked a black-fletched arrow, casting his gaze towards the caverns only a few hundred paces distant.

'How does one hunt troll?' he asked.

'Some of my lads will go in and flush it out,' said Snorri. 'Or it'll chase them out… One way or another, best to lure it into the open first.'

'And where does one aim for the killing shot?' said the prince.

Snorri laughed.

'This is no bear or stag that can be brought down with a single shaft,' the dwarf said. 'Their brains are exceptionally small, and I've seen a troll carry on fighting with three bolts through its thick head. Their heart is in the chest behind strong bone. Fire is a good bet, for burnt flesh does not regrow.'

In illustration, the king handed one of his bolts to Malekith and pointed to the tip. A small rune was inscribed into the sharpened iron, flickering with a distant flame.

'It might take some bladework to finish it off,' the king added, taking back the bolt.

Malekith pondered this as more than a dozen dwarfs headed across the open ground, flaming brands in their rough fists. He felt no fear, for there was no creature in the world that he could not best. His heart did beat a little faster in anticipation, and the prince could see that Snorri was equally eager to get a sight of their prey.

The High King felt Malekith's gaze and turned to wink at the elf.

'Good fun, eh?' Snorri chuckled.

The torch-bearing dwarfs had now entered the caves and the light from their brands disappeared. Soon enough there came the echo of shouts and three dwarfs came running from a cave entrance to Malekith's left. They glanced over their shoulders, not in panic but to ensure their quarry was following.

A dozen paces behind them emerged the troll.

It was tall and gangling, easily twice Malekith's height, with wiry, muscled limbs and a bulbous stomach. Its head was large and ungainly, with a flattened nose and small, unintelligent eyes. Its hide was like a thick grey scale, hairless save for clumps upon its head and shoulders. Large and frayed pointed ears framed its hideous face, and its mouth was wide and filled with cracked teeth. Its long arms ended in club-like hands, its bony fingers tipped with broken, filthy claws.

The troll gave a keening howl as it lolloped after the dwarfs, stooping to knuckle forwards every few paces, sniffing the air.

Snorri took the first shot, at a distance of some three hundred paces. His crossbow twanged loudly and as the bolt flew forwards its tip erupted with flame. The shot took the troll in the left shoulder and elicited a pained grunt.

The dwarfs scattered further as the troll broke into a run down the gentle slope towards Malekith and the High King. Calming himself, Malekith took aim, his breathing shallow, his senses tuned to the swirl of the wind. He muttered a simple incantation and his arrowhead flickered with blue flame. With a sigh, Malekith released the bowstring and the arrow sped across the open ground and struck the troll directly in the left eye.

The troll fell to the ground with flailing limbs, screeching and gurgling. The prince turned to Snorri, who was still winding back the string on his crossbow.

'No killing shot?' said Malekith with a smile.

'Don't count your gold until the ore's been smelted,' grunted Snorri, not looking up from his task.

Malekith turned back to the troll and stared openmouthed as it pushed itself back to its feet. The prince's shaft was intact, piercing the eye socket, its flaming tip protruding from the top of the troll's head. It turned its good eye on the hunters and gave an angry roar before breaking into a bounding run that covered the ground with surprising speed.

'Oh…' said Malekith.

Regaining his composure, Malekith loosed three more shots at the fast-approaching monster, each arrow bursting into blue fire as it slammed into the creature's chest. Now even more angry, the troll lowered its head into a reckless charge, its clawed feet churning clods of thin earth from the ground.

Snorri fired another bolt, which punched into the creature's right leg, just above the knee. It stumbled and fell. It stayed on all fours for a moment, shaking its head groggily, before rising once more and resuming its attack.

The other dwarfs began to shout to each other and a flurry of bolts converged on the troll, some missing, others biting into flesh but with little effect. The troll turned on the closest of its attackers, a dwarf by the name of Godri who was one of the king's closest companions. Claws raked across the thane's armour, sending iron rings scattering across the floor with droplets of blood, the dwarf hurled onto his back.

The troll then veered back towards Malekith and Snorri, crimson splashed across its face and arms.

Snorri was still winding back the string of his crossbow and the troll was only a score of paces away. Malekith drew Avanuir and leapt to the attack, the shining blue blade carving a furrow in the creature's ribs as the elven prince darted past. The troll ignored him and bore down on Snorri.

The High King threw his unloaded crossbow into the creature's face and swept out a hand axe from his belt. His first chopping blow lodged into the creature's gut and the troll's momentum barrelled them both over. The two rolled down the slope, the troll biting and slashing, Snorri hacking with his axe.

Malekith dashed after the High King even as the other dwarfs closed in with axes ready. The troll was now on top of Snorri and reared its head back, jaws open wide to bite off the face of the High King.

Seizing his opportunity, Malekith threw Avanuir, guiding the blade with the power of magic. Spinning horizontally, the magical sword scythed through the air. It struck the troll at the base of its skull and sheared off the top of its head, leaving nothing but neck and lower jaw. Avanuir continued swirling past, over Snorri, before looping back again and lancing into the troll's chest.

With a shudder, the troll pitched forwards, pinning Snorri beneath its lifeless bulk.

Malekith was at the High King's side in a moment, and was relieved to see Snorri was still breathing. The dwarf's eyes flickered open, and between the two of them they hauled the troll to one side, allowing the High King to regain his feet.

Foul blood and mucus had spilled onto the dwarf king, matting his beard and staining his mail armour. Drips of gore hung from the brow of his helm, seeping into his braided hair. Snorri used a gauntleted hand to distastefully scrape what he could from his person, and then turned to Malekith and adopted a regal pose, shoulders set, chin held high.

'Congratulations,' said the High King. 'You've killed your first troll!'

THE GROWING FRIENDSHIP between prince and High King was cemented during the latter part of the summer, some twenty days before the negotiations were due to begin in earnest. Word had come to the capital that an army of beastmen was gathering south of the massive mountain lake known as Black Water, and was of such a size that the kings of Karak Varn and Zhufbar feared an attack against one hold or the other.

Upon hearing this news, and having spent much of the season idle in the halls of Karaz-a-Karak, Malekith's spirit was roused. Learning that King Snorri planned an expedition against these Chaos creatures, Malekith went before the High King in his throne room and offered to lead his company alongside the dwarfs. Snorri looked doubtful at first.

'The throng of Karaz-a-Karak stands ready at my command,' said Snorri. 'What need do I have for fifty more warriors?'

'In prosperity allies may learn much about each other, but in hardship they learn what is most important,' said Malekith.

'This is true,' Snorri said with a nod. 'However, we stand upon the brink of important times, and I would not have my descendants remember me as the dwarf who risked the lives of his new-found friends.'

'Do not fear for our safety, for we are each warrior-born, none more so than I,' replied Malekith. 'The army of Nagarythe is the most splendid in all of Ulthuan and, saving perhaps the throng of your hold, the most powerful force in the world. Though I have but a relative handful of my warriors present, I would like to demonstrate this to you. We may well become partners in trade, but in these dangerous times it is as important that we become comrades upon the battlefield.'

'There is much truth in what you say,' said Snorri with a smile. 'Let it not be said that I was unwilling to show the elves the true worth of a dwarf with an axe! In battle we see the proper qualities of courage and discipline, and perhaps it is time that we had this measure of the elves.'

'And we of the dwarfs,' countered Malekith with a smile.

'Yes, that too,' said Snorri with a meaningful look. Both understood that to see the other in battle would give each a better appraisal of their prospective allies, their strengths and, if things went ill, their weaknesses.

So it was that two days after the audience, the Naggarothi readied themselves for battle once more and marched out with the army of Karaz-a-Karak. Snorri led the dwarfs, and an impressive host it was. Positioned at a rampart just above the gate, the elven prince had a magnificent view of the wide road leading down the mountainside, and the rank after rank of warriors issuing forth.

Every warrior was different, for each provided his own wargear. Some carried axes, others hammers, while many carried bows or the mechanical crossbows that the dwarfs now favoured. Upon their shields were a wild variety of blazons and runes, though common themes of the different clans became evident as Malekith stood at the gate of the hold and watched the throng pass out.

Malekith stood with Aernuis, watching the host as it marched forth. The rival prince and his companion would not be accompanying the army; Malekith considered it better that the military spectacle and prowess of his Naggarothi not be undermined by the presence of the two Eataine-born elves. Though Malekith had been careful never to claim that all elves were as brave and strong as the folk of Nagarythe, it was his intent that King Snorri be left with the impression that this was the case.

The dwarfs were gathered into regiments of warriors from the same clan, and marched forth beneath the banners of their families and ancestors. Drummers boomed out martial beats and hornblowers sounded low, mournful dirges. Some carried newly forged weapons, others wielded heirlooms passed down from their forefathers, whose names and histories were as renowned as those that had once wielded them.

Snorri was the most striking individual in the army. He marched at its head flanked on each side by standard bearers, carrying banners woven from metallic threads and icons inscribed with magical runes.

'The one that goes before him bears the icon of the High King,' explained Aernuis. 'The dwarf to his right holds the clan standard of Snorri. On his left is carried the banner of the hold, and the fourth belongs to Snorri himself.'

The king was protected by an all-encompassing suit of armour, under which could be seen a layer of heavy mail.

Magical sigils were carved into the polished iron, and these glimmered with energy. His axe was no less spectacular, for three runes of angular design were cut into its blade to bring death to the High King's foes. The two-bladed axe glowed with mystical power and the king held it above his head as if it were no more than a feather, and with it waved the throng forwards on the march. Snorri's war helm was also golden and likewise inscribed with magical symbols bestowing courage and kingship.

'The king's helm was made by Valaya, or so the dwarfs believe,' said Aernuis. 'The runes upon it cast a spell so that any who look upon the High King are inspired and awed; to enemies, the High King appears as a terrifying nightmare that fills their hearts with dread.'

'I feel nothing, nor do I see any nightmarish vision,' said Malekith.

'Then perhaps you are neither friend nor foe,' said Aernuis.

The prince of Nagarythe looked sternly at Aernuis but could see no hint of mockery or insult.

'Perhaps I am simply too far away,' said Malekith.

About Snorri and his standards were gathered many of the hold's thanes, and with them the bodyguard of the king made up of the finest warriors the clans contained. They were armed with great axes and hammers burning with fell runes, and wore mail and plates thick enough to ward away all but the most telling of blows.

These venerable dwarfs had long beards that reached to their ankles; to protect this precious hair they wore segmented armour tied to the braids of their beards so that no enemy cut would deprive them of their fine facial hair. Malekith had learnt much about dwarfs and their beards in his time at Karaz-a-Karak and it was something of remark, indeed suspicion, that the elves grew no facial hair at all. 'Beardling' was a phrase oft-used to describe young dwarfs, and 'beardless' was tantamount to dishonourable, a grave insult amongst dwarfkind.

'They are somewhat of a rabble,' remarked Malekith, watching the dwarfs walk out without particular time or rhythm, each sauntering along at his own rate. They ambled out smoking pipes, eating, chatting and behaving in other un-warlike fashions that gave Malekith the impression that while visually impressive, the dwarfen host lacked the gravitas of his own legions. There was little of the precision and finesse he associated with the steady ranks of his spear companies.

It also told him a good deal about the dwarf attitude to war, for they appeared to be no more concerned that they were marching to battle than if they were out for a pleasant afternoon stroll. Having seen the savage beastmen and wild orcs, Malekith suspected that the dwarfs had faced little opposition to their might, and safe in their holds had not truly been tested in the many years since they first wrested control of the mountains.

It was while considering this that another thought occurred to Malekith. The lack of concern showed by the dwarfs might betray an underlying motive for this expedition. If the confidence of the dwarfs were due to some prior knowledge concerning the nature of their foe, then might not it be the case that all of this display was for the benefit of the elves?

'What have you heard concerning this horde of beasts?' Malekith asked.

'Only that it is sizeable,' replied Aernuis.

'It is awfully convenient that the High King feels it necessary to march out at this time,' said Malekith. 'Perhaps they hope to intimidate me with this display of strength?'

'That could be,' said Aernuis, though there was doubt in his voice.

Malekith laughed inwardly at the thought that the dwarfs believed they could overawe him with such manoeuvres. He had to admire their spirit though, and regretted not having seen the opportunity himself. Perhaps if he had allowed a few dwarfs to travel west with his messengers, to return with tales of how quickly the elven realm was expanding and the size of her armies, then some of the dwarfen truculence might have been dislodged.

'When they see the Naggarothi in battle, they will understand that such tacit threats are fruitless,' said Malekith.

'I am sure that they will, Malekith,' said Aernuis, his tone and expression betraying nothing of his own opinion on the matter.

Perhaps the most intriguing aspect of all the army, and the one that caused Malekith the greatest pause for thought, was its engines of war. While the elves had machines that could hurl spear-sized bolts from the decks of their ships or the walls of a castle, the dwarfs had all manner of ingenious contraptions for the field of battle. Some were small and carried upon the backs of the dwarfs themselves: spring-weighted slings that hurled pots of fire and windlass-loaded bows that fired half a dozen darts with a single shot. Others were grander and were pulled along by teams of ponies upon specially built wagons with broad wheels and sprung-loaded axles.

'These machines, what is their purpose?' asked the prince of Nagarythe.

'Each is built individually by the carpenters and smiths of the hold,' said Aernuis. 'They view the craft of engineering with the same passion as we would a jewelsmith or poet. Each pours his own labour and inspiration into his construction.'

'So each engine is unique?' said Malekith, watching the long line of wagons and limbers winding their way out of the huge gate.

'Yes,' Aernuis replied. 'Like everything else the dwarfs design or make, each engine is named and recorded in their histories, its exploits as vaunted as those of a flesh-and-blood hero.'

'That seems indulgent,' said Malekith. 'I would say the dwarfs dwell too much on the past and do not look to the future keenly enough. That will be their loss, for forward-thinking elves such as I will be able to seize better the opportunities that lie ahead.'

'They plan meticulously, if not with vision,' said Aernuis. 'Though perhaps they lack your flair, they see their rise in strength as inevitable.'

'What is that?' Malekith said, choosing to ignore Aernuis's warning. He pointed at a gigantic bolt thrower that fired projectiles so long that three dwarfs were required to load it.

'*Wolfspear*,' answered Aernuis after a moment's thought. 'If I recall correctly, *Wolfspear* was the first machine to guard the gates at Karaz-a-Karak. The legend has it that it slew four giants when first the hordes of Chaos poured south to besiege the hold.'

'And what about that catapult thing?' said Malekith, indicating an enormous trebuchet followed by a wagon loaded with cunningly carved rocks as large as horses.

'Ah, that is *Gatebreaker*,' said Aernuis. 'A mysterious engine. I once heard an engineer say that it had smashed the dark citadel of Thagg-a-Durz. When I inquired as to who else but the dwarfs had the means to create such castles that required attack, the dwarfs fell silent. Their surly expressions discouraged me from any further inquiry.'

'So, there are enemies of the dwarfs that we do not yet know about?'

'I have heard no other mention of such a race or nation in my time with the dwarfs,' said Aernuis. 'But even when appearing open, there is much that they do not say to us.'

'Well, we shall soon see the mettle of our potential allies,' said Malekith. Without further acknowledgement of the Eataine prince, he turned away and swept down the steps from the rampart, his cloak swirling behind him.

THE DWARFISH AND elven host marched north along a winding road of brick, which soared over wide valleys on extraordinary bridges that arced over the gorges in breathtaking spans hundreds of feet above the jagged rocks and swirling rivers below. In places, the road seemed to barely cling to the steep sides of the mountain peaks, supported on piles and columns dozens of feet high driven into the mountainside with immense bolts and supported by silver-plated scaffolding.

The air was crisp and sharp, even with the full heat of the sun upon their faces, but the dwarfs walked on relentlessly, seeming never to tire nor complain. They ate on the march, which Malekith thought efficient but uncouth, and as he had seen before, when they made camp every dwarf knew his role and duties and carried out his tasks with little supervision or communication from his leaders.

It was this quiet independence that gave the dwarfs their real strength, Malekith admitted to himself as he watched them break camp the following morning. Each could rely utterly upon his fellows, and the sense of community and brotherhood bound the dwarfs together as a kindred.

The people of Nagarythe he praised for their discipline, their attention to duty and their unending dedication, but he knew his folk would never be lauded for their friendship and hospitality, or for a love of others.

ONWARDS AND NORTHWARDS marched the army, crossing vale and peak with monotonous but speedy advance for two more days. Scouts were despatched by the king to locate the bestial foe, and they returned shortly before nightfall to report that they had seen fires some miles to the north-east.

The king was content to allow the army to rest for the night, though he took pains to point out to Malekith that this was not because the dwarfs could not march straight to battle, but was rather so that he could spend the darkest hours in deliberation with his lieutenants, so that all might know the plan of battle for the coming day.

Before dawn the scouts were again sent out to locate the foe, and they returned just as the army was ready to march, the breakfast fires having been extinguished and the wagons packed with their gear. The beastmen, a savage horde numbering several thousand creatures of greater or lesser size, had spent the night carousing and celebrating, for it seemed that they had recently overrun an isolated brewery further north.

News of this attack was greeted by many curses and much wagging of beards by the dwarfs, who until then had seemed more like the head of a family dealing with an unruly cousin than an army marching to death and bloodshed. Now in the belief that these creatures had attacked their lands, the dwarfs became very serious and Malekith found the change not only swift but extraordinary. The thought that beastmen had assailed their realm filled the dwarfs with a simmering anger.

In a few moments the beastmen had been transformed from potential annoyance to hated enemy, and the dwarf throng made their remaining preparations in what seemed to be considerable haste, eager to attack lest their enemies somehow elude them. Speculation about the attack spread through the army, and as the dwarfs marched out there was a grim mood utterly unlike the atmosphere that had pervaded the host when it had left Karaz-a-Karak.

There was little conversation and a solid purpose had now taken hold. Instead of pipe-smoking the dwarfs ran whetstones over their axe blades and tested the strings on their crossbows. Gear was checked and re-checked, and the thanes moved about the throng issuing gruff commands and reminding the warriors of their oaths.

Steadily the host strode northwards, following the lead of the scouts. Their route took them into a deep valley, with thick stands of pines to either side amongst the rocky outcrops. For several miles the gorge cut through the mountains, its walls becoming ever more heavily wooded.

The column was called to battle order as it neared its quarry, the king and his veterans taking their position in the middle of the host while crossbow-armed dwarfs and more lightly armoured troops made their way forwards. The fire-throwers were sent out to guard the flanks, while the engineers began preparing their machines to be unlimbered.

BEFORE MIDDAY THE gorge opened up into a vast craggy bowl circled by rocks and tall firs. Here the beastmen remained, lazing amongst the smoking remnants of their fires, the smashed and clawed ruins of their spoils littering the ground. Broken barrels and splintered staves lay all about the rocky ground, and upon the pyres could be seen the charring corpses of dwarfs, their flesh ripped and hacked from the bodies.

At the sight of this a deep growling emanated from the throng, and there was much cursing.

A few of the more conscious beastmen saw the army issuing from the gorge and ran about the debris-strewn camp howling and shouting. One picked up a horn from the ground and brought it to up its lips.

Before a note could be sounded, the horned thing collapsed to the ground with a black-shafted arrow in its neck. The dwarfs turned in amazement to see Malekith plucking another arrow from his quiver.

Though the hornblower had been silenced, the beastmen were quickly rousing and rising to their feet, snatching up crude clubs, jagged blades and roughly hewn wooden shields. Their appearance and variety defied description, for each was subtly different from the next.

Many had goat-like heads and legs, with long spiralling horns of an antelope, or curling tusks jutting from their mouths. Others were reminiscent of rams, or scorpions, or serpents. Shapeless things with many limbs and eyes lumbered towards the dwarfs, their mewling cries and senseless roars echoing around the rocky basin.

As the alarm was taken up there came a great cacophony of grunts and shrieks, baying and barking. As well as this clamour, the wind also brought the stench of the camp to Malekith. He almost retched as his senses were overwhelmed with the stink of carrion, rotted blood and dung. His fellow elves coughed and spluttered, and even the dwarfs wrinkled their noses and covered their faces with gauntleted hands.

In size as well as in shape, no two beastmen were alike, for some were in height like the dwarfs, though less broad, with thin, twisted faces and stubby horns. Most seemed of a similar size to the elves, though wider of shoulder and larger of limb. Several were much taller, perhaps twice

Malekith's height, with bull heads, bloodstained fangs and huge chests thick with muscle.

Some were almost hairless, others albino or with brightly patterned skins; more still were covered in patches of thick fur of reds, browns and black, or were striped like tigers or spotted as leopards. Long beards trailed from bulging chins, and eyes of black, red and green regarded the approaching dwarfs with a mixture of hatred and fear.

Hooting and wailing drowned out the tramp of dwarfish iron-shod boots as the beastmen gathered into groups about their leaders and came forwards to meet the assault.

As they marched on, the dwarf column spread into a line as space permitted, the missile regiments to the flanks, the more solid clansdwarfs holding the centre. The war machines were dismounted from their carts upon hillocks and rises so that they could oversee the whole battlefield, and as Malekith suspected would happen, all of this was done with few shouted commands, only the occasional beating of a drum or short horn blast. Now that battle was almost upon them, the dwarfs were much more cohesive in their movements, though they still lacked the precise drill and organisation of the Naggarothi.

Malekith positioned himself and his warriors close to the High King's bodyguard, in the hope that Snorri would have a full view of their excellence in battle even once the fighting had commenced. Lacking the numbers for a properly organised line, Malekith arranged his warriors in a single block of bows and spears, the better-armoured warriors to the fore, the archers ready to fire past them at approaching enemies. He stood at the centre of the front rank, Alandrian beside him.

'I see little challenge here,' said the prince. 'A disorderly mob against so many engines and bows will perish without a fight.'

'A shame indeed, highness,' said Alandrian. Like the rest of the company, the captain bore a spear and tall shield. His helm covered most of his face, so that only his mouth was visible and Malekith could not see his lieutenant's expression. Alandrian's tone had been less than enthusiastic.

'I think perhaps you have spent too much time talking and not enough with a blade in your hand,' the prince said sharply.

Alandrian turned, his mouth pursed with anger.

'I am Naggarothi, highness,' the captain declared. 'Warrior-born and fearless. Do not mistake my desire for peace for cowardice.'

Malekith smiled to himself at the venom in Alandrian's retort and was content that his captain would be as fierce a fighter as he had been in the many long years of their acquaintance.

THERE WAS STILL some considerable distance between the beasts and the dwarfs when the first of the war machines loosed its deadly load. A cluster of rocks each as large as a dwarf's head sailed through the air, and then fell amongst the mustering beastmen, crushing skulls and snapping bones.

A great jeer rose up from the dwarfs at the striking of this first blow, which was to be followed by many more as boulders and bolts began to rain down upon the filthy encampment.

Spurred into decisive action, the Chaotic horde ran forwards, the fastest outpacing the slowest so that there was no line or formation but simply separate groups hurtling towards the dwarfs. Malekith sighed, knowing that even against the dwarfs such a lack of tactics would see the beastmen slain or hurled back before a sword was swung or spear was thrust.

As rocks and bolts continued to take their toll, joined now by crossbow quarrels, and arrows from the elves, Malekith saw that his prediction would be correct. In face of such devastating volleys the beastmen could not maintain any momentum and their charge petered out as they turned away, and in small groups fled from the death unleashed upon them.

A few of the least intelligent creatures continued their attack and the dwarfs concentrated their missiles upon them. Shambling, slithering monstrosities impervious to fear or pain lumbered forwards driven by the instinct to slay, but were eventually cut down as dozens of rocks and arrows pounded and pierced their scaled and leathery bodies.

Malekith returned his bow to its quiver with another sigh and glanced over at Snorri, wondering if the king would sally forth to hunt down the survivors of the barrage. Malekith was sorely tempted to lead his warriors on into the enemy to display their brilliance at arms, but sudden concern stayed his command.

The High King's attention was focused upon the unfolding scene ahead, but now and then he glanced to his left or right, and at one point turned fully around to stare back towards the valley walls behind the host. Some of the other dwarfs were doing likewise, and Malekith felt a tingle of apprehension.

In the Annulii Mountains of his homeland, the prince knew every sound and scent, but here his senses were unaccustomed to the particular hissing of the wind in the trees, the rattle of rocks and the smell of the air. For the dwarfs, though, this was their home and Malekith knew that their instincts here would be as keen as his were in Nagarythe. Their sudden interest in the surroundings gave Malekith a sensation he had not felt since the daemons had been defeated: worry.

It came to him all at once just how little he knew about this place, and how ignorant he was of its dangers and denizens. He was just mastering his concern when there came a sound that turned his worry to an emotion he had not felt in over three hundred years: apprehension.

It was a horn blast, flat and short. It was not the sound itself that caused Malekith such anxiety, but the direction from which it came. It resonated down the valley, but the prince's sharp hearing told him that it had originated in the trees that covered the eastern wall of the valley, behind the host.

A moment later it sounded again and this time there were answers; other atonal blasts and harsh cries were carried on the wind. Hearing this, the beastmen in the rocky hollow slowed in their flight, then turned and started to come back towards the dwarfs.

Now Malekith saw fully the discipline and cohesiveness of the dwarf army. Snorri barked out orders and received acknowledging shouts from his thanes. The engines and crossbow regiments began to pour their shot into the beastmen again, while the king's bodyguard and nearly two-thirds of the throng turned about and began to array themselves for battle at the valley mouth.

Uncertain what plan was being enacted, Malekith split his company, sending the archers forwards to support the attack against the encampment and turning his spears to face this new threat.

Malekith's mind was racing. How was it that they had become so easily trapped? Had the dwarf scouts not wit or skill enough to detect the ambushers?

Then a darker thought entered the prince's mind; perhaps some greater intelligence, some malign intellect, guided their foes.

There was little time to ponder such questions, for amongst the shouts and the thunder of war machines, there came a new sound. Malekith felt it through the soles of his boots before he could hear it. A trembling of the ground, like the distant rumbling of a waterfall.

He could see nothing amongst the closely growing pines, but the growing thunder in the ground intensified and with a rising sense of unease Malekith realised that it was the pounding of thousands of feet.

A blur of darkness in the air caught his attention and he looked up to see a boulder hurtling through the skies towards the dwarfen line. Armour screeched and bones snapped beneath its weight as the stone crashed into the dwarfs, bouncing and rolling through their ranks.

At first Malekith thought that some strange dwarf machine or other had malfunctioned, or that the beastmen had mastered the use of catapults as he had seen orcs employ such crude engines. More movement drew Malekith's eye up the valley's eastern side and he spied a large figure. It was easily ten times the height of an elf. It was naked but for misshapen rags of tattered hide and bloody sheepskins.

As Malekith watched, the giant stooped and picked up another rock, then hurled the projectile far out over the trees into the army beneath.

From the western woods poured the beastmen, hundreds of them swarming and shouting as they burst from the trees hurling stones and other improvised missiles. They erupted from the cover of the forest close to where a battery of engines had been positioned, and the crews abandoned their machines and formed up to defend themselves. Against such numbers their resistance was brief, and Malekith watched as the bestial horde continued down the hillside towards the dwarf line.

The dwarfs moved to counter this attack, the clan warriors locking their shields together as they advanced to meet the threat. As the distance was closed, the dwarfs hurled throwing axes into their enemies, and in return unwieldy javelins were launched into their armoured ranks. Beastmen fell by the score during this exchange, but only here and there did the sturdy armour of the dwarfs fail.

On and on came the tide of twisted evil, a seemingly unending stream of bloated, frothing beasts and animalistic, howling warriors.

With a shattering clash the charging beastmen met the defiant dwarf line and vicious fighting broke out across the breadth of the army. Though the dwarfs held firm and hacked down their foes with relentless ferocity, still more came, savage and shrieking with the joy of slaying. The beastmen spread out as more and more clambered over the dead to reach the dwarfs, and Snorri sent forwards more of his followers to extend the flanks of his force lest the bestial deluge of vileness surround his army.

While his attention was drawn to the ongoing battle to his left, Malekith recalled that the first horn had sounded from the east, to his right.

He looked over towards Snorri and saw that the High King was deep in consultation with his thanes. Seeing that all the efforts of the dwarfs were directed to the west, Malekith decided the best way to draw attention to the danger from the east was through action.

'Naggarothi, with me!' he shouted, drawing his sword. As one the spearmen raised their shields with an affirmative shout. 'Advance!'

Malekith led his soldiers forwards, towards the spine of the mountainside where the valley met the deep crater of the basin. At another command, they broke into a trot, jogging along swiftly to swing wide of the dwarfs' flank. Dwarfish shouts of anger followed them, but Malekith ignored the noise, judging rightly that the dwarfs mistakenly thought the elves were fleeing.

Snarling and howls now sounded from the woods, and Malekith called his troops to a halt, remembering Aernuis's first encounter with goblins.

Sure enough, dozens of wolves sped from the treeline, carrying goblins upon their backs. The wolves were larger than any normal beast, with foaming maws, dark fur and red eyes. The goblins carried spears and small round shields. From under fur-trimmed helmets, their pinched green faces were split by vicious snarls and hungry leers. Many carried short bows and they loosed off erratic shots as they closed in.

The Naggarothi raised their shields to head height as one, and the small arrows clattered harmlessly aside, lacking the punch of a true elven bow. Still, the goblins made up for in numbers what they lacked in quality and more arrows rained down in wavering and corkscrewing fashion, many falling short. Even as their comrades closed, the goblins paid no heed to the risk of hitting their own kind and continued to shower the elves to little effect.

'Spears to guard!' shouted Malekith.

The Naggarothi lowered their shields just as the first of the wolves raced forwards and leapt to the attack, to be skewered on a spear point, its diminutive rider shrieking as it leapt clear. Another elf thrust forwards his spear, lancing its tip through the goblin's throat. With a twist, the warrior pulled his weapon free and returned to the guard position.

More of the wolves tried a direct attack, seeking to jump amongst the elves to wreak havoc, yet the wall of spears held firm and they and their riders suffered the same fate as the first.

A second wave attacked more cautiously, turning at the last moment to ride in front of the regiment hacking at spear tips, but the Naggarothi pressed forwards a few paces and caught them unexpectedly, slaying many on the points of their spears.

The wolf riders ran back and forth, darting in to attack when they thought the elves' guard was down, but not a single greenskin nor their lupine mounts landed a wound upon the Naggarothi. For all that their attack did no direct harm, Malekith could see more goblins leaving the woods on foot, and saw that his small company would quickly become encircled.

With a snarl, he reached out to the winds of magic and drew power into himself. He felt it writhing within him, crawling under his skin, pouring through his veins. With a chant to focus the unwieldy energies, the prince moulded the coiling magic with his mind.

A golden spear dripping with sparks formed in his left hand, and with a curse upon his lips Malekith hurled the spell at the wolves. The magical spear tore straight through three of the creatures and exploded with a shower of yellow flame. Panicked, the wolves yapped and yelped and turned heel, urged to flee even faster by their cowardly riders.

None too soon, Malekith reorganised his troops to face the goblins now marching out of the woods. The green-skins attempted to circle around the elves, jabbing their weapons towards them and screaming jibes and curses in their foul tongue.

The Naggarothi turned and expanded their formation with ease, spreading out into a semi-circle that presented no flank to the enemy, their backs secured by the outcrop of rock at the valley's entrance. Hissing and spitting, the goblins did not attack at once, and they eyed their slaughtered kin and the dead wolves, the corpses of which lay in heaps about the elven regiment.

'I think they have reconsidered their position,' laughed Alandrian from beside Malekith.

The prince's eyes did not leave the goblins, as more of their number flowed from the woods. Soon there were several hundred of the spiteful little creatures, shouting and taunting, but approaching no closer than a stone's throw.

Something immense crashed through the trees behind the goblins, smashing through branches and splintering trunks.

With a bellow the giant strode out into the valley, having evidently grown bored of hurling rocks from above. In its right hand it held a tree limb studded with shards of broken armour, blades of axes and swords, and bent pieces of shield. Buoyed by their gigantic companion, the goblins began to run further forwards, beating their weapons upon their wooden shields and shouting in their shrill voices.

Above the cries and the clamour of battle, Malekith heard a sudden whistling of air. Turning, he saw a great metal shaft arcing over the dwarfen army, from the direction of *Wolfspear*. The engine's crews had turned the gigantic bolt thrower about upon its hillock in the midst of the dwarf army, much to Malekith's relief.

He followed the trajectory of the massive bolt until it struck the giant full in the chest, smashing through its monstrous breastbone, heart and spine. With an astonished gurgle, the giant lurched forwards two steps and then crashed to the ground, flattening a dozen goblins beneath its bulk. Wails of dismay flooded up from the horrified greenskins, who looked at each other in their panic.

'Kill them,' snarled Malekith, breaking into a run.

Needing no further encouragement, the Naggarothi surged forwards, running hard and fast towards the foe.

Like some small animal frozen with terror as the hawk swoops down, the goblins remained unmoving for several heartbeats. With pitiful shrieks they turned to run as the elves came within a few dozen strides, heading for the safety of the woods.

For all their fright-driven speed, the goblins' small legs carried them across the ground much more slowly than the loping run of the elves, and Malekith overtook the slowest of the greenskins with ease. Striking out to right and left, his sword cleaved through heads and spines. Then the Naggarothi caught up with the bulk of the fleeing rabble, and the butchery began.

Malekith felt the Khaine-fever taking over as he slashed and cut, caring not for the acrid blood that spattered on his lips nor the gore splashed across his golden armour.

His warriors were likewise filled with battle-lust, having spent many long days in the hold of the dwarfs without vent for their energy. Heads and limbs were scattered in the orgy of death, and with rage fuelling their steps the elves chased down the goblins and killed every last one of them.

Only when nothing but entrails and bloodied remains were left did they stop, panting hard not from exhaustion but excitement.

Finally tasting the bitter filth upon his face, Malekith wiped the blood clear of his mouth and looked around. The dwarfs were still fighting hard with the beastmen, and were falling back towards the valley basin, drawing them further from the elves.

Malekith did not know if there were more goblins in the woods, or any other loathsome creature for that matter, and turned the company around to head back to the main battle. From this direction they would drive into the rear of the bestial horde.

Malekith could see the four standards of Snorri White-beard above the melee, and chose a line of attack that would see the elves cut through the Chaotic filth to meet up with the High King in the melee.

Now calmed by the bloodletting of the goblins, the Naggarothi advanced steadily, cutting down the beastmen in their path. The largest of the beasts were now fighting hard at the front, leaving the smallest and most cowardly to face the attack of the elves. Most ran before they could be hewed down, though some did not see their peril until it was too late. Their lives ended spitted upon spear shaft or cleaved in twain by Avanuir.

As he cut his way through the beastmen, something disturbed Malekith's concentration. There was shifting in the magic around him. It was dark and heavy and hugged the ground, but something was causing it to sluggishly swirl into the air.

Stopping for a moment and waving his warriors to advance further, the prince focussed his attention on the mystical energy. It was definitely being drawn somewhere else. Following its flow, he looked out over the sprawling battle. Like an eagle seeking its prey, Malekith allowed the magic to guide his eyes, until his gaze alighted upon a peculiar beastman.

Its skin was a pale green, blotched with strange moss-like growths amongst mangy patches of fur, and it wore a tattered cloak of what looked like skin. It was hunched over and a grasping hand protruded from its back. Its horned head was covered with a thick hood of rough, mucus-encrusted cloth. In its gnarled, clawed grip the thing held a long piece of wood to which were bound shards of evilly glowing stone. They scorched into Malekith's magical sense, burning with dark magic.

The shaman lifted its staff and pointed the end towards the elves. Too late, Malekith realised what was happening.

Exerting his will, Malekith tried to seize back the magical power being leeched by the shaman, but he could not stop the vile spell. A thick black cloud of flies erupted from that staff, its buzzing deafening, blotting out all other sound. The swarm lifted above the beastmen and flew straight for the Naggarothi, but it was not the sight of the droning cloud that so disturbed Malekith. He could sense the dark energies writhing within the living fog; like the stench of rot or soured milk the magic flooded Malekith's unearthly senses.

The fly cloud descended on the elves with an ear-splitting hum. Where each fly landed, it brought decay. Armour began to spot with rust, and wooden spear shafts grew weak with mildew. Malekith saw an elf flailing at the swarm with his shield, but within moments it had split and disintegrated into orange dust. Plates of armour cracked, leather split and frayed, and scale links turned to a rusted mass.

Suddenly, like a great inhalation, the magic disappeared. Like a cleansing wind blowing through thick smoke, something new disturbed the mystical flow of energy, dissipating it. The swarm dissolved in the air, leaving the Naggarothi swinging rusted gauntlets and broken spear staves into thin air. The breeze became stronger and then grew into a consuming immaterial whirlwind, like a great gulf that had opened up under the sea to swallow all the waters.

A blazing light caught the attention of the prince, and over the bobbing heads of the embattled beastmen he could just about see a dwarf wielding a metallic globe, stood beside the king. White light poured from runes engraved into the strange sphere, and it was to this that the magical winds were being drawn.

A counter-current formed in the ethereal energy of the magical winds as the shaman tried to fight the power of the dwarfen globe. Something went wrong, though. Malekith could feel the magic becoming barbed and dangerous, like a mellow beast suddenly enraged and revealed to have razor-sharp fangs.

For a moment, Malekith fancied that he saw something on the edge of his vision, a shadow of a shadow not unlike some great daemon in form. It appeared above the shaman and seemed to reach into the beastman with an indistinct hand. Then it was gone, and Malekith fancied that perhaps he had simply imagined it.

With a detonation of magical energy that shredded beastmen and dwarfs for many yards in every direction, the shaman exploded. The ground cracked beneath its falling corpse and the air churned with invisible force. Malekith felt the expanding magical field buffet him as surely as any storm or wave, but the prince gritted his teeth and allowed its gnawing energies to pass him by.

Though Malekith's magical blade and Vaul-forged armour were untouched by the horrifying spell, his warriors were now in poor shape. Some were stuck in their rust-seized armour and rolled upon the ground trying to free themselves; many were pocked with boils and lesions left by the horrific biting of the daemon-flies. Most were now weaponless, amongst them Alandrian, and Malekith could see no option but to order a retreat, much as it bit deeply at his pride to do so. Before he had a chance to issue the command, a new horror emerged for them to face.

* * *

THERE WAS A rumbling of thunder overhead and storm clouds gathered with unnatural speed above the valley. Lightning crackled across the dark canopy and shot to the earth in blinding bolts. A wind from nowhere began to howl down the gorge, bending the trees and whipping grit and droplets of blood into the air.

Pines were sent hurtling in every direction as a terrifying monster erupted from the woods to the east. In form it was not unlike a dragon, though perhaps a little lesser in size, with the scaled legs, body and tail of such a creature. Its hide was a deep crimson, but its talons were of a black as dark as coal. The gigantic centaur-like monster had a red-skinned torso and a pair of arms where the dragon's neck and head would have been. Its head sat upon broad shoulders that were encased in plates of studded armour. Two serrated horns coiled out of its skull and its mouth was little more than a fang-filled slit.

It wielded a pair of identical swords, larger than anything Malekith had ever seen, but true-forged blades rather than the improvised weapons of the beastmen. Energy flickered and crawled upon those cruel swords, whose hilts and crossguards were fashioned from fused spines and whose pommels were made from real skulls. The gigantic beast's eyes were wide and filled with the energy of the storm.

'Shaggoth!' cried one of Malekith's soldiers, and the prince knew it to be true.

The oldest legends of the dragons spoke of such creatures, but Malekith had considered them to be myths from before the rise of the elves; before even the coming of the Old Ones and the banishment of the elven gods. Cousins to the dragons who had ruled the world before the coming of the gods, the shaggoths had bartered their souls to Chaos long before the Dark Gods had arisen to claim this world. If the dragons were to be believed, they had warred with the shaggoths for an eternity until finally the dragons had triumphed and driven their foes into hiding.

With the coming of Chaos, Malekith guessed, the shaggoths had been roused from their lairs, and now one of the titanic creatures stared down at Malekith with death-filled eyes. Lightning arced down from the storm clouds above, striking the shaggoth full on the chest. The creature was invigorated rather than harmed, as coruscating energy rippled across its gnarled skin.

'Our allies watch!' cried Malekith to his elves as those that could move backed away in terror from the apparition. 'Do not shame yourselves! Show no fear! Strike without hesitation! Slay in the name of Nagarythe!'

With lightning still flickering across its flesh, the shaggoth lunged forwards and snatched up one of the Naggarothi in a foreclaw, splintering rusted armour and crushing bones and organs. A sweep of a sword carved through three more warriors, sending their remains spinning through the air. With Malekith's command still ringing in their ears, the Naggarothi closed ranks and attacked, but even those whose weapons had not been undone by the shaman's curse could find no weakness in the scales and hide of the beast.

With a deafening roar, the shaggoth cast the remains of the unfortunate Naggarothi in its claws, so that he smashed back into the company, toppling several more elves. Its swords blazing with energy, the prehistoric monster hacked and chopped with savage glee, slicing great bloody wounds into the regiment.

Summoning what little magical power remained after the dwarfs' counterspell, Malekith charged in to the attack, Avanuir trailing blue flames as he swept the magical sword towards the beast's underbelly.

The creature reared with an angry bellow and Malekith was forced to leap backwards to avoid a raking claw aimed for his throat. Ducking beneath the swipe of a monstrous sword, Malekith took hold of Avanuir in both hands and hacked at the beast's legs, though even the enchanted blade of Nagarythe bit only lightly into the armoured skin of the terror.

Alerted by his preternatural senses, Malekith tried to dodge another swinging blade, but was caught on the shoulder by the shaggoth's fist and sent wheeling through the air. Landing heavily, the wind knocked from him, Malekith struggled to regain his feet. Pouncing with unlikely speed, the shaggoth grasped Malekith in one of its foreclaws and wrenched the prince aloft. Its right arm swung back ready for the death blow, energy arcing from the blade it held.

With a wordless shout, Malekith drove Avanuir deep into the flesh of the creature's foreleg, causing it to spasm and drop him to the ground. Crawling forwards, Malekith ducked beneath the creature's bulky body and then stood, raking the tip of Avanuir along the softer skin of its underside. Thick, dark blood dripped from the wound and the shaggoth tried to back away so that Malekith would not be hidden by its own body. The prince rolled between its thrashing legs, avoiding an immense sword that dug a great trench in the earth where he had been stood, and drove Avanuir into the base of the shaggoth's tail.

Such wounds would have been grievous against any other foe, but the shaggoth was not even slowed by them. Malekith rolled beneath another attack and barely brought up Avanuir in time to deflect another blow, though the parry sent the magical sword spinning from Malekith's fingers.

Unarmed, Malekith stood up to face the beast, staring defiantly into its black eyes. Intelligence flickered in those inky depths, a recognition of what Malekith was. Other Naggarothi jabbed and hacked at the shaggoth with swords and knives, trying to draw its attention away from their prince. It turned quickly and swept them away with a swing of its tail, hurling them from their feet. Malekith remained where he was stood, hands balled into fists that glowed with magical flame.

The shaggoth loomed over the lord of Nagarythe, its twin swords held high above its head. More lightning arced down from the storm clouds it had summoned, earthing into the tips of those primordial blades. It crossed its blades in front of it in a mocking salute, its mouth twisted with an evil smile.

The first strike caught Malekith full in the chest, lifting him from his feet with an explosion of electricity. Sparks of energy flew from the prince's magical armour as he sailed a dozen feet into the air and then crashed down onto the rocky ground. Pain lanced along his spine and his ribs felt shattered, but Malekith's pride would not let him die on his back.

With a grunt, he pushed himself to his feet, his injuries sending spasms of agony through his body. The prince turned to face the shaggoth once more.

'I am Aenarion's son.' Malekith spat blood onto the ground at the shaggoth's feet. 'My father slew the four greatest daemons that the Dark Gods could send. Armies were laid low by his blade. The world trembled at his tread. All will remember me as they remember him.'

The shaggoth brought down its leftmost blade and Malekith raised his arm to protect himself, the ensorcelled gold of his armour screeching and blazing with light at the impact. The shaggoth's smile died, and its brow furrowed in frustration and anger. Another blow that would have felled trees and shattered stone sent Malekith skidding backwards, his arm broken, a slash across his face.

Spitting more blood, Malekith stood again.

'Your time is long past,' Malekith taunted the beast. 'Our time is now. Go back to your dark hole and pray to your filthy gods that we do not hunt you down.'

With a roar of anger, the shaggoth lashed out wildly, allowing Malekith to easily avoid the blow. Malekith ducked beneath the sword, and then leapt high, fuelled by anger and magic, his blazing fists smashing the shaggoth across the face. Reeling from the blow, the shaggoth took several steps back, shaking its head.

Landing lightly, Malekith readied himself to strike again when the shaggoth let out a great howl of pain. It whipped around, and the prince saw that its tail had been half-severed. There was a flash of light from some source obscured by its gigantic body, and a clawed foreleg whirled into the air in a fountain of thick gore.

Ducking so that he could see beneath the creature's heaving gut, Malekith saw the dwarf High King, blazing rune axe in hand. Each blow cut through flesh and bone without pause, sending the shaggoth staggering from side to side.

Determined that he would not be upstaged by Snorri, Malekith leapt to where Avanuir had fallen and snatched up his blade. Though his left arm was shattered and his insides burned from injuries that could not be seen, Malekith sprinted forwards and leapt upon the shaggoth's back. As it bucked and turned, Malekith ran up the bony crests along its spine. Spitting through gritted teeth from the pain, the prince grabbed one of the shaggoth's curling horns with his crippled left hand and planted a foot upon its shoulder.

With a triumphant cry, he brought down Avanuir across its neck, chopping deep into the thickly muscled flesh. Thrice more Avanuir bit, until the beast shuddered and spasmed and then collapsed to the ground. With a final effort, Malekith sawed the head free and tossed it to the ground beside Snorri, who was awash head to foot with the entrails and sinews of the monster. The beast's remains toppled to the ground, tossing Malekith unceremoniously into the blood-slicked mud next to Snorri.

The High King looked down at Malekith, his eyes glittering behind the visor of his helm. He then gave the curious thumb-up signal the prince had seen the dwarfs use as a sign of approval.

'We'll share this one, I think,' Malekith said magnanimously.

Only then, with his point proven, did Malekith allow himself to pass out.

◄ SEVEN ►

An Alliance Forged

WITH THE SHAGGOTH slain and their goblin allies routed or slaughtered, the beastmen had little stomach for the continuing battle and quickly slunk back into the woods. Neither elf nor dwarf was prepared to venture after them, the dwarfs knowing they would never catch their swifter foes, the elves utterly undone by the shaman's spell and the shaggoth's attack.

It was a much slower and wearier march back to Karaz-a-Karak for Malekith. His whole body ached and his back and arm flared with pain every time he took a step. The dwarfs offered to carry him upon one of the war machine limbers, but Malekith refused such indignity. Agonising though it was, he walked alongside the dwarfs, hiding his pain as best he could.

It was a source of pride that those of his warriors still capable of standing did likewise, though seven of them were so badly wounded that he allowed them to be carried on the wagons. The bodies of nineteen others were carried with dignity amongst the dwarfen dead.

The dwarfs were similarly determined to prove their resilience, though a good many had suffered broken bones and deep cuts. Bandaged and hobbling, they marched back to the capital with their heads held high, as high as any dwarf's head could ever reach.

Malekith spent most of those following days with the High King, and was pleased that the heroic display of his warriors and himself had earned much respect in Snorri's eyes. Snorri was much more talkative, and seemed eager that the coming negotiations went well.

To CHEERS AND great clamour, the throng returned to Karaz-a-Karak and strode through the gates. The dwarfs chanted Snorri's name and came forwards to congratulate their returning warriors. The elves were greeted with similar enthusiasm and were presented with all manner of small gifts and tokens of the dwarfs' appreciation by wide-eyed beardlings and smiling dwarf maidens.

That same night, the High King hosted a banquet for the victorious army, and lavished his warriors and the elves with food and beer. He bid Malekith the honour of sitting at his right-hand side, and gave the prince his own royal drinking tankard. There were many toasts raised, and more speeches, though on this occasion Malekith was far more complimentary to his hosts than he had been in Karak Kadrin. He thanked the dwarfs for their hospitality and spoke of their courage and honour. He pledged his lifelong friendship to their people, and swore an oath of brotherhood with the High King.

This last was a great occasion and marked the dwarfs' absolute acceptance of the elves as their comrades and friends. Whatever the negotiations and trade talks would bring, Malekith now knew that he would forever be an ally of Snorri, and found himself glad that this was so, not only for the power and prestige this would surely bring, but also because Malekith genuinely liked and admired the dwarfs' ruler.

THE DAY AFTER the celebratory feast, Alandrian was summoned to Malekith's chamber. The prince gave him a very personal mission. The lieutenant accepted his orders without question and sought out Aernuis. He found the Eataine prince in one of the upper galleries.

'There is something important we must discuss,' Alandrian said with a conspiratorial tone. 'Come with me.'

Aernuis followed without question as the Naggarothi captain led him out of the hold via one of the many secondary gates, and they walked out onto a windy rampart high up the mountainside.

'Where are we going?' asked Aernuis finally, as Alandrian took them up a winding stair that led up to a cliff face.

'We cannot risk being overheard or seen,' Alandrian confided.

Saying no more, Aernuis ascended the steps and they stood side-by-side upon a wide ledge. Beneath them a swift river had cut a deep ravine, and gushed over a steep fall into a pool surrounded by jagged rocks some two hundred feet below. Spray filled the air and the roar of the water masked all other sound.

'What is it that you have to say?' asked Aernuis.

'I have a message from Prince Malekith,' said Alandrian.

'What is it?' replied Aernuis.

Swifter than a striking snake, Alandrian stepped behind Aernuis and pulled a curved blade from his belt. Grabbing the prince by the chin, he drove the point of his blade into

Aernuis's back, cutting through his spine. Aernuis struggled as he collapsed to his knees, his cries muffled by Alandrian's hand.

'You are no longer useful to him,' Alandrian hissed in his victim's ear. 'Malekith has the ear of the High King now, and he remembers the slights against him. He is not known for his forgiving nature.'

Aernuis writhed and wept, but Alandrian's grip was as tight as a vice.

'My prince cannot allow you to live,' the Naggarothi explained. 'He would willingly let his light shine upon your life, but he cannot share power with you. You are beneath him, and your petty ambition would undermine all that he hopes to build.'

The Eataine prince flailed at his assassin but Alandrian easily batted away his grasping fingers. Without any hint of pleasure or regret, the Naggarothi drew his knife across Aernuis's throat and pushed him from the ledge. He stepped forwards to watch the body tumble into the spume. The trail of arterial blood spewing from the wound was soon swallowed up by the fury of the waterfall. Tossing the blade casually after the Eataine prince's corpse, Alandrian turned back towards the stair. He wondered where he might find Sutherai.

FIFTEEN DAYS LATER, the audience chamber of Snorri was filled with a crowd of dwarfs and elves. Though ostensibly mingling and getting to know each other, the two peoples were keeping to their own and only a few brave souls of either race ventured over to talk to the opposite delegation. The High King sat upon his throne and watched all of this with amusement, Malekith stood upon his right.

'It is a shame that your two companions are not here to witness the culmination of their efforts,' Snorri remarked.

'A shame indeed,' Malekith replied without pause. 'I cannot comprehend what possessed them to venture from the city without an escort.'

'Nor I,' said Snorri.

Malekith detected no hint of accusation in the High King's voice, though perhaps the prince's ignorance of the dwarfish language masked some implication in the words.

'I am glad that their disappearance has not caused problems for the negotiations,' Malekith said smoothly. 'It is good that their sudden departure has not formed unfounded suspicions between us. Such an occurrence could have unravelled many months of careful planning.'

'Do you think there is cause for suspicion?' said Snorri, turning a questioning eye upon the prince.

'I think not, but I can see how one might view such matters with suspicion. I do not think that there is any conspiracy at work. Prince Aernuis has long been in self-exile and perhaps the impending talks got the better of his nerve.'

'Whatever his reasons, he is probably troll-fodder by now,' said Snorri, returning his attention to the throng below. 'Or worse.'

'A regrettable end for a prince of Ulthuan,' said Malekith.

They both allowed the hubbub of the hall to wash over them for a while until Malekith felt the need to break the silence.

'Shall we join our parties and bring them together?' the prince said.

'Yes, let's get this pony moving,' said Snorri, stepping from his throne.

* * *

FOR MORE THAN a year the talks between the elves and dwarfs progressed, and there were many treaties signed and oaths sworn on both sides. While the rulers and diplomats haggled, the common people of both races got on with the business of the actual trade, reaching local agreements and personal bargains with their opposites.

Malekith recovered from his wounds in time to see the negotiations concluded. Once fit again, he divided his time between Athel Toralien and Karaz-a-Karak, and led the elves to numerous celebrated victories over the creatures of darkness. Bel Shanaar sent the prince a mighty gift in recognition of his achievements: a white dragon from the mountains of Caledor. As his father had done in the time of the daemons, Malekith led the armies of the elves from atop this mighty beast and his foes fell before him. Many times more over the following centuries did the prince of Nagarythe march forth beside the High King, and their friendship was a symbol of the unity between the races of elf and dwarf.

THE ALLIANCE WITH the dwarfs heralded the golden age of the elves; their colonies spread across the globe and the wealth of distant lands flowed into their coffers. Their fleets travelled wherever the elves' desires took them, and cities of gleaming marble and alabaster rose up in the wildernesses of the world.

From Ulthuan the elves spread to every corner of the world, settling in the steaming jungles of Lustria, the savage forests across the great ocean, and upon volcanic isles in the east. The cities of Ulthuan grew with the empire, so that even the meekest of their kind lived in grand mansions amidst great luxury. Everything from the sea to the mountains became the domain of the elves, and in the peaks the dwarfs reigned supreme, their own empire growing vast upon the spoils of the alliance.

Only one land remained free of elvish influence. Eastwards, beyond the mountains of the dwarfs, lay the blasted wastes of the Dark Lands. No elf wished to venture further east, for there was plenty enough for both peoples to enjoy and the dwarfs warned that there was nothing but death and misery in the barren desert.

Thus the elves named the high peaks Saraeluii: the Mountains at the Edge of the World. Truly they were masters of all that they surveyed. Their armies marched at will under the command of the princes, and the evil orc and goblin tribes, vile beastmen warbands and unnameable Chaos creatures were driven into the far north.

Only here, at the very roof of the world, would the elves not venture. It was here that the Realm of Chaos touched upon the world, disgorging its tide of magical energy, warping and corrupting the lands. Having suffered greatly at the hands of daemons before, the elves had no desire to war against the Dark Powers upon the doorstep of their otherworldly realm, and were content to corral the nightmare mutants and monsters upon the bleak ice and keep them from the cities in the south.

Malekith found that his spirit was not quelled by these battles, for his foes were now of little threat, scattered remnants of the huge tribes and armies that had once made the woods their homes. His dragon was slain by a monstrous giant whilst the Naggarothi fought against the last great horde of orcs to beset the elves' lands, and with reluctance the prince realised an age had ended. Elthin Arvan had been tamed, and with that his chance for greater renown would ebb away. So it was that Malekith finally turned his attention to the north, and first went into the cold lands of the Chaos Wastes.

⊰ EIGHT ⊱

The Passing of an Age

HOPING TO REGAIN some of his former passion, Malekith renewed his friendship with the dwarfs of Karak Kadrin, and alongside them took the fight to the monsters and mutants that came south from the Realm of Chaos. On occasion the High King would join Malekith in these conquests, and together they forged along the mountains and across the tundra to bring civilisation to the icy wilderness.

For a while Malekith was content, his turmoil soothed by the comfort of battle and his isolation from the politics of the elven princes. With sword in hand he became master of his own fate once more, and the legends of his exploits grew in proportion so that again his name was spoken of in awe by the high and the mighty of the colonies and Ulthuan.

It was here in the bitter cold of the northlands that Malekith first encountered the tribes of men. Some were savage in the extreme, and either took flight at first sign of the elven and dwarfen host, or sallied forth from their caves and crude huts to wage pointless battle against their far superior foes. At first Malekith took them to be nothing more than another barbarian people, no different or better than the orcs or beastmen.

However, as Snorri and Malekith led an army of dwarfs and elves into the very north of the Saraeluii, a group of humans came forth timidly from their rough dwellings to greet them. The humans brought with them gifts of simple bread and roasted meat. Though they had little more than stone weapons and heavy sticks, they confronted Malekith and Snorri without fear, grunting in their basic language.

The High King took the proffered food and in return gave the human chieftain a golden band from his wrist. The man took it and held it up, admiring the gleam of the metal, and a smile cracked his grimy, bearded face. With a shuffling gait, the tribal leader beckoned for the two to follow him back to their caves.

Malekith at first ignored the man, but Snorri was as inquisitive as ever and followed the elder. Relenting, Malekith walked after them, gesturing for his warriors to stand ready should anything untoward occur. Barriers of crudely split wood and curtains of woven grasses and raw animal hides barred the entrance to the largest of the caves, and smoke billowed out of the entrance from the cooking fires within. Ducking through the skins, Malekith found himself in a high, deep cavern.

Half a dozen human females were clustered within, suckling their young. Older women tended a fire over which roasted half the carcass of an enormous deer. The humans looked at their visitors with curious, intelligent eyes, and immediately Malekith recognised that these creatures were not like the orcs or the beastmen. There was something in their gaze that spoke of wisdom and emotion, utterly unlike the unthinking enmity of an orc's stare.

Snorri tugged at Malekith's arm and pointed excitedly to the cave walls. They were painted with many different scenes, interspersed with abstract symbols and crude pictograms. In particular the High King drew the prince's attention to a painting of a small figure, rotund in form and wielding what looked to be an axe. He had a shock of red hair and a long red beard, and fought against a band of daemon-like stick figures with horns and long claws.

'Grimnir,' Snorri said with a grin, and Malekith nodded.

The daubings did look somewhat like the Ancestor God of the dwarfs, who had dyed his hair a fiery orange and wielded a rune axe as he had ventured into the Realm of Chaos to fight the daemons. That had been more than a thousand years ago, but the cave paintings seemed no more than a few years old. Had these humans passed down what they had seen all those centuries ago, Malekith wondered, leaving paintings and tales for the next generation? If it was true, it spoke loudly about their character and intelligence, and Malekith was quietly impressed.

The pair spent a mostly wordless afternoon with the humans, sharing their food and showing them various trinkets and weapons that they carried. The humans were awkward and filthy, but Malekith could see in them a certain nobility of spirit. After they left the camp, promising through signs and gestures that they would return, Snorri and Malekith fell into a long debate concerning what to do with these people.

'They are children of the Old Ones, just as we are,' the High King said. 'They are not creatures of Chaos or darkness, though they are simple and have little civilisation yet.'

'Yet?' said Malekith.

'For sure,' said Snorri. 'Without guidance or protection, they have survived the fall of the Old Ones and the coming of the Dark Gods. With but a small amount of education from us, they will no doubt become useful. They are quick to learn, I reckon, and will be attentive to our lessons.'

'And to what purpose would you educate them?' laughed Malekith. 'Would you have them as clever labourers, or is there a greater intent to your proposal?'

'I would teach them language and writing,' Snorri replied earnestly. 'Not the language of the dwarfs perhaps, but a tongue that we can all understand. They are here for a reason; I can feel it in my bones. It is our duty to shield them from the worst perils of the world and ensure that they prosper.'

'Who are we to judge what should and should not happen?' countered Malekith. 'They have survived thus far by their own wit and strength, and perhaps it is right that we leave them to find their own path. We cannot know the will of the gods and the Old Ones, and I agree that they have a purpose here, but we cannot guess at what it might be. Is it our place to interfere, or to let things take their course?'

'Hmm, there is much in what you say,' said Snorri. 'However, whatever their destiny, I cannot see that it was to be consumed by hideous creatures nor swallowed up by the dark legions of Chaos. Does it not strike you as odd that they thrive here, under the very shadow of the Chaos Wastes? I know from kin who have travelled further north that there are many of these tribes, in the mountains and upon the icy plains. Is it not preferable that we guard against their corruption, so that perhaps they might become a bulwark against the armies of the Chaos Gods?'

'I would sooner see them as backward friends than clever enemies,' said Malekith. 'What if they take what we can teach them and turn our own knowledge against us? With stone axes and flint-tipped spears, they are no threat to us, but who can say what would happen if they learned the means to work metals, to grow into a nation that might one day look upon our domains with envy?'

'There is much we do not know,' agreed Snorri. 'This is no matter to be decided in the course of a single day.'

So the two were in accord, and decided that their peoples would wait and watch. There was much promise in the race of men, but also much that could be perverted and turned to darkness. The elves and the dwarfs would treat their barbaric neighbours with a light touch, allowing them the shelter of their two empires but otherwise only guiding and shaping their future with their presence alone.

FOR AN AGE the world turned and Malekith was content. War and adventure were plentiful and he returned only seldom to Athel Toralien, preferring the wild lands to the increasingly managed and austere realms of his colony. The Naggarothi prince was lauded across all of the colonies, and here he was king in all but name, for even the other princes admired what he had achieved.

Let Bel Shanaar rule over dull Ulthuan, Malekith would tell himself. Let the Phoenix King fill his days settling the arguments of spoilt princes. Glory and renown forever beckoned to the prince of Nagarythe and he grasped his opportunities with both hands.

All was to change.

* * *

FOR MORE THAN twelve hundred years the colonies grew and endured, and in that time Malekith's power abroad knew no rival, except perhaps in Karaz-a-Karak. Then came word that Bel Shanaar, now rich beyond measure upon his trade and taxes, planned to travel to the dwarfen capital to meet his peer, the High King. For most in the cities of the forests this was heralded as an event worthy of much celebration. However, Malekith was not pleased.

'What is his purpose in coming?' Malekith demanded of Alandrian. He had just received a letter from Morathi warning of Bel Shanaar's intent.

The two of them sat in a wide chamber at the heart of the prince's winter palace, Malekith's retreat during the season of ice when his armies could no longer march. A fire burned in the dwarf-built grate, and the two elves reclined upon long couches, wrapped in warm woollen robes.

'I cannot know his intent, highness,' replied Alandrian.

'Do not be coy with me,' snapped Malekith. 'What do you think he is up to? My mother claims his rule is weakening on Ulthuan and he seeks to bolster his popularity.'

'Your mother is better placed than I to judge events on Ulthuan, highness,' said Alandrian, and then quickly continued after receiving a cold stare from his master. 'What she says confirms my own belief. Though Tiranoc grows rich, there are some princes who feel that Bel Shanaar does not lead his people. The true glory of our people is in the colonies. On Ulthuan, life has become so luxurious that none need fight nor labour. Fields are not tilled, no game is hunted. All she now desires is sent from the cities across the world: sacks of grain, spiced meats, cut gems and dwarfen trinkets. Ulthuan grows indolent and her people lose themselves in poetry and song, wine and debauchery.'

Malekith frowned and stroked his chin.

'I cannot refuse him directly,' the prince said. 'The other cities are keen for his patronage still.'

'Many are jealous of you, beneath their smiles and plaudits,' said Alandrian. 'They seek strength from the Phoenix Throne so that they might become more independent of Athel Toralien.'

'They simply swap one master for another,' snarled Malekith. 'I helped build them. I keep their lands safe. How do they repay my dedication? They cry to Bel Shanaar and hope that he will shield them from the cruel reality of the world.'

'Perhaps there is opportunity here,' said Alandrian. 'If the dwarfs see Bel Shanaar as weak compared to your greatness, your position grows stronger.'

'No, that will not do,' said Malekith. 'King Snorri believes our people to be united, as are his. If Bel Shanaar is seen as weak the High King will see all elves as weak, including me. He believes that all of Ulthuan and her princes are as strong as Nagarythe and me. We cannot undermine that useful illusion by showing him otherwise.'

'I cannot see how we can turn this to your advantage, highness,' admitted Alandrian.

'Why now?' Malekith mused to himself. 'Why, after one thousand two hundred years does Bel Shanaar visit us now?'

IT WAS A question that was to vex Malekith over the long winter months as he brooded in Athel Toralien. The prince was painfully aware that all the talk in the colonies was of the Phoenix King's visit, his own exploits and glory now forgotten by the fickle, gossiping elves of the other cities.

The prince was further insulted by the news that Bel Shanaar planned to visit the city of Tor Alessi first. Taken at face value, this was reasonable, for the city had been founded by princes from Tiranoc, the Phoenix King's own realm. Yet Malekith knew that this was in fact a subtle slight, for Athel Toralien was paramount in size and power in Elthin Arvan. Athel Toralien was a capital in all but name, more than equal in power to Tor Anroc. Bel Shanaar's intent was to show that despite this, there were lands still beyond Malekith's control.

It was mid-summer when the Phoenix King and his entourage arrived at the Naggarothi city. Malekith ensured that his welcome of the Phoenix King left Bel Shanaar in no doubt as to where the rule of Elthin Arvan truly lay. He recalled the greater part of his army, some two hundred thousand Naggarothi, and lined the road to the city with regiments of black-clad archers, magnificently armoured knights and grim-faced spearmen.

Such military spectacle had never before been seen, on Ulthuan or anywhere else. The Naggarothi host dwarfed the guard of the Phoenix King, even bolstered as the Tiranoc force was by troops from Tor Alessi. Malekith hoped the comparison between the two armies was not lost on the other princes.

Not to be outdone by the Phoenix King's wealth, Malekith lavished his guests with the finest gifts and hosted banquets in their honour for thirty days. Herein was another subtle snipe, for Malekith dedicated each night of festivities to a different guest: one for the Phoenix King and one each for the twenty-nine princes who accompanied him. Malekith's message was clear: Bel Shanaar was the first amongst equals, no greater than any other.

The day before Bel Shanaar was due to leave, Malekith invited the Phoenix King to inspect the warriors of Athel

Toralien. They drilled before the city walls, where Malekith stood with his rival upon the massive northern gate tower with his rival. A dozen other princes watched with them, forcing Malekith to choose his words carefully.

'I see that you are impressed, majesty,' said Malekith.

'Against what threat do you maintain such a force?' asked Bel Shanaar, turning his gaze from the marching columns of spearmen filing past far below the gatehouse.

'The lands of Elthin Arvan are still home to beasts and orcs,' Malekith said. 'I maintain garrisons in dozens of citadels between the ocean and the realm of the dwarfs. There is also the ever-present threat from the north.'

'Bands of marauders, scattered tribes of thuggish humans?' Bel Shanaar laughed.

'The Dark Gods and their daemonic legions,' said Malekith, and was pleased to see the princes momentarily fearful.

'Caledor's vortex remains strong,' Bel Shanaar said dismissively. 'Such caution is unnecessary.'

'I inherited a duty from my father,' Malekith said, his voice pitched so that it easily carried to the gathered nobles. 'I shall protect my people against any threat, and stand ready to do the same for Ulthuan.'

Bel Shanaar cast a sideways glance at the princes and said nothing. The Naggarothi continued their manoeuvres until the sun was setting over the ocean.

'Well, that was enlightening,' said Bel Shanaar with a clap of his hands. He turned towards one of the gate towers and then spun back on Malekith. 'I regret that I must depart so soon, but there are others who have begged me to attend their cities and palaces. The Naggarothi cannot have me all to themselves, you know.'

Before Malekith could retort, the Phoenix King had moved away and was surrounded by a gaggle of princes.

The Naggarothi prince stormed off in the opposite direction. He felt the need to vent his frustration and wondered where Alandrian would be hiding.

THE CULMINATION OF this tour was the Phoenix King's arrival at Karaz-a-Karak. Wishing to display his splendour and power, Bel Shanaar arrived with an entourage of three thousand elves, and a bodyguard of ten times that number. The most high-ranking were housed by the dwarfs, and the others lived in a huge camp that spread for miles along the road that led to the hold.

The greeting ceremony was like nothing either dwarf or elf had ever seen before, as both sides attempted to outdo each other in grandiosity and spectacle. The High King summoned all the kings of the holds to gather to greet Bel Shanaar; hundreds of lesser princes and nobles and every ruling prince of Ulthuan attended the Phoenix King – including Malekith. It was Snorri's wish that Malekith introduce him to the Phoenix King, and out of friendship Malekith therefore attended the reception of the Phoenix King, backed by five thousand of his Naggarothi knights.

The procession was almost a mile long, and more than a hundred banners fluttered above the column as it made its way up the road to Karaz-a-Karak on the appointed day. The dwarfs lined the highway cheering and clapping, and many had been drinking for days on end beforehand to get in the right spirit. Five hundred kings and thanes stood as guard for the High King, each accompanied by his banner and shield bearers, while great runelords and master engineers stood proudly with their guild standards, surrounded by the clan elders of every hold.

As was to be expected there was a huge feast and many speeches, so that the whole thing took more than eight days to complete, for every king and thane had to meet and be formally introduced though many had fought and even lived beside each other for hundreds of years.

Throughout the celebrations Malekith was on hand to offer whatever advice and information the Phoenix King required; he deigned to act as translator for Bel Shanaar. The climax of all this activity came on the eighth night, as the High King and Phoenix King finally stood together upon the throne dais of Snorri's audience hall. Bel Shanaar spoke at length upon the benefits of the alliance and the splendid welcome of the dwarfs. He praised the princes for the creation of this corner of the vast empire, and concluded with an announcement that tested Malekith's tolerance to the limit.

'Elf and dwarf shall be bound forever in immortal friendship,' Bel Shanaar declared. 'As long as our empires endure, may we know peace between us. As a sign of our dedication to this common cause, we shall appoint an ambassador to this court, one of our greatest sons. He is the architect of my empire and the forger of this alliance, and his authority in these lands shall be as mine. His words will be my commands. His will shall be my wish. I name Prince Malekith as embassy to Karaz-a-Karak, and bestow the blessings of all the gods upon his endeavours.'

Malekith fumed inside at these words, and had to fight to keep his expression one of gratitude. 'My empire,' Bel Shanaar had said. 'His will shall be my wish,' a voice raged inside Malekith's head. All that he had laboured and fought to create these many centuries, Bel Shanaar had taken from him with those few words. What right did the Phoenix King have to claim anything that Malekith had made possible?

Ambassador? Malekith already had absolute authority over these lands; he needed no permission from Bel Shanaar. The colonies had been his, wrested from the wilderness and the hordes of darkness by his own hands. Blood he had spilt and agonies he had known in the birth of this great empire, while Bel Shanaar had sat upon his throne in Tor Anroc and gorged himself upon the spoils of Naggarothi endeavour. Holding his ire in check, the prince turned and bowed stiffly to the Phoenix King, avoiding Snorri's gaze lest he recognise some hint of the anger that burned within.

For the remainder of the visit, Malekith excused himself from Bel Shanaar's company, claiming that he was needed back in Athel Toralien. In reality, he sought the sanctuary of the forests, for such was Malekith's anger he could not look upon the face of another elf for several months.

EVENTUALLY THE PRINCE calmed and tried as best he could to return to a normal life. In the five decades that followed Bel Shaanar's visit Malekith sent messages to Morathi frequently, and she replied with equal regularity. Always she was keen to praise her son for his achievements, but there was also gentle admonishment that he ignored his father's legacy on Ulthuan. Ever she had insisted that he return to the isle to take up his birthright, and her writing became even more strident following Bel Shanaar's visit to Karaz-a-Karak. She too had felt the slight caused by the Phoenix King's words and deeds, and Morathi had ranted at length in her next letter, decrying the hypocrisy of Bel Shanaar, who spoke out against supposed decadence in Nagarythe.

In this last matter, Malekith's intuition was roused and he secretively took more interest in affairs back on Ulthuan. He subtly inquired over the coming years as to the nature of life in Nagarythe, both through his missives to Morathi and from loyal Naggarothi who still sailed between the isle of the elves and the colonies.

The news from the merchants worried him on occasion, for there was talk of cabalistic cults dedicated to the more sinister elven gods, and of pleasure sects that lost themselves in luxury and excess. Malekith's suspicions were tempered by the letters of Morathi.

'Jealous of Nagarythe's prominence despite the Phoenix King's court being in Tor Anroc,' she explained in one of her letters, 'many of the ruling princes are waging a subtle and insidious campaign against me and my council. They will not accuse me outright of any misdeed, but through innuendo and rumour imply that we are in league with some unknown dark power.'

Malekith could imagine how the envy of the princes would lead them to such actions, and believed his mother when she assured him that the so-called pleasure cults and dark sects were nothing more than ancient rituals the Naggarothi had always undertaken for the appeasement of the less fondly regarded elven gods.

'The Phoenix King has even hinted that he looks unkindly on the Naggarothi's connections to Khaine,' she continued. 'Our oldest gods he would see forgotten, while he decorates his halls with gold brought to his coffers by the spears of our warriors.'

In his reply Malekith told his mother to do nothing to antagonise the princes or move openly against the Phoenix King, and she promised him it was so, though her tone was ever defiant to their authority.

Something of what Malekith had heard began to seep into life in the colonies. Always the elves had enjoyed wine and song, and the reading of poetry both beautiful and satirical. However, Malekith stayed for months, sometimes years at a time away from the cities, and so the slow but subtle changes wrought upon them seemed more stark to him upon his returns.

A softness of spirit and a laxity that Malekith had detested in Ulthuan began to creep into the culture of Athel Toralien. Many of his subjects were now second- and even third-generation colonists, who had not had to raise a sword in anger to defend their lands, and Malekith feared that the very stability he had fought to bring to this realm was undermining the heart of his people. Not wishing to appear tyrannical, Malekith did not openly oppose the many wine houses and pleasure dens that now seemed to be found in every other building of the city.

Instead, he commanded his council to institute a formal practice of inducting Naggarothi who came of age into the ranks of his army. What once had been tradition Malekith now enforced with law, in the hope that discipline and military life would breed into a new generation the will and power of the elves who had first followed him here.

Malekith's growing contact with mankind awoke his inquisitive spirit, and he was filled with a passion to deepen his knowledge of this race, and also of the shadowy powers that held sway over the Chaos Wastes. Deeper and deeper into the north he ventured, sometimes alone, other times with a host of his warriors. Though the wild forests had all but been tamed by the elves, Malekith drove his armies northwards possessed by a bloodthirsty spirit that worried those who knew the prince well.

It was upon returning from one such campaign that the prince visited his dwarfen allies in Karak Kadrin. The mood in the hold was sombre as Malekith entered the throne room of King Brundin, who had inherited the hold's rule from his father a few years previously. The king was surrounded by solemn-faced nobles, amongst them the venerable Kurgrik whose fortunes had risen considerably since his days of humble logging.

Malekith's oldest dwarf companion turned and hurried down the steps towards the prince, stroking his exceptionally long beard in an agitated fashion.

'What is amiss?' asked Malekith.

'The High King lies upon his deathbed,' said Kurgrik, wringing his fingers through his beard. 'Messengers scour the northlands searching for you. He asks for you, elven prince. You must go to Karaz-a-Karak!'

Malekith glanced up at the throne dais and saw the crowd of earnest, grief-stricken faces, and knew that this was no exaggeration.

'Convey my regrets to King Brundin, but I leave now,' said Malekith.

The prince turned on his heel and ran from the hall. He dashed through the doors, ignoring the shouted concerns and questions of his companions. Down tunnel and across gallery sped Malekith, until he came upon the great gate. Outside, the elves' steeds were corralled on the hillside. Malekith leapt the fence and headed straight for the tallest of the horses, his own mount. He did not wait for saddle or bridle and instead leapt onto the steed's bare back. Malekith turned southwards and the horse broke into a thundering gallop at a whispered word from her rider. Vaulting the corral, the pair sped down into Peak Pass.

Though Malekith journeyed swiftly south, fear that he might arrive too late gnawed at him. When his steed was all but dead from exhaustion, he turned westwards until he came upon one of the elven towers that guarded the borders of the great forest of Elthin Arvan. Here he commandeered a new mount and continued southwards. Driven by worry, Malekith did not eat or sleep, and rode by the light of the moon as much as the sun. After three days he neared the hold of Zhufbar. Dwarfs laboured digging a fresh mineshaft not far from the road, and the prince wheeled his steed towards them. The dwarfs looked up in astonishment, unexpectedly confronted by the ambassador of the elves.

'What news from Karaz-a-Karak?' Malekith demanded.

'No news,' replied their gangmaster, a rugged, tanned dwarf with a greying golden beard and a hook for a left hand.

'The High King still lives?' said Malekith.

'The last we heard, he does,' said the dwarf.

Without further word Malekith heeled his mount into a fresh gallop and sped towards Black Water, where so many years before he had fought alongside the High King. His mind was devoid of fond memories, so possessed was Malekith to see his ally before he passed away. Along the shore he raced, his horse throwing up a wave of spray in its wake as the prince urged his mount on at dangerous speed.

The following day Malekith took the southern road from Karak Varn direct to Karaz-a-Karak. Wide enough for many carts, the road was built of brick and stone, and his passage was swift. He weaved amongst the dwarfen carts until he spied an elven caravan. Bringing his tired steed to a halt before the lead caravan, Malekith dismounted and signalled for the driver to stop.

'Prince Malekith?' said the driver. 'What brings you here?'

'I need one of your horses,' said Malekith, already untying the traces on the foremost of the three beasts drawing the wagon.

'You can ride with me, highness,' offered the driver, but the prince paid him no heed and away he galloped without explanation or payment.

Two more days Malekith rode hard until finally he came before the great gates of Karaz-a-Karak. For the first time he did not marvel at their golden majesty, nor regard with awe the huge towers and buttresses that flanked the huge doors. His steed sweating hard, he galloped up the road. The guards at the gate made to step forwards to bar his route but he did not slow. Recognising the prince and seeing his intent, the guards hurled themselves out of his path, pushing away other dwarfs to clear a passage.

Through the gate raced the prince, the clatter of his horse's hooves on the tiles echoing from the high vaults. Dwarfs were sent ducking into doorways and scurrying in every direction as he pounded through the winding tunnels towards the king's chambers. Only when he saw a crowd of the king's advisors pressed around the door to one of the king's rooms did he slow down. Leaping from the back of the horse, he ran forwards and grabbed the closest of the nobles, a loremaster called Damrak Goldenfist.

'Am I too late?' he demanded.

The stunned dwarf said nothing for a moment and then shook his head. Malekith let go of Damrak and slumped against the wall.

'You misunderstand me, ambassador,' said Damrak, laying a gnarled hand on Malekith's arm. 'The king still awaits you.'

THE SOLEMN BEATING of drums could be heard echoing along the halls and corridors of Karaz-a-Karak. The small chamber was empty save for two figures. His face as pale as his beard, King Snorri lay on the low, wide bed, his eyes closed. Kneeling next to the bed, a hand on the dwarf's chest, was Malekith. He had stood vigil with the ancient dwarf for three days since arriving, barely sleeping or eating in that time.

The room was hung with heavy tapestries depicting the battles the two had fought together, suitably aggrandising

Snorri's role. Malekith did not begrudge the king his glories, for was not his own name sung loudly in Ulthuan while the name of Snorri Whitebeard was barely a whisper? Each people to their own kind, the elf prince thought.

Snorri's eyelids fluttered open to reveal cloudy, pale blue eyes. His lips twisted into a smile and a fumbling hand found Malekith's arm.

'Would that dwarf lives were measured as those of the elves,' said Snorri. 'Then my reign would last another thousand years.'

'But even so, we still die,' said Malekith. 'Our measure is made by what we do when we live and the legacy that we leave to our kin, as any other. A lifetime of millennia is worthless if its works come to naught after it has ended.'

'True, true,' said Snorri with a nod, his smile fading. 'What we have built is worthy of legend, isn't it? Our two great realms have driven back the beasts and the daemons, and the lands are safe for our people. Trade has never been better, and the holds grow with every year.'

'Your reign has indeed been glorious, Snorri,' said Malekith. 'Your line is strong; your son will uphold the great things that you have done.'

'And perhaps even build on them,' said Snorri.

'Perhaps, if the gods will it,' said Malekith.

'And why should they not?' asked Snorri. He coughed as he pushed himself to a sitting position, his shoulders sinking into thick, gold-embroidered white pillows. 'Though my breath comes short and my body is infirm, my will is as hard as the stone that these walls are carved from. I am a dwarf, and like all my people, I have within me the strength of the mountains. Though this body is now weak, my spirit shall go to the Halls of the Ancestors.'

'It will be welcomed there, by Grungni and Valaya,' said Malekith. 'You shall take your place with pride.'

'I'm not done,' said Snorri with a frown. His expression grim, the king continued. 'Hear this oath, Malekith of the elves, comrade on the battlefield, friend at the hearth. I, Snorri Whitebeard, High King of the dwarfs, bequeath my title and rights to my eldest son. Though I pass through the gateway to the Halls of the Ancestors, my eyes shall remain upon my empire. Let it be known to our allies and our enemies that death is not the end of my guardianship.'

The dwarf broke into a wracking cough, blood flecking his lips. His lined faced was stern as he looked at Malekith. The elf steadily returned his gaze.

'Vengeance shall be mine,' swore Snorri. 'When our foes are great, I shall return to my people. When the foul creatures of this world bay at the doors to Karaz-a-Karak, I shall take up my axe once more and my ire shall rock the mountains. Heed my words, Malekith of Ulthuan, and heed them well. Great have been our deeds, and great is the legacy that I leave to you, my closest confidant, my finest comrade-in-arms. Swear to me now, as my dying breaths fill my lungs, that my oath has been heard. Swear to it on my own grave, on my spirit, that you shall remain true to the ideals we have both striven for these many years. And know this, that there is nothing so foul in the world as an oath-breaker.'

Malekith took the king's hand from his arm and squeezed it tight. 'I swear it,' the elf prince said. 'Upon the grave of High King Snorri Whitebeard, leader of the dwarfs and friend of the elves, I give my oath.'

Snorri's eyes were glazed and his chest no longer rose and fell. Malekith's keen hearing could detect no sign of life, and he did not know whether his words had been heard. Releasing Snorri's hand, he folded the king's arms across his chest, and with a delicate touch from his long fingers, Malekith closed Snorri's eyes.

Standing, Malekith spared one last glance at the dead king and then walked from the chamber. Outside, Snorri's son Throndik stood along with several dozen other dwarfs.

'The High King has passed on,' Malekith said, his gaze passing over the heads of the assembled dwarfs and across to the throne room. He looked down at Throndik. 'You are now High King.'

Without further word, the elf prince picked his way gracefully through the crowd and out across the nearly empty throne chamber. He stopped halfway towards the throne and gazed up at the high dais. He remembered perfectly the first time he had been here. At the time Malekith's attention had been focused on Aernuis; the High King had barely registered in his thoughts. Now all he could think about was the dwarf now lying still in that small bedchamber.

The throne was empty. Everything was empty. The wars against the orcs and the beasts had been won. The forests had been tamed by the elves and the mountains conquered by the dwarfs. Bel Shanaar had robbed him of rulership of the colonies. It was as if Snorri had unknowingly taken the last days of glory to his grave. His friend was dead and there was nothing else to fight for.

Nothing except the Phoenix Throne.

OVER THE FOLLOWING decade, Malekith became ever more distant from his court in Athel Toralien. As he had done so in Nagarythe, he appointed a wise and well-regarded council of fellow princes and other dignitaries to rule in his stead, and passed on the mantle of ambassador to Carnellios, a prince of Cothique who had been part of the original talks and whom the dwarfs had come to trust. Once content that all was in order, the prince declared that he would go into the north again, for many years, perhaps never to return, and he asked for volunteers to accompany him.

After issuing his proclamation, Malekith set out on a tour of the castles and citadels that protected the lands of Athel Toralien, to extend his offer to all of their garrisons. He picked the finest captains, knights and archers from amongst their number and returned to the city with seventy warriors.

Riding upon the west–east road to Athel Toralien, the prince and his company came upon a great encampment outside the city's walls, stretching for almost half a mile. Great marquees and pavilions housed rich nobles, while more moderate tents were numbered in the many hundreds.

Yeasir was at the east gate to greet his master.

'Thank the gods you have returned,' said the captain, grabbing the bridle of Malekith's steed to allow the prince to dismount.

'Some emergency?' said Malekith, handing the reins to one of his companions. 'An orcish horde perhaps? Beasts from the north?'

'No, no,' said Yeasir. 'There is no threat.'

'Then why do I have an army of vagabonds and princes at my gate?' demanded Malekith, turning to stare at the tent-city stretching along the road.

'They all wish to accompany you on your voyage,' Yeasir said breathlessly.

'All of them?' said Malekith, eyebrows raised.

'Six thousand seven hundred and twenty-eight,' said Yeasir. 'Well, according to the roll of volunteers that Alandrian was forced to begin. They filled the city at first and there was no room in the docks or markets. We had to send them outside, and provided many with shelters.'

'I cannot take more than five hundred,' said Malekith. 'Send away any that have wives or children, and any that have never drawn blood in battle. That should thin out the numbers a little.'

'Yes, highness,' said Yeasir. 'Many are not Naggarothi, do you wish them to accompany you?'

'Only if they swear loyalty to Nagarythe,' said the prince with a frown. 'And I don't want anyone under three hundred years old. I need experience; seasoned veterans.'

'There are eighteen princes of various realms,' Yeasir said. 'What shall I do with them?'

'They seek to glorify themselves in the glow of my deeds,' snapped Malekith. 'Any that are not of Nagarythe, and I mean Nagarythe, not this city, send them home. I will talk to any you feel are worthy of my attention.'

'As you wish, highness,' said Yeasir, bowing as he left.

Malekith stared out along the road as news of his return began to spread through the camp. Horns sounded, and more and more elves came out of their tents and began to converge on the city. Hundreds of them soon packed the road, crying out to the prince for his attention. Malekith turned his back on them and walked into the city. He turned his head to one of the guards.

'Shut the gate until they go away,' the prince snapped.

FIVE HUNDRED ELVES Malekith chose to be his companions; enough to man a ship and fight, but few enough to feed and supply out in the wilds. Almost half were nearly as old as Malekith and some had journeyed with him from Ulthuan. All were without family, for Malekith knew that he ventured into the truly unknown, and whatever perils lay ahead he was determined that his wanderlust would not leave a legacy of widows and orphans.

Alandrian organised the provisioning of the expedition and the repatriation of those who had been turned away. Amongst his many duties he managed to catch up with Malekith one evening.

'Is all ready?' asked the prince, sitting on a low chair upon the balcony of his city house. He gestured for Alandrian to help himself to the contents of a crystal decanter perched on a small table. Alandrian poured himself a goblet of golden wine and sat down.

'If I could make a suggestion, your highness,' Alandrian said delicately. 'Perhaps five hundred and one companions would be better for you.'

'Five hundred and one?' said Malekith, and then he gave a laugh and a nod of understanding. 'You wish to offer your service?'

'I do, highness,' said the lieutenant. 'Yeasir accompanies you, and so would I.'

'It cannot be done,' said Malekith. 'Yeasir has no family. You have a beautiful wife who has borne you two equally beautiful daughters. I could no more rob them of their father than I could cut off a limb.'

'You are destined for great glory,' said Alandrian. 'I have served well and attended my duties with vigour and loyalty. I ask only that I be allowed to continue my service.'

'Your time of service is no more,' said Malekith. He held up a hand to stop Alandrian's protest. 'I have had papers drawn up, declaring you a prince of Nagarythe and the ruler of Athel Toralien.'

'A prince?' stammered Alandrian.

'That is right,' said Malekith, laughing at his friend's stunned expression. 'I was going to wait a while before making an announcement but you have forced my hand. You will be my regent in Elthin Arvan. Yeasir is a soldier first and last, and I will name him commander of

Nagarythe, the title I once held when my father was alive. You are a leader, with a patience to match your wisdom and your gift with words. You can best serve me not with spear point but with quill point. Rule Athel Toralien in the finest traditions of Nagarythe. Be ever ready to come to the aid of your homeland. Most of all you must enjoy yourself and take what reward you can from the life the gods have given you!'

Malekith raised his goblet in toast to his companion, who half-heartedly lifted his own, still shocked by the prince's declaration.

━━━ NINE ━━━

A Delayed Departure

In the months of preparation before his departure, Malekith received an unexpected visitor. He was sitting in the uppermost chamber of his tower overlooking the harbour of Athel Toralien, reviewing an agreement on the succession of power to his followers. Though he had a palatial mansion, several in fact, within the city and out in the forest, he chose to conduct his business here, in a tower built over the part of the old wall where he had first defended the city against the orcs.

Malekith was just re-reading a particularly complex passage for the third time when he was disturbed from his study by noise from the street far below the open window. There was also much commotion from within the tower, as doors slammed and he heard a great many feet pounding upon the stairs. He tried to ignore the excited shouts and concentrate on the legalistic wording of the document he held, but the ruckus persisted and in frustration he threw the parchment onto his desk and stood up. At that moment there was a hurried knocking at the door.

'What?' he demanded.

The door was flung open by Yeasir, who stepped into the room with a hasty bow.

'I am trying to concentrate,' the prince growled.

'Forgive the disturbance, your highness,' said Yeasir breathlessly, bowing again with more decorum. 'Please look out of your window.'

'My window?' said Malekith.

The prince turned and strode to the open casement and stepped out onto the small balcony beyond. He stared down at the street below and saw crowds of elves hastening through the streets towards the docks, some of them running in their excitement. Raising his head, Malekith looked out over the roofs of the warehouses to the harbour beyond.

It was a sunny spring day and the calm waters of the bay glittered in the afternoon light. Dozens of ships bobbed at anchor in the middle of the port, but all seemed calm and Malekith could see nothing amiss. Then he turned his gaze further to the south and saw a line of black sails approaching past the harbour wall.

Shielding his eyes against the glare, Malekith looked at the approaching ships. There were ten of them, nine unremarkable but for the fact that they flew silver and black pennants of Nagarythe at their mastheads. The tenth was what caught Malekith's attention, and the cause of so much interest from the city folk below.

It glided across the waves without effort, four huge lateen sails filled with the breeze, surf crashing around the gold-plated ram at its prow. It was larger than any ship Malekith had ever before seen, in size as large as a castle keep, spread over three hulls – one central structure flanked by two outrigger hulls that were each the size of a warship. Upon its deck stood high towers of dark-stained wood banded and trimmed with shining gold. It was the finest vessel ever to have crossed the seas, and Malekith was dumbstruck by its majesty and elegant lines.

Like a lion amongst scavenging dogs, the ship surged through the surf at the heart of its fleet, before trimly tacking across the wind and gracefully gliding towards the longest pier. The sound of clarions rang out from across the waves from the other nine ships, heralding the arrival of their leader.

Malekith fought the urge to leap straight from the balcony and run to the docks, and instead turned and instructed Yeasir to fetch his cloak and sword. He stood there tapping his fingers impatiently on the curved parapet of the balcony, watching as the immense ship slid closer and closer. He could now see the crew upon the deck, dressed in smart smocks of red and white, straining at stays to keep the sails full. At some unheard command, they jumped into action to furl the mainsail, slowing the ship's passage as it neared the wharf.

Yeasir entered again and fixed Malekith's scabbard to his belt and hung his purple cloak from his shoulders. Perhaps more hurriedly than he realised, Malekith strode from the room and descended the long winding stair at the centre of the tower. Guards at the doors flung them open at his approach, and Malekith swept past them without a glance, intent on the street outside.

It was thronged with people, and though many parted as they saw him approach, some were so intent upon reaching the docks that they did not note his appearance. Yeasir trotted ahead of his lord to clear them out of the way, and as they realised their error they fell to their knees in apology, and begged Malekith's forgiveness as he strode past. In this way, Yeasir swiftly cleared a path to the docks, but upon arriving at the wharfs found the route utterly blocked by the press of elves who had gathered here from all over the surrounding buildings.

A few realised the unmannerly obstruction they were causing, but could only shrug and bow in apology, as they attempted to get out of the way but could not due to the crowds behind them. Such was the hubbub that Yeasir's shouted commands were barely heard, and in the end Malekith resorted to drastic measures.

Drawing Avanuir from its sheath, he held the fabled sword aloft, its tip pointed towards the cloudless sky. With a word, the prince sent a pulse of magic along the blade. The sorcery erupted into a bolt of flame that shot high up into the air with a piercing screech, attracting the attention of all.

Thus warned of their ruler's approach, the elves began to make way as best they could for the prince, some of them awkwardly leaping onto boats that stood at the water's edge, others pushing into buildings or climbing onto awnings and balconies. As the waves parted before the prow of the approaching ship, so the elves parted in the path of their prince. With a satisfied nod, Malekith sheathed his sword and strode forwards along the widening line between him and the docking vessel.

Malekith walked to the end of the curving pier of white planks and stood with his hands on hips as the immense ship slowly slid around and came alongside. Elves with thick hawsers in hand leapt lithely over the side to the quay to secure the vessel. Amidships, a length of the gunwale soundlessly swung upwards and a wide set of steps slid out of the gap to touch down upon the pier. Malekith walked along the quay to stand at the foot of the docking stairs.

Looking up onto the ship, the sun was behind the vessel, throwing the sails and rigging into stark silhouette. A figure appeared at the top of the ramp, tall and elegant, draped with silky ribbons that danced in the sea breeze. As she strolled cat-like down the ramp, Malekith could see his visitor more clearly, as young and beautiful as he had ever remembered her: Morathi.

The widow of Aenarion walked languidly down from the ship and stopped before Malekith, holding out a hand for him to help her down the last step. He kissed the back of her hand and led her onto the quay, sweeping his cloak out of the way as he did so. Morathi turned her face towards him as they walked along the pier back to the dockside, and she smiled.

'My wonderful son,' she purred.

'Precious mother,' replied Malekith with a formal nod of the head.

As the crowd upon the harbour side could see more clearly, there was shocked whispering, which spread from the end of the pier and out through the assembled elves. A respectful silence then descended and the only sound that could be heard was the cry of gulls in the air and the lapping of the waves against the piles of the quays. Now the elves surreptitiously crowded forwards again, those further back leaning forwards and straining to get a look at the queen-regent of Nagarythe. Many had been born in Athel Toralien and had never seen the seeress.

Mother and son walked serenely towards the tower where the prince had been working, Morathi's hand upon Malekith's. Neither looked at the other, but both gazed out to the crowd with beatific smiles. Malekith's expression was a mask hiding his true feelings, for inside he was in turmoil but he could not show weakness.

Morathi's arrival was most unexpected, and he feared what news she brought. He could think of no reason that was pleasant why she would have abandoned the comforts of Anlec for the colonies. Had she finally driven Bel Shanaar too far and been forced into exile with her son? Was Nagarythe threatened? The ship too was an enigma. It was clearly of Naggarothi design, but no shipyard outside of Lothern was capable of building such a behemoth. How had she come by such a prize, and what was her intent?

Craving the answers to these questions, Malekith forced himself to pace slowly through the streets, accepting the bows and waves of the adoring crowds that were even now still growing in number.

The prince detected a certain smugness in his mother's manner: a pride that he felt was not wholly down to a mother meeting her son. Certainly she had caused quite a stir with her arrival, and Malekith suspected that this was in great part the source of her pleasure. Ever since Malekith had been old enough to notice his mother, he had seen how attention focused upon her, and how only Aenarion's light had shone brighter than hers. As a rock absorbs the heat of a summer midday sun, so Morathi bathed in the quiet adulation of the elven masses of Athel Toralien.

It was some time before they reached the tower overlooking the bay. Glancing over his shoulder as they passed though the doors, Malekith saw that Alandrian had joined Yeasir. He waved Morathi to proceed him up the stairs and turned to his lieutenants.

'Leave us for the moment,' Malekith instructed them. 'Do not go too far, I will be calling for you shortly. Yeasir, please send someone to the docks to ensure that my mother's luggage and servants are taken to the Palace of Stars. We will join her entourage there this evening.'

As the pair bowed and turned to leave, Malekith thought of something else.

'Best send word to my servants at the palace too, and the farmers,' Malekith said, drawing confused looks from Alandrian and Yeasir. 'My mother will have brought many hangers-on, advisors and other menials. There will be a lot of mouths to feed.'

Nodding in realisation, the pair left Malekith, who closed the doors to the tower behind them, shutting out the gaping crowds.

Turning, he leapt up the stairs three at a time, chasing after his mother. Despite his haste, Morathi was already standing beside the balcony window by the time Malekith reached the top of the tower. She turned and smiled as he strode into the room, and held out an arm for him to hold. Sighing, the prince allowed his mother to lay her hand upon his, and led her out onto the balcony. This time, the seeress-queen and prince of Nagarythe were greeted with rapturous cheers and applause. The streets were packed with elves in every direction, and windows and balconies were full as the people of Athel Toralien sought the best vantage point to see their mysterious, glamorous visitor.

'What are you doing here?' Malekith whispered as he waved to the adoring crowds.

'I have come to visit you, my wonderful son,' replied Morathi, not turning her smile from the masses below. 'A mother worries, you know that. Word came to me that you were heading off into the wilds for some ridiculous adventures, so I thought it best that I finally visit your new home before you left.'

'You will not dissuade me,' Malekith warned her. 'I am ready to leave within days.'

'Dissuade you?' said Morathi with a faint laugh. 'Why would I not want you to go? Was it not me that stood upon the quayside when you left Nagarythe, and told you to earn glory and renown for yourself and your people? Have you not done so, and have I not looked upon all that you have achieved with great love and pride?'

'Forgive my misunderstanding,' said Malekith. 'If you are here to lend your support, then I am very grateful.'

Morathi did not reply straightaway, but instead indicated discreetly that they should retire inside. With a final wave and a grin, Malekith stepped off the balcony and his mother followed. Closing the window, Malekith rounded on his mother.

'So why is it that you are here?' he asked, not with accusation but with genuine curiosity.

'It is not my support that you need, at least not in any physical way,' Morathi replied.

Seeing his mother wave a hand towards the bottle upon the desk, Malekith took a clean glass from one of the many cabinets in the room and poured wine for Morathi. She took it with a nod, had a sip and then continued.

'You have been away from Ulthuan for too long. I was of a mind to persuade you to return rather than gallivanting across the wastes, but then I realised that such a course of action would be a fool's errand and only earn me your enmity, perhaps even your disdain.'

'You are right, I will not return to Ulthuan,' said Malekith. 'Why do you think it is so important that I do so now?'

'Not now, but soon,' Morathi said. 'I sense that Bel Shanaar's rule is fading. His usurpation of your relationship with the dwarfs was an attempt to bolster his flagging fortunes. Now that the colonies are well established, all of the kingdoms enjoy the comfort and wealth that the realms overseas bring to us, Tiranoc no less so, nor more so than any others. Nagarythe's most adventurous spirits have departed the shores of the isle, for new generations look to the likes of you to emulate, not to the staid, overly sincere Bel Shanaar. In comfort there is frailty, for a sword must be forged in the burning fires before it can rest in its scabbard. There is no more fire in Ulthuan. Even as her empire continues to grow, Ulthuan herself is diminishing.'

'If Ulthuan has become lessened, then it is the fault of the princes who rule there,' said Malekith, pouring himself some wine.

'That is my point,' snapped Morathi. 'There is none capable of succeeding Bel Shanaar; his court is as weak as he is. Your achievements here have been rightly lauded, but your success has been copied and appropriated and demeaned by others. If only you had returned to us before Bel Shanaar accorded himself and his rule with the dwarfs and stole your victory. It is time to create a new legend for yourself, and return in triumph to reclaim what is rightfully yours.'

'What would you say if I told you that I wish never to return to Ulthuan?' said Malekith. 'What if I have decided that my life is out here, away from the coddling embrace of Ulthuan?'

'Then I would curse you for a fool and cast you out of my life,' said Morathi. 'But that is not really how you think. You do not like Ulthuan, and I cannot blame you. She is like a maiden that you love, gripped tightly within the arms of a less-deserving amour. But, just as you turn away from that sight, within your heart still lingers that love for the maiden, no matter what she does.'

'You are right, of course,' admitted Malekith. 'She is like to me as a lover who has spurned my attentions many times, and yet her gaze lingers upon me always, tempting me with the notion that one day she will accept my advances. However, if what you say is true, then perhaps it is too late for me; the beauty of youth has faded and Ulthuan perhaps is on the decline into infirmity and then a swift passing away. Perhaps it is better this way, that we break our ties to that small isle, and reach out to the wider world.'

Morathi strode across the room, her face a mask of fury, and slapped Malekith across the cheek. In instinct he raised his hand to reply in kind, but Morathi was as quick as a serpent and snatched his wrist in her fingers, her long and sharpened nails digging so deep into the flesh that blood trickled across her hand.

'How dare you!' the seeress hissed. 'Your father gave his life for Ulthuan, and it took his death to save her! I thought I had raised you better than this. I thought that you had not become one of those prancing, preening fools that pass as princes in Bel Shanaar's court. How dare you condemn Ulthuan to death by indifference! Your father laid down his life to protect our isle, who are you to do different?'

Malekith snatched away his wrist with a snarl and made to turn, but Morathi was relentless and grabbed his arm and spun him around to face her.

'You dare to turn your back on me, just as you turn your back on your homeland!' she snarled. 'Perhaps the First Council was right not to choose you; not because of a darkness upon you, but because you are weak and undeserving.'

'What more could I do?' demanded Malekith. 'I have conquered new lands in the name of Nagarythe, and brokered the greatest alliance our people will ever see. What more can I give to Ulthuan?'

'Yourself,' said Morathi. 'When Aenarion died, he left Ulthuan a legacy, and you are part of it. To rule is also to serve, Aenarion understood that. He served Khaine, for there was no other master worthy of his fealty. You must be prepared to serve a high purpose, a great power.'

Morathi paused and took a deep breath, calming herself. When she continued her voice was low but insistent.

'Serve Ulthuan and you will be Phoenix King. Protect her from enemies outside and within and she will embrace you in return. Go into the north and learn of the race of men. Head into the chilling wastes and confront the Dark Gods that hunger over our world. Then return to Ulthuan and take up your place as ruler, to shield us against their unnatural thirst. I fear that only you can protect us against the dangers I have foreseen. I see fire and bloodshed sweeping Ulthuan again. The colonies will burn and all that we hold dear will be cast upon the rocks and be for naught.'

'What have you seen, when will this happen?' asked Malekith.

'You know that there is no future that is certain,' replied Morathi. 'I have simply cast my gaze ahead along the path of my life, and I see death. War will come again and the Naggarothi will be called upon as they were by your father. I warned the First Council that it would be so, but they did not listen. You must learn what you can of Chaos, and of humans, for our future is entwined with both. When you are master of your fate, then return to us and take what has been kept from you for so long. Let Anlec be a beacon of hope again.'

Malekith saw desire and fear in equal measure in the face of his mother, and his love for her stirred him. He laid an arm about her shoulders and pulled her close to him. She quivered, though whether from anxiety or excitement he could not tell.

'It shall be as you say,' said Malekith. 'I shall go into the north and seek whatever destiny awaits me there. I will return to Ulthuan, and I will guard her against whatever comes to pass.'

'And I have a steed worthy of such a journey,' said Morathi, pulling away from her son and leading him by the hand back to the window. She pointed out towards the bay, to the huge ship that now lay in a berth along the quayside.

'She is *Indraugnir*, named after the dragon whom your father befriended and from whose back he fought against the daemons. The two of them died together upon the Blighted Isle, after Aenarion returned the Godslayer to its black altar. It is not yet time for you to ride upon the dragon, but this dragonship shall suffice in the meantime. That fabled name will not go unnoticed by the folk of Ulthuan.'

'She is a magnificent vessel,' said Malekith. 'Yet for all of her glory, she is beyond the means of the Naggarothi to build. I do not understand how she came to be made.'

'We spoke of Ulthuan as a coquettish maiden, and she is,' said Morathi. 'There are many princes who admire her, and who are willing to aid her when she asks in return for the promise of favour. Prince Aeltherin of Lothern is one such admirer, and it is he who built the first of the dragonships and gifted her to you. Others will be built in the shipyards of Lothern over the coming years, but *Indraugnir* is the first and ever will be the greatest in the eyes and dreams of our people.'

'So, you have allies outside of Nagarythe,' said Malekith.

'Many,' replied Morathi. 'Some of the princes of the First Council are dead, by war or age, and their sons now wonder whether their fathers chose rightly. Not all were happy at the time, and a thousand years is a long while to be reigned over by a lesser ruler than Aenarion. There is support for us in every kingdom and across the colonies. The frustration of the common folk builds, for while they live in comfort, their inner spirits are unsatisfied. I do what I can to lift them, to provide their lives with purpose and meaning, but they now live in a world far removed from the times of hunger, fear and deprivation that we knew many centuries ago. They live in idyllic palaces surrounded by a garden paradise, yet many see it for the gilded cage that Ulthuan has become. We pray to the gods for direction, and they answer me through their visions and dreams.'

'I hear much that concerns the gods and your prayers,' said Malekith. 'You tempt fate by courting the twilight pantheon. The likes of Morai-heg and Nethu are not to be toyed with. My father paid a heavy price for the favours of Khaine; do not underestimate the forces you play with.'

'There is no need to be afraid,' said Morathi. 'Only true priests and priestesses perform the actual dark rituals. For the most part these ceremonies are little more than gatherings for feasting and gossiping. Only Bel Shanaar and his deceptively pious coterie feign outrage at some of the rituals, but they know as well as you and I do that Atharti, Hekarti and others cannot be ignored. It is only because we still value the old traditions and the ancient customs in Nagarythe that we are able to perform these rituals at all. Someone must be guardian of the forgotten paths, and if that means that the other kingdoms must turn to us on occasion, then that is all the better.'

'If you move against Bel Shanaar, it will be treason,' said Malekith. 'I know that you seek to undermine his power and influence. Be careful that you do not destroy Nagarythe in the process. No prince of Ulthuan will betray the Phoenix King, and if you move too fast, you will leave Nagarythe friendless and weak.'

'I will make no moves at all,' said Morathi, sitting down in the chair behind Malekith's desk. She swept her long black hair over her shoulder and looked at her son. 'The position of Phoenix King should always command great respect and authority. I would not erode the power of the Phoenix King and leave you a tarnished crown worth less than a copper cap. It is Bel Shanaar that will be found weak, not his rank, and in time the princes will entreat us to help them. Upon the wave of their desire and need will you be swept to the Phoenix Throne and the power of Anlec rightfully restored. I am merely the means for you to achieve this. I cannot become Phoenix King. Only you, the son of Aenarion, can claim what is yours; it cannot now be given, it must be taken.'

Malekith pondered these words in silence, refilling his glass. He walked to the window and gazed at *Indraugnir*. It was well named, for just as the dragon of his father was a foundation of the stories told about him, so too would this ship become a pillar upon which to build the story of Malekith. His mother was deft at manipulating popular opinion, and recapturing the imagination of Ulthuan with this new ship, stirring up the oldest tales of courage and heroism from the time of the first Phoenix King, would set the stage for whatever adventures next befell Malekith.

Yet there are only so many times and so often one can return to the well before it eventually runs dry, and Malekith knew that Morathi's sway over the other princes waned the more she used it. If Bel Shanaar was replaced by another elected Phoenix King, not of Aenarion's line, the precedent set by Bel Shanaar would be sealed in tradition; it would end all hope for Malekith to see Anlec as capital once more.

'And what of the Everqueen?' asked Malekith after much thought. 'Should I succeed Bel Shanaar, I cannot marry my half-sister.'

'It is of no consequence,' said Morathi. 'I have persuaded many of your fellow princes that Bel Shanaar's marriage to Yvraine is merely a technicality required because the Phoenix King must be of the line of Aenarion. You are his son and have no need to marry into the bloodline. If we oppose it, there will be little support for such a sham marriage to be repeated. Though there was once a dream that we might return to the peace of the Everqueen's reign shortly after the war with the daemons, there are few of us surviving now that can even remember the time before Aenarion. The Everqueen is a figurehead and nothing more, the real political power of Ulthuan lies not in Avelorn but in Tor Anroc. She is irrelevant, a priestess raised above her station.'

'What of Morelion?' said Malekith.

'Aenarion's first son lives in solitude in the islands to the east,' Morathi said. 'He has no will to succeed Aenarion, and even if he did he has not the resource nor influence to make a serious bid for the Phoenix Throne. Trust me, and trust in Nagarythe. When you wish to resume your father's duties, there will be those of us ready to raise you up to where you belong.'

'Then I shall await the will of the gods,' said Malekith. 'When the sign comes, I will know it. I shall bring Ulthuan back to greatness and the memory of my reign will echo down through the centuries as loudly as my father's.'

'Good,' said Morathi with an amused smile. 'Now, which of your palaces do you recommend to your weary mother?'

As MALEKITH HAD expected, Morathi was accompanied by a great many retainers: guards, cooks, entertainers, gardeners, food tasters, painters, poets, chroniclers, actors, costumiers, handmaidens, dressmakers, acolytes, soothsayers, priests and priestesses. There were nearly seven hundred in all. All came directly from Nagarythe, and were unlike anything the colonists of Athel Toralien had seen before.

For several decades there had been fewer and fewer émigrés from Ulthuan, and so the most recent styles and fashions remained unseen. Morathi deplored the sheep-like mentality of those elves that followed court styles so slavishly, but was never one to miss an opportunity and so she exploited the somewhat fickle nature of elven taste whenever it suited her.

The seer-queen had carefully cultivated a reputation as a trend-setter and paragon of exquisite aesthetic. She was always at the forefront when it came to patronising an up-and-coming singer or poet, or endorsing some risqué but popular movement. In this way, Morathi managed to appear to move with the times, while Bel Shanaar and his supporters seemed outdated and staid. It helped that through her sorcery, Morathi never appeared to age a single day, even less so than any long-lived elf, while almost imperceptibly the years crept up on the Phoenix King. To young and old alike, Morathi was ever the perfect blend: a guardian of tradition whilst also being a forward-thinking visionary.

Her huge entourage reflected the wide variety of concerns and movements with which Morathi involved herself. From satirical poets who moped about the wine houses hidden behind white veils, to outlandishly tattooed jugglers and fire-eaters who entertained in the plazas, the hundreds of Morathi's followers made their presence felt all across Athel Toralien. Most prominently it was the arrival of the priests and priestesses that changed the city.

Malekith had resisted such developments in Athel Toralien, having been raised by his father to be distrustful of the priesthoods who had denied Aenarion the guidance he had sought. Although Malekith never openly opposed any temple or shrine, he ensured that a priest establishing any such building within the boundaries of his lands soon fell out of favour. Followers were hard to come by under such circumstances and most priests left within a season of their arrival. With the coming of Morathi's entourage it was as if a flood gate had been opened as priests and priestesses of all descriptions began plying their trade in the city.

In the earliest days of the Everqueen, the elves had worshipped and placated their gods at certain places on Ulthuan sacred to each of them. Elves would travel to these holy grottos, auspicious streams and sinister caves and peaks to entreat with the gods or to offer their praise.

With the elves now spread across the world, Morathi had slowly revolutionised the role of the priesthood. Once they had tended to the shrines that had grown over the sacred sites down through the years. Through Morathi's manipulation, now they were vessels of the gods' power. All were ordained in the time-honoured fashions of the past, but now rather than elves making pilgrimages to the holy places, the priests took the blessings of their gods out across the globe, so that all might still worship Asuryan and Kurnous, Isha and Lileath. Priests could now find spots sacred to their gods in the wider world, and even in the cities of Ulthuan shrines and temples were founded.

Long denied a spiritual release, the citizens of Athel Toralien embraced these newcomers and flooded to their rituals. When the prince complained to Morathi one morning, she laughed away his concerns.

'Your distaste for religion is quite unnatural, Malekith,' the seeress-queen said. The pair walked upon the outermost wall of the city, gazing out across the wind-tossed ocean. 'If you are to rid yourself of your loathing, you will have to overcome your unspoken fears.'

'I am not afraid of priests,' Malekith snorted.

'Yet you never enter a shrine, nor give a moment's praise to the gods,' said Morathi, stopping and leaning her back against the parapet so that the low sun blazed down onto her fair skin. 'Perhaps it is the gods that scare you?'

'The gods have never favoured Nagarythe, I see no reason to debase myself in their name,' the prince countered.

'Yet the gods have their part to play in your life,' Morathi warned. 'It was Asuryan's blessing that made your father the Phoenix King. It was the blade of Khaine that he wielded to free our isle. His first wife was the chosen of Isha. Your blood calls to the gods, and in turn they call to your blood.'

'There are other, stranger and stronger gods now,' said Malekith, his gaze unconsciously straying to the north, to the unseen Realm of Chaos. 'I fear that even Asuryan is now humbled.'

'Then if not for your spirit, embrace the gods for your power,' Morathi said. 'By participating and sponsoring religion, as I have done, you will come to control that from which you are currently distanced. It matters not whether you believe the gods are listening. The important point to remember is that your people do. If they believe you have the favour of the gods, their dedication and loyalty is that much stronger.'

'I will not rule with falsehood,' Malekith said. 'One day we will be free of the gods and the better for it.'

Morathi said nothing in reply, but her face expressed her doubt without words.

* * *

As THE TIME to leave Athel Toralien approached ever closer, Malekith fretted more and more, wishing to be gone. Morathi's arrival had disrupted all routine and semblance of order in the city, as Malekith knew it had been intended to. Knowing how fickle elves could be at times, Morathi had ensured that the spectacle of her arrival, her gift of *Indraugnir* and Malekith's departure would all blend together into a story that would stick in the memory and be debated in the city for many years to come.

Of her vast entourage, only a few handmaidens and gifted seers were returning to Ulthuan with the queen. The rest were, as she put it, her gift to Athel Toralien and the other cities of the east. She had ensured that though Malekith was leaving the colonies that he had almost single-handedly created, his name would live on there in his absence.

When it came to the time for the expedition of Malekith to leave, the Naggarothi prince stood upon the deck of *Indraugnir* as she swayed at anchor in the harbour of Athel Toralien. Alandrian stood with him, as did Yeasir. Morathi was in one of the spacious cabins preparing for the voyage. The three of them looked out over the city, which was more than ten times the size it had been when they had first sailed into the anchorage more than thirteen hundred years before. All knew how much things had changed in that time, and they shared the memory of it without having to say a word.

'Where will you go?' asked Alandrian.

'Out to the snow and the ice,' Malekith said, pointing to the north and west. 'I go to meet my fate, whether glorious or ignoble.'

'It will be glorious, of that I am sure,' said Alandrian with good humour. 'You have been marked by the gods for great things, my prince. It is in your blood to bestride history like a colossus while we mere mortals must labour in your immense shadow!'

'Well, my shadow and I will be moving along shortly,' said Malekith with a smile. 'Feel free to enjoy what warmth and light you can in my absence. If what you say is true, then when I will return I shall eclipse the sun and the moons from several miles away!'

The tide was fair and the prince bid Alandrian farewell. The two parted with Alandrian promising he would keep the city safe, and renewing his loyalty to Nagarythe. Morathi came up on deck just as they were about to depart, to wave to the adulalatory crowds who again lined the dockside to see her. With the wind filling her sails, *Indraugnir* got under way, and by noon the city was out of sight below the horizon.

— TEN —

The Call of Khaine

WEST THEY SAILED, as Malekith had said they would. Across the Great Ocean *Indraugnir* carried them, towards an uncharted world. Yet for all their grand destiny, there was a more mundane duty to perform first. Morathi was returning to Nagarythe, and would need to be taken to Galthyr before Malekith's host could continue westwards. Thirty days after setting out from Athel Toralien, aided by a strong wind and *Indraugnir's* swift lines, they sighted the northern isles of Ulthuan.

Standing out from the tossing sea as pinnacles of rock, the northern isles protected the coast of Nagarythe and Chrace from the heavy swells and high waves that were stirred up by the north wind. In their midst rose one island larger by far than all the others, and most westerly of the archipelago: the Blighted Isle. It was here that the Shrine of Khaine was located, a black table of rock from which protruded the Widowmaker, the weapon of Khaine.

Morathi knew it well, and she stood at the port rail looking south as the Blighted Isle came into view through the fog and crashing surf. Malekith joined her.

'You think of my father,' said the prince.

'I do,' replied Morathi. 'It was more than a thousand years ago that he flew here upon the real Indraugnir and breathed his last. He is but a memory now, a myth to be told to children who will gasp in awe at his feats, yet not wholly believe them. Even I only truly knew the legendary Phoenix King, for we did not meet until after he had drawn the sword. Even I knew of him only by reputation before that, and of the time before his blessing by Asuryan there is nothing left but mystery. He is gone from us now, he who was the greatest. There is nothing left of him but you.'

Malekith stood there a while, the spray from the sea wetting his face as he looked at the bleak, dark rocks.

'There is something else that remains,' he said finally.

'What is that?' asked his mother. 'Something that remains of what?'

'Of my father,' said Malekith. 'No one has been to the Blighted Isle since Aenarion returned the sword. He and Indraugnir lie there to this day. We should return their bodies to Anlec where they can lie in state, and all the princes from all over the world will come to pay their respects to the first of the Phoenix Kings. Even Bel Shanaar will have to kneel before his remains and pay homage. All the princes will see that, and when my father is interred in a mausoleum that will rival the pyramid of Asuryan, with the bones of the largest dragon of Caledor standing guard at its entrance, I shall take his armour. The princes will remember Bel Shanaar bowing before that armour and the people will see anew that I am Aenarion's son; Aenarion reborn.'

'Is this the sign for which you have been waiting?' said Morathi. 'Will you now return with me to Nagarythe?'

'Not without my father!' said Malekith.

Calling for a boat and crew to be made ready, the prince then ordered the ship's master to bring *Indraugnir* to a stop. Malekith then changed out of his fine robes and garbed himself in his golden armour, ready to be taken over to the Blighted Isle. Morathi stood at the ship's side as the boat was lowered into the water. She smiled at her son as he leapt up to the rail and seized hold of a rope. With a boyish grin of excitement that Morathi had not seen for hundreds of years, the prince of Nagarythe slid down the rope into the waiting boat.

The boat pushed away and was instantly carried from the ship's side by the surging waves. The fifteen elves of the boat crew erected the mast quickly and turned the boat south, heading towards the south-east end of the isle, the part most sheltered from the prevailing wind and waves. Finding a small inlet, they made the boat secure but only Malekith leapt ashore while the crew tried their best not to touch the cursed rock.

THE BLIGHTED ISLE was devoid of all life; a bleak upthrust of crags that was home to neither plant nor animal. No grasses clung to life in crevasses. No beetles scuttled in the shade beneath toppled boulders. No crabs dwelt in the dark pools of water by the sea's edge. The wind seemed to quieten as Malekith walked inland, picking his way through scattered rocks and stones.

Having no particular course or goal, Malekith wandered for a long while, absently making for what he deemed to be higher ground towards the west of the island, so that he might spy the location of his father's remains. Pulling himself up a rocky ridge, the prince looked to the west and saw that the afternoon had all but passed and the sun was not far from the horizon. Though dismissive of the superstitions of the sailors, Malekith had no desire to be out on the Blighted Isle in the dark, and resolved to find his father's remains and return to the boat before nightfall.

With more purpose, Malekith continued his search, his eyes scanning the valleys and hollows for a glimmer of metal or glint of bone. He found nothing, and was despairing of success as the long twilight shadows surrounded him. He was just beginning to think about returning to the boat and resuming his search the next day when he suddenly paused, caught by a strange instinct.

Though he heard no voice, nor saw no sign, Malekith felt a pull to the south, as if he were being called. The lure was strong, like a singing in his blood. With a last glance towards the setting sun, Malekith followed the strange sensation and turned south, bounding over the rocks at speed.

It was not long before Malekith came to a wide, flat expanse near to the centre of the Blighted Isle. Here jagged black rocks veined with lines of red thrust up into the ruddy skies like a circle of columns. The ground within was as flat as glass and black as midnight. At the centre there stood a block of red-veined rock and something only partly visible shimmered above it. This was clearly the Shrine of Khaine, but as Malekith looked around he could see no sign of his father's resting place nor any remains of Indraugnir. They must have come here, for Aenarion had returned the Sword of Khaine to the very altar close to which Malekith now stood.

Even as his thoughts touched upon the Godslayer, there came to Malekith's ears a distant noise: a faint screaming. Now that it had attracted his attention, the prince looked at the altar of Khaine more closely. As he did so, the sounds around him intensified. The screams of agony were joined by howls of horror. The ring of metal on metal, of fighting, echoed around the shrine. Malekith heard a thunderous heart beating, and thought he saw knives carving wounds upon flesh and limbs torn from bodies on the edge of his vision.

The red veins of the altar were not rock at all, but pulsed like arteries, blood flowing from the altar stone in spurting rivers of gore. He realised that the beating heart was his own, and it hammered in his chest like a swordsmith working at an anvil.

A keening sound, like a note sung by a sword's edge as it cuts the air, rang in Malekith's ears. It was not unpleasant, and he listened to it for a while, drawn by its siren call to take step after step closer to the altar. Finally, the prince of Nagarythe stood transfixed before that bloody shrine just as his father Aenarion had been.

The thing embedded in the rock shimmered before Malekith's eyes, a blur of axe and sword and spear. Finally a single image emerged, of a bulbous mace studded with gems. Malekith was confused, for this was no weapon, but rather reminded him of the ornamental sceptres often carried by other princes. It seemed very similar to the one borne by Bel Shanaar when he had visited the colonies.

It was then that the meaning came to Malekith. All of Ulthuan would be his weapon. Unlike his father, he needed neither sword nor spear to destroy his foes. He would have the armies of an entire nation in his grasp, and would wield them however he pleased. If he but took up Khaine's sceptre, there would be none that could oppose him. Like a vision, the future unfolded before Malekith.

He would return to Ulthuan and go to Tor Anroc, and there cast down the gates of the Phoenix King. He would offer up the body of Bel Shanaar to Khaine and become undisputed ruler of the elves. He would reign for eternity as the bloody right hand of the God of Murder. Death would stalk in his shadow as he brought ruination to the empire of the dwarfs, for such was the power of the elves that they need not share the world with any other creature. Beastmen were put to the sword by their thousands, and the carcasses of orcs and goblins spitted upon poles lined the roads of his empire for hundreds of miles.

Malekith laughed as he saw the rude villages of humans being put to the torch, their menfolk tossed onto pyres, their women with their hearts ripped out, while babies had their heads dashed in upon the bloodied rocks. Like an unstoppable tide, the elves would conquer all that lay before them, until Malekith presided over an empire that covered the entire globe and the fumes of the sacrificial fires blotted out the sun. Malekith was carried forwards on a giant palanquin made from the bones of his vanquished enemies, a river of blood pouring out before him.

'No!' cried Malekith, breaking his gaze from the sceptre and hurling himself face first to the rocky ground.

He lay there for a long while, eyes screwed shut, his heart pounding, his breathing ragged and heavy. Slowly he calmed himself, and opened an eye. There seemed to be nothing amiss. There was no blood or fire. There was nothing but silent rock and the hiss of the wind.

The last rays of the day bathed the shrine in orange, and Malekith pushed himself to his feet and staggered from the circle, not daring to look back at the altar. Knowing that his father would not be found, Malekith gathered his senses as best he could and made for the boat, never once looking back.

Even when he was back aboard *Indraugnir* he ordered the captain to sail north with all speed until the Blighted Isle could no longer be seen. None questioned this command, although Morathi regarded her son with renewed curiosity as he strode to his cabin with unseemly haste.

Sailing further, they came upon the trade lanes of Ulthuan's western ports. Having found none of his father's remains, Malekith refused to return to Ulthuan and instead transferred his mother to one of the many merchant ships returning to Ulthuan from the east. Despite her protestations, Morathi was seen off *Indraugnir* with very little ceremony, and the shocked master of the eastern trader found himself gifted with a small fortune of gold and gems in return for taking the seeress-queen to Galthyr.

By the time they had completed the short journey, during which Morathi had complained constantly and her sorcerers had terrified more than a few of the crew, the ship's captain wished he had asked for more.

—‹ ELEVEN ›—

The Finding of the Circlet

FOR MALEKITH, HIS new freedom was as intoxicating as wine. He turned *Indraugnir* north and headed for the lands of ice that girded the Realm of Chaos. For several years Malekith and his crew explored the coastline of the frozen northlands, foraying eastwards and westwards in attempts to make charts for future visitors. It proved impossible, as the proximity of the Chaos Wastes and the ever-shifting nature of the ice itself changed the landscape with the passing of every season.

Likewise, any attempt to map the scattered human settlements proved fruitless, for they were nomadic and followed the erratic migrations of elk and other animals. Unlike the men who lived just north of the colonies, these humans were both fierce and terrified. Their weapons and armour were more advanced, forged of bronze, yet there was something about the elves that filled them with horror and they would flee whenever Malekith landed with a shore party.

There was good hunting on the outermost edges of the snowy plains: deer, bears and birds aplenty. The elves fished also, but were forced to head south in the coldest parts of the year, where they traded with other ships for grain and wine. Though some of his followers grumbled about the conditions, most were content, as was Malekith. For many this was the opportunity for them to wrest control from the elements, to forge something entirely new out of the unforgiving wilderness, just as they had done in the forests east of Athel Toralien.

For all the enthusiasm of the Naggarothi, these lands were harsh and resources were scarce. These were not the bountiful forests of the east, but a bleak expanse of unrelenting snow and rock. That the crude humans could survive here was testament that there was some worth in these lands, but Malekith knew that there would be no glittering cities of marble and alabaster. However, he was determined that the north would yield to his will.

Many years after setting out from Athel Toralien, Malekith landed upon an icy coast with the greater part of his followers. They carried their food and tents upon sleds pulled by teams of sturdy horses and were wrapped in coats of fur, and wore thick gloves and boots to protect them from the freezing wind. A few souls were left aboard *Indraugnir* and told to return to this place every fifty days to watch for the expedition's return. With that, Malekith and his warriors forged inland to see what secrets the northern blizzards concealed.

In the Chaos Wastes, the Naggarothi found foes more fell than any they had met before. The lands teemed with monstrous creatures warped by the power of Chaos, and every time that the elves made camp the sentries would be tested by some terrifying winged beast or mindless, shambling thing.

The men of this realm were also far in advance of their cousins further south. Whether from unknown allies or gifted dark knowledge by the Chaos Gods, these humans had thick armour of leather and bronze, and hardened weapons. They wielded swords and axes with surprising skill, and some had shamanic powers and assailed the Naggarothi with spells drawn from the dark magic that swirled in great strength throughout the north.

Many of the humans showed signs of Chaos corruption, and had bloated muscles or bestial faces. No few carried ensorcelled weapons gifted to them by the Chaos gods. Malekith slew a chieftain with bat-like wings and scales instead of skin, who wielded a jagged sword that constantly screamed in some arcane and dreadful language. Avanuir also took the life of a tribal champion who had a snake's body and was clad in armour made of iron-hard bone.

Though Malekith never ventured into the Realm of Chaos itself, often his expedition came close to its uncertain borders. The air shimmered with magical aurorae and crackled with mystical energy. Vast and insane landscapes hovered upon the edge of vision: nightmarish forests of flesh, mountains of bones, rivers of blood and burning skies all lurked beyond the invisible boundary. Even in the Chaos Wastes, the blasted shadowlands surrounding the Realm of Chaos, the daemonic and the unnatural held sway. For the first time in over a thousand years, Malekith pitted his sword against the blades of the daemonic legions of Chaos.

Malekith took ever greater risks, searching for some doom or myth that never materialised. The prince drove his army further and further westwards and northwards, seeking some sign that only he would recognise.

In truth, Malekith was growing ever more despondent. Nearly fifteen years had passed since he had left Athel Toralien and it seemed to the prince that he was no closer to achieving the great glory he desired. There was no army to overthrow, just scattered warbands of humans and transient daemonic apparitions to banish. There were not boundless riches to send back to Ulthuan, just the unending bleakness of snow, rock and ice: an eternal grinding battle of attrition.

With his company much reduced by hardship and fighting, Malekith felt his search growing ever more in vain. Northwards they pressed once more, unto the very edge of the Realm of Chaos. Though he shared his despair with no one else, the Naggarothi could sense Malekith's growing frustration and worried what desperate act he might be considering.

For days they were engulfed by a mighty tempest of wind and snow, and though the Naggarothi struggled onwards eventually Malekith called them to a halt to wait out the unnaturally savage storm.

DURING THE NIGHT, the tents of the Naggarothi camp buffeted by blizzard, Yeasir confronted his lord. The two were alone in Malekith's pavilion, wrapped in their heavy furs as they sat upon the cold ground around a burning magical stone; the only fire that could be lit. Canvas cracked and slapped around them, and the wind howled all about.

'If you but let us know what it is you wish, then we would help you,' said the Naggarothi captain.

'What if I was to tell you that I would dare the Gate of Chaos itself?' said Malekith. 'Would you still follow me?'

Yeasir did not answer immediately but his look of horror was all the reply Malekith needed.

'So there is a boundary across which the Naggarothi dare not cross?' said the prince.

'I would counsel against it, your highness,' said Yeasir, picking his words carefully. 'Yet, if after my protestations were heard you were still intent upon such a course, I would follow you as would the others.'

'And what arguments would you make to dissuade me?' asked Malekith.

'That no living soul has ever entered the Realm of Chaos and returned,' replied Yeasir.

'Is that not the point of such an endeavour?' said Malekith. 'Were we to venture into the heart of Chaos itself and return, would that not be a legend worth telling for a thousand years?'

'If we return,' cautioned Yeasir.

'I did not know that the cold had cut so deeply into your veins, Yeasir,' said Malekith with scorn.

'It is not fear that holds me back,' said Yeasir sharply. 'I would gladly march against any foe, mortal or daemonic, but there is no valour in matching a hundred spears against the might of the Dark Gods! If we were to dare such a thing, we would be remembered as fools led by stupidity and vanity, not glory. Worse still, we would not be remembered at all, for if we should cross over to the worlds beyond and not return, then our tale will end with nothing. "They were lost in the snows of the north," the chronicles would read, and our names would go unremembered.'

Malekith scowled, not out of anger but frustration. He knew that Yeasir's points were valid, but in his heart he yearned for something more. The longer he remained in the north, the more chance that Bel Shanaar would be succeeded by another prince before Malekith's return. The prince of Nagarythe could not bear the thought of slinking back to Ulthuan after all this time, to spend his days living out the fading glories of an age past.

'I will make no decision now,' Malekith declared. 'The morning sun may bring fresh counsel.'

And it did.

BEFORE DAWN, THE storm abated and a calm settled upon the tundra. Yeasir came to Malekith's tent as the sun was breaking, much excited. Following his captain, Malekith emerged from his pavilion to see what had stirred the camp.

To the north, in the growing light of the day, could be seen distant structures. Upon a snow-swept hill, outlandish buildings rose up from the ice, carpeted with white but unmistakable nonetheless. Their exact shape could not be discerned from this distance, but grey and black rock hewn by hand rather than nature jutted at strange angles from drifts and hills of snow. The early morning sunlight sparkled from icicles hanging from strange balconies and glinted from odd-shaped domes. Malekith gave the order for the company to break camp and make ready to march with all speed.

What Malekith had taken to be a few miles turned out to be several leagues, the distance deceptive in the otherwise featureless snow plain. It took hours of marching before the Naggarothi came upon the outskirts of the strange buildings. No outer wall guarded their border and they seemed deserted. In design they were unlike anything the elves had seen before; not of elven, dwarfish or human hand.

The buildings were made of solid stone, but appeared not have been carved from the naked rock but fused seamlessly from some other stone. The walls met at strange angles, and the empty doorways and windows formed odd shapes of darkness, with no corner square. There were no curves either, no rounded arches or elegantly pointed arcs. Some buildings were low, so that their roofs were no higher than Malekith's head, while others had several storeys, each of which was a dozen feet high or more.

To begin, the Naggarothi wandered the wide, uneven streets, up sweeping terraces and lines of stairs that changed in height at every step. The roads joined at irregular intervals, and met in uneven, star-shaped plazas. Other than the cold stone there was nothing else, no wood nor metal, and Malekith judged the settlement to be ancient indeed. After an hour's searching it was clear that the city was vast, larger than anything Malekith had ever encountered.

Here on the edge of the Realm of Chaos, distances could be perversely extended or contracted, and so it was within the city. Short pathways seemed to widen as the elves approached, streets appeared to take longer to walk along than the buildings around them would imply, while eerie avenues that seemed to stretch for miles could be walked along in a matter of moments.

Eventually Malekith and the others ventured inside one of the buildings. It was a grand structure of five storeys, which widened unnaturally as it soared towards the grey skies, its flat walls pricked with hundreds of tiny, dark windows. The lower floor was open, with no internal walls, and the only feature was a wide stairwell that led downwards; there appeared to be no means to reach the upper levels.

Bringing out dwarf-made lanterns that glittered with silver fire, the elves descended the steps. These brought them into a contorted network of passages and rooms, and very quickly Malekith feared they would get lost. He ordered a warrior to stand at each junction with a lamp held aloft, so that no elf was ever out of sight from the route back. In this way, they slowly explored the windowless catacomb. They found no sign of the city's builders, just blank stone devoid of carvings or colour.

After an hour of searching – far longer than Malekith would have suspected by the size of the building above – they came upon another stair. It rose steeply upwards and double-backed and criss-crossed itself in a disturbing way. That it reached far higher than the ceiling was indisputable, though its position, as far as Malekith could tell, put it in the centre of the storey above where no stair had been seen.

Their breath carving clouds upon the cold air, Malekith and his warriors mounted the steps, continuing to leave sentries at each twisted landing so that no elf was out of sight of another. The elves scaled the stairway in a surprisingly short time, and it opened out onto another empty floor, with wide windows through which they could only see the cloudy skies.

Walking to the nearest window, Malekith looked out and then stepped back with a gasp. The stairwell had brought them up to a floor above where they had entered the building, for down below he could see a few of his warriors standing guard at the doorway where they had come in. The city stretched out in every direction as far as he could see, going on and on until it was lost in a grey haze.

Disorientated, Malekith closed his eyes and took a deep breath. Having recovered himself a little, he leaned out of the glassless window, avoiding looking towards the horizon, and hailed the Naggarothi some sixty feet below. They looked up with startled shouts, and their voices came back impossibly distant.

Disturbed, Malekith ordered the Naggarothi to leave, though it took another hour for them to climb down the winding stairway and trace their way back out of the labyrinthine catacomb. There was much distressed murmuring by the Naggarothi, and Malekith's usual confidence had been eroded by the unnatural surroundings. Looking up into the sky, he could see no sign of the sun and so only his internal awareness gave him any sense of the passage of time.

He reckoned it to be mid-afternoon, and knew that in these northern climes the sun would set early at this time of the year, barely passing above the horizon for a few hours. Malekith declared that they would leave the city before night fell and seek out its secrets with renewed vigour the following day.

However, with no sun to guide them, none of the Naggarothi knew from which direction they had entered the city. They retraced their steps as best they could from the footprints in the snow, but these soon petered out and could be found no more, though no snow had fallen since their arrival as far as they were aware. Now even more unnerved, Malekith called for the company to gather, and found that five of their number were missing. None could recall where they had last been seen, and the prince feared that they were lost in the city somewhere, perhaps forever.

Sensing the unease in his warriors becoming panic, Malekith bid them to stay where they were, somewhere amidst the criss-crossing arteries of the city's maze-like roads. Clearly the proximity of the Realm of Chaos was addling their senses, and Malekith could not trust his own eyes. Instead he turned to a deeper sense, of the magic that flowed across the world from the Gate of Chaos.

Closing his eyes and blanking out all other sensation, the prince entered a meditative trance he had learnt from Morathi in his youth. Normally he needed no such concentration to harness the winds of magic, but now he desired finesse and focus and so looked to the lessons of his childhood to give him a centre upon which to concentrate.

Imagining himself as a small speck, a grain of dust upon the ground, Malekith allowed his othersense to reach outwards just a small distance. Magic swirled in all directions, without form or rhythm. Edging out his sphere of awareness, he allowed his mind's eye to encompass a greater part of the city. Here he could detect a more regular stream of power; an underlying flow that poured from one direction. Fixing that point in his mind, Malekith opened his eyes.

Composed once more, Malekith could feel the gentle but persistent surge of Chaos unconsciously, and knew in which direction north now lay. Turning to the south, he ordered the Naggarothi to follow him.

They had walked for perhaps an hour when Malekith felt a different current in the flow of magic. Something close at hand was causing an eddy to form, much like the dispelling stone of the dwarfs. More confident that he could lead his warriors from the city if necessary, Malekith decided to make a detour and investigate this phenomenon. Now that he was aligned with the winds of magic again, Malekith marched unerringly between the grotesque buildings, guiding the company directly to the source of the anomaly.

There was something about the building that disturbed Malekith even more than the others. It was not as tall as some, but very broad and rose up like a five-levelled ziggurat, though each successive step was slightly misaligned in comparison to the one beneath, so that the whole structure seemed to have been twisted by a god's hand in some prehistoric time. There were archways all around its bottom floor, though nothing could be seen of the upper floors. Though he could not reason exactly why, the building brought Malekith to mind of a temple; to what deity or power, he could not fathom.

Malekith commanded half of his warriors to form a perimeter around the building, which stood alone just off-centre in a huge irregular eight-sided plaza. The other half of the company, Malekith led through one of the slanted archways. They followed the corridors, stairs and tunnels within for some time, but ever their path led them outwards so that they stood in rooms and galleries on the outer edge of each level. Malekith felt magic bubbling around him, and could sense a ward upon the inner walls keeping the magic at bay from somewhere within.

Eventually he found a spot where the magic churned violently, though looking about Malekith could see no physical source for such a disturbance. Holding up a hand to command his warriors to wait, he walked to the point where several streams of energy collided with each other. He stood on that exact spot, nauseated by the clashing magical waves.

Looking around he could see a triangular door that could be seen from nowhere else. He pointed and told Yeasir to follow his directions. Confused but obedient, the captain stalked across the floor of the room, following Malekith's gestures. To Yeasir it seemed as if Malekith guided him towards a solid wall and he hesitated, just a pace from the stone, before the prince's snarling voice bid him to walk forwards once more. With a grimace, his eyes half-closed in expectation of thudding into the wall, Yeasir took a step; he nearly fell over as he found himself atop a strange angular stair, much like the one they had found in the first building.

Through cunning artifice and magic, the stair was impossible to see, as if the door to it stood slightly apart from the world. Once Yeasir had stepped through, he had disappeared from sight, but he returned in moments and waved for the others to follow him.

The stairs led down for a comparatively short stretch, though such concepts as time and distance were becoming increasingly irrelevant in this impossible city. They led into a chamber, utterly black but for the glimmer of the elves' lanterns. The air seemed to suck all the light into itself, and even with the radiance from the lamps Malekith could see barely ten paces ahead.

Stepping cautiously forwards, he found himself treading upon a tiled floor, arranged in a seemingly haphazard mess of geometry yet every tile still fitting perfectly in the insane mosaic. The tiles were as grey as the stone of the rest of the city, but were slightly soft to tread upon, like a thin carpet. Casting the light of his lantern to the right and the left, Malekith could make out dim shapes rising in the gloom: figures stood upon pedestals lining a wide concourse that led away from the door. Malekith raised a hand to halt those following behind, and turned left to inspect the statues more closely.

By the silvery light of the lamp, they looked to be made out of some dull alloy, but as he came within a few paces Malekith could see more clearly that they were skeletons of greying bone. They were not unlike the bones of an elf, or for that matter a man, or dwarf; in proportion they were short of torso and long of limb like an elf, but had the thicker bones of a man, and were of a height little more than a dwarf. Their faces were slender, with a mouth, two eyes and two nostrils that were so disturbingly familiar yet not quite like any skull he had seen, causing Malekith to pause a moment before continuing his inspection.

They were clad in black shrouds that were wrapped about the bodies and shoulders in identical fashion, with hoods raised up on their skulls. Every cadaver wore chains of dark beads, perhaps black pearls, which hung limply from bony wrists and about throatless necks. Each held a serrated, angular sword in its right hand and a triangular shield upon its left arm, both free of any design that Malekith could discern.

The tiles stopped at the line of plinths, and beyond them the floor seemed to be made of the same stone as the rest of the building. Malekith could see nothing in the darkness, the lantern light reflected off no edge or surface, and he had no idea whether there were any other features or if the rest of the chamber was utterly empty.

Walking along the line of inanimate sentries, Malekith could not guess at how far the two lines stretched, but sensed that their course narrowed almost imperceptibly, bringing them together at some distant point as yet out of sight.

Glancing back towards the others, Malekith had another surprise. Though he was sure that he had walked no more than fifty paces, in as straight a line as made no difference, the glimmer of his companions' lanterns was like distant starlight in the gloom, and quite some way off to his left and higher up than his current position.

The prince called out for them to send a party to join him, and his voice echoed off distant walls, bouncing and resounding within a space he judged to be much vaster than the building in which it was supposedly enclosed. With a shiver, Malekith waited for the others to reach him, the light from their lanterns swiftly growing brighter with every heartbeat as if they covered a dozen paces with every stride.

Yeasir was with them and he gazed wide-eyed at the skeletal parade. He said nothing, but his look of concern was not lost on Malekith. With a reassuring nod, the prince turned along the line once more and followed the skeleton-flanked concourse. The pathway did indeed narrow gradually, and led the Naggarothi to a great stepped plinth the summit of which lay in the gloom beyond their lights. Ascending the first few steps and walking around them, Malekith saw that five other lines of skeletons joined the central feature at irregular angles. He rejoined his comrades and ordered a handful of them to stand guard at the bottom of the steps, while the others followed him up the steep dais.

It led onto a plateau, which was impossibly, maddeningly as wide as the base of the steps below. Seven figures sat upon low square stools, more opulent versions of the skeletons below with more dark pearls and brooches of the same black material. Six sat facing outwards, each one facing one of the lines upon the ground below as far as Malekith could tell. They had no hoods but instead wore simple crowns consisting of a narrow band about the skull with a black gem that reflected no light upon their foreheads.

The seventh figure sat facing Malekith, though the prince suspected that he would have faced the intruders regardless of which direction they had approached from. His crown was much larger, of a silver-grey metal, with curling, horn-like protrusions; the only organic shape they had seen since entering the city.

'Highness!' snapped Yeasir, and Malekith turned, his hand on his sword hilt. It was only then that he realised that his other hand had been reaching out towards the skeletal king, to pluck the crown from his skull. Malekith had no recollection of having crossed the dais, and shook his head as if dazed by a blow.

'We should touch nothing,' said Yeasir. 'This place is cursed, by the gods, or worse.'

Malekith laughed and the noise seemed stifled and flat, with none of the ringing echoes of his earlier shout.

'I think this great king rules here no more,' said Malekith. 'This is my sign, Yeasir. What greater statement about my destiny could I make? Imagine returning to Ulthuan with such a crown upon my head, an artefact of the time before.'

'Before what?' asked Yeasir.

'Before everything!' said Malekith. 'Before Chaos, before the Everqueen, before even the gods themselves. Can you not feel it, the great antiquity that fills this place?'

'I feel it,' growled Yeasir. 'There is ancient malice here, can you not sense it? I say again, there is a curse upon this place.'

'You were willing to follow me to the Gate of Chaos,' Malekith reminded his captain. 'Would you rather we left this treasure here and continued north?'

Yeasir's muttered reply was inaudible, but Malekith took it to be his captain's acquiescence. Not that the prince needed the permission of anyone to take whatever he wanted, from wherever he wanted. Magic had guided him to this place and Malekith knew that there was purpose behind it. Whether it was the gods or some other will that had led him here, it was to stand before this prehistoric king and take his crown.

With a smile, Malekith lifted the circlet from the dead king's skull; it was as light as air and came away with no difficulty.

'You have it, now let us leave,' said Yeasir, fear making his voice shrill.

'Calm yourself,' said Malekith. 'Does it not make me kingly?'

With that, the prince of Nagarythe placed the circlet upon his head and the world vanished.

* * *

GOLDEN LIGHT BLAZED throughout the immense hall. It did not appear to have a single source, but simply radiated out from all of the walls. Yeasir blinked in the sudden brightness, trying to clear spots from his eyes. As his vision returned, he saw more clearly where they were.

The chamber was vast, larger than any hall he had ever seen on Ulthuan or in the realm of the dwarfs. The walls were impossibly distant, and as Yeasir turned about to look around, he swore that their number increased and reduced, so that at one moment he was standing in a great irregular octagon, at others a triangular chamber.

Disorientated, he looked up and saw a vast ceiling stretching out to the horizon, so immense that he could not see where it met the walls. Huge angular stalactites jagged downwards at strange slants. The ceiling itself was made up of immense plates and surfaces that formed bizarre vertices, and perspective seemed to bend and contract depending on where he looked. Tearing away his gaze from the maddening vista, Yeasir turned his attention to his lord.

To Yeasir, it seemed as if Malekith had been frozen. He stood next to the regal skeleton at the centre of the dais locked in his pose, the crown upon his head, his fingers still touching the strange iron-like headgear. Yeasir leapt forwards with a shout, fearing some bewitchment had befallen his master. Another cry from one of the warriors distracted him and he turned his head to see several of the Naggarothi pointing out across the hall.

Following their fingers, Yeasir saw what he had feared ever since they had entered the ancient hall: the skeletal figures stepping down from their plinths and turning towards the central dais. They also glowed with light, and stalked purposefully forwards, their shields and weapons held ready. Yeasir cast a quick glance at the figures seated around them and was relieved to see that not one of them stirred. Ignoring his transfixed prince, Yeasir dashed to the opposite side of the platform and saw that skeletal warriors were advancing from every direction.

'Form up for defence!' Yeasir commanded, and the Naggarothi came together in a ring of spears and shields that encircled the top of the high podium.

'Prince!' the captain cried out, crossing the dais and laying a hand on his shoulder as if to wake him.

As soon as he touched Malekith, sparks of energy exploded across Yeasir's body and he was flung backwards across the dais, clattering and rolling across the hard stone. His body was numb and his muscles jerked and spasmed as magical energy coursed through him. Gritting his teeth, he fought to control his juddering limbs but felt drained of all strength. He lay there groaning, his arms and legs as heavy as lead, his ears ringing, his vision hazy.

There were more alarmed shouts but Yeasir could not discern the words. In momentary flashes of clarity he could see the Naggarothi archers raising arrows to their bowstrings and loosing them out from the edge of the dais, but he could not see if their shots had any effect. Moaning, he managed to roll to his stomach, and the numbness began to dissipate, replaced instead by gnawing pain in every joint and bone.

He tried to speak, but all he could do was clench his teeth and hiss, as pain shot along the captain's spine and exploded inside his brain. Amongst the buzzing and squealing that filled his hearing, Yeasir caught snatches of shouts and the dreadful clatter of thousands of bony feet marching upon the stone. A panicked thought shot through his pain-clouded mind: we are doomed.

TWELVE

Primordial Foes

A KALEIDOSCOPE OF clashing colours swarmed around Malekith. He was filled with the peculiar sensation of rising high up into the air whilst at the same time plummeting down towards some bottomless depth. His head swam and his skin tingled with power. He was lost in sensation, his whole being pulsing and vibrating with unknown energy.

In time – moments or an eternity, Malekith could not tell – the swirling colours began to coalesce around him. They formed into a nightmarish landscape above the centre of which floated the elf prince. The skies boiled with fire and black clouds, and beneath him stretched an arcane plateau that stretched on for infinity: the Realm of Chaos.

In one direction Malekith spied an unending garden, forlorn and decaying, filled with drooping willows and sallow grasses. A miasma of fog and flies drifted up from the overgrown copses of bent and withered trees, and rivers of oozing pus gurgled between fronds of clinging fungi and piles of rotted corpses. Marshes bubbled and boiled and pits of tar gurgled, spewing gaseous vapours into the thick air.

At the centre of the unkempt morass rose up a mansion of titanic proportions: a grandiose but tottering edifice of crumbling stone and worm-eaten wood. Peeling paint and flaking brick stood upon cracked stone and bowed beams, crawling with sickly yellow ivy and immense black roses. Fumes belched from a hundred chimneys and gargoyle-headed pipes spat and drooled gobbets of ichor across cracked tiles and mouldering thatch.

In the smog and gloom shambled daemons of death and plague; immensely bloated creatures with pustulant flesh and pox-marked skin, and slobbering beasts with slug-like bodies and fronds of tentacles dribbling noxious emissions. Swarms of boil-like mites scrabbled over the sagging walls and roofs of the manse, while a legion of cyclopean daemons, each with a single cracked horn, meandered about the wild gardens chanting sonorously.

Turning his gaze from the filth and squalor, Malekith then looked upon a mighty citadel made up of glimmering mirrors and crystal. Its surface shimmered with a rainbow of colours, translucent yet transparent, shifting with eddies and swirls of magic. Doors yawned like devouring mouths and windows stared back at the prince like lidless eyes. Fires of all colours billowed from the spires of thin towers, sending fountains of sparks trailing down to the ground below.

All about the bizarre palace was an immense maze, of shifting walls of crystal. The twisting, contorted pathways overlapped above and below, and passed across each other through unseen dimensions. Arcing gateways of flame linked parts of the immense labyrinth together, flickering from blue to green to purple and to colours not meant to be seen by mortals.

The skies about the horrifying tower were filled with shoals of creatures that climbed and swooped upon the magical thermals, shark-like and fearsome. Formless, cackling things cavorted and whirled about the maze, flashing with magical power. Daemons with arms that dripped with fire bounded manically along the winding crystal passages, leaping and bouncing with insane abandon. Malekith felt his eyes drawn back to the impossible fortress and saw that a great gallery had opened up.

Here stalked arcane things with multi-coloured wings and bird-like faces, with contorting staves in their hands and robes of glistening pink and blue. One of the creatures paused and looked up at him. Its eyes were like pits of never-ending madness, deep oceans of swirling power that threatened to draw him into their depths for eternity.

Breaking that transfixing stare, Malekith then looked upon a blasted wasteland, surrounded by a great chain of volcanoes that spewed rivers of lava down their black sides and choked the air with their foul soot. Immense ramparts were carved from the mountainsides, huge bastions of dread hung with skulls and from whose jagged battlements fluttered a thousand times a thousand banners of red.

Within the encircling peaks the land was rent by great tears and chasms that welled up with blood like wounds, as if it had been constantly rent by the blows of some godly blade. The skeletons of unimaginable creatures were piled high amongst lakes of burning crimson, and all about were dunes made of the dust of countless bones. Hounds the size of horses with red-scaled flesh and enormous fangs prowled amongst the ruination, their howls

tearing the air above the snap and crack of bone and gris-
tle.

At the heart of this desolation grew a tower of unimaginable proportion, so vast that it seemed to fill Malekith's
vision. Of black stone and brass was it made, tower upon
tower, wall upon wall, a castle so great that it would hold
back the armies of the whole universe. Gargoyles spouted
boiling blood down its brazen fortifications, and red-
skinned warriors with wiry frames and bulbous, horned
heads patrolled its ramparts. Upon its highest parapet
there stood a thing of pure fury; rage given bestial, winged
form. It beat its broad chest and roared into the dark skies.

Shuddering, Malekith turned fully about and stood
bewitched by a panorama of entrancing beauty. Enchant-
ing glades of gently swaying emerald-leafed trees bordered
golden beaches upon which crashed white-foamed waves,
while glittering lakes of tranquil water beckoned to him.
Majestic mountains soared above all, their flanks clad in
the whitest snow, glistening in the unseen sun.

Lithe creatures clad in the guise of half-maidens
cavorted through the paradise, laughing and chattering,
caressing each other with shimmering claws. Across emerald meadows roamed herds of sinuous beasts whose
bodies shimmered and changed colour, their iridescent
patterns hypnotising to the elf prince. Malekith felt himself drawn onwards, ensnared by their beauty.

Suddenly realising his peril, Malekith tore his gaze away
from the mesmerising vision. He became distinctly aware
that he was being watched and could feel the attention of
otherworldly beings being turned in his direction. Feeling as
if his soul were about to be laid bare and flayed before the
gaze of the Chaos Gods, Malekith felt terror gripping him.
He sought somewhere to flee, but in every direction spread
the domains of the Dark Gods. With a last dread-driven

effort, he wished himself away and was surrounded again by the twirling energies of magic.

When his vision had cleared again, Malekith found himself hovering far above the world, as if stood upon the edge of creation itself and looking down upon the realms of men and elves and dwarfs and every other creature under the sun. He could see the jungle-swathed forests of Lustria where lizardmen scuttled through the ruins of the Old Ones' cities. He saw orc tribes massing in the blighted wilderness, carpeting the ground in tides of green.

Over everything drifted the winds of magic, now more clear to him than they had ever been. The prince saw them streaming from the shattered Gate of Chaos in the north and spreading out across the northlands. He saw the vortex of Ulthuan as a great swirl of power, drawing the energy out of the world. He saw sinkholes of darkness and blazing mountains of light.

In that instant it all became clear to Malekith. The whole world was laid out before him, and he saw as perhaps only his mother had before seen. There were torrents of power that swept across the lands untapped by mortal kind. The very breath of the gods sighed over oceans and plains, down valleys and across forests. From Chaos came all magic, whether good or ill. It was stunning in its beauty, just as a storm-tossed sea can enthral those not caught in its deadly grip.

Malekith lingered awhile, now aware of the crown burning upon his head. It acted as some kind of key, some artefact created by the races that had come before the rise of elves, before even the coming of the Old Ones. It would be easy for him to stay here forever, marvelling at the rich, random choreography of the dancing winds of magic. He could spend an eternity studying their heights and depths with the circlet and still not unlock all of their secrets.

Something nagged at his mind however, a sensation deep within his soul that threatened to break his reverie.

YEASIR STRUGGLED TO his knees, still weak from the magical blast that had cast him down. The alarmed shouts of his comrades grew more urgent as the skeletons began to advance up the steps towards the Naggarothi. Crawling to the edge of the uppermost level, he looked down to see the unliving legion marching implacably onwards, each stepping in synchronicity with all the others, guided by common purpose or will. The arrows of the elves had little effect, most bouncing harmless from the glowing bones of their enemies, others simply passing through them as if they were nothing more than ghosts.

As the first line of skeletons reached the uppermost step, the Naggarothi struck out with their spears, driving silvered points into skulls and ribcages. This had more effect than the arrows and no few skeletons crumbled into bones, their golden light ebbing and then disappearing. Their advance was as inevitable as the coming of the tide though, and even as the first rank fell the second stepped forwards, and the third, and the fourth.

The skeletons' blades were as keen as the day that they had been forged, despite the passage of ages, and they bit into shield and flesh as the skeletons attacked back. Cries of pain and fear began to reverberate around Yeasir as he struggled to pull free his own sword, but the scabbard was pinned beneath him and he had not the strength to lift himself from it.

The elf to Yeasir's left gave a cry and toppled down the steps as an unearthly blade slashed through his throat. The skeleton took another pace forwards into the space the elf had occupied and turned its grinning face towards Yeasir. It raised its arm above its head, the wicked black blade in its hand sparkling with golden light. Yeasir gave a cry and tried to push himself away, but the skeleton stepped forwards again, ready to strike. The captain pulled his shield in front of him just as the sword swung down, and the undead thing's blade rang against it with a dull crash.

Again and again the sword smashed upon the shield, with relentless, metronomic ferocity. After the tenth blow, all the strength was gone from Yeasir's arms and the eleventh strike smashed the top of the shield into his face, stunning him. Dazed, he could do nothing as the skeleton's sword arm rose high again. He stared into the guardian's eyes, seeing nothing but pits of darkness.

The golden light that filled the room flared into white intensity, blinding Yeasir. He shrieked and knotted his eyes shut, expecting to feel the bite of the unnatural blade any moment. No blow came and Yeasir opened a single eye, fearful of what he might see. The skeleton still loomed above him, arm upraised, but its aura had dimmed to a faint glow and it stood utterly motionless.

Yeasir opened his other eye and dared to let out his breath. The captain then heard harsh laughter from behind him and turned his head slowly, wondering what other fearful apparition awaited him.

Malekith stood in the centre of the dais, the circlet upon his head blazing with power. His face was drawn but he was filled with a glow of energy. His expression was one of disdain, divine yet strangely cruel. His gaze was distant. The prince looked at Yeasir for a long while but did not appear to actually see him. The prince flung out an arm and with the gesture the skeletons came to life once more, turning upon their heels and marching back down the steps. Panting with relief, Yeasir watched as they returned to their plinths and once again took up their immobile vigil.

* * *

WITH THE POWER of the crown, Malekith could see the magical forces binding the skeletons together and the ancient commands that blazed within their empty skulls. It was simplicity itself to order them to stop, and then with another thought the prince bid them to return to their eternal slumber. All about him the hall was filled with great golden arches and glittering pillars, unseen to all except him.

Given extraordinary awareness by the circlet he could look upon the magic of the ancient architects of the city, the curving galleries and arching balconies constructed from mystical forces that even he had been unaware of. This was why the chamber was devoid of other magic, for it contained its own power, far stronger than that of the fitful winds of magic. Just as air cannot pass into a solid object, so too the winds of magic found no room to creep into the enchantment-filled chamber.

Now gifted the insights granted by the crown, there was no telling how acutely the Naggarothi prince might master the power of Chaos. With the circlet to act as his key, Malekith could work such spells as would make the witchery of Saphery seem insignificant. Had he not looked upon the realm of the Chaos Gods itself? Did he not now know their lands, and had he not dared them and survived?

Elation filled Malekith, more majestic than any triumph he ever felt before. His mother had warned that Chaos was the greater enemy; the perils of orcs and the armies of the beastmen paled into insignificance against those legions of daemons that Malekith had seen. The Chaos Gods plotted and waited, for they had an eternity to ponder their plans and to make their schemes. The elves could not shelter behind the power of the vortex forever, Malekith realised, for he had felt the slowly growing power of the Chaos Gods even as he had stood in their midst.

It all came together in the prince's mind. The men of the north were vassals of the Dark Gods, and as they prospered and multiplied, so too would the influence of their ineffable masters. There might come a day when the bulwark of the vortex would fail, and again the hordes of Chaos would be unleashed upon the world. Ulthuan was utterly unprepared for such an eventuality. Bel Shanaar could not hope to meet such a threat. It was an apparent truth to Malekith that he alone, with the power of the circlet, now bore the means by which the elves might be protected from this greater doom.

Slowly, with much effort, Malekith took the crown from his head. The great magical architecture faded from his vision and he found himself back in the strangely angled hall beneath the prehistoric city. His Naggarothi surrounded him, staring at their lord with eyes full of wonder and fear.

Malekith smiled. He now knew what he must do.

PART TWO

The Cults of the Cytharai; the Return of the Prince; Anlec Restored; the Will of Asuryan

◄ THIRTEEN ►

The Malaise of Luxury

EVEN AS MALEKITH embraced the destiny revealed to him by the Circlet of Iron, far to the south on Ulthuan another elf started upon a path that would see him brought into the fates of the most powerful princes of the isle. An unassuming captain of the Lothern Guard, Carathril led a handful of his company along the harbour road. His mission was secret, known only to a few amongst the court of Eataine, but its import was beyond reckoning. That night would set in motion a series of events that heralded the end of the elves' golden age.

White light blazed across the night sky, shining from the thousand windows that pierced the walls of the Glittering Tower. Surf sparkled as it crashed against the rocks upon which the lighthouse was built. By the light of the Glittering Tower ships moved to and fro across the bay, passing into and out of the great portal of the Emerald Gate, beyond which lay the still waters of the Straits of Lothern.

Their white sails cast a ghostly shimmer over the calm waters, bathing the sea with radiance.

Past rearing cliffs lined with towers and walls, where the spear tips of sentries could be seen moving endlessly on their patrols, rose up the bulk of the Sapphire Gate, its wrought silver dazzling under the magical light of the giant gems set upon it. In the starlight beyond the Sapphire Gate, a lagoon opened out, tranquil in its stillness, where white beaches climbed out of the quiet waters.

Piers and wharfs crowded with ships of all sizes curved elegantly across the waters. Small jolly boats and pleasure craft hung with golden lanterns drifted along the shore, the laughter and conversation of their revelling passengers echoing across the softly lapping waves. Amidst the forest of tall masts and slender spars of white-decked merchantmen and sleek-sided yachts, the mass of warships loomed large. Immense dragonships rode confidently at anchor, their golden rams and silver-chased bolt throwers shining reminders of their bloody purpose. Darting hawkships tacked back and forth through the sea traffic, their Sea Guard crews ever alert to any danger.

Around the lagoon, the city of Lothern stretched up into the hills. Verdant terraces, abundant vineyards and low-built villas dotted the hillsides, linked together by winding paths of silvery grey that meandered from the shoreline up to the great mansions and slim towers built upon the peaks of Lothern's twenty hills. Quiet reigned over the city; not the peace of contentment but a hush of apprehension.

A languid malaise blighted Lothern, just as it gripped all of the island of the elves. Many elf-folk of Ulthuan had lost themselves in debauchery and excess. What had begun as aesthetic gatherings, readings of darkly poetic works and ceremonies of mutual solace, had become something far more sinister. With blood sacrifices and twisted rituals of debasement, the cultists now pleaded with forbidden powers for release from their woes.

The pleasure cults had drawn in others by offering the simple thrill of experience, for the elves had always been a people who felt sensation and emotion strongly. Let loose from the civilities of polite decorum, some elves had lost themselves in the raw hedonism enjoyed by the cults of excess, indulging every perverse whim and partaking of any forbidden deed.

Few suspected the true extent of the cults' inveiglement into their society, nor the secret machinations that fuelled the midnight conferences of their shadowy leaders. Even fewer knew the true extent of their network, for in outlook each appeared individual and disparate, unique emerging counter-cultures within each realm and city with no connection to the travails of the other kingdoms. So it was that Bel Shanaar and his princes sought to quell the rising power of the cults through political and spiritual means, hoping to forestall the recruitment of new followers and rebalance the distressed psyche of the elven people.

Carathril was intent upon the destruction of a cult recently uncovered in Lothern, and to this purpose he led his warriors along the winding streets of the city.

IN THE MANSE of Prince Aeltherin on the outskirts of the city of Lothern, hidden amongst carefully tended orchards and perfectly appointed gardens, a vile ceremony was reaching its climax.

The air in the marble hall of the elven lord swirled with purple and blue vapours, which billowed from braziers wrought from the twisted bones of animals. Intoxicated by the narcotic fumes, a sea of elves writhed upon the red-carpeted floor. Fishermen and nobles, servants and lawmakers lay together, rendered equally low in their depravity. Some wept at nightmares only they could see, others laughed hysterically, while a few simply moaned in ecstatic pleasure.

Around and about the seething mass stood a dozen priestesses, stripped to their waists, their exposed bodies daubed with symbols drawn in the blood of a fox, their long hair teased into dramatic spines with the fat of the same animal.

The high priestess, Damolien, whispered a low chant, her voice all but lost in the cacophony of joy and misery that filled the high hall. She wore the skin of the slain fox about her shoulders, and on occasion, she would pause and stroke her hands through its fur. Her keen senses further heightened by the narcotic fog, Damolien quivered at the feel of the hairs on her palms and fingers.

A quiet descended as the attendees one-by-one lapsed into a stupor, some still sobbing quietly, others sighing with satisfaction. With a nod, Damolien sent one of her priestesses to fetch Prince Aeltherin, the master of the house, so that he could partake of the ceremony's final stage. Just as the priestess turned towards the double doors that led from the hall, there was a tumult outside. Raised voices and a shriek caused the priestesses to turn as one towards the doorway. Damolien slipped the serrated sacrificial dagger from her waistband a moment before the doors crashed open.

Prince Aeltherin careened into the room, lurching over the somnolent bodies of his guests. Blood spilled from a cut across his chest and crimson droplets flew from his fingertips onto Damolien's face as the prince tripped over a supine figure and sprawled to the ground. Warriors in silver scale armour and wearing white sashes burst through the doorway, their bared swords in hand. Their captain, his tall helm decorated with threads of gold in the likeness of leaping lions, held a sword dripping with blood. He pulled a sliver of parchment from his belt and allowed it to fall open to show the seal of Phoenix King Bel Shanaar.

'PRINCE AELTHERIN of Lothern!' the captain called out. 'I am Carathril, captain of the Lothern Guard, and I have a decree for your arrest. Surrender to the judgement of the Phoenix King!'

Like a fish flopping upon a riverbank, Aeltherin dragged himself across the now-comatose elves littering the floor. His eyes looked pleadingly towards Damolien.

'Protect me,' Aeltherin hissed.

'Lay down your weapons and surrender in peace,' said Carathril, his voice calm. 'Give yourselves over to the Phoenix King's mercy.'

Damolien smiled. Her tongue flicked out like a serpent's as she licked the blood of Aeltherin from her lips.

'Mercy is for the weak,' she purred, and leapt lithely across the room.

Shrieking like harridans, the other priestesses followed their mistress, their hands flexed like talons, their fingernails sharpened to long points. Carathril leapt back from the assault, the point of Damolien's dagger narrowly avoiding his eye. One of his soldiers leapt forwards, sword arm straight, and lanced his blade into the high priestess. She fell without a sound as her disciples hurled themselves at the guards.

The priestesses were vicious and two of Carathril's elves had fallen to their raking claws, their throats opened up, before the killers were despatched by the swords of their fellows. As Carathril stepped distastefully between the unconscious pleasure-seekers, he sheathed his sword and reached a hand out towards Prince Aeltherin.

'Prince, you are wounded,' Carathril said gently. 'Come with us and we will see that your injuries are tended to properly. Bel Shanaar wishes you no ill, only to help you.'

'Bel Shanaar?' snarled the prince. 'An upstart! Usurper! His judgement is that of the crows feasting on a rotted carcass. I curse him! May Nethu take him and cast him to the blackest chasm!'

With a final effort, Aeltherin, hero of Mardal Vale and protector of Linthuin, pulled himself to his feet. With a contemptuous sneer upon his lips, the prince snatched up one of the bone braziers, spilling its fuming coals onto his robes. The diaphanous cloth ignited like tinder, quickly engulfing the prince in blue flames. The flames caught on the carpet as Aeltherin fell and soon the fire had leapt to the tapestries hanging upon the white walls.

Running nimbly amidst the billowing smoke and deadly flames, Carathril and his company dragged to safety as many of the insensible cultists as they could, but the flames grew too intense and still a dozen elves lay helpless amidst the inferno. As one of his soldiers sought to go back into the hall, Carathril grabbed him by the arm.

'It is too late, Aerenis,' Carathril said. 'The fires will claim them. Perhaps they will now know the peace they were seeking.'

◄ FOURTEEN ►

The Phoenix King's Court

MAJESTIC EAGLES CIRCLED overhead, their vast shadows flickering across the rough stone of the mountain pass. These were no ordinary birds of prey; they were great eagles, capable of seizing a mountain lion to devour, each wing twice an elf's height in breadth. Carathril reined his steed to a halt and sat there for a moment, gazing up into the blue skies, watching the birds swoop and climb around the snowy peaks of the Annulii. The jingle of harnesses broke his reverie as his accompanying bodyguard, Aerenis, brought his mount to a stop beside him.

The two elves were clad in blue woollen cloaks to guard against the cold of the high mountains, Carathril's edged with golden thread as a symbol of his rank as captain. Each wore a skirt of light scale mail, split at the waist and hemmed with bleached leather, and wide belts decorated with gems and silver. Long white shields hung on their saddlebags, Carathril's painted with the face of a roaring lion, Aerenis's decorated with a single golden rune – sarathai, the symbol of defiance and unyielding defence. Both of the riders wore the tall helms favoured by elven warriors across all of the kingdoms, Carathril's decorated with the lion crest of his family, Aerenis's plain but for the azure plume of a single feather.

They carried leaf-bladed spears and long recurved bows in their saddle packs, and each carried a quiver of white-fletched arrows. Fortunately, they had not had reason to wield such wargear, for their passage had been uneventful.

Despite the seeming tranquillity of the pass neither elf was relaxed. They were crossing through the highest range of the Annulii, where the magical vortex of Ulthuan drew a ring of mystical energy through the mountains. Here magic infused the air and ground; it pulsed and ebbed around the two elves with a barely felt quiver of power. Carathril and Aerenis, attuned to the mystical breezes and flows of the world, unconsciously sensed its presence and strength.

Other creatures were drawn here also, grown large on the unnatural energy like the eagles, but of an entirely less friendly nature. Griffons, with the bodies of massive lions and the heads and wings of giant birds, made their lairs in the mountaintops, while gigantic serpents and bizarre cockatrices lurked in the caves and gulleys swept by the magical winds.

The lieutenant's eyes glimmered from the darkness of his visor as he looked at Carathril.

'Captain?' Aerenis spoke quietly, shielding his eyes against the sun as he followed his captain's gaze. 'What troubles you?'

'It is nothing,' Carathril assured his second-in-command. 'Just a passing fancy, a whim.'

'How so?' asked Aerenis.

'Nothing disturbs them, the great eagles, that is,' Carathril said quietly. 'They eat, and they breed, and they raise their chicks, far removed from our woes. Such freedom, to soar and to hunt, unfettered by anguish or strife. You know, they say that the mages in Saphery can transform themselves into doves or hawks.'

'You would glide upon the breeze as a bird?' Aerenis sounded dubious. Carathril was not known for poetic flights of fantasy. '"They" say a lot of things about those Sapherians, and they are a strange folk that is for sure. But I doubt that they could transform themselves into a bird. Magic does not work so simply, or so I believe. Anyway, why would you want to be a bird? You are not carefree and capricious. What of your duty to Lothern, and your pledge to the Phoenix King? Do these things not give you solace in these dark times?'

'They do, for sure,' said Carathril, turning to Aerenis with a grim smile. 'And with that in mind, we should be on our way to bear tidings to King Bel Shanaar.'

Carathril and Aerenis rode down the winding path of the pass, their horses delicately picking their way along a narrow path of grey cobbles as the valley narrowed into a defile no more than a stone's throw wide. The light of the morning sun had not yet breached the canyon tops, and they plunged into cool shadow.

Above them, the air danced and shimmered and a faint magical aurora played about the barely visible mountain peaks. Occasionally the distant silhouette of an eagle would pass overhead. The rock here was pale and broken, and tumbles of scree and pebbles littered the crevasse floor, so that the two elves were forced to ride slowly, their steeds picking their way carefully between the patches of debris. Scattered whitethistle bushes clung to life under rocky overhangs, the last few brilliant blooms still opening their petals, the first deep red berries bursting into colour on slender, thorned stems. Here and there thin trickles of meltwater from the higher slopes meandered across the path.

Silence descended, broken only by the occasional sighing of the wind across the rocks. They rode on without word for some time, each elf alone with his thoughts. To Carathril's familiar eye, Aerenis seemed distant, perturbed. He rode with a tenseness the guard captain had not seen before.

'Dark thoughts?' Carathril asked, reining his steed across the path to ride alongside his lieutenant. 'The events at the prince's manse disturb you.'

'They do,' admitted Aerenis.

'I am sorry we could not save them all,' Carathril said, guessing his companion's guilt.

'It is more than that,' Aerenis replied. 'Before you pulled me back, I recognised a face I knew. A friend of my sister, Glarionelle, she was there.'

'The flames were too strong; you could not have rescued her,' Carathril said, leaning across to place a comforting hand on his friend's shoulder.

'That I know,' Aerenis said with a nod. He turned his face skywards and spoke as if to himself. 'Though it grieves me it is not the cause of my pain. Why was she there at all? She always seemed so full of life when I saw her. Her laughter came fast and lasted long. What drove her to seek the solace of the forbidden gods?'

Aerenis closed his eyes for a moment and then turned his gaze on Carathril, his dark blue eyes moist with tears.

'How could someone so fair have fallen to such depths?'

Carathril did not reply immediately, but thought for a moment, choosing his words. There was little comfort he could offer Aerenis, for he could not begin to understand his suffering. Carathril was the last of his family, his fore-fathers had died fighting the daemons and he was without wife or heir. Since the fall of Aenarion only duty and dis-cipline had filled his heart.

'I do not know,' he said, removing his hand and brush-ing a lock of silver hair from his face. 'Perhaps it was curiosity that lured her, and then passion that kept her snared. I have heard tales, no more than rumours, that not all go to such gatherings willingly. Some are fooled by the coven leaders, others forcibly taken from their homes, drugged and abducted. Those who might have the answers you seek are now dead, for good or ill. Find solace in the fact that we saved some, even if we could not save them all.'

'You are a strong leader and a wise counsellor,' said Aere-nis with a rueful smile, meeting Carathril's gaze. A sombre expression replaced the smile and Aerenis glanced away. 'Perhaps it should have been you and not Aeltherin who was prince.'

Carathril laughed with genuine amusement and Aerenis shot him a shocked glance.

'What do you find so amusing?' demanded Aerenis with a frown.

'The blood of princes does not run in my veins,' Carathril explained. 'My father and grandfather did not draw weapons alongside Aenarion, they were not warrior-princes fit to rule these lands. For all my station, for all my swordcraft and authority, I am content to be a servant, for I am the son of farmers, not fighters. While Aenarion and the princes fought, my family sheltered behind their blades, thankful for the protection of their betters. They were slain in fields of corn, not upon fields of blood. I do not feel ashamed, for no matter how mighty a prince becomes, he still needs water to drink and bread to eat. I believe that life and destiny finds a place for us all, and that is a comfort to me.'

'Well, let us hope life has beds for us in Tor Anroc this night!' joked Aerenis, eager to lighten the mood.

Carathril gave his lieutenant a playful shove.

'And one of those golden-haired Tiranoc maidens to warm it for you, no doubt!'

Their laughter echoed along the defile, sending a flock of birds darting into the darkening skies.

THE AUTUMNAL SUN was low on the horizon as Carathril and Aerenis rode through the long grass of Tiranoc. Their descent from Eagle Pass had been swift and they had made good time over the last two days. Once out of the mountains they had allowed their horses full rein and galloped swiftly over the many miles, glad to be lost in a blur of meadows and woodlands.

In Tiranoc, as in all of the Outer Kingdoms, the weather was colder than that of the inner realms, being more exposed to the sea winds than those lands within the circle of the Annulii. Still, the sun had been warm enough to make the ride pleasant for Aerenis and Carathril, and in each other's company they had passed many miles in constant yet trivial conversation.

Ahead, no more than two leagues distant, the city of Tor Anroc rose from upon a white-stoned hill, bathed in the setting sun. About the foothills of the mount clustered white buildings roofed with red tiles, nestled amongst freshly tilled fields, and thin smoke drifted from the farm chimneys. Orange and pink in the dusk light, the foundations of Tor Anroc towered above the plain, and two great roads curved away to the left and right, spiralling around the hilltop to the summit.

From high walls, the blue and yellow flags of Tiranoc hung limply on their banner poles, barely stirred by the still evening air. Towers and citadels carved from the white rock broke above the curving crenellations of the curtain wall, but these in turn were dwarfed by a central spire that pierced the twilight like a shining needle.

Heartened by the closeness of their destination, Carathril and Aerenis guided their steeds into a gentle trot and forged through the wild meadows; before long they came upon a roadway, flagged with hexagonal red tiles, which cut straight as an arrow towards the city.

Ahead lay walled orchards, where rows of apple and cherry trees clung stubbornly to their golden and red leaves. The harvest had passed and the fields were quiet, peacefully descending into their winter sleep behind hedges of callow flower and kingwood. They had left behind the livestock pastures in the foothills, where shepherds and goatherds had been moving their flocks down from the higher slopes. Soon the droving would begin and the herds would be brought to the markets of the towns surrounding Tor Anroc, and eventually to the capital itself.

The proximity of the city changed the landscape, just as a great tree might dominate a patch of woods or an island break the flow of a river. Here the farms were protected by high walls of white stone, and stood along the road behind gates of silver and gold.

Further back, away from the turnpike and reached only by meandering trails across the fields, stood tall mansions with many-roofed halls and slender towers. Here the nobles of Tiranoc lived in the summer, away from the city. Now only a handful trailed grey smoke from their chimneys; most of Tiranoc's princes had retired back to their city homes to the warmth of open fires, the excitement of winter balls and the intrigue of court life in Tor Anroc. Their horses' hooves clattering on the road, the riders made good speed and the sun was still loitering in the western sky as they rode into the shadow of the high rock of the city.

A great gatehouse barred the road, a bastion upon a wall twice the height of an elf that arched backwards into the mount itself, all carved from the naked rock. Two pale towers flanked the roadway, devoid of openings except for high arrow slits that looked upon every approach. On each of the flat tower tops stood a bolt thrower, mounted upon an assembly of bars and thin ropes so that that they could be swung with ease in any direction.

The golden gate of Tor Anroc lay open, but passage was barred by two chariots, stood side-by-side. Their fronts were carved in the likenesses of eagles and golden wings swept back to form their sides. Two pale grey horses stood motionless in front of each, bound by black leather harnesses; upon the back of each chariot stood two stern warriors, one with a long silvered spear, the other with bow bent and arrow nocked. The sentries watched cautiously as Carathril and Aerenis slowed their mounts to a walk and approached, hands held out from their sides.

'Who approaches Tor Anroc, city of Tiranoc, seat of the Phoenix King?' the spearman on the left called out.

'Captain Carathril of Lothern, bearing missives for his majesty Bel Shanaar,' Aerenis replied as the two halted a dozen paces from the gateway. 'And I, his aide, Aerenis, lieutenant of Lothern.'

'Come, Firuthal, why such caution?' Carathril called out as he dismounted. The spearman stepped down from the back of his chariot and approached; his face was grim.

'It is not for me to say, friend,' Firuthal said, extending a hand in greeting, which Carathril gripped firmly. 'The guard is doubled on the orders of Bel Shanaar. We are told to patrol the roads and borders, to keep watch for strangers. It is not my place to question our commands.'

'But I am no stranger,' Carathril said, turning and waving Aerenis to join him. 'I bring important news for the Phoenix King, and then perhaps when your watch is complete we can share a jug of wine and speak more freely.'

Firuthal nodded but still did not smile.

'Perhaps,' the charioteer said. 'My watch finishes at midnight; I shall come to find you at the palace.'

'Be sure that you do,' Carathril said, pulling himself back into his saddle with a jingle of harness.

Firuthal quickly trotted back to his chariot and nimbly leapt aboard. With a word, he urged the horses forwards and guided them past Carathril and Aerenis.

'Go quickly, I will send word to the Phoenix King that you are here,' Firuthal told them as he passed, with a glance over his shoulder towards the rising pinnacle of the palace tower. 'He will be eager to hear your messages.'

With a wave, Carathril rode on under the gateway, Aerenis following closely. Beyond, the road split into two and they took the left fork, climbing the hill along its southern slope. The screech of a bird attracted their attention and they looked up to see a hawk racing towards the tower of Tor Anroc: Firuthal's message. As they rode higher, the plains and meadows were laid out around them, stretching from mountain to coast and ruddy in the swiftly falling twilight. Soon low buildings enclosed the road and they were swallowed up by the outskirts of Tor Anroc.

The clatter of pots and the scent of cooking reminded Carathril that it had been some hours since they had eaten, and he hoped that he could swiftly conclude his business with Bel Shanaar and seek a hostelry.

He noted immediately the quiet and calm of Tiranoc. As they passed under a second gateway, through the curtain wall and into the city proper, he noted the lack of people on the streets. Within the city, the road continued its same swirling ascent, curling tighter and tighter about the hilltop, the buildings growing taller with each loop until they passed over the road itself and the pair found themselves riding through a long, lantern-lit tunnel. For a short while, they rode in twinkling lamplight, the jangling of the horses' harnesses and the clipping of their hooves echoing from walls occasionally pierced with high, thin windows and narrow doors.

Frescoes broke the monotony of the white walls, painted in vivid colours, showing harvest scenes and chariot races, deer hunts and marketplaces. Alleys and side streets broke the all-enclosing shaft, but these too offered no view of the sky. The city was now carved out of the stone of the mount, every room, window and door fashioned by masons from the heartrock of the hill. Having been raised in the open avenues of Lothern, Carathril felt a little unnerved and he only realised how uncomfortable he had started to feel when they finally exited the tunnelway out onto a broad plaza surrounding the palace.

Tiled with the same red stone as the road, the courtyard stretched for three hundred paces and it was filled with market stalls and crowds. The cries of stall keepers hawking their wares mixed with the hubbub of bargaining and general conversation. Dressed in flowing robes of white and wrapped with cowls, scarves and cloaks dyed in the same vibrant hues as the tunnel paintings, the folk of Tor Anroc weaved between the stalls at leisure, crossing each other's paths in a slow, complex dance of commerce. In the centre, the tower of the Phoenix King's palace soared into the darkening skies, golden light glimmering from its narrow windows.

'This way,' Carathril said, pointing to the left. A road was kept clear to the doors of the tower, and here a company of charioteers stood guard, fifty of them arrayed in two lines that flanked the approach to the palace.

NONE ATTEMPTED TO bar their arrival, and a retainer came forwards to take the reins of their horses as they dismounted outside the palace gate. The high wooden doors opened before them, showing a vaulted entrance hall lit by gold lanterns. At the far end, a marble stairway spiralled out of sight. A deep red carpet stretched along the hallway and up the stair, and Carathril self-consciously lifted up the hem of his cloak, covered as it was with the grime of many days' travel.

An elf swathed in a flowing robe of blue embroidered in gold with flowing birds came into view, walking swiftly down the stairs.

'Captain Carathril, I am Palthrain, chamberlain to his majesty,' the elf introduced himself with a deferential nod as they met at the bottom of the stairs. His cheeks were sharply angled and his wide eyes dark under a shock of black hair. His movements were measured and precise as he gestured for them to accompany him.

He spoke as he led them swiftly up the steps, his eyes fixed on Carathril's as he did so.

'His majesty is most keen to hear of events in Lothern,' said Palthrain. 'It has been many weeks since we have heard word from Prince Aeltherin, or any of his court, for that matter.'

Carathril hesitated a moment, casting a glance at Aerenis.

'Rest assured, captain, that whatever you tell the Phoenix King I shall know immediately,' said Palthrain.

'Our news will not bring any joy, I am afraid,' said the captain.

Palthrain took this with no more reaction than an understanding nod, though his eyes never left Carathril's.

They passed several landings during their ascent: wide archways leading from the stairs to the hallways and galleries that made up the greater part of the palace. On the fourth level, Palthrain turned them aside and ushered them through the arch into a wide indoor amphitheatre. Wooden benches, empty for the moment, surrounded a central circular floor. At the far end of the hall, in the gap made by the horseshoe of seats, the Phoenix King sat upon a high-backed golden throne; about him stood several other elves of regal disposition.

As THEY APPROACHED, they saw that Bel Shanaar was deep in conversation, his gaze not once straying to the new arrivals. He was dressed in his formal robes of office: layers of white and gold, delicately embroidered with silver swirls and runes. From his shoulders hung a long cloak of white feathers, which draped over the arms of his throne, hemmed with a band of golden thread and sapphires. His face was faintly lined, the only sign of old age any elf endured, and a golden band studded with a single emerald swept back his pale blond hair, showing a forehead creased with a frown. His eyes were bright blue, and he pursed thin lips as he listened intently to the words of his counsellors.

'His majesty, Bel Shanaar, Phoenix King of Ulthuan,' Palthrain whispered reverentially as they crossed the lacquered wooden floor.

He waved his hand gently towards a short, young elf to the Phoenix King's left, who stood with his arms crossed, his expression one of displeasure.

'Elodhir, son of the Phoenix King, heir to the throne of Tiranoc,' said the chamberlain. The family resemblance was clear.

On the other side stood a tall, broad elf dressed in a long sweep of gilded scale armour, bound with a thick black belt, a sword hanging from his hip.

'Imrik of Caledor, son of Menieth,' Palthrain said. 'He is the grandson of that great mage, Caledor Dragontamer.'

'All know of Imrik,' said Carathril, thrilled to see such a legendary warrior in the flesh.

'The third and last of the Phoenix King's advisors is Thyriol,' said Palthrain. 'He is one of the most powerful mage-princes, ruler of Saphery.'

Thyriol's silver hair hung to his waist in three long tresses bound with strips of black leather. He wore multi-layered robes of white and yellows, which constantly shimmered as he fidgeted from foot to foot.

'Thyriol who presided over the First Council?' asked Aerenis, awe in his voice.

'The same,' said Palthrain. His voice rose in volume. 'Captain Carathril of Lothern, your majesty.'

'Thank you, Palthrain,' Bel Shanaar said, still not looking at them.

The chamberlain bowed and left without further word. Carathril and Aerenis were left standing on their own, listening to the discussion.

'We cannot show mercy,' said Imrik with a shake of his head. 'The people need our strength.'

'But many of them are victims as much as they are perpetrators,' cautioned Bel Shanaar. 'They are brought low by their own terrors, and the priests and priestesses play on their fears and manipulate their woes. I have spoken with some who claim that they did not realise how debased they had become. There is dark magic in this, some more evil purpose that we have not yet seen.'

'Then we must find their ringleaders and question them,' suggested Elodhir. The prince took a pace towards his father. 'We cannot simply allow the cults to spread unchecked. If we should allow that to happen, our armies will be eaten away by this menace, our people consumed by their own desires. No! Though it is perhaps a harsh judgement on some, we must prosecute your rule with firm determination and relentless purpose.'

'That is all well and good, Elodhir, but against whom must we prosecute it?' asked Thyriol. As always, Thyriol's words were quiet and meaningful.

As he carefully considered his next words, the elf lord ran thin fingers through his silver hair. His deep green eyes fixed on each of his fellows in turn. 'We all know its root, yet there is not one of us speaks its name. Nagarythe. There, I have said it and yet the world still turns.'

'Tales and rumour are no basis for policy,' replied Bel Shanaar. 'Perhaps our guests bring tidings that will aid our discussions.'

Carathril stood dumbly for a moment, taken aback by his sudden inclusion in the conversation. The Phoenix King and three princes looked at him with inquiring eyes, and the guard captain cleared his throat and gathered his thoughts.

'I bear ill tidings, your majesty,' Carathril said quietly. 'I and my companion have ridden hither with all haste to bring you the news that Prince Aeltherin of Lothern is dead.'

A scowl crossed the face of Imrik, while the others present bowed their heads for a moment.

'It is our misfortune that the great prince fell from grace, your majesty,' continued Carathril. 'I know not how, but

Prince Aeltherin became a member of the pleasure cults. For how long, we do not know. It appears that for some time the prince was in league with the dark priestesses of Atharti, and from his position misdirected our efforts to uncover the plots of the cult. Only a chance happening, a name whispered by a prisoner in her sleep, started us on a sinister path that led to the doors of the prince's manse itself.'

'And how is it that Prince Aeltherin does not stand here to defend himself against these accusations?' asked Elodhir. 'Why is he not in your custody?'

'He took his own life, highness,' explained Carathril. 'I endeavoured to reason with him, implored the prince to put his case before this court, but he was gripped with a madness and would not consent. I know not what caused him to act in this way, and I would not dare to speculate.'

'A ruling prince party to these covens of evil?' muttered Thyriol, turning to the Phoenix King. 'Matters are even graver than we would have dared admit. When news of Aeltherin's fall spreads, fear and suspicion will follow.'

'As is the intent of the architects of this darkness, I have no doubt,' said Bel-Shanaar. 'With the rulers of the realms no longer to be trusted, to whom will our citizens turn? When they cannot trust those with authority, the greater the dread upon the minds of our people, and the more they will flock to the cults.'

'And who shall we trust, if not our own?' asked Imrik, his demeanour dark.

'The defection of Prince Aeltherin casts a cloud over every prince,' said Bel Shanaar with a sorrowful shake of his head. 'If we are to lead the people from the temptations of the cults, we must be united. Yet how can we act together when the doubt remains that those in whom we confide may well be working against our interests?'

'To allow ourselves to be divided would bring about a terrible age of anarchy,' warned Thyriol, who had begun to pace back and forth beside the king's throne. 'The rule of the realms is fragile, and the greatest of our leaders are beyond these shores in the colonies across the ocean.'

'The greatest of our leaders sits upon this throne,' said Elodhir, his eyes narrowing.

'I spoke not of one individual,' said Thyriol, raising a placating hand. 'Yet I would wish it that Prince Malekith were here, if only to settle the matter of his people in Nagarythe. In his absence we are reluctant to prosecute investigations within his realm.'

'Well, Malekith is not here, while we are,' said Bel Shanaar sharply. He paused for a moment, passing a hand across his forehead. 'It matters not. Thyriol, what is the counsel of the mages of Saphery?'

The mage-prince ceased his pacing and turned on his heel to face the Phoenix King. He folded his arms, which disappeared within the sleeves of his voluminous robe, and pursed his lips as if in thought.

'You were correct to speak of dark magic, your majesty,' Thyriol said. 'Our divinations sense a growing weight of evil energy gathering in the vortex. It pools within the Annulii Mountains, drawn here by the practices of the cults. Sacrifice of an unnatural kind is feeding the ill winds. Whether it is the purpose of the cults or simply an unintended result of their ceremonies, we cannot say. This magic is powerful but dangerous, and no mage will wield it.'

'There is no means by which this dark magic can be spent safely?' asked Imrik.

'The vortex dissipates some of its power, and would cleanse the winds in due course were the dark magic not fuelled further,' explained Thyriol. 'Unfortunately, there is nothing we can do to hasten this, other than to stop the cults practising their sorcery.'

'And so we return again to our main question,' sighed Bel Shanaar. 'How might we rid ourselves of these cults?'

'Firm action,' growled Imrik. 'Muster the princes; send out the call to arms. Sweep away this infestation with blade and bow.'

'What you suggest threatens civil war,' Thyriol cautioned.

'To stand idle threatens equal destruction,' said Elodhir.

'And would you lead this army, Imrik?' Bel Shanaar asked, turning in his throne to stare intently at the Caledorian prince.

'I would not,' Imrik replied sharply. 'Caledor yet remains free of this taint, and I seek to maintain the peace that we have.'

'Saphery has no generals of renown,' said Thyriol with a shrug. 'I think that you will find the other realms reluctant to risk open war.'

'Then who shall lead the hunt?' pleaded Elodhir, his exasperation clear in his voice.

'Captain Carathril,' said Bel Shanaar. Carathril started, surprised that his presence was still remembered. He had assumed the princes had heard all that they needed, and had been waiting for leave to be excused.

'How might I be of service, your majesty?' Carathril asked.

'I dispense with your duties to the Guard of Lothern,' said Bel Shanaar, standing up. 'You are loyal and trustworthy, devoted to our people and the continuance of peace and just rule. From this moment, I appoint you as my herald, the mouth of the Phoenix King. You will take word to the princes of the realms. I will ask if there is one amongst them who is willing to prosecute the destruction of these intolerable cults. This peril that besets us is no less than the division of our people and the destruction of our civilisation. We must stand strong, and proud, and drive out these faithless practitioners of deceit. The gratitude of our lands and this office will be heaped upon the prince that delivers us from this darkness.'

‐‐◄ FIFTEEN ►‐‐

A Bold Oath

CARATHRIL FELT WEARIER than he had ever felt before in his long years. For eighty days since becoming the herald of the Phoenix King, he had ridden across the length and breadth of Ulthuan. He had crossed back and forth over the Annulii Mountains; south to the mountains and hills of Caledor where the Dragonriders lived in tall castles amidst the mountain peaks; north to Chrace, where the warriors wore the pelts of fierce white lions hunted by their own hands.

Carathril had crossed the Sea of Dusk and the Sea of Dreams to Saphery, where mages ruled and the fields were tilled by enchanted ploughs and lanterns of ghostfire glittered in the towns. He had taken ship to Avelorn, the beautiful forests of the Everqueen, though he had not met the ceremonial wife of the Phoenix King on his visits, only her stern guard of handmaidens and the priestesses of Isha. In Yvresse, he had sailed amongst the eastern islands and camped under the wooded boughs of the Athel Yvrain. He had become accustomed to the long rides and nights spent under the stars or in strange beds, driven on by his duty to the Phoenix King.

He had borne the tidings of Bel Shanaar to the princes, and as winter closed her chill grip upon the Outer Kingdoms, Carathril had reluctantly returned with their replies: none was willing to lead the soldiery of Ulthuan against the pleasure cults.

Now he rested, as he had done for the past seven days, sitting upon one of the benches in the audience chamber of the palace, lulled half-asleep by the droning of the princes' voices below. For weeks they had arrived and left, seeking counsel from Bel Shanaar and each other, bringing tidings, mostly grim, of events across the realms of Ulthuan.

As far as Carathril could tell, the conflict with the cults of pleasure and excess was growing in intensity. From his own experience in Lothern he knew that it seemed that another sect would emerge even as one was destroyed. It was becoming evident that for some time now, many years likely, the cults had been prospering outside of the cities and large towns. Distant farms and isolated hunting lodges had become meeting places for those drawn to the forbidden rituals of these cults, and here thriving communities had established themselves. Cult members had spread far and wide, and there was no telling how many figures of authority, how many nobles and commanders were now in their grip. Carathril had wanted to believe that the insurgence of dark practices and loathsome ceremonies had been halted, but each revelation dashed his hopes a little further.

The fundamental problem was that each kingdom was confident in its own abilities to combat the emerging

fanaticism of the cults, but was suspicious of its neighbours. Even though united under the rule of the Phoenix
King, each realm was a sovereign territory of its princes,
ruled over in the Phoenix King's name.

The princes had a great amount for which to be worried,
and each had a vested interest in protecting the fortunes
of his kingdom, for all the ruling families were powerful,
militarily, politically and economically. They were
descended from the bravest and strongest of Aenarion's
captains, who had wielded the magical weapons of Caledor Dragontamer against the daemon hosts. They had a
bloodright to rule their lands, and each jealously guarded
his domains with the ferocity of a she-lion protecting her
young.

No prince could agree to allow another to control the
armies of their house, nor could they comfortably consent
to having the troops of another realm stationed in their
lands. To Carathril's simple mind it seemed as if they ever
postured and manoeuvred for aid whilst never offering
their own. Once enamoured of these lofty rulers, Carathril
was quickly tiring of their political ways. In short,
Carathril realised, the majority of the princes – both those
that ruled over a realm and those that served them – considered the wider purging of the cults to be somebody
else's problem.

It seemed as if a few of the princes felt the same as the
herald. Of all the princes, Carathril considered Imrik to be
closest to the herald in outlook and opinion. He was
plain-speaking, thought of as gruff, even rude, by some of
his peers, and feared inaction more than anything.

As the grandson of the great Caledor Dragontamer, he
was considered the noblest of all the princes, and this
stirred jealousy in the hearts of others. They all feared the
power of the kingdom of Caledor, for it was from here the

dragon knights hailed, a force greater than any mustered by other realms. As was the way of powerful individuals, many of the princes were loath to surrender control of their forces to another, and for his part Imrik was unwilling to shoulder the responsibilities he thought were being shirked by the other princes.

Carathril missed Lothern dearly. He had passed through his home city some fifty days earlier to bear news to Prince Haradrin, now ruler of the realm of Eataine. What he had seen, the suspicion and fear in the eyes of his people, made Carathril long to be dispensed from the Phoenix King's service so that he might return and aid his folk. Yet it was not to be, for Bel Shanaar ever sought more diplomacy with the princes, and Carathril was required to be on hand at short notice.

Carathril felt alone amongst these high-ranking personages, for Aerenis had left for Lothern only a few days after they had first arrived. Those few elves that Carathril knew in Tor Anroc were cordial enough, but it quickly became evident that his position as herald not only denied him much time for personal matters and socialising, but also made those around him wary of speaking their mind. They persistently enquired of delicate matters from Carathril, seeking confirmation of rumours and nuggets of information from the Phoenix King's court, and Carathril was reluctant to confide what little he really knew for fear of being seen as a gossip, unworthy of the trust bestowed upon him.

The more Carathril learned of the secretive nature of the cults – of how many of the members led plain and normal lives on the surface but performed hedonistic and despicable acts in private – the more he became distrustful. Eventually, he had decided to forego his rare excursions to the rest of the city and now stayed solely within the confines of the palace when he was in Tor Anroc.

A STIR AMONGST the court roused Carathril as two more joined their number. He recognised them immediately as Prince Finudel, ruler of Ellyrion and his sister, Princess Athielle. They had arrived only two days ago and caused much commotion with promises of cavalry and spearmen for the cause. Carathril leaned forwards, his chin cupped in his hand, and listened to what was being said.

'It matters not if the horsemasters of Ellyrion stand ready to ride forth,' Prince Bathinair of Yvresse was saying. 'Who are they to ride forth against, my dear Finudel? You can hardly lead a cavalry charge through every village and town in Ulthuan.'

'Perhaps you seek to upset the harmony between the realms for your own ends,' added Caladryan, another of Yvresse's nobility. 'It is no secret that of late the fortunes of Ellyrion have waned. War suits those with little to lose, and it costs those who have the means. Our endeavours across the oceans bring us wealth and goods from the colonies; perhaps Ellyrion is jealous of that.'

Finudel opened his mouth to speak, his anger etched in creases across his brow, but Athielle quickly laid a hand on her brother's arm to still him.

'It is true that we have perhaps not prospered as much as some,' the Ellyrian princess said quietly. 'In part that is because we of the Inner Kingdoms must pay the taxes of Lothern to pass our fleets into the Great Ocean. If not for those taxes, I suspect that the Outer Kingdoms would perhaps have less of a monopoly of trade.'

'We cannot be held to account for the quirks of geography,' sneered Prince Langarel, one of Haradrin's kin from Lothern. 'The sea gates must be maintained, and our war fleet stands ever ready for the benefit of all. It is fitting, then, that all should contribute to the cost of maintaining these defences.'

'And against whom do you defend us?' growled Finudel. 'Men? Hut-dwelling savages who can barely cross a river, and an ocean divides us from them. The dwarfs? They are content to dig in the mountains and sit in their caves. The slaves of the Old Ones? Their cities lie in ruins, their civilisation swallowed by the hot jungles. Your fleet is not required, a token of the hubris of Lothern kept gilded by the labours of the other realms.'

'Must every old slight and rankle be dredged up before me every day?' demanded Bel Shanaar, his voice cutting sharply through the raised voices of the princes. 'There is nothing to be gained from this bickering, and everything to be lost. While we argue over the spoils of our growing colonies, our cities here at hand are being devoured by decadence and forbidden pursuits. Would you have us abandon our roots and settle in the newly grown branches of our realm? The world has riches enough for us all, if we could set aside these incessant arguments.'

'The power of the cults grows, that much is clear,' said Thyriol, from where he sat upon one of the ring of innermost benches surrounding the hall. All turned to the mage in expectation.

'The vortex holds the winds of magic in check for the moment, but dark magic is gathering in the mountains. Strange creatures have been seen in the highest peaks, unnatural things spawned from the power of Chaos. Not all things of darkness were purged by the blade of Aenarion and the vortex of Caledor. Hybrid monsters of flesh, mutant and depraved, dwell still in the wilderness. The dark magic feeds them, emboldens them, makes them stronger and cannier. Even now, the passes become ever more dangerous to travel. In the winter when the hunters and soldiers cannot keep these growing numbers of beasts at bay, what then? Will we have manticores and hydras descend into the lowlands to attack farms and destroy villages? If we allow the cults to grow unchecked, perhaps even the vortex itself will fail and once more plunge the world into an age of darkness and daemons. Is there one here with the will to prevent that?'

The assembled princes stood in silence, eyeing each other, avoiding the gaze of the Phoenix King.

'There is one perhaps that has the will,' a voice called out, echoing along the audience chamber from the doorway. Its timbre was firm and deep, filled with authority.

A ripple of gasps and whispers spread through the court as the newcomer strode purposefully across the lacquered floor, the fall of his riding boots sounding like the thunder of war drums. He was dressed in a long skirt of golden mail and his chest was covered with a gold breastplate etched with the design of a dragon, coiled and ready to attack. He wore a cloak of shadow-black across his shoulders, held with a clasp adorned with a black gem set into a golden rose. Under one arm he carried a tall war helm, fixed with a strange circlet of dark grey metal that had jutting, thorn-like spines. A complex headband of golden threads swept back raven hair that fell about his shoulders in twisted plaits tied with rings of rune-etched bone. His eyes were piercing, dark, as he stared at the nervous princes and courtiers. He radiated power, his energy and vigour surrounding him as surely as light glows from a lantern.

The princes parted before the newcomer like waves before a ship's prow, treading and stumbling upon robes and cloaks in their eagerness to back away. A few bowed stiffly or nodded heads in unthinking deference as he swept past to stand in front of the Phoenix King, his left hand, gloved in supple black leather, resting on the golden pommel of a sword hanging in an ebon scabbard at his waist.

'Prince Malekith,' said Bel Shanaar evenly, stroking his bottom lip with a slender finger. 'Had I known of your coming I would have arranged suitable welcome.'

'Such ceremony is unnecessary, your majesty,' replied Malekith, his tone of voice warm, his manner as smooth as velvet. 'I thought it prudent to arrive unannounced, lest our enemies be warned of my return.'

'Our enemies?' said Bel Shanaar, turning a hawkish look upon the prince.

'Even across the oceans, as I fought against vile beasts and brutal orcs, I heard of the woes that beset our home,' Malekith explained. He paused and turned to face the princes and their counsellors. 'Alongside the dwarfs, beside their kings, I and my companions fought to keep our new lands safe. Friends I had that gave their lives protecting the colonies, and I would not have their deaths be in vain, that our cities and our island here would fall to ruin even as we raise sparkling towers and mighty fortresses across the length and breadth of the world.'

'And so you have returned to us in our hour of need, Malekith?' said Imrik haughtily, stepping in front of Malekith with his arms crossed defensively.

'You must also have heard that which vexes us most,' said Thyriol softly, standing up and pacing towards the prince of Nagarythe, stepping between Malekith and Imrik. 'We would wish to prosecute our war against these insidious evils across all of Ulthuan. *All* of Ulthuan.'

'That is why I have returned,' replied Malekith, meeting the mage's keen gaze with his own piercing stare. 'Nagarythe is gripped by this torment no less than other lands;

more I have heard on occasion. We are one island, one realm under the rule of the Phoenix King, and Nagarythe will not be party to insurrection, nor shall we tolerate black magics and forbidden rituals.'

'You are our greatest general, our most sound strategist, Prince Malekith,' said Finudel, his voice hesitant with hope. 'If it pleases all present, would you take up the banner of the Phoenix King and lead the fight against these miserable wretches?'

'In you runs the noblest blood of all princes,' gushed Bathinair, one of the Yvressian princes present. 'As you fought the darkness alongside your father, you could again bring the light back to Ulthuan!'

'Eataine would stand by you,' promised Haradrin with a clenched fist held to his chest.

A chorus of pleading and thanks bubbled up from the assembled nobles, but fell silent the moment Malekith raised a hand to still them. The Naggarothi prince turned his head and looked at Bel Shanaar, saying nothing. The Phoenix King sat in thought, his lips pursed, steepling his slender fingers beneath his chin. Bel Shanaar then looked at Imrik's stern expression, an eyebrow raised in question upon the Phoenix King's face.

'If it is the will of the Phoenix King and this court, then Caledor will not oppose Malekith,' Imrik said slowly, before turning away and stalking from the room.

An almost imperceptible expression of relief softened the furrows in Bel Shanaar's frown, and he sat back and gave a perfunctory nod towards the prince of Nagarythe.

'As it pleases this court, so shall I act,' declared Malekith. 'A company of my finest warriors, fighters hardened by war across the seas one-and-all, rides even now to Anlec to announce my return. The army of Nagarythe shall be roused, and no hall nor cave nor cellar shall avoid our gaze. The raven heralds shall ride forth again, and all rumour shall come to our ears so that our foe might not hide. With mercy we shall temper our vengeance, for it is not our desire to slay needlessly those who are simply misguided. By trunk and root we shall tear free this tree of rotten fruit that feeds upon our fair nation, and we shall set free those trapped beneath its dark bower. No matter how high that tree reaches, no matter how powerful or prominent its leaders are, they shall not escape justice.'

‑◄ SIXTEEN ►‑

A Journey to Darkness

NORTHWARDS MARCHED THE caravan of Malekith. At their head, the prince led the column from atop an immense black steed bridled with silver and black leather. Behind him rode six hundred knights of Nagarythe, their silver and black pennants snapping in the chill autumn air. With them, they had brought news that already many cultists had surrendered to Malekith's soldiers, throwing themselves upon the mercy of the prince. The people of Nagarythe, long cowed by the cultists who had held sway in Malekith's absence, had come forth from their homes in celebration. Many of Nagarythe's citizens had been forced into serving the cults against their will, enslaved with threats of sacrifice and violence. As if unshackled from a great yoke, they had thrown off the tyranny of the dark priests and priestesses and taken to the streets to proclaim the victorious return of their rightful ruler.

Not only fair wishes from Bel Shanaar accompanied Malekith on his march north; three hundred chariots of Tiranoc went with him as a symbol of the Phoenix King's support. More horsemen had recently arrived from Ellyrion, despatched on the orders of Finudel. Seven hundred reaver knights had crossed the Annulii Mountains along the Unicorn Pass, the Eyin Uirithas, and met the caravan some one hundred leagues from Anlec. In their wake came ten thousand spearmen, assembled from across Eataine and Yvresse; even now they crossed the Inner Sea to join the host that marched against the dark cultists.

With them came a long baggage train, as any army on the march needed an unending tide of supplies to keep it on the move. The wagons of Tor Anroc were as larger versions of their sleek chariots, each pulled by four high-stepping steeds, the backs of the wains covered with gaily covered awnings and hung with pennants and flags of the kingdom. A hundred in all followed in the army's wake, filled with cooks and fletchers, smiths and ostlers, bakers and armourers and all the gear of their trades. Priests and priestesses came also, of Asuryan and Isha, and astromancers of Lileath, diviners of Kourdanrin and other such soothsayers, chroniclers and clerics as Bel Shanaar had seen fit to grant the expedition.

Though the elves of Tiranoc and Ellyrion were glad of such mystical companions, the Naggarothi, and in particular Malekith, paid them little heed and avoided their gatherings.

Amongst the host rode Carathril, still under oath as Bel Shanaar's herald, to act for the Phoenix King in this endeavour. He felt as much relief and anticipation as the princes, and riding alongside the prince of Nagarythe filled him with a confidence he had never before felt.

* * *

ONE BRIGHT MORNING they came upon a stone bridge that soared elegantly across a frothing river. This was the Naganath, which spilled straight from the mountains and across to the sea in a sweeping torrent. Beyond its foaming waters lay Nagarythe.

Malekith's gaze was distant, directed even further north, towards Anlec. His face betrayed no emotion, yet inside his thoughts were mixed. For almost his entire life he had sworn never to set foot here again until he was ready to take his rightful place. Excitement bubbled up inside him at the prospect of the events he saw unfolding in his head. Yet they were tinged with sadness, and not a little regret. Just before they crossed the bridge, Malekith signalled the column to halt and swung down from his saddle. Sensing Carathril's gaze upon him, Malekith turned to the herald and smiled.

'It has been more than thirteen hundred years since I last trod upon those lands,' Malekith said, his voice quiet. 'It has been more than one-and-a-half thousand since I took up the crown of Nagarythe, under the shadow of my father's sacrifice. Of that time, I have spent more of my life upon foreign soil than I have my homeland.'

'It must feel good to return,' said Carathril.

'Yes, it does feel good,' said Malekith with a nod. He nodded even more firmly and then grinned. Then he broke into a laugh and his eyes glittered. 'Very good!'

Carathril laughed with him, realising how much of an understatement he had uttered. Malekith's mood swiftly turned sombre though, and once again he cast his gaze northwards.

'I have been remiss in my duties as ruler,' Malekith said. 'It is in my absence that these depraved and reckless cults have flourished. From my lands, from the realm forged from the blood of my father, has grown a dark canker that poisons the heart of Ulthuan. That is a shame I cannot bear, and I will expunge it.'

'You cannot be blamed for the weaknesses and corruptions of others,' Carathril said with a shake of his head. 'The guilt for this malaise is not yours.'

'Not mine alone, I accept that,' replied Malekith. 'Yet we all bear some responsibility for this degeneration of authority and tradition, and I bear more than most.'

The prince swung himself back upon his steed and turned to face the halted column. His voice rang loud and crisp in the morning air.

'Remember that these are the sovereign lands of Nagarythe,' he cried. 'It is here that Aenarion the Defender built Anlec, and from here that he rode forth to battle the daemons. I do not return to lead an invasion. We do not come here as conquerors. We are liberators. We are here to free this realm from the dark and terrible grip of its depression and immorality. We are here to bring light where darkness has settled. None shall be slain who offers repentance for his misdeeds. None shall be punished who turns from his wayward path to rejoin the side of the righteous. Fight first with your hearts before your swords. Pity those that stand against us, but do not fear them, and do not hate them. It is fear and hatred that has laid them so low, so we shall bring them hope and we shall bring them salvation.'

Malekith drew his sword and held it aloft; its rune-etched blade glimmered with blue fire. His voice rose to a triumphant shout.

'The blood of our forefathers stains this earth! This is Nagarythe and she bows to no darkness! I am prince here, these are my lands! I am Malekith!'

A great roar erupted from the assembled army, from the throats of both Naggarothi and elves of other realms.

Malekith sheathed his sword and snatched the standard from the hand of his aide. Wheeling his steed with a flourish, Malekith urged on his mount and galloped across the bridge, the silver and black banner of Nagarythe fluttering above him. Still chanting, the column surged after him.

As the company made their way through Nagarythe, the truth of the situation became ever clearer. In the first village they entered, cheering crowds cast petals and blossoms, and a choir of children sang praises to the soldiers accompanied by flutes and harps. The village elder, a venerable elf with silver hair whose tresses reached her waist, presented Malekith with a garland of mountain laurel, and showered thanks upon Carathril and the others as they passed.

Dark-haired maidens presented the marching warriors with bundles of flowers, and a few leapt upon the chariots to hug and kiss the crews. Not even on the carnival days of Isha had Carathril known such celebration, and his heart soared to see the joy in the eyes of the villagers.

As they reached the central square, the mood changed. Here the white-washed buildings were stained with soot, their doors and windows charred. In the centre of the plaza huddled a group of some thirty elves, surrounded by villagers with knives and spears at the ready.

The black dresses and robes of the captives were tattered and bloody, and many bore grazes and bruises. A few bore more severe injuries, cradling broken arms and bandaged cuts. Some had crudely shaven heads, while others had runes of Asuryan daubed with white dye on their exposed flesh.

A handful of cultists regarded the soldiers with defiant and sullen eyes, their faces twisted with sneers; most had vacant gazes of shock, and a few looked down in shame and buried the heads in their hands, weeping. Pity, Malekith had said, and it was pity that filled the prince as he looked upon these poor wretches. Malekith signalled for Carathril to stop, and waved on the rest of the troop. The ruler of these desperate people sat upon his majestic steed and looked down at the prisoners, his face unmoving.

'Traitor!' shouted one of the cultists, a young elf clad only in a loincloth, his bare flesh cut with dozens of small incisions; self-made rather than inflicted by his captors. 'Khaine shall not forgive such treachery!'

Malekith did not react but simply continued to stare at the cultists, though from the corner of his eye he saw Carathril flinch at the mention of the Lord of Murder.

'Ereth Khial will devour you, son of Aenarion!' spat another degenerate, an old man whose black and dark blue robes were torn to shreds.

'Silence!' said Carathril, drawing his sword and urging his steed forwards. The cultists shrank back, cowed by his anger. 'We do not openly speak these names for a reason. That you consort with such gods is proof of your guilt. Save your hexes and curses!'

A lissom elf, her hair waxed into long spines and dyed orange, stood and bared herself to the company with a lewd smile. Scenes of licentious acts were painted in blue dye across her breasts, stomach and thighs.

'Perhaps Atharti's blessings would please you more, my lord,' she said, running a hand over her pale skin. 'There are those here who can attend to your pleasure, whatever your desires may be.'

Malekith waved Carathril back and dismounted. He stood in front of the consort of Atharti. Though she was attractive, it was disgust rather than ardour that Malekith felt. Dark magic polluted her comely body. Hiding his feelings, the prince calmly took off his cloak and wrapped it around her, covering her naked form.

'There is no pleasure in the degradation of others,' Malekith said, stroking the girl's hair. 'It is love not lust that we bring with us. I see fear in your eyes, and that I understand. It is the retribution of mortals not gods that fills you with dread. And I say to this, do not be afraid. We are not here as executioners. We have not come to seek vengeance in blood. Whatever your crimes, you shall be treated fairly and with dignity. We do not judge you for your doubts and your desperation. Your weakness is regrettable but no cause for punishment. Some, I have no doubt, have trodden upon this path willingly and with malice, and in time justice will find them. But even for them, there is mercy and forgiveness. Healers shall attend to your ills, both physical and spiritual. We shall bring forth the darkness that lingers within you, and free you from its grip. In time, you will know peace and harmony once more.'

Malekith ordered that the villagers bring fresh clothes for the captives, and food and water. While the prince marshalled this activity himself, he sent the greater part of the column onwards towards Anlec. Once fed and clothed, the cultists were taken under escort and Malekith resumed the march.

From the village, the road turned north-east, towards the mountains, and rose steadily for several miles before cutting into thick woodland. Tall pines formed a wall on either side of the column, and as the day wore on the caravan was swathed with long shadows. No sound could be heard; an eerie quiet stilled all noise from bird and mammal.

'This is a queer land,' Carathril remarked to himself. One of the knights of Anlec heard him and heeled his horse over beside the herald.

'This is Athel Sarui,' the knight told him. 'Forest of Silence' the name meant, but Carathril had not heard of this place before.

'I see why it is so named,' said Carathril. 'Are you from this land?'

'No,' the knight replied quickly, taken aback by Carathril's question. 'No living souls save for the trees live here. It is said that beyond the forest, at the feet of the mountains, there is a great cave. It is one of the Adir Cynath, a gate to Mirai, the underworld. To wander close to the mountains is to risk the gaze of Ereth Khial, and to be taken into her darkness by the rephallim.'

Carathril shuddered at the mention of these forbidding names, of the dark goddess of the dead and her bodiless servants. To hear them spoken openly was unheard of in Lothern, for the cytharai, as the deeper gods were known, were not openly worshipped by right-thinking folk. The cults had embraced the dark promises of these thirsting entities, and by that act even now plunged Ulthuan into turmoil. The knight recognised Carathril's expression of concern.

'Fear not, captain,' he said calmly, and produced a silver amulet from beneath his mail shirt. It was shaped in the symbol of yenlui, the rune of balance, and studded with three shining diamonds. 'This was a gift from a friend in Saphery, it will protect us. Those of us who dwell in the north must oft speak these distasteful names, for many of the darkest shrines to the dwellers beneath lie in our lands.'

'And how is it that the heartland of Aenarion allows such practices?' asked Carathril.

'The cytharai must be appeased, from time to time,' said the knight. 'One does not ignore the gods without peril, especially those of vile and short temper. And does not that blackest of places, the shrine to the God of Murder, lie beyond our northern coast? Once it was that a single priest or priestess would tend the shrines of the nightly lords and ladies. He or she would entreat them to still their vengeance, and placate them with sacrifices.'

The knight cast his gaze downwards.

'On occasion, in desperate times, one must visit these dire abodes, for there are some things beyond even the knowledge of Asuryan and Isha. Even Aenarion sought their wisdom, and that is not to be undertaken lightly. Many are the wards and blessings the priests can bestow upon those who would supplicate themselves before the cytharai.'

'Yet how did worship of gods so abhorrent spread so widely?' said Carathril.

'In indolence or sorrow, more of our people turned to the cytharai to ease their minds, to seek answers to questions perhaps best not asked,' the knight told him. 'Of loved ones long dead; of secrets lost in time; of joys forgotten with the coming of Chaos. Fortified and gratified by their indulgences, these misguided souls opened up the dark mysteries and learned their ways. They perverted the rituals of appeasement and turned them into ceremonies of praise. These dark acts they took with them, ever in secret, and founded new shrines in other lands. In the shadows, beyond the sight of right-minded folk, they practised their evils, perfecting them, luring others into their depravity. For more than five hundred years they have spread across Ulthuan, insinuating themselves into homes and hostels, from the lowliest to the highest. Be aware, the task we now undertake will be neither swift nor easy.'

'And you, how did you not become ensnared or enslaved by these pernicious shrine-folk?' asked Carathril.

The knight tucked his talisman back beneath his shirt and then pulled back his long black hair from the nape of his neck. A scar was there, etched into his skin, in the shape of a curved dagger.

'Who said that I did not?' the knight said. 'For many years I laboured with the blades of Khaine, a holy executioner in Anlec. My father had raised me within the cult, and I knew no different. It was only when he asked me to cut out the heart of my sister that I slew him and fled with her. We travelled across the sea to escape those that hunted us, and in time I met with the prince and told him of the travails of our people. I am Maranith, captain of Nagarythe under oath to Malekith, and it was I he sent to rouse this army ready for his return. I cannot hope to expunge the stain upon my spirit, but if my labours free others from its trap, I shall die content.'

'And I am proud to labour beside you,' said Carathril, extending a hand. The knight gripped it firmly in his own gauntleted fist and shook it firmly.

'What we have started here will change Ulthuan forever, Carathril,' Maranith said. 'Fight with the prince, and history will remember you for eternity.'

CARATHRIL GAVE A nod and rode away. Filled with curiosity, he dropped down the column and pulled his horse to a walk beside the prisoners, observing them. The girl who had so brazenly offered herself to him now seemed demure, wrapped in white linen, her blonde hair washed and plaited, her skin cleansed of its obscene marks. She cast coy glances occasionally at Carathril, the wildness that had filled her eyes before now utterly gone. Carathril smiled at her and waved for her to approach. He dismounted and led his horse as she stepped up beside him.

'Tell me your name,' said Carathril.

'I am Drutheira,' she replied hesitantly.

'I am Carathril, from Lothern,' the herald told her. 'It is uncommon for the maidens of Nagarythe to have straw hair such as yours.'

'I am not from Nagarythe, my lord,' Drutheira said.

'There is no need to call me lord; I am no prince, merely a captain of the guard. You may call me Carathril, or captain, as you please. How come you to be here, then?'

'I am from Ellyrion, captain,' she told him. 'A while ago, twenty years or more, my brother and I were running the herd in the foothills of the mountains. Riders came, clad in black cloaks, and we thought that they had come for the horses. Galdarin, my brother, tried to fight them, but he was slain. They left the horses, but took me. They bore me here, where they had built a temple to Atharti.'

'Twenty years?' gasped Carathril. 'It must have been hideous, enslaved to such diabolic rites.'

'At first I was terrified,' admitted Drutheira. 'They beat me and whipped me, until I could no longer feel pain, I no longer cried. I cared not what happened to me. Then they brought me calmleaf and black lotus, and we feasted and dined in honour of Atharti. I learned the skills of the consort, and daily gave myself to the pleasures of Atharti. When Helreon died, I succeeded her as priestess and learned the inner mysteries of our goddess.'

Her voice had become strident and defiant, but suddenly she paused. Without warning, she began to sob.

'Oh, captain, today is the first day in twenty years I have seen clearly what I have become,' she moaned. 'Other girls I ordered brought to the shrine, and enslaved them as I was enslaved. What terrible things I have seen; have witnessed with joy in my heart. I was lost in the bliss of Atharti, never looking upon those vile acts in the way I see them now. What have I done?'

Carathril hushed her and laid a comforting hand upon her shoulder. She did not look up at him, but instead hung her head and continued to cry. He searched for the words to ease her, but could find none. He was not gifted with a lyric nature, and part of him still reviled what she had become. To give herself, body and spirit, so wholly to the forbidden gods was an idea he found utterly abhorrent. Unable to marry the loathing he felt with the pitiful sight of her so distraught, he chose to remain silent.

They walked thus for some time, until her crying ceased. He turned to see her gazing at him, her face streaked with tears, her eyes shot with red.

'What is to become of me?' she asked.

'As Prince Malekith promised, you will not be harmed,' Carathril assured her. 'In all likelihood, when you are fully cured of this affliction you can return to Ellyrion. I am sure your family think you dead, and would be overjoyed to find you alive and well.'

She said nothing but simply nodded.

'Tell me of Ellyrion,' Carathril said, uneasy with the prospect of more silence between them. He has visited many realms as herald, but wished to hear how Drutheira remembered her land of birth.

'It is fairest in the evening, as the sun sinks upon the mountains and bathes the meadows in gold,' Drutheira told him. 'Pastures of grass as high as your waist, as green as emeralds, stretch out as far as one can see. White horses run wild through the foothills, calling to our herds and leading them astray. We listen to their voices on the breeze; hear them taunting their cousins who are caught beneath bridle and saddle.'

'Does that not make you sad?' asked Carathril. 'Would you not have all horses run free like their wild cousins?'

She laughed, a startlingly beautiful sound to Carathril's ears.

'You are silly, captain,' Drutheira said. 'The steeds of Ellyrion are proud of our friendship, and call their wild cousins stupid and backwards. They love the jangle of harness and the glitter of silver tack. You should see them prance and hear them laugh when they ride forth. They have lush grass to eat and warm stables at night, and call upon their cousins to join them when the winter rains come.'

Carathril was about to say more when he heard his name called from ahead.

'Forgive me, it appears that I am needed,' he said with a rueful smile. 'I would like to talk to you again soon.'

'And I, you,' Drutheira replied. 'Perhaps you could tell me of Lothern.'

'I shall,' he promised, and swung himself upon his horse. He was about to flick the reins and ride ahead when a thought struck him. 'Tell me, Drutheira of Ellyrion, what does my horse think of me?'

She frowned slightly and then smiled. Laying a hand upon the horse's cheek, she leaned close and whispered into his ear. She giggled as the horse neighed and whinnied.

'What?' said Carathril petulantly. 'What did he say?'

'He is very happy to bear you,' Drutheira informed him. 'You have ridden far together, and you look after him well.'

'What is so funny?'

'He said that for all the riding you have done, you have grown to be a heavier not lighter burden to bear with each trip. He thinks you have become a little plump on grain.'

Carathril gave an indignant snort, before laughing himself.

'The palaces of princes would never live to see a herald of the Phoenix King go hungry,' he said. 'Perhaps I need to learn how to say no.'

With a word, he encouraged his steed forwards, breaking into a swift trot. Behind him, Drutheira's smile went unseen; it was a sly expression, filled with a cunning amusement. She returned to the other prisoners and they began to whisper amongst themselves.

AS CARATHRIL NEARED the head of the column, Prince Malekith was deep in conversation with one of the raven heralds. The newcomer was mounted upon a jet-black steed and upon his shoulders he wore a long cloak made of dark feathers. He was hooded, revealing only glimpses of his pale, drawn face. The rider held a long-hafted spear, and he had a compact bow tied amongst his saddlebags next to a quiver of black-fletched arrows. The prince of Nagarythe turned to Carathril.

'May I present Captain Carathril of Lothern, herald of Bel Shanaar,' said Malekith. 'This is Elthyrior, one of the raven heralds of Nagarythe.'

'I am honoured,' said Carathril, receiving a silent nod from Elthyrior as his only reply.

'Very well,' said the prince to the raven herald. 'Call your brethren to Anir Atruth, and watch for spies and agents of the cults. We shall meet you there in three days, and then march upon Ealith.'

Malekith commanded his horse into a trot and Carathril did likewise.

'You have never met one of Elthyrior's order before?' asked the prince. 'Not on all your long travels?'

'I know little of the heralds of the northlands,' said Carathril. 'I cannot say what is fact and what is myth, but all I hear is sinister.'

Malekith laughed.

'There is something of a darkness about them, I would agree,' said Malekith. 'Few elves ever meet one of their kind: ever solitary figures only seen on lonely moors and wild mountain passes, and the stories of such encounters are whispered around campfires, and in hushed tones in the wine halls.'

'Where do they come from?' asked Carathril.

'From Nagarythe,' said the prince. 'While we laud the exploits of the greatest heroes of the past, the raven heralds are content to be forgotten. It was my father who founded their company, when the lands were beset by hosts of daemons. Formed of pure magic, the daemons of Chaos could arrive and attack at will, and it was the raven heralds who watched for their appearance and took swift word to the army of Aenarion.'

'And they are loyal to you?' said Carathril.

'They are loyal to Nagarythe,' said Malekith. 'For the moment I am content that their cause and ours are the same. Elthyrior brings grave news from ahead. It seems that we have sparked our foes into action. Upon word of our crossing into Nagarythe, a great many cultists quit Anlec and have marched south. They have made their lair in Ealith, south of Anlec. It is an old fortress, one of the ancient gatekeeps built by my father to protect the road we now travel. We cannot reach Anlec without confronting them.'

'There will be a battle?' said Carathril.

'The raven heralds will act as our outriders, and warn of any ambush ahead,' Malekith said, ignoring the obvious question. 'There are none with eyes as keen as the northern riders, and our enemies will not mark their passing. Our foe will not surrender Ealith meekly back to my rule. Send word to the other captains to gather at my tent tonight, for we must make plans for battle.'

Malekith noticed Carathril frown.

'It is right that we be troubled,' the prince said. 'We should not seek this confrontation gladly, but we must prosecute our cause willingly.'

'I am willing,' Carathril assured him. 'I would cast out this blackness with my own life, were that possible.'

'Be not too hasty to surrender life,' Malekith warned. 'It is not through death but through life that we prevail. I have defended this isle for more than a thousand years, and I have seen many of my comrades sell their lives for no gain while those that survive go on to victory and prosperity. I was raised in Anlec, even as daemons slaughtered and corrupted all about me. My first memories are of spear, sword and shield. My first words were war and death. I was anointed with bloodshed and grew up beneath the Sword of Khaine, and I have no doubt that its shadow lies upon me still. Perhaps it is true that my father's line is cursed, and that war will haunt us for eternity.'

'I cannot imagine what it was like to live in those times,' said Carathril. 'The fear, the sacrifice, the pain of so many lost. I must admit, I offer thanks to the gods that it has been so, and ask that I must never endure what you and others endured.'

'You are wise to do so,' said Malekith. 'One does not seek war for its own end, for it leaves nothing but ashes and graves. However, always remember that though civilisation is built upon foundations of peace, it is only protected through the efforts of war. There are forces and creatures that would see us crushed, driven from the face of the world and dragged into an eternity of darkness. These forces cannot be reasoned with, they cannot conceive of liberty, they exist only to dominate and destroy.'

'But the foes we face are not daemons, they are our own people,' said Carathril. 'They breathe, and laugh, and cry as we do.'

'And that is why we shall show them mercy where possible,' Malekith assured him. 'I have faced grave enemies for my entire life. These last years I have wandered far and wide and seen many amazing and terrifying things. In the forests of Elthin Arvan, our companies fought goblin-fiends that rode upon gigantic spiders and I have battled with stinking trolls that can heal the most grievous wounds. Monstrous winged creatures tossed soldiers aside like dolls in the cold wastes of the north, and savage men caked in the blood of their fellows hurled themselves upon our spear tips. We wept at some of the horrors that confronted us, and I have seen seasoned warriors flee in abject terror from foes not of flesh and blood. But I have also seen such heroism that the greatest of sagas cannot do them justice. I have seen a bowman leap upon the back of a bull-headed beast and strike out its eyes with an arrow in his hand. I have seen a mother gut a dozen orcs with a knife to protect her children. I have seen spearmen hold a narrow pass for twenty days against an endless horde of misshapen nightmares. War is bloody and foul, yet it is also full of courage and sacrifice.'

'I hope that I have such bravery,' said Carathril. 'I do not know if I would have the strength to master my fear in the face of such sights.'

'I have no doubt that you do,' Malekith said. 'I see the fire that burns within your heart, the dedication to your duty, and I would have no hesitation in having you fight by my side, Carathril of Lothern.'

As THEY RODE, the path veered westwards and brought them from the forest, and by mid-afternoon the head of the column travelled along a high ridge overlooking the northern domains of Nagarythe. Beneath them was spread Urithelth Orir, the great wilderness of Nagarythe.

For sixty leagues westwards and twenty leagues to the north stretched a desolate moorland, broken by stands of withered trees and majestic outcroppings of black rock. Patches of hardy grasses dotted the dark, thin soil, and banks of reeds found purchase along thin rivulets that cut through the hard earth.

To the east the mountains of the Annulii rose abruptly from the bleak flatness, towering in steep cliffs above the lowlands and rising ever higher and higher to the north, the most distant peaks tipped with a permanent white cap. Clouds were gathered about the mountain peaks, but above Urithelth Orir the skies were blue and clear, and the air bit with autumn chill.

The road broke northwards again, as straight as any arrow across the plains, rising and falling gently, crossing the many streams by wide bridges. As sunfall approached, the column halted and made camp. The light of dozens of campfires soon blazed as night swiftly approached, and streamers of smoke obscured the starry skies. Malekith's pavilion was erected at the centre of the camp, within a ring of tents housing his knights. Silver lanterns were brought out and hung on poles, throwing pools of deep yellow upon the bleak ground.

Here and there, the sound of a lute or harp broke the gloom, but their sound was mournful not cheering. Low voices sang old laments, bringing to mind the woes of the past, preparing the warriors for the sorrows that lay ahead.

—◄ SEVENTEEN ►—

The March to Ealith

As DUSK SETTLED, Carathril wandered the camp, seeking out the imprisoned cultists, wishing to speak again to Drutheira. Yet he could not find them and all of his inquiries were met with ignorance. The elves of Ellyrion and Tiranoc assumed they were in the camp of Nagarythe, while the Naggarothi curtly denied any knowledge of their whereabouts. Reluctantly, Carathril returned to his tent, alone and disheartened.

His camp was not far from the central circle. As he ate a supper that was of basic fare brought from Tor Anroc, for there was no hunting to be had in these parts, he heard sounds of laughter and celebration from the Naggarothi encampment. He heard old battle hymns written during the times of the daemon war, lauding the greatness of Nagarythe and its princes. As he washed down a meal of crisp bread and soft cheese with water from his canteen, a messenger arrived from Malekith to take him to the prince's war council.

As the guards waved him inside, he ducked beneath the canopy of the pavilion and found himself standing upon thick red carpets laid upon the bare earth. The tent was high and golden lanterns hung from chains around the cloth ceiling, bathing all in a yellow glow. Warmth filled the pavilion from a dozen glowing braziers that gave off no smoke, and the air was filled with excited chatter.

Retainers clad in simple blue coats passed through the assembled captains with ewers of wine. Carathril waved aside a proffered goblet and searched the crowd for a familiar face. There were at least a dozen elves, some dressed in the finery of the Anlec knights; a couple from Tiranoc wore blue and white sashes across their armour, as did Carathril; a trio of elves on the far side of the pavilion wore cloaks of deep red and Carathril recognised them as the leaders of the Ellyrian reavers.

He spied Malekith's second-in-command, Yeasir, talking to the Ellyrians, and Carathril cut his way towards them through the scattered clusters of elven warriors, repeatedly turning down more offers of wine.

'Friend Carathril!' Yeasir called out as he approached. He waved a hand at each of the Ellyrians in turn, as he continued. 'Do you know Gariedyn, Aneltain and Bellaenoth?'

'Not by name,' said Carathril with a nod of greeting.

'I have hoped to speak with you, herald,' said the elf identified as Aneltain. 'But you spend so much time closeted with Prince Malekith, I have not had the opportunity. It must be good to have the ear of a prince.'

'I would not say that I have the prince's ear,' replied Carathril, somewhat taken aback. 'Though I do enjoy Prince Malekith's company.'

'And he yours, I would say,' said Yeasir. 'I have barely exchanged five words with him this past week.'

'It was not my intent to monopolise the prince…' began Carathril, but Gariedyn waved away his protestations.

'Do not apologise,' said the Ellyrian captain. 'We are just jealous, that is all. I am sure that if any of us had been chosen as Bel Shanaar's herald we would enjoy similar attention.'

'So, what does the prince have in mind, then?' asked Bellaenoth. 'Who will he choose to lead the attack on Ealith?'

'The knights of Anlec will have that honour, I am sure,' said Yeasir. He thrust his empty goblet towards one of the waiting servants and had it quickly refilled. Swallowing a mouthful, he continued. 'Ealith belongs to Nagarythe, after all, and it would not do for us to be seen skulking at the back like some timid Yvressians.'

'For my part, I would gladly give you the honour,' said Bellaenoth with a sorrowful shake of the head. 'By all accounts, it is a fearsome stronghold. I would not like to be first in line when we come up against its high walls.'

'That is because you do not know Malekith,' Yeasir assured them. 'He is as brave as a Chracian lion, and as strong as a Caledorian dragon. But, most importantly, he is also as cunning as a Sapherian fox. He would not throw us against such daunting fortifications with no plan. No, I am sure that our noble prince has a scheme for rooting out these troublesome cultists without us having to dash ourselves needlessly against the walls of Ealith.'

'Perhaps the good herald has some insight into this clever ploy?' suggested Gariedyn, and all eyes turned to Carathril.

'Me?' he stammered. 'I am not privy to the counsels of Prince Malekith, much as you may seem to think otherwise.'

Their expressions remained unconvinced.

'Besides,' Carathril added, 'it would not be my place to announce such matters when the prince has chosen not to do so. As a herald, my discretion is paramount.'

'So, you do know something,' said Bellaenoth. Something caught his gaze past Carathril's shoulder and Bellaenoth nodded towards the pavilion's entrance. 'Well, we may find out soon enough anyway.'

MALEKITH STRODE INTO the pavilion, swept up a goblet from the tray of a nearby attendant and downed its contents in a long draught. As he placed the goblet back upon the golden tray, his eyes swept the room, lingering on no one person for any length of time.

'My noble captains,' he said, glad that he had their attention immediately. 'My trusted companions. I must beg your forgiveness for an unavoidable act of perfidy. In these troubled times it is hard to judge who one can trust, and so I judge to trust no one. At least, I must say, I did not trust anyone until now. I could not be sure that the spies of our enemies were not within my camp, and so I have been forced to mislead you all.'

A startled murmur crept around the room, and then died away as the prince continued.

'I have known since I left Tor Anroc that Ealith was held by our foes,' Malekith revealed, pacing further into the pavilion. 'I did not want our enemies to be aware of this knowledge, and so I have kept secret counsel with only the raven heralds, whom I would trust with not only my life, but my realm. As I had hoped, it appears that our foes are confident in their position, knowing that we have not marched forth prepared for siege. To their minds, we must labour to make towers and rams to attack their fortress, and await reinforcements and bolt throwers in order to assault their walls. They believe that they have time aplenty to shore up their defences, and for more of their numbers to gather. Secret covens lurk within the forests and hills around Ealith, ready to sally forth to attack our siege works, ambush our supplies and harass our forces. They are wrong.'

The whispering recommenced, this time excited and intrigued. Two servants brought forth a chair of deep red wood, its high back carved with the likeness of a mighty dragon encircling a slender tower, the throne's arms and legs fashioned as the be-scaled and clawed limbs of the drake. Malekith unclasped his black cloak and cast it upon the throne, but did not sit. He turned to face the assembled captains, his eyes narrowed.

'Knowing the deceit upon which our enemies thrive, I have spread false rumour through their minions,' the prince told them. 'Two of our prisoners have escaped upon stolen horses, bearing news to Ealith overheard from the incautious lips of our warriors. News that we march to Enith Atruth, two days to the west, and another two days' ride from Ealith. The citadel itself lies no more than a day's ride to the north, and our escaped captives will have reached its walls before midday tomorrow. Confident that we tarry in our attack, they will not be ready for our strike. By dusk, Ealith will be ours.'

'Excuse me, highness, but an army does not move as swiftly as a solitary rider,' said one of the Ellyrians. 'Even if we could reach Ealith within the day, it would be impossible to conceal our approach.'

'That is true, Arthenreir,' replied the prince, enjoying his theatrical performance. 'It matters not whether we come to Ealith in a day or a hundred days, we have not the strength of arms to force victory through open battle. And it would not be desirable even if it were so, for I wish there to be as little bloodshed as possible on both sides. Guile shall see our fortunes ripen where might alone proves fruitless.'

'I told you,' whispered Yeasir with a smile. Carathril ignored him and listened intently as Malekith continued.

'Our enemies think Ealith secure against attack, but they are wrong. For many centuries the citadel has been abandoned, and its secrets have been forgotten by most. Not by me, nor the raven heralds. Ealith sits upon a spur of rock, reached only by a single causeway that is overlooked by towers and walls. Or so it would seem to our foes.'

Malekith now dropped his voice to a whisper, and met the gazes of those elves closest at hand, as if confiding in each of them alone.

'In fact, there is another entrance to Ealith,' said the prince. 'There is a passage, carved from the rock itself, which leads from the citadel to the outside. It was built as a means for defenders to sally forth to attack a besieging army from the rear, and leads to a hidden cave more than half a mile from the walls. We shall ride before daybreak, a company of no more than a hundred, and under cover of darkness enter this ancient passageway. It will take us into the heart of the enemy, where we will strike with absolute surprise. The army will march in our wake and there will be no escape. We shall slay or capture their leaders and force the rest to surrender. Without the puppeteers to pull their strings, our enemies are cowardly, decadent hedonists with no stomach for battle.'

'Who is to ride, highness?' asked Yeasir.

'The company shall be split thus: forty of Nagarythe, thirty of Ellyrion, and thirty of Tiranoc's finest riders. No more can we guarantee to approach Ealith unseen, and our strength lies in speed and stealth, not numbers.'

Malekith noticed disappointment well up on the face of Carathril. The Lothern captain was an average rider at best, trained to fight with spear and sword, not with lance and horse. However, he was the herald of the Phoenix King and potentially a useful ally. Malekith raised a hand to attract Carathril's attention and smiled.

'My noble comrade Carathril, you will ride with us, as an honorary knight of Nagarythe. I would not have such a fine heart and sure arm left behind on this adventure!'

'You have my eternal gratitude, highness,' said Carathril with a deep bow. 'It will be my honour to ride amongst such noble companions.'

Once the assembled warriors had departed, Malekith sat on his throne. A few moments later, Yeasir led in a small group of elves covered with dark robes. As they pulled back their hoods, Malekith saw that they were the cultists who had surrendered to him.

The prince of Nagarythe smiled. He had more work for them to do.

DARKNESS STILL SWATHED the camp as Malekith set forth with his riders; the sun was hidden behind the mountains and would be for some time to come. Before they had left, the company had assembled on the outskirts of the encampment and three shadow-swathed raven heralds had passed along their line, blackening harnesses and securing loose tack so that no glint or jingle would give them away. They had handed out long, black cloaks for the riders to wear over their armour, and thus concealed, Malekith's expedition had departed in silence and secrecy.

Now the hundred horsemen followed one of the raven heralds along a winding path northwards, heading down the ridge upon which the army had spent the night. They rode swiftly but not recklessly, and Malekith was glad of the sure-footedness of his mount. Late stars glimmered overhead in the pre-dusk grey, visible now that they had left behind the smoke of the camp. The thudding of hooves in the dirt was the only sound to break the still, and Malekith began to relax, calmed by the steady drumming.

As dawn slowly broke above the mountains, Malekith found that they were riding along an overgrown herder's trail through an expanse of low hills that rose up under the long shadow of the mountains. Their path was crisscrossed with rivulets and streams and the soil was more fertile, giving rise to stands of low bushes and thick clumps of sturdy grasses.

They slowed to negotiate this trickier ground, and at points rode in single file to follow in the tracks of the raven herald who led the way. The second rode sentry at the rear, and of the third there was no sign: he had departed in darkness to scout the way ahead.

They halted briefly mid-morning to ease tired limbs and make a hasty breakfast of bread and cold meats, before riding on. By this time, they had cleared the foothills once more and had made good progress across the rocky moors. Between the heat of the sun high in a clear sky, the thin yet warm cloak wrapped tightly about him and the effort of riding, Malekith did not feel the chill touch of autumn, though the breath of the riders and their steeds steamed in the air.

THEY SAW NOT a soul as they rode, although here and there they passed tumbled-down remains of ancient cottages and towers, scattered across the landscape as if discarded by the hand of some god. There was no road to follow, not the slightest track nor path, and it was clear that these lands had long ago been abandoned. They paused once again in the middle of the afternoon, allowing their mounts to water from a swift-moving brook. A few scattered stones marked the remains of an ancient mill beside the waterway; of its wheel and gears, nothing remained.

Carathril's gaze was drawn to a lone hill, not far from the stream, which rose steeply from the yellowing grass: a mound of bare, blackened rock. At its summit, Carathril could just about see a tumbled monolith, its white stone stark against the darkness of the hillock.

'Elthuir Tarai,' whispered a deep voice, causing him to start. One of the raven heralds stood directly behind him. His black horse stood close by, neither grazing nor resting, but alert and ready. The rider's face was all but hidden in the shadow of his deep hood, but Carathril could see a pair of emerald green eyes. It was Elthyrior.

'What did you say?' said Carathril.

'Yonder hill,' said the raven herald, pointing towards the barren knoll. 'It is the Elthuir Tarai, where Aenarion first wielded the Godslayer in battle. A thousand years ago, there was a town here, called Tir Anfirec, and all the lands about were farms and meadows. The daemons came and unleashed foul sorcery upon the ground, and their curse lingers here still. Upon that mount, Aenarion first drew the Sword of Khaine in anger, and struck down a host of the daemons. I am grandson to Menrethor, who fought here beside the king.'

'Then you are a prince?' said Carathril.

'In name only,' said Elthyrior, looking away. 'These were once the lands of my family, now they belong to nobody.'

'What happened to the town?' asked Carathril.

'It is said that the unnatural blood of the daemons seeped into the earth and poisoned it. The filth of their existence stained the fields and rivers, and Tir Anfirec withered and died like a plant without water. Dark magic saturated every granule, root and leaf, so that cattle died of fever, babes were stillborn and no living thing could flourish. Caledor came to this place and erected a lodestone, even as he planned his creation of the vortex. The waystone, like all the others, siphoned away the dark energy of the daemons, and over the centuries life slowly returned. Not enough for people to return, but sufficient for a few blades of grass and the odd insect nest. Then, perhaps fifty years ago, worshippers of the darkness came here and toppled the stone and undid its enchantments. Now the dark magic is returning, gathering again.'

'Why not raise up the stone again?' said Carathril.

'None in Nagarythe have the knowledge or means,' said Elthyrior. 'At least, none with the will or desire to do so. Perhaps there are loremasters in Saphery that have understanding of such things, and when peace prevails once more, they can restore the waystone. I fear that no living thing shall ever grow again upon Elthuir Tarai, for it was upon that slope that Aenarion sealed his pact with Khaine, and the God of Blood will share it with no other.'

Malekith was calling for the riders to mount up once more. With no further word, Elthyrior leapt into his saddle and his horse quickly wheeled away, leaving Carathril alone with his thoughts. He looked again upon that desolate hill and shuddered, pushing from his mind the frightening images the raven herald's tale had conjured.

As THEY WENT further north, the lands became more welcoming, now covered here and there with high yellow grass that reached to the riders' knees as they rode. In the full light of day, this dreary heath was more cheering than the dark wilds they had passed through, and the mood of the company lightened considerably. There were scattered conversations along the column, and here and there the riders even joked and laughed, as if to ward away the apprehension that had grown.

Carathril found himself riding alongside the squadron of Ellyrian reaver knights, beside Aneltain who had been chosen by Malekith to lead them. They were more lightly armoured than the knights of Anlec, wearing only breast-plates and shoulder guards and trusting in their speed and agility to avoid the foe. Their high helms were crested with long feathers taken from the tails of colourful birds. The Ellyrion steeds were uniformly white, not as broad nor tall as the Naggarothi mounts, and were harnessed with blue-lacquered tack. Each reaver knight carried a short thrusting spear with a broad, leaf-shaped head, and a small but powerful bow, with arrows fletched with blue feathers.

Of all the assembled elves, they were the most garru-lous, and chatted freely amongst themselves as they rode. Aneltain was no different and quickly struck up conversa-tion with Carathril.

They talked at first about their homelands, as warriors from different realms naturally do: compared the beauty of their women, the quality of wine and the relative mer-its of their people. Soon their talk moved on to their current surrounds, as both were strangers in these lands, and then onto the Naggarothi themselves.

'They are taciturn, that is for certain,' said Aneltain. 'Of course, by Ellyrian measure, all other elves are tight-lipped, but these Naggarothi will utter only a single word when ten would be natural, and nothing when one would suffice.'

'Prince Malekith seems eloquent enough,' countered Carathril.

'The prince? Sure, he can weave a speech with the best of them,' admitted the Ellyrian. 'But then, he has been Bel

Shanaar's ambassador to the High King of the dwarfs, and from what I hear they are a race not known for their wagging tongues. I suspect he's spent the last two hundred years having to talk just to fill their silence. No, there's something different about these Naggarothi, some shadow upon their spirit that makes me feel uneasy.'

'You distrust them?' said Carathril, his voice dropping to a whisper as he glanced at the knights of Anlec only a short distance ahead.

'That is too strong a word for it,' replied Aneltain. 'I would gladly fight beside them, and I would trust them to watch my back. No, they just make me feel uneasy. There is a grimness about their mood that disturbs me. They don't laugh enough for my liking, and when they do it is with dark humour.'

'It is impossible to understand them, I admit,' said Carathril. 'We cannot hope to think what drives such folk. They are people of Aenarion. Many of them, like the prince, fought at his side. Even those too young to have been raised in those benighted times were raised by parents that were. Perhaps they are right not to laugh, for they have much still to grieve for. They suffered more than most, and their scars run deep.'

'Laughter cures all ills,' said Aneltain. 'It lifts the spirits and banishes dread.'

'I fear there are some ills too heavy to be lifted,' said Carathril. 'I for one am glad that I ride beside them and not against them. A great many of them quit these shores for the new colonies, driven by the need for battle, keen to escape the peace. I cannot understand the mind of one who seeks such peril, but it is the way of the Naggarothi to hail the warrior above other callings. I have no doubt that each one of those riders ahead has drawn more blood across the seas than either of us will do in our lifetimes.'

'That is for sure, and it makes them no less disconcerting,' said Aneltain. 'I have heard that in Anlec they still practise the rites set down by Aenarion: that a spear and sword are forged upon the birth of every child and they are presented to them upon their twentieth year. They learn the names of their weapons before those of their parents, and for their first years sleep upon the inside of a shield as a crib. But, as you say, it is better that we ride to battle with them than against them.'

Having come to this agreement, they then descended into a debate concerning the unique customs of their own homes, and the afternoon passed swiftly.

THE LEAGUES SWEPT past as they rode ever northwards, and the sun was fast dipping towards the west when Malekith called them to halt once more. The company gathered in a circle about their leader. None of the raven heralds were to be seen.

'Night comes quickly, and we must be ready,' the prince announced. 'We are yet out of sight of Ealith, and the raven heralds clear a path through the pickets of the foe so that we might pass. Once they return and bring word that all is well, we ride with all speed. Sariour rises above the mountains before midnight and we must be within the passageway before she spills her celestial light upon us. We cannot know what awaits us inside, and once we move on, I cannot give you clearer orders, for we must move as silently as ghosts.'

Malekith turned about on the spot, meeting the gazes of his company with a fierce stare.

'I have but these words for you,' he said. 'Spare those that surrender, spare not those that resist. I cannot say what horrors we might face, what depravities these cultists have already performed within the walls of their fortress.

Let nothing distract you. Guard your fellows and they will guard you. Look to your swords for guidance, for though we are merciful I would have none of us fall this night. Pray to Asuryan, offer thanks to Isha, but remember to save a word for Khaine, for it is into his crimson realm that we must ride tonight!'

With these grim words still ringing in their ears, the company waited in silence, as the sun dropped beyond the sea and plunged them into starlight. A wind grew steadily, blowing chill from the north, and Malekith hugged his cloak tighter about himself. The riders checked each other's gear, to ensure no metal would catch the light and no rogue piece of harness would make noise at an untimely moment.

Malekith dismounted and stretched his legs, pacing to and fro as he waited for the order to move on. He did not linger long, for soon one of the raven heralds returned, almost invisible in the darkness. The prince mounted again, his legs sore from many days spent riding, and soon they were off at a trot on the last stage of their journey.

⤙ EIGHTEEN ⤚

A Foe Revealed

THE RIDERS OF Malekith skirted eastwards before heading south, having circled around Ealith to come at the fortress from the north. Through the gloom, the prince could see the castle in the distance, lit by fires from within so that the walls seemed to glow yellow and red. The keep was upon a great spur of rock that jutted several hundred feet from the surrounding grasslands. Laughter and shrill cries could be heard in the distance and strange shadows danced about the towers.

Upon its highest pinnacle a slender tower reached into the stars, and a strange green light emanated from its narrow windows. Malekith flinched as that light flickered for a moment, filled with the unshakeable belief that he had somehow been seen. Such a thing was impossible though, for the company were as shadows, swathed as they were by the dark cloaks of the raven heralds.

A stand of trees obscured Ealith from view, and Malekith was forced to duck as they rode beneath the boughs into the heart of the copse. Here was almost utter blackness, save for a few glimmers of starlight that broke through the almost solid canopy of leaves. The company dismounted, following the lead of their prince, and walked their steeds further into the trees.

At their centre there rose a great oak, as mighty as a guard tower, and Malekith led his horse between two massive roots and to the others he seemed to disappear. In fact where they thought there was earth and tree was a large opening, as wide and as high as a city gate, the roots of the ancient oak forming a twisting archway. Beyond lay the passageway, walled with grey stone, high enough to mount once more and for three riders to move abreast. At their head, Malekith drew his sword and its blue flame glimmered in the darkness like a beacon. Lanterns were passed down the line and one rider in ten set a glimmering light upon his saddlebags so that those behind could follow. As will o' wisps the company wound along the corridor, plunging deeper and deeper beneath the earth.

Soon the cut stone of the entrance gave way to bare rock, carefully but plainly carved by unknown hands. Malekith felt the corridor rising again and it began to turn to the right in a tightening spiral, and narrowed to the point that they had to ride single file for a short while. As the passage levelled out, at the same height as Ealith's inner walls, it widened again so that five horses could walk side-by-side. Malekith raised a hand to halt the column.

Ahead was a wall of bare rock, with no sign of door or gate. Malekith sat upon his horse in front of the wall and began to chant softly; ancient spell-words whose meanings were lost on the others. As the prince spoke, he traced lines through the air with the tip of his gleaming sword and where it passed a flickering trail of blue fire lingered, sparkling in the darkness. A rune of fire hung in the air, growing in intensity. With a final word, Malekith slashed through the sigil with his blade and a blinding flash filled the corridor. A wide archway now stood where the wall had been, and beyond lay the courtyard of Ealith.

'Ride forth!' shouted Malekith, heeling his mount into a gallop and leaping through the archway.

THE COMPANY BROKE into a charge, lowering spears and lances as they thundered from the secret passageway into the castle. Malekith held his blade at the ready, unconsciously ducking slightly as he passed through the portal though it was easily high enough for a rider to pass.

The courtyard was thrown into pandemonium. A dozen fires burned in bronze braziers, giving off an acrid smoke. Vile runes had been daubed in blood upon the white walls, and clusters of wailing prisoners were chained to each other in small groups. The cultists were taken completely unawares; some had been tending the braziers, others tormenting their captives.

Everywhere cultists leapt up with cries of alarm and shouts of terror as the knights crashed across the pale flagstones with a wall of lances and spear tips, striking down all within reach. Malekith bellowed wordlessly as he cut left and right, despatching a cultist with each blow. The ringing of steel echoed from the high walls, mixed with war cries and the screams of the wounded. Malekith singled out a fresh target: an elf with a pair of serrated daggers in his hands, naked but for a brightly patterned cloak and kilt, standing menacingly over a cowering elf maiden. The cultist turned his head as Malekith charged, his face a mask of dread. The prince did not hesitate, and as he raced past, he slashed downwards with his blade, catching the cultist a deadly cut across the neck.

Panting with excitement, Malekith slowed his steed and cast about for another foe. Dozens of bodies littered the ground, pools of blood spreading across the white paving. Everywhere enemies were flinging down their blades and hurling themselves to their knees with shouts of surrender. A few tried to resist further and were swiftly and mercilessly overwhelmed by the knights. Malekith jumped from his saddle and dashed towards the doors of the central citadel, which towered two hundred feet above the courtyard.

'Ellyrians, stand guard!' the prince shouted. 'All else, follow me!'

The gate had been barred from the inside, but this proved little barrier to the prince of Nagarythe. His sword blazed with magical energy as he raised it high. He brought the enchanted blade down and struck a mighty blow against the door in an explosion of blue fire that shattered the keep gate into charred planks. Without hesitation, Malekith leapt into the hallway beyond.

Though mere moments had passed since the attack had begun, the cultists were recovering quickly. Inside the citadel was a great staircase that spiralled to the upper levels of the tower. Archways led from the entrance hall to chambers all around, and scores of cultists poured from these rooms in a shrieking wave that engulfed Malekith and his company.

Screeching like a wild cat, a female cultist with red body paint and a shaven head hurled herself at Malekith, spitting and biting. He smashed the back of his hand across her face and sent her hurtling to the ground, where she lay unmoving. He barely parried a dagger aimed for his throat, and cut down the ranting zealot who wielded it.

All around the elves of Malekith fought back to back, as more of their companions tried to press through the splintered doors to aid them.

As the prince swept out with Avanuir there was another detonation of magical fire, and a dozen cultists were launched high through the air, trailing smoke and burnt flesh, to crash against the walls. Malekith raised up his left hand and blue flame danced from his fingertips. With howls of pain and fear the cultists hurled themselves away, some prostrating themselves and gibbering abjectly, others running back through the doorways to escape the wrath of the prince.

'Upwards!' cried Malekith, pointing towards the stairway.

Carathril joined the prince as he leapt up the steps three at a time, followed by a handful of knights. Others led pursuits into the chambers below. The next level of the citadel was devoid of life and they continued upwards until they reached a wide chamber at the top of the tower. The stairs led them into the middle of a circular room that filled the space of the tower. Here lanterns blazed with the green radiance Malekith had seen from outside, and the eerie light showed scores of elves in horrifying acts of torture and debauchery; a plateau of vileness that would be forever etched into Malekith's memory. All that he heard and all that he had yet seen was not enough to prepare him for the horrors he witnessed in his own lands.

A high priestess, lithe and athletic, presided over the despicable ceremony from a dais littered with corpses and blood. Her white robes were spattered with gore, and a daemonic bronze mask covered her face. Her eyes glowed with a pale yellow light from within, and her pupils were tiny points of blackness in pools of luminescence.

In one hand, she held a crooked staff, wrought from bones and iron, and tipped with a horned skull with three eye sockets. In the other, she wielded a curved dagger still slick with the blood of many sacrifices.

Malekith charged across the chamber, cutting down any cultist who barred his path. He was but a few steps from the dais when the priestess thrust forwards the tip of her staff, and a bolt of pure blackness leapt out and struck the prince full in the chest. The prince's heart felt like it would explode. With a cry of pain torn from his lips, Malekith faltered and fell to his knees. He was as much shocked as hurt, for he knew of no wizard who could best the sorcerous abilities granted him by the Circlet of Iron.

He gazed in amazement at the priestess. She stepped down from the dais with languid strides and walked slowly towards the injured prince, the tip of her staff fixed upon him.

'My foolish child,' she sneered.

THE PRIESTESS LET the sacrificial dagger slip from her fingers to clatter in a shower of crimson droplets upon the floor. With her hand thus freed, she pulled off her mask and tossed it aside. Carathril gave a yelp of astonishment. Though caked with blood, the priestess's lustrous black hair spilled across her bare shoulders. Her face was pristine, the very image of beauty. In her were aristocratic bearing and divine magnificence combined.

Carathril felt himself spellbound. Around him, the other knights gazed dumbly at this apparition of perfection, similarly ensorcelled.

'Mother?' whispered Malekith, his sword slipping from his numb fingers.

'My son,' she replied with a wicked smile that sent a shiver down Carathril's spine; of lust and fear in equal measure. 'It is very rude of you to butcher my servants so callously. Your time amongst the barbarians has robbed you of all manners.'

Malekith said nothing but simply stared up at Morathi, wife of Aenarion, his mother.

'You have been weak, Malekith, and I have been forced to rule in your stead,' she said. 'You trot across the world at the bidding of Bel Shanaar, ever eager to risk your life for him, while your lands fall into ruin. You grovel on bended knee to ask this upstart Phoenix King to rule your own realm. You are a cur, happy to eat the scraps from the tables of Tiranoc, Yvresse and Eataine while your people starve. You build cities across the ocean, and navigate the wide world, while your home festers in filth and decay. You are not fit to be a prince, much less a king! Truly your father's blood does not run in your veins, for no true son of Anlec would allow himself to be so cowed.'

Malekith looked up at his mother, his face twisted with pain.

'Kill her,' he managed to spit through gritted teeth.

As if those words had broken a spell, Carathril found himself able to move again. Sheathing his sword, he snatched his bow from the quiver across his back and set an arrow to the string. As he pulled back his arm, Morathi swung her staff towards him and he leapt aside just as a dark bolt cracked the stone of the floor where he had been standing a heartbeat earlier. As if also broken from trances, the cultists lounging around the room leapt to their feet with snarls and shouts. Malekith pushed himself to his feet, but another blast of Morathi's sorcery hurled him across the floor with a clatter of armour.

This inner coven fought with a feral tenacity, deranged from narcotic vapours and their dedication to Morathi. Carathril tossed aside his bow and drew his sword again as an elf with gem-headed pins piercing her lips and cheeks ran at him with a flaming brand in her hands. Shouts and shrieked curses filled the room and pungent smoke billowed as braziers were knocked over in the struggle. Carathril felt the heat of the brand in the cultist's hands wash over him as he ducked a sweeping attack.

He struck out at the elf's naked legs and cut her down at the knee, sending her toppling to the floor. Even lying upon her back, Carathril looming over her, she hurled abuse and thrust the brand at him. He pushed the tip of his blade into her chest and she slumped to the marble flagstones.

'There will be no welcome for you in Anlec,' Morathi snarled above the din, having retreated to the dais. 'Go back to that usurper and do not return.'

Malekith gave a roar that nearly deafened Carathril and hacked with wild abandon at the cultists who had surrounded him, dismembering and decapitating with wide, sweeping blows. A gap opened up in the melee between the prince and his mother and he stalked towards her, his sword shining with magical energy. A look of panic swept the sorceress's face and she began to back away. Even as Malekith's front foot fell upon the dais, Morathi raised her staff above her head in both hands and a shadow enveloped her, spreading like diaphanous wings to either side. Her body melted and dissipated as those spectral wings beat thrice and swept upwards, and then she was gone.

More knights of Anlec raced up from the stairwell and soon the remaining cultists were slain or pacified. Carathril looked at Malekith, where he still stood upon the dais. Where he had expected to see the prince still in shock or perhaps wrought with grief, instead Malekith was a picture of cold fury. The flame of his blade burned white-hot as he gripped it in both hands before him, and his eyes glittered with barely controlled magic.

The prince's stare moved across the room until it fell upon Carathril, who flinched at Malekith's fell gaze. Carathril was locked in that stare, fixed by two raging orbs of hate, and for a long heartbeat the captain thought that the prince would attack him. The moment passed and Malekith slumped, his sword falling from his fingertips to ring upon the stone floor.

'Nagarythe has fallen into darkness,' he whispered, and now his eyes were filled with tears.

AT DAWN, MALEKITH stood upon the rampart of Ealith and watched the sun rising over the Annulii. In the light of day, the events of the past night seemed dim, distorted. He could barely bring himself to believe that Morathi had been the architect behind the rise of the cults. Now that he considered it, he realised he should not have been at all surprised. It was just like his mother: a network of spies and agents across all of Ulthuan, power over the weak princes and their armies. He cursed himself for allowing Morathi to spread her dark touch into Athel Toralien and feared what he had left behind in Elthin Arvan.

Yet there was logic to her plan that Malekith could not dispel. Had he not already started to use the cultists to his own end? The army of Nagarythe was but one weapon, an unsubtle one at that; the cults of luxury were a far more insidious force and all the more dangerous for it. Morathi had told him as much on her visit to the colonies. Religion and belief could be exploited for power, he had but to steel himself against his distaste to wield them.

A shadow moved up the road towards the citadel and Malekith saw that it was a swift-moving rider: one of the raven heralds. He watched as the dark figure raced up the causeway and through the gates. It was not long before Elthyrior strode up the steps to the wall and gave the prince a nod of acknowledgement.

'Grave news, Malekith,' said the raven herald. 'Ealith is ours, but Nagarythe rises up in support of Morathi.'

'How so?' demanded the prince.

'Some of my company have been corrupted by your mother,' Elthyrior admitted. 'It was they who brought us here, to lure you into the clutches of Morathi. We cannot know her intent, but I believe she sought to turn you to her cause.'

'In that she has failed,' said the prince. 'I have escaped her trap.'

'Not yet,' warned Elthyrior. 'The cults are strong and much of the army is loyal to your mother. Even now they march on Ealith, seeking to surround you and destroy you. There is no sanctuary here.'

'Thank you, Elthyrior,' said Malekith. 'If I could ask but another favour of you. Ride forth with those you know to be loyal to me. Gather what warriors and princes you can and send them south to Tiranoc.'

'And you?' asked Elthyrior.

Malekith did not reply for a moment, for what he was about to say pained him more than any physical wound.

'I must retreat,' he said after a long while. 'I am not yet ready to challenge Morathi and we cannot be caught here.'

As MALEKITH ORDERED, so it was. The army marched westwards with all speed, ever aware that ahead and behind the worshippers of the forbidden gods were gathering in greater numbers. At Thirech Malekith faced a motley army of several thousand, but the cultists were poorly led and easily shattered by the charges of Malekith's knights, quickly fleeing into the fields and forests around the town.

For four days and five nights Malekith's host marched onwards without relent, seeking the harbour at Galthyr.

Just after dawn on the fifth day after the battle at Ealith, the army rode into sight of Galthyr. Malekith ordered the army to wait out of bowshot from the walls. On the prince's orders, Yeasir rode slowly towards the gate, shielding his eyes against the glare of the morning sun reflected from the white walls. Figures moved upon the parapet, with bows drawn. Yeasir reined his horse to a halt less than a stone's throw from the gate tower.

'I am Yeasir, captain of Malekith!' he called out. 'Stand ready to receive the prince of Nagarythe!'

There was no reply for quite some time, until several new figures appeared upon the gatehouse battlement and stared down at the newcomer. There was a brief consultation between the group, and then one raised a curled golden horn to his lips and let free a clear, resounding note. At the same time, a pennant broke free and fluttered from the flagpole, silver and black.

'The clarion of Anlec!' laughed Malekith. 'And the banner of my house!'

A great cheer welled up from the army as Malekith waved them forwards and the gates opened before them. At a gallop they raced along the road, passing swiftly into the town beyond, the rest of the amy marching with haste behind them. No sooner had the last of them passed than the gates swung closed again with a mighty crash.

Galthyr was half-ruined, with many buildings burnt or collapsed. Wounded soldiers were gathered in the city's squares, tended to by healers of Isha. Malekith spied Prince Durinne walking amongst the casualties and hailed Galthyr's commander as he dismounted.

'I see that we have not been fighting alone,' said Malekith.

'Indeed not,' said Durinne, shaking Malekith's hand. 'Your fleet is safe in the harbour, though only by the valiant efforts of my warriors.'

'Morathi's cultists?' asked Malekith.

'Some amongst the city's populace were her creatures and we drove them out,' explained Durinne. 'They returned two days ago with the armies of Prince Kheranion and Turael Lirain. The prince demanded that I open the gates and surrender Galthyr to his authority. He did not take kindly to having arrows shot at him...'

'You have my thanks,' said Malekith. 'It seems that the list of my allies grows shorter each day. I have not room on my ships for many more, but you are welcome to leave with me.'

'Galthyr can stand for a while yet,' said Durinne. 'When you have left there is little of value here for Morathi to covet. There are other ports already under her sway.'

'Yet she might wish to see you destroyed out of spite for resisting her,' said Malekith. 'Come with me.'

'I will not abandon my city or my people!' Durinne said. 'When the time comes to leave, I have the means to make it happen. Do not spare any more thought on my wellbeing, Malekith.'

Malekith laid a hand on Durinne's shoulder, the gesture expressing the gratitude he felt better than any words he could say.

MALEKITH WAS IN no mood to tarry in Galthyr, for he was sure that even now other ships would be making their way down the coast to blockade the port. Only a few hundred townsfolk remained, but Malekith trusted them not and would not allow them to evacuate upon the ships. The tide and wind were fair, so that no sooner had the host arrived at Galthyr than they left upon *Indraugnir* and another two great dragonships, and seven hawkships. Three more hawkships Malekith sent north, to forestall any pursuing fleet.

Heading south for several days, Malekith's weary force was met by ships from the Tiranoc fleet and escorted to the port of Athel Reinin. Here Malekith left the greater part of his knights, and sent the Ellyrians back to their homeland, warning them not to attack Nagarythe on their own, but to protect the passes across the mountains. Carathril and the charioteers of Tiranoc, who had been forced to burn their chariots at Galthyr, formed a guard for the prince and they rode with all haste. Messages were sent ahead by hawks from the watch towers of Athel Reinin, carrying brief word of what had happened and counselling Bel Shanaar to send troops to his northern border.

ELEVEN DAYS AFTER fighting for his life in Ealith, Malekith found himself back once again in the council chamber of the Phoenix King. He was still shocked at all that had happened; it hardly seemed possible that his world could have changed so much in so little time. He felt sick at the thought of the treachery of Morathi. The prince had requested private audience with the Phoenix King, and had asked Carathril to accompany him in his role as herald to Bel Shanaar, to provide unbiased account. The king was sat upon his throne, dejected and weary, while the prince and Carathril sat upon chairs in front of him.

'You understand that while Morathi holds power, you will never regain Nagarythe?' Bel Shanaar said upon the conclusion of Malekith's tale. 'And to end her grip, she must be imprisoned or slain.'

Malekith did not answer immediately but stood up and paced away from the throne. He despised Bel Shanaar, and despised himself more for needing his help. Whatever his feelings for the Phoenix King, it was clear to Malekith that he would never take his rightful place unless he reigned over Nagarythe once more. He could not fight Morathi alone, and so he was forced to humble himself before this usurper who now sat before him. The simple truth was that Malekith needed Bel Shanaar and would have to put aside his own ambitions for a time. Morathi had abandoned her son and he no longer owed her any loyalty.

'I disown her!' Malekith declared, spinning on his heel. 'Ever she has clawed for power, and whispered in my ear that it is I who should wear that cloak and crown. From the moment of Aenarion's death, she has ceaselessly pushed me to rule this isle. You remember how she screamed and railed when I was the first to bend my knee to you, and ever since she has sought to control me, to force me to power so that she might be queen again. I know not why my father wed her, for she is conniving and vain, and for all my life I remember nothing but her sharp tongue and unbridled ambition. She has cast me aside, and even now, I suspect, she raises up some other puppet in my place. She will not relent until she holds sway over all of Ulthuan, and that is something that I shall not abide.'

'And yet, she is for all that, still your mother,' said Bel Shanaar with concern upon his face. 'If it comes to such, would you be able to drive your blade through her heart? Would your sword arm remain strong as you struck off her head?'

'It must be done, and I would have no other do it,' replied Malekith. 'There is a wicked irony that I should send from this world she who brought me into it. Such considerations are yet far from our immediate concern, for Nagarythe must be reclaimed first. I do not know what hold she has over the other princes and nobles of Nagarythe. I hope that some still resist her, but they will be scattered and few. She will twist and distort my actions to those who waver, so that it appears that it is I who is the aggressor. Our folk are loyal but they are not imaginative. We are raised to obey orders, not to ask questions, yet there are many still who would raise their banners beside their true prince. I shall march to Anlec and overthrow the witch-queen!'

─◄ NINETEEN ►─

Malekith's War

IT WAS TOO late in the year for Malekith to mount another expedition into his homeland, and so he spent the winter gathering what troops he could from the other princes, while all the while the raven heralds slipped across the border to bring news of what passed in the north. Such reports were disquieting, for it seemed that now she had revealed herself as the witch-sorceress she had long been, Morathi had thrown aside all regard for pretences and now wholly embraced her dark nature.

Nagarythe seethed with activity and to Malekith's further dismay, when spring finally came, unsettling word arrived from the colonies that the same racial ennui that had so beset Ulthuan was now taking hold in the cities to the east. In response to Malekith's requests for troops, Alandrian could only send a fraction of the Naggarothi army from Athel Toralien; the rest he needed to guard against growing numbers of orcs moving into Elthin Arvan from the south.

Other fighters joined the prince's army from Nagarythe; individually and by company they had cautiously made their way south into Tiranoc, risking not only the wrath of Morathi but also the ire of the Tiranoc army guarding the border against any who crossed. Malekith had hoped for many more, but it seemed as if a good many of his former captains and lieutenants were content to serve his mother, either in loyalty or out of fear, while a cadre of princes still faithful to Malekith were isolated in the mountains of Nagarythe, gathered under the banner of the lords of House Anar.

Malekith had learned well the lesson of Ealith. He knew that the army under his command could not march directly from Tiranoc to Anlec, for the host of Nagarythe would be prepared for such an attack. Yet Malekith did not let despair grip his counsel, and as he sought for support from the other princes, he paid especial attention to befriend Haradrin of Eataine, who had at his command the greatest fleet of the elves and the staunch Lothern Sea Guard. Malekith still had *Indraugnir* under his charge, and with several more dragonships from Lothern he was sure that he would be able to overpower the Nagarythe fleet. Malekith brooded a long while on what few advantages he had, and by the time spring began to thaw the snow in the mountains he had envisioned a bold plan of action.

It began with the army of Tiranoc forming into hosts not far from the Naganath. Knowing well that Morathi's spies and magic would discern such movement, Malekith hoped to lure the Naggarothi into believing that an attack was imminent, and thus draw their forces southwards.

* * *

IN THE LAST days of winter, Malekith rode alone into the Annulii east of Tor Anroc. He took with him the Circlet of Iron, and headed into the high peaks. He found himself a sheltered spot and sat upon the ground out of the biting wind. Placing the circlet upon his head, Malekith closed his eyes and allowed the ancient artefact to direct his mind.

Malekith's view raced over the plains of Tiranoc, where frost still clung to the grass. To the Naganath his mind's eye flew, over the icy waters into Nagarythe. He saw the armies of Morathi assembling in the Biannan Moor, and pickets stationed along the length of the river to watch the movements of the Tiranoc hosts. Westwards he spied an army encamped about the walls of Galthyr, though the besiegers seemed content merely to contain Durinne and his army. Further northwards towns and villages were ransacked for supplies and the cultists presided over bloody ceremonies in praise of the cytharai.

Then to Anlec came the prince's vision. In cages of iron throughout the city great beasts from the mountains prowled and roared: savage manticores and screeching griffons, many-headed hydras and hissing chimerae. Around the cages clustered beastmasters with vicious goads and barbed whips, tormenting their captives and feeding them on raw elf flesh. Smiths laboured at magically white-hot fires upon armour plates for the gigantic war beasts, and forged spiked collars with heavy chains. Leatherworkers fashioned sturdy saddles and harnesses studded with rivets and adorned with bones.

Around and about the city were grisly altars to the likes of Ereth Khial, Meneloth, Nethu and other grim deities. Bloodstained chalices stood upon tables draped with cloths of skin, and braziers sputtered with bloodied hearts and charring bones. Wretched and crying, lines of elves in chains and tattered rags were dragged before those savage sacrificial shrines to be cast upon blazing pyres or shredded with wicked daggers in praise of hungry gods.

All was watched over by the cruel nobility of Nagarythe. Princes in dark robes sat upon black destriers draped with silver caparisons, while masked priests with daubed runes upon their naked skin chanted supplications and pleas. The stones of the pavements were stained red, and piles of bones gathered rotting in the gutters to be gnawed upon by impish familiars and scrawny hounds.

As he turned his gaze upon the central tower, the palace of Aenarion, Malekith found his view obscured by a great shadow. He heard a whispering voice: his mother's. He strained to hear what she was saying, but could discern nothing but a murmur. The power of the circlet granted Malekith unprecedented power, and he shuddered to think what unspeakable pacts his mother had made for her own sorcery to blind him.

THE PRINCE SENT word to Bel Shanaar that the Phoenix King should move a greater part of his army to the border. Over the following days Malekith spied upon the movements of the Naggarothi with the circlet. Once he was sure that the legions of Nagarythe marched for the border to protect against attack, Malekith returned to Tor Anroc. He sent swift-flying message hawks to Lothern, ordering *Indraugnir* and a sizeable fleet to set sail and head northwards around the western coast of Ulthuan. Their course was set for Galthyr. Once more using the crown from the north, Malekith saw the Naggarothi fleet gathering about the port, expecting an attack from the sea. More warriors were drawn to the siege, to contest any landing that might be made.

Guided by secret commands from Malekith the raven heralds sowed fear and confusion in the midst of the enemy. They attacked supplies and waylaid companies marching to join the scattered armies. They burned freshly growing crops in the fields and intercepted messengers riding between the Naggarothi commanders and Anlec. Their attacks were concentrated to the west and south, to further the illusion being spun by Malekith's manoeuvres.

Malekith's true attack came not from the west or the south, but from the east. In small companies, under cover of darkness over the course of many nights, the prince moved the greater part of his host into the mountains of Ellyrion. They hid in farms and villages close to the mountains, supported by food stockpiled by Prince Finudel.

When the first moon of the new spring rose, Malekith rode to Dragon Pass, the Caladh Enru, two hundred miles south of Anlec. There he unfurled the banner of Anlec and rallied his army for the attack.

Many thousands strong numbered the host, and amongst them rode princes of Nagarythe and Tiranoc, Ellyrion and Eataine. Sapherian wizards had joined the venture, Thyriol amongst them. As Malekith had foreseen, the possibility of him creating an alliance with Ellyrion had not been envisaged by Morathi and the attack came as a total surprise. In a single day, the garrison of Arir Tonraeir at the western end of Dragon Pass was overrun, and the army of Malekith marched for Anlec.

The army turned northwards, past the twin peaks of Anul Nagrain and across the river Haruth into the plains of Khiraval. Here there had once been farms and pastures for the herds of Nagarythe, but now all had fallen into ruin under the rule of Morathi and the cults. The tumbled remains of abandoned farmsteads jutted from the overgrown fields like broken teeth, and packs of ferocious wolves and monstrous bears had come down out of the mountains to claim Khiraval as their own. The army marched along a highway broken by weeds and marred by cracks and holes. It took them through deserted villages, the empty doors and windows gaping at them like accusing black eyes. The more he saw of what had befallen his proud kingdom, the greater was Malekith's ire.

The Naggarothi commanders in the south were now caught in a horrifying situation. If they were to move north to counter Malekith's attack, they would turn their backs on the Tiranoc hosts at the border. In the end they opted to keep their positions, trusting to the army and defences of Anlec to fend off Malekith's force.

With news coming from the raven heralds that the way ahead to Anlec was clear, Malekith and his army pressed on. Across Khiraval and then north-east towards Anlec through the muddy fens of Menruir they marched. Within fifteen days of crossing into Nagarythe, Malekith's host reached mighty Anlec, the immense capital.

Malekith trusted to the valour of his followers and the poor training of the defenders, who for the most part he reckoned to be wild cultists and not the professional warriors he had artfully drawn far to the south. There was no time to waste, for it would not be long before companies were brought back from Galthyr, and the captains in the south realised that Bel Shanaar had no desire for a costly assault across the Naganath. There was no time for siege to be set, nor any reason to expend energy on pointless parley.

As he had so often done before, Malekith struck hard and fast in his attempt to secure victory.

As the army of Malekith arranged itself for the attack, a clear spring sky bathed the black marble buildings of Anlec, glimmering on a coat of late frost. Silver and black banners snapped in the cold wind from atop the many towers around the high walls, while sentries patrolled back and forth clad in blackened scale and golden helms. The fortress-city reverberated to the tramp of booted feet and the scrape of metal as regiments practised drills in the open squares. The cries of their lieutenants echoed from the stone walls and mingled with the crackle of sacrificial pyres and screams of howling prisoners.

Fearsome was the citadel, for it had been built by Aenarion with the aid of Caledor Dragontamer and was so wrought that no approach was left undefended. Eighty high towers and many miles of thick walls surrounded the city, yet only three gates controlled access in and out, each surrounded by bastions filled with war machines and troops.

The approach to each gate was fraught with peril, for walls extended outwards from the curtain of Anlec and provided points from which the defenders could shoot upon the road for half a mile. Isolated towers, each surrounded by stake-filled ditches, were built in a ring of outer defences, each positioned so that its war engines could cover the next.

Within the circle of towers there was dug a great moat, fifty paces wide. No mere water filled this obstacle, but magical green flames that hissed and crackled fiercely. Only one drawbridge crossed the fire ditch on each road, and this was protected by a keep every bit as fearsome as the gatehouses of the city.

For all the forbidding defences of Anlec, Malekith showed no fear. He sat astride his steed at the front of his army, clad in his golden armour, the circlet of sorcery upon his head, Avanuir blazing in his hand. Behind him were two thousand of his knights, veterans all, hardened in the colonies to the east and led by captains who had fought with Malekith in the chill northlands. They were garbed in golden scale armour and cloaked with purple and black. Their lances glowed with enchantments and runes of protection burned upon their shields. Grimfaced, they eyed the dark citadel of Anlec without dread.

To the north and south of the knights were Malekith's companies of spears, seven thousand in all. Led by Yeasir, they formed up into ranks ten deep, pennants fluttering above them, the sounds of silver horns ringing out the orders. Yeasir strode back and forth along the line, reminding them that they fought for the true ruler of Anlec, exhorting them to show no mercy and to stay firm in the face of their despicable foes. Behind the spears were the lines of archers, three thousand of them, their black bows strung, their quivers heavy with arrows.

Further to the north rode the reaver knights of Ellyrion. Prince Finudel and Princess Athielle had eagerly offered to join Malekith's host, and they trotted forwards at the head of two thousand of their followers. In his hand Finudel held Cadrathi, the starblade lance his father had wielded in battle alongside Aenarion. Athielle waved forwards her troop with the shining white blade Amreir, the winterblade that her mother had used to slay the daemon prince Akturon. White and blue banners flew above the cavalry, emblazoned with images of golden horses. The Ellyrians' steeds were eager, stamping and neighing, and the reaver knights chatted amiably amongst themselves, showing no sign of concern at the imposing fortress confronting them.

The southern wing of Malekith's army was led by Bathinair, prince of Yvresse. He sat astride a monstrous griffon, taken from the mountains of the Annulii as a hatchling and raised to be his war mount in Tor Yvresse.

Redclaw was its name and it was a majestic beast. Its body was that of an immense hunting cat, thrice the size of a horse, patterned with black and white stripes. Its head was that of an eagle, with a high crest of red and blue feathers, and its forelegs were as the talons of some mighty bird of prey, with crimson claws like curved swords. Two wide wings of grey and black feathers swept out from its broad shoulders, between which Bathinair sat mounted upon a throne of white wood, the banners of Yvresse and his house fluttering from its back. He held the spear of ice, Nagrain, its silvered shaft gleaming in the morning light, its tip a blazing crystal stronger than any metal. Redclaw threw back its head and gave a deafening screech, and clawed at the earth in anticipation of the hunt.

Bathinair had not come alone from Yvresse and with him stood another two thousand warriors armed with long spears and carrying blue shields, clad in white robes of mourning.

Charill, one of the princes of Chrace, had come also. He stood upon the back of a chariot pulled by four majestic lions from the mountains of his lands. Each was the size of a horse, and as white as snow. They roared and snarled, pacing eagerly in their harnesses. He wielded the fabled axe Achillar, whose double-headed blade crackled with lightning in his hands. Beside him stood his son, Lorichar, bearing the banner of Tor Achare: the head of a lion in silver thread upon a scarlet background. Both wore long cloaks of lion fur, edged with black leather and hung with many jewelled pendants. Other nobles upon lion chariots flanked the prince, each dour warrior armed with axe and spear and clad in golden mail.

With them came huntsmen from the mountains: blue-eyed warriors with long locks of golden hair bound into plaits, with lion pelts upon their shoulders. They wore silvered breastplates with lion designs, and short kilts threaded with gold. The lion warriors carried heavy axes of differing designs, etched with runes and hung with braided tassels. Their demeanour was as fierce as their namesakes, and they gripped their weapons with eager determination.

Lastly came the princes of Saphery: Merneir and Eltreneth, led by Thyriol. They were mounted upon pegasi: winged horses taken from the highest peaks of the Annulii. Glittering capes of many colours streamed from their shoulders and each bore sword and staff that gleamed with magical power. They circled above the host of Malekith, the sun gleaming from the golden harnesses of their flying steeds.

Malekith saw that all were arrayed ready for battle, and his heart soared at the sight. Not for centuries had he commanded such a host, and the call of his blood sang within his veins. For good or ill, the fortunes of the day would resound down through history, and his name would be recounted for generations to come. The prince was not content merely with posterity, though, and was determined to win victory. He ordered the army to a halt just outside of bowshot from the closest towers and wheeled his steed to face the army. Raising Avanuir above his head, Malekith called out to his army, his voice ringing clearly the length and breadth of the host.

'Look upon this citadel of dread!' he cried, pointing to Anlec with his magical blade, sapphire fire licking along its length. 'Here once hope sprang for our people, and here now glowers our doom! In these halls the ghosts of our fathers reside, and how they must howl at the sight of seeing what was once so great now brought so low! Here was lit the bright beacon of war by Aenarion, now a blackened flame of malice and domination! We are here to extinguish that baleful flare and restore anew the light of the phoenix! You may look and see the unending walls and the cruel towers, but I do not. The might of Anlec is not in her stones and mortar, but in the blood of her defenders and the courage of their hearts. No such strength remains in this benighted city, for all vigour and honour has been crushed from her by the choking chains of misery and slavery.'

The prince then turned his sword upon his army and its point swept along the long rows of warriors.

'Here I see the true spirit of our people!' Malekith declared. 'None come here by bond or bribe, but have marched forth for great and noble cause. We would not see such dark cities across our realms, and all here know in their spirit that today we shall halt the spread of the malignant shadow. Fell Charill! Noble Finudel! Majestic Thyriol! Know these names, and be proud to fight beside them, as I am. In time all here shall be remembered and their names shall be lauded. Unending shall be the appreciation of our people, and cherished shall be the memories of those that fight here this day! Look to your left and look to your right, and fix in your mind the face of your brothers-in-battle. You shall see no weakness there, only determination and bravery. Each here today claims his right to be a prince, for reward comes to those willing to risk all, and never have such dignified companions been assembled since the time of my father. Heroes one-and-all, you are, and as heroes shall the gods heap their praises upon you.'

Malekith then raised his sword in front of his face in salute.

'And forget not that it is I, Prince Malekith, who leads you!' he shouted. 'I am the true lord of Anlec! Scion of Nagarythe! Son of Aenarion! I know not despair, nor fear, nor defeat! With this blade I carved a new kingdom to the east. By my hand our people made grand alliance with the dwarfs. These eyes have looked upon the Dark Gods and did not flinch. Monsters and horrors I have faced and bested, and today will be no different. We shall win, because where I lead, victory follows. We shall win, because it is my destiny to triumph. We shall win, because I will it!'

Malekith then stood in his stirrups and raised Avanuir high above his head. A great cry erupted from the throats of his warriors, shaking the ground. Malekith waved the army forwards.

'Glory awaits!' he cried.

⫷ TWENTY ⫸

The Battle of Anlec

AT MALEKITH'S SIGNAL, the army advanced in line, heading towards the bridge across the river of fire. Arrows arced from the roofs of the outlying towers, and the battle began.

With a wild screech, Redclaw beat his wings and bore Bathinair high into the air. The Yvressian prince soared higher and higher, climbing far above the range of the enemies' bows. Likewise did the Sapherian mages circle upwards into the cloudless sky. Behind their shields, the spearmen marched forwards, not once breaking their stride even as more and more arrows rained down upon them.

With a fearsome shriek, Redclaw dived down from the heavens towards the closest of the towers. The archers atop its summit turned their bows towards the descending beast, but their arrows caused no lasting wound upon the griffon's thick hide. Bathinair's lance flashed with power as its point drove through the chests of the defenders, even as Redclaw's talons and beak savaged others upon the tower, rending and tearing.

Another tower suffered at the wrath of Thyriol, who streaked down from above, the tip of his staff blazing with green fire. As his pegasus swooped low over the tower, the mage unleashed his spell, the flames roaring from his staff in the shape of a hawk diving for the kill, exploding amongst the archers and tossing their bodies over the parapet.

More elves rushed up to the tower roof from within, only in time to be blasted by a bolt of red lightning from the staff of Merneir, which shattered the granite bricks of the tower and sent burning bodies and cracked stones tumbling to the charred earth. The army of Malekith surged through the gap between the two towers, while Bathinair and the mages wheeled above their heads, the cheers of the army ringing out to greet them.

The fortified bridge seemed altogether a more daunting obstacle. It consisted of four immense towers, with a drawbridge between each pair, so that the fiery moat could only be crossed by the bridges on each side both being lowered. Atop each tower was a powerful engine, which hurled immense bolts far out across the barren plain. Before his army came within range of these fearsome machines, Malekith signalled for his host to halt.

He rode forwards alone a short way, as if daring the defenders of the towers to direct their machines against him. It was a strange scene; the solitary prince upon his steed staring at the grim castlebridge like a golden lion standing its ground before a gigantic black bear.

Calmly, Malekith raised an open hand into the air. He felt the swirl of magic coursing around him and fixed his eyes upon the moat of flames. Upon his head throbbed the circlet, and the prince could sense the bubbling mystical energies within the flame-filled ditch across his path. He had been master of Anlec and knew the commanding words of the flames, but he could feel other enchantments had been bound into the moat; his mother had known he would try to use the spell words to break this defence. She had not reckoned with the power of the circlet, though, with which Malekith's power was increased five-fold.

In him built energies that would have torn asunder a lesser mage, and as the tide of magic grew, he began to quiver from the surging excitement that filled him. Speaking the command spell, he opened the dam of his mind and unleashed a tide of magic that flowed out of him and into the fire moat. The flames turned black and rose higher as the Naggarothi prince poured all of his will and determination into them, until they climbed a hundred feet into the air.

Now sweating with the effort, Malekith raised up his other hand, his limbs shaking with strain. The magic of the fires wriggled and writhed, trying to escape the grasp of his spell. With gritted teeth, Malekith began to bring his hands closer together and in response the flames of the trench began to coil into tall waves, one on each side of the bridge house.

Malekith brought his hands together with a thunderous clap and the two tides of flame rushed towards each other, utterly engulfing the castle across the entrenchment. Black fire scorched through arrow slits and poured over the roofs of the towers. Ebon flames incinerated elf and machine in an instant, reducing them to clouds of ash that billowed up into the air above the bridge. Even as the ancient planks of the drawbridge began to smoulder, Malekith pulled apart his hands and let loose his grip on the enchantment, the fires washing away and returning to their normal colour.

With a shout of relief and joy, Malekith turned to his army and waved them forwards, his face split by a wide grin. As the spearmen of Nagarythe reached him, he reined in his horse beside Yeasir. The captain looked up at him with suspicious eyes.

'Did you know that was going to work?' Yeasir asked.

'Well,' said Malekith with a smile. 'It's a long walk back to Ellyrion. I would not have wanted to have come all this way for nothing.'

Yeasir's laughter rang in the prince's ears as he wheeled his steed away, riding south to consult with Charill and his Chracian hunters. While Malekith outlined the next stage of his plan to his fellow prince, the Sapherian wizards alighted upon the smoking towers of the bridge and set free the bindings upon the huge drawbridges. They crashed down over the moat of fire, and the path to Anlec was open. Malekith was the first to ride across, his horse cantering forwards with jaunty high steps as the prince made a confident show for his followers.

In truth, the next phase of the attack was the most worrisome for the prince. It was five hundred paces to the closest outcrop of the walls and a further hundred paces through a corridor of arrows and bolts to reach the gate towers. Bathinair and the mages would do what they could to occupy the defenders upon the ramparts, but Malekith knew that speed was their greatest ally here, and even if they moved swiftly, casualties would be high.

As Yeasir led the advance towards the eastern gate, spear-sized bolts from engines upon the walls shrieked into his spearmen, slaying half a dozen warriors with each shot, their fury so powerful that no shield or armour was defence against them. Yeasir shouted himself hoarse urging on his followers in the face of clouds of black arrows, knowing that although there was no true weakness in Anlec's defences, the war machines could not target foes within a short distance of the walls. If the army could reach the safety of the wall's shadow the greatest danger would be passed.

A thousand elves fell as they raced across the bloody field on foot, the knights held in reserve to attack once the gate had been breached. Yeasir was still unclear as to how this was to be accomplished, but after the feat with the fire moat, Yeasir was willing to trust that his lord had an equally accomplished ploy. In fact, Yeasir realised, he was about to wager his life on it.

Some respite was earned for the spearmen by the warriors from the colonies, who moved forwards behind thick wooden pavises. They were armed with new weapons – repeating crossbows made by the dwarfs, which could fire a hail of short bolts in a short space of time. From behind their movable palisades, they unleashed volley after volley of darts at the walls, pinning down the bolt thrower crews and forcing the defending Naggarothi archers to seek cover. The shots did not go wholly unanswered though, as heavy bolts split the timbers of their wheeled shields and punched through to maim and slay those sheltering behind.

Those enemy warriors out of the crossbows' range were beset by the spells of Thyriol, Merneir and Eltreneth. Storms of purple and blue lightning tore along the battlements, leaping from one warrior to the next. Fire spells in the shape of hawks, dragons and phoenixes left a charred ruin of the defenders in their wake. Bolt throwers shattered into splinters under their enchantments and armour glowed with fiery heat, scorching those within. Daggers of white magic sliced through flesh while swords conjured from nothing hacked and slashed at the cultists upon the wall.

Bathinair played his part too. He and Redclaw left a swathe of dismembered and headless bodies along a stretch of the wall north of the gate, until the weight of bow fire from the defenders against him grew so much that he was forced to soar away, both he and his mount bleeding from many wounds. Crimson dripped from the griffon's beak and claws, falling onto Yeasir and his spearmen as the winged beast glided overhead.

The captain had no time to marvel at such spectacles. A third of his warriors lay dead or wounded upon the killing ground, and they were only halfway to their target. Close enough, it appeared, for the defenders to worry that they might yet reach the wall, for the massive gate yawned open in front of them.

From under its great arch there spilled a tide of wild depravity that Yeasir recognised all too well. Nearly naked but for loincloths and gauzy rags, their long hair spiked with gore, cultists of Khaine screamed and shrieked as they charged forwards. A mix of male and female worshippers, their skin daubed with blood, wearing grotesque jewellery made from sinew and innards, the cultists wielded long, serrated daggers and wicked-looking swords. They poured forth from the open gate in a stream of flesh and blood, hundreds of fanatical bloodworshippers.

Yeasir remembered well the feral snarls and wide eyes of the Murder God's chosen disciples, and knew that they were oblivious to everything but the spilling of blood, their battle-frenzy fuelled by the vapours from narcotic incense and potions brewed by the priestesses who ruled their cult.

The Commander of Nagarythe called for the spearmen to slow and rank up, ready to receive the Khainites' charge. In such formation they were more vulnerable to the arrows stinging down from the walls above, and Yeasir had no doubt that the defenders would not hesitate to fire into the forthcoming melee, heedless of the risk to their own comrades; such was the point of unleashing the cultists. With a crash, the gates closed once more.

A thundering of hooves attracted Yeasir's attention, and he turned to see the reaver knights of Ellyrion galloping forwards. They swept around the spearmen, ducking and swaying in their saddles to avoid the arrows raining down from the ramparts. Expertly loosing their bows as they dashed in, the reavers began to pour arrows into the cultists. In-and-out, left-and-right they galloped, sometimes turning nearly all the way around to fire backwards as they raced past their foes. Some turned their weapons upon the walls, their aim impeccable even at speed, their shots picking out any head or limb that could be seen.

The riders formed two circles running counter to each other around the spearmen, and under the cover of their bows Yeasir ordered the advance to begin again, the circles moving forwards to keep position with the spearmen.

When only a few dozen Khainites remained, the Ellyrians broke off their shooting and stored their bows, taking up their spears instead. With Finudel and Athielle at their head, their famous weapons in hand, the Ellyrians charged in. The Khainites would not break before their attack: so intoxicated with blood-frenzy had they become that they fought until the last of them lay dead upon a heap of bodies, his dying breath a curse upon his enemies.

The path was open to the gates and the Ellyrians directed their steeds away, leaving passage for Yeasir and his warriors to enter between the high walls that led to the immense portal. Behind them came Charill and his hunters of Chrace, and behind them the spearmen of Yvresse stood ready to push forwards through any breach.

As the shadows of the walls loomed above them, the spearmen began to glance upwards at their forbidding heights, expecting death to be unleashed upon them at any moment. Yeasir risked a glance backwards, seeking some sign of Malekith's intent. The prince was sat upon his horse a little way back, arms casually folded across his chest. Malekith somehow felt the eyes of his lieutenant upon him and gave a playful wave, before pointing towards the gatehouse.

Yeasir looked up at the menacing towers and saw black-hooded figures appearing at the battlements. They carried bows in their hands and looked down upon the spearmen with arrows nocked.

'Stand ready!' Yeasir shouted, hefting up his shield.

At that moment, the black banner that flew above the gatehouse fluttered and then fell, as if its pole had been cut. In its place there was raised a new standard: white threaded with silver, with a blazon of a clawed griffon's wing upon it. Yeasir stumbled, almost losing his footing in disbelief, for he recognised it as the banner of House Anar.

The warriors of the Anars tossed bloodied corpses over the battlements, and Yeasir saw it was the bodies of cultists and warriors loyal to Morathi, their throats and bellies slit open. The gate ground open again before Yeasir, and he let out a great roar of triumph.

Fearing that the way in might close any moment, he broke into a run, his spearmen close behind. With the lion warriors of Chrace and the spearmen of Yvresse close on his heels, Yeasir was the first to cross the threshold into Anlec. He shouted again as he passed under the shadow of the gate of his home city, exalted at his return.

* * *

INSIDE, THE CITY was utterly unlike the home Yeasir had left behind many centuries earlier. The great square beyond the gate had once been dominated by a large statue of Aenarion seated upon a rearing Indraugnir; now instead it was lined with statues of the cytharai. Atharti cavorted naked atop a marble stone, snakes twining themselves about her limbs. Anath Raema, the huntress, held her bow in one hand and the severed head of an elf in the other, her waist girded by a belt of severed hands and heads. The god Khirkith was depicted crouched upon a pile of bones, a jewelled necklace in his hands as he admired his looted treasure.

There were many others, of gods of destruction and death, and goddesses of strife and pain. A brazier burned before each, sputtering with dire contents, the bloodstains upon the statues' plinths testament to the foul practices of the cultists.

When Yeasir had left Anlec, the buildings around the square had been busy trading forums, bustling with wares from all across the globe. Now the open-fronted facades had been turned into animal pens, with bars across their high arches, and all manner of unnatural beasts in the darkness beyond.

Mutated bears growled and gnawed at their cages, while two-headed orthruses howled and a stinking fume drifted into the square from the pens of half-bull bonnakons. Gaseous clouds issued forth from the cages of wild chimerae and hideously large serpents spat venom through the bars. Other things wailed, cavorted and roared menacingly from the shadowy confines of their prisons.

From one cage there billowed a great cloud of smoke, and licking tongues of flame could be seen lighting the smog. A gate was thrown open and there came a great screeching, as of many creatures shrieking in concert. From out of the gloom there emerged a titanic beast, a seven-headed hydra with flames flickering from its nostrils. Its scales were of deep blue, and many welts and scars upon its flesh told of its ill treatment by its keepers. Its heads were protected by plates of golden armour, as was its spined back and muscled flanks.

Behind the hydra came a pair of handlers wielding vicious goads and whips, with which they urged the monster forwards, shouting and hurling abuse. Enraged, the hydra stalked forwards, its claws gouging rents in the stone flags of the plaza, its heads swaying and writhing like a nest of serpents. From the cage came another of the huge beasts, of red flesh and silver armour, with blades and barbs hammered into its scales, and spiked collars about its five necks. Its tail was likewise armoured and beweaponed, and thrashed left and right as its handlers scourged its sides with the tines of their long spears and the cruel thorns of their lashes.

Not since the shaggoth had Yeasir known such dread as he looked at the two behemoths crashing across the square towards his spearmen. Mastering his fear, he called out for his warriors to form a shield wall, though he doubted such a manoeuvre would be any defence against the monstrous creatures bearing down upon the Naggarothi.

Growls and roars sounded to the right and the lion chariots of Charill raced forwards, the prince at their front. The handlers of the foremost hydra turned their beast towards the Chracians and with another lash from their whips sent it charging forwards.

Seven blasts of yellow fire gouted from the creature's throats, directed towards Charill's chariot. A shimmering blue aura leapt up around the Chracian prince and his lions, a jewelled amulet hanging upon his bared chest glowing bright with power, and the flames lapped around the prince's magical ward without harm.

The lions leapt to the attack, biting and clawing at the hydra's scaled flesh. The hydra's heads snapped forwards, their dagger-like fangs tearing chunks of bloody ruin out of the lions, whose yelps of pain resounded around the square. The hydra reared up with two lions clamped in its fearsome jaws, wrenching them into the air amidst the tangle of their frayed traces, overturning the chariot. Charill and Lorichar leapt free from the splintering wood and twisted metal, and regained their feet as the other chariots attacked.

The Chracians raced past the monster, axes and lion's fangs scoring wounds upon the creature's hide before they swerved away from its whipping tail and snapping heads. In their wake came the hunters, swinging their axes in wide arcs, lodging their blades deep into the creature's tough hide. Though blood streamed from dozens of wounds, the hydra was relentless, powerful jaws and savage claws wreaking red furrows through the Chracians.

Charill bellowed his war cry and joined the attack, Achillar burning with white light in his hands. With the fabled axe he smote a great blow upon one of the creature's necks, severing it utterly, so that neck and head fell to the floor and continued to writhe for a while like a snake. Blood spumed briefly from the injury, but to the Chracian's horror, the great wound swiftly closed over. Flesh bubbled, veins and arteries, muscle and sinew knitted and grew afresh, so that within moments a new head had grown in the place of the old.

Several dozen hunters and the shattered remains of three chariots now surrounded the beast as the Chracians were hurled back by its savagery. With a wordless shout,

Lorichar ran forwards, the speared tip of the household banner aimed towards the monster's chest. Lorichar drove the point of the standard deep between the creature's scales, all of his weight behind the blow. His thick muscles straining, his face a mask of effort, Lorichar drove the banner point deeper and deeper.

Yeasir had not the time to see what happened next, for the second hydra was almost upon the Naggarothi.

'Where's Prince Malekith?' Fenrein asked from beside the captain.

Yeasir did not answer, although the thought had also occurred to him. He had not seen the prince since they had entered the city, and the Naggarothi captain dearly wished his lord was beside him; sorcery and Avanuir would make short work of the horrendous creature that now loomed above the Naggarothi.

Unearthly chattering and screeches briefly distracted the lieutenant as he saw more cultists unbarring the other cells. All manner of beasts and monsters ran forth, howling and yammering. Scaled and feathered, majestic and misshapen, the captured denizens of the Annulii poured forth from their dens like a nightmare made real. The Yvressians moved forwards, spears at the ready to meet the bizarre horde.

Yeasir could spare them no more thought as he turned his attention back to the hydra now just two dozen paces away.

He saw it drawing its heads back, and yelled a warning to his warriors. As one they dropped to a single knee and raised up their shields just as the hydra's fire roared out. Yeasir felt his shield heating in his hands, burning at his fingers as the flames engulfed the spearmen. There were cries of pain and the smell of charred flesh filled the captain's nostrils. Surrounded by a pall of smoke, the

Naggaroth captain looked up and saw that a great swathe of his company now lay burning upon the ground; many thankfully dead, others screaming and sobbing as they clutched scorched limbs or rolled about on the stone, their hair and clothes alight.

Black-fletched arrows whickered overhead as the archers of House Anar shot from the gatehouse. Their aim was not for the monstrous hydra, but for the cultists cowering behind its bulk. Several arrows unerringly found their marks and the two handlers dropped, bodies and necks pierced and bloody.

Suddenly free of the goading whips and spears of its handlers, the hydra slowed. Three of its heads bent back to examine their unmoving corpses, the other four rose into the air, nostrils flaring as they caught the scent of basilisks and khaltaurs. Fiery venom dripping from its maws, the hydra heaved around its bulk and spied its enemies from the mountains. With deafening hisses issuing from its many throats, the hydra lumbered into a run, heading for the other monsters.

Its closest prey was a gigantic wolf with glowing eyes and iron fangs, which turned at the hydra's approach and leapt at one of its throats. No longer under any control, the hydra tore apart the wolf-thing and barrelled forwards, tail and claws smashing and crushing the lesser creatures before it. All control disappeared as the beasts of the mountains fell upon each other; blasts of fire and lightning danced amongst the mutated creatures and blood of all colours stained the square as the ferocity of the monsters was unleashed. The Yvressians retreated with shrieks of alarm as the ragged corpse of a basilisk was hurled into the ranks, its poisonous blood burning their skin.

Yeasir could not help but laugh, out of relief more than humour. A glance told him that the Chracians had finished off their monstrous foe, though they stood about its body chopping and hacking with their blades to ensure that it regenerated no further.

Malekith's whereabouts still a mystery, Yeasir turned and looked for the prince. He spied him then upon the wall, talking with Eoloran, the prince of House Anar. Telling his spearmen to stand guard for fresh attack, Yeasir left the company and headed towards the steps.

MALEKITH SAW YEASIR striding up the stairway to the gate wall, and waved him forwards. With the prince stood Eoloran, his son Eothlir and his grandson Alith. All were dressed in silver armour and black cloaks, and carried bows etched with magical sigils. The three were grim-faced, but Malekith was in good humour as he looked at the bloody savagery being unleashed in the plaza below. He introduced Yeasir to his companions, clapping a hand to his second-in-command's shoulder in an encouraging fashion.

'Well done!' the prince exclaimed. 'I knew you would not let me down.'

'Highness?' said Yeasir.

'The city, you fool,' laughed Malekith. 'Now that we are in, it is only a matter of time. I have you to thank for that.'

'Thank you, highness, but I think you deserve more credit than I,' said Yeasir. He looked at the Anars. 'And without these noble warriors, I would still be stood outside, or perhaps lying outside with an arrow in my belly.'

'Yes, well, I have thanked them enough already,' said Malekith. 'It would be best not to give them too much credit, otherwise who knows what ideas they might get.'

'How did they come to be here?' asked Yeasir.

'Malekith sent word to us many days ago,' said Eoloran. He was an ageing elf, of hawkish features and a deep voice. 'When he told us of his intent to attack Anlec, at first we thought him mad. By secret means, he outlined his plans for the attack, and it became clear that this was to be no idle gesture. We were only too happy to play our part in ridding Nagarythe of this wretched regime of darkness. Ten days ago we came into the city, dressed in the manner of Salthites and Khainites, and all manner of other vile worshippers of the cytharai. We met in secret and gathered together to await Malekith's attack. We could not open the gates sooner for the square below was filled with Khainites... Well you know that, since you faced them. Once the square was undefended, we struck as swiftly as we could to take the gate.'

'Well, you have my gratitude, prince,' said Yeasir with a deep bow. He turned to Malekith with a frown. 'I must admit to being somewhat hurt that you did not feel that you could trust me with this counsel, highness.'

'Would that I could have,' said Malekith airily. 'I trust you more than I trust my own sword arm, Yeasir. I could not divulge my plan to you lest it affect your actions in battle. I wanted the defenders to know nothing was amiss until the gates were opened, and foreknowledge of the Anars' presence may well have meant that you held back until the gates were already flung wide. We needed to keep the pressure on so that all eyes were turned outwards rather than inwards.'

Malekith then turned to Eoloran.

'If you would excuse me, I believe my mother is waiting for me,' the Naggarothi prince said, now empty of all humour.

THERE WAS STILL fierce fighting in the plaza, and the knights of Anlec arrived to take their share of the glory, driving hard into cultists and beasts with their lances.

Designed as a fortress, Anlec was laid out in a fashion so that there was no direct route to the central palace. Along twisting streets, harassed by archers from roofs and windows, the army of Malekith advanced cautiously, aware that by alley and underground passage there were many ways by which a foe could come at them from every direction and then melt away into the city.

Fortunately for Malekith, the defenders had committed a greater part of their strength to the defence of the walls, confident that no enemy had ever passed into the city by force of arms. This left the remaining defenders scattered, and as most were simple cultists they attacked in haphazard, uncoordinated fashion and were easily dealt with.

At one stage the advance was halted, as a fearsome figure atop a manticore descended on the column from the skies. Malekith recognised him as Prince Kheranion, and knew him of old.

He wore armour of ithilmar inscribed with protective runes and bound with enchantments of warding, forged in the Shrine of Vaul, against which it was said no mortal weapon would draw blood. The beast upon which the prince rode had the body of a gigantic lion, with bat-like wings that swathed the street in shadow as the traitor plunged down from the air, his mount roaring ferociously.

The knights at the head of the advance were taken by surprise as the prince dropped from above, their armour gouged by his monster's teeth, their horses cast down upon the cobbles.

In his hand the prince wielded the fell lance Arhaluin, the shadowdeath that Caledor had forged for Aenarion before he had wielded the Sword of Khaine. Seeing the weapon in the hands of his foe sent Malekith into a rage. He raced forwards, his steed's hooves striking sparks from the pavement as the prince gathered magical power for a sorcerous blast.

Before Malekith could confront Kheranion, Morathi's captain steered his mount into the air once more and swooped over the rooftops. Moments later he dived into the attack once more, crashing into the Yvressian spearmen further down the road.

For several minutes the prince hit-and-ran in this fashion, halting the advance and allowing other defenders to gather in numbers around the column. Doorways and windows spat arrows into the attackers. Red-robed cultists leapt from hidden trapdoors to snatch warriors and drag them from sight before their comrades could react. Chilling screams began to echo through the streets, unnerving the attackers further.

Beset from above and below, Malekith shouted in frustration and urged the army to move onwards.

The Naggarothi prince knew that ahead lay a wide killing ground, where his army would be vulnerable to attack, but there was no option but to press on towards the palace. Soon the winding streets led them to a rectangular space lined on all sides by high walls punctured with murder holes. As arrows rained down from these narrow slits, Malekith summoned the energy for a spell.

Here, in the heart of Anlec, there was much dark magic, drawn here by the murder and suffering of the cultists' victims. Aided by the circlet, Malekith was able to tap into this flowing energy and harness it. He tried to form a magical shield around his troops, but the dark magic contorted and thrashed in his mental grasp, refusing his will.

With a snarl, Malekith allowed his frustration full vent and let loose a stream of magic as a cloud of black darts that exploded outwards, each small missile twisting and turning to seek out an embrasure or opening. Screams and shouts resounded from the corridors within the walls around the cloister as the darts found their targets, and blood from the slain dribbled from windows and under door.

Kheranion attacked again, plunging downwards with lance ready. Malekith hurled a bolt of lightning at the stooping monster, but Kheranion raised his silvered shield and the spell earthed itself harmlessly within the enchanted guard.

Kheranion was not without some sorcery himself and a dark nimbus surrounded him before erupting into a flock of evil crows that descended upon Malekith's army, pecking at eyes and exposed skin, causing disarray and panic. With a contemptuous sweep of his arm, Malekith dispelled the curse and the crows evaporated into burning feathers.

So intent was Kheranion on his magical duel with Malekith that he did not spy a shape coming upon him from the clouds. It appeared first as a speck, but rapidly grew larger until the shape of Bathinair's griffon could be seen. Hearing its screech, Kheranion turned, but too late. In Bathinair's hand, Nagrain trailed icy shards and its crystalline point bit deep into the muscle and bone where the manticore's right wing met its body. With a strange yelp, the manticore twisted and raked its claws across the chest of Redclaw, and the two snarled and snapped at each other as they dug in their long claws.

Bathinair avoided a thrust from Kheranion as the two monsters locked together and spiralled towards the ground. Nagrain leapt again but Kheranion deflected the attack with his shield, his own magical lance piercing the throat of Redclaw. In its death throes, the griffon clamped its beak about the left foreleg of the manticore and both beasts and riders crashed into a tiled roof before spinning onto the cobbles of the open ground.

The manticore lashed its tail sting forwards, catching Bathinair a raking blow across the chest and sending him flying from the throne upon which he had been seated. Discarding Arhaluin, Kheranion drew a sword whose blade was made wholly of flame. The prince advanced purposefully towards the stricken Bathinair. The manticore righted itself and lunged forwards lopsidedly, its wounded wing trailing uselessly behind it.

Malekith drew Avanuir and urged his horse forwards, eyes intent on Kheranion.

Another shadow eclipsed Malekith for a moment as Merneir swept across the square atop his pegasus, his staff blazing with golden light. With a shout, the mage unleashed a ball of blue fire that hurtled across the open space and detonated with a flash beside Kheranion. The prince was hurled into the air and the manticore flung sideways by the blast. The gold-shod hooves of his steed flailing, the mage descended upon the manticore with his sword, hacking away at its venom-tipped tail while Kheranion shook his head and groggily stood.

Behind the renegade prince, Bathinair rose to his feet also, Nagrain grasped in both hands. His face was a mask of anger as blood trickled across the left side of his face from a cut on his forehead. He swept the point of the spear towards Kheranion and a hail of icy shards erupted from the weapon's tip, slamming into the prince's armour and smashing him from his feet once more. The firesword spun from his grip.

Out of desperation, Kheranion flung forwards an outstretched hand and a blast of power caught Bathinair full in the chest, sending him crashing into the wall a dozen paces distant. The prince collapsed to one knee, panting hard, while Kheranion scrabbled on all fours to reclaim his blade.

Just as Kheranion's fingers curled around the hilt of the accursed sword, Malekith arrived. He leaned low in the saddle and Avanuir carved a furrow into the renegade's armour and bit into his spine. Malekith leapt from the back of his horse as it galloped on and landed cat-like next to the stricken prince. Kheranion stared into Malekith's eyes and saw the prince of Nagarythe's murderous gaze.

'Spare me!' begged Kheranion, falling to his back and tossing away his magical sword. 'I am crippled and no more a threat!'

Malekith saw that this was true, for the prince's legs hung limply from his body as he dragged himself away across the cobbles.

'Perhaps you would have me end your suffering?' said Malekith, taking a step forwards, the point of Avanuir aimed towards his foe's throat.

'No!' cried Kheranion. 'Though I am undone, perhaps my wound is not beyond that of the finest healers.'

'Why would I allow you to live, so that like a pet serpent you could rise up and bite me again?'

Kheranion sobbed with pain and fear, and held up an arm as if to ward away the killing blow.

'I denounce Morathi!' Kheranion shouted, his voice reverberating around the courtyard. 'I will swear anew my oaths to Malekith!'

'You are a traitor, and yet have not the conviction to stand by your treacherous path,' snarled Malekith. 'Betrayal can be forgiven, cowardice cannot.'

With that, Malekith drove the point of Avanuir downwards and Kheranion shrieked, but the tip of the sword stopped a fraction from the fallen prince's throat.

'Yet I also swore to be merciful,' said Malekith, lifting away his blade. 'Though you have done many wrongs against me, I must stand by that oath and offer clemency to those who repent of their misdeeds. Perhaps I will find a way even for a creature as craven as you to make amends.'

With an agonised grunt, Kheranion threw himself forwards and grasped Malekith around the leg and whimpered meaningless gratitudes. Malekith kicked him away with a sneer.

'Pathetic,' the prince rasped, turning away.

◄ TWENTY-ONE ►

A Destiny Manifested

THE CLOSER MALEKITH and his host drew to the central palace, the more disturbing Anlec became. Many of the buildings here had been turned into immense charnel temples, their steps stained dark with blood, the entrails and bones of the cultists' victims hung upon their walls as decoration. Hundreds of braziers burned fitfully, spewing noxious, acrid fumes through the streets. The air itself clung with the stench of death and all was silent save for the crackling of flames and the tread of the warriors on the bloodstained tiles of the streets. They came at last upon the palace of Aenarion, a large building that doubled as the central citadel of Anlec. It appeared deserted, and the broad doors were opened wide. Dismembered skeletons, rotting organs and other detritus littered the steps leading up to the entrance.

Malekith stopped at the foot of the steps and looked up into the beckoning door, seeking an ambush. Lanterns glowed with ruddy light from within, but there was no sign of any other living thing.

Slowly, Malekith ascended the steps, Avanuir in hand. His knights dismounted and followed a short way behind, similarly ready for attack. Malekith paused before he stepped across the threshold and checked one more time for hidden attackers. Satisfied that there was no immediate threat, he strode through the doors into the chamber beyond.

It was as he remembered from a millennium ago. A long colonnaded hall led away from the doors, much like a larger version of the entrance of Ealith's keep. There was no evidence of the murder and slaughter of the rest of the city here. The floor was a vast mosaic of a golden blade upon a storm-filled sky, and Malekith remembered it from when he was a child.

He had crawled upon this floor and happily stroked the golden tiles even as his father had told him of its story, for it was a depiction of a dream, the vision that had beset Malekith's father and spurred him to take up the war against the daemons. Though his father had not known it at the time, it had been the Sword of Khaine calling to him, from hundreds of leagues distant, suddenly awoken from its eons-long slumber by the anger of Aenarion.

The slamming of the doors behind him shattered Malekith's thoughts and he spun around, expecting attack. He heard thuds and thumps as his followers outside attempted to open them, but Malekith knew it would be fruitless; the tinge of ancient magic hung about the portal, spells laid upon it in the time of Caledor.

'Come to me,' a voice echoed along the empty halls, and Malekith recognised his mother's tone.

Still wary of attack, Malekith stalked along the hallway, all childhood thoughts forgotten. His eyes roved across the archways and high galleries, seeking any sign of a hidden assassin, but there was none. Passing through the great doorway at the end of the entrance hall, Malekith came to an antechamber from which two sets of stairs spiralled upwards to the left and right.

The one on the left led to the bedchambers, guardhouses and other domestic rooms on the first floor, while the stair to the right wound higher to the throne room of Aenarion. Without hesitation, Malekith turned to his right and slowly ascended the marble stair, a carpet of deep blue running down its centre. His footfalls made no sound as he walked, and in the silence there came a noise on the very edge of his hearing.

It was weeping, a constant low sob. Stopping, Malekith listened more intently but the noise could be heard no more. Walking again, Malekith heard a distant, dim shriek and a yammering for mercy. Halting once more to listen, the sound faded away again, leaving only silence.

'Spare us!' said a voice behind Malekith, and he spun, sword in hand, but there was nothing there.

'Mercy!' pleaded a whisper in Malekith's right ear, but turning his head he saw only empty air.

'Not the blade!'

'Free us!'

'Give us peace!'

'Justice!'

'Show us pity!'

Malekith twisted left and right, seeking the source of the voices, but he was alone on the stairway.

'Begone,' the prince growled, holding up Avanuir.

In the flickering glow of the blade, Malekith finally saw movement: ghostly figures dimly reflecting the blue glare of Avanuir's fire. He could see the spirits only in glimpses, and saw flashes of headless bodies, children with their hearts ripped out, mutilated women and victims of all kinds of vile torture. They reached out with broken hands, skin hanging in flaps from mutilated arms. Some were eyeless, others had their mouths stitched shut or their cheeks pierced with spikes.

'Get away from me!' snarled Malekith, turning and leaping up the stairs, casting glances over his shoulder as he hurried upwards. The swirling ghosts chased the prince up the steps and he slashed at them with Avanuir, parting their insubstantial forms with its glowing blade.

Panting, he reached the upper landing and stood before the high double doors that led to the throne room. Soundlessly, they opened inwards, bathing Malekith in the golden light from many lanterns within.

At the far end of the hall sat Morathi, clad in a draping wind of golden cloth that obscured very little of her nakedness. She held her staff of bone and iron across her lap, her fingers toying with the skull at its tip. Morathi sat in a simple wooden chair next to the mighty throne of Aenarion; which was cut from a single piece of black granite, its back shaped like a rearing dragon, of which Bel Shanaar's throne was but a pale imitation. Magical flame licked from the dragon's fanged maw and glowed in its eyes.

Malekith's eyes were drawn to the throne above all other things, ignoring even his mother, for this was the strongest memory he had of this place; of his father girded for war sat upon that immense chair, in counsel with his famed generals.

The memory was so vivid that Malekith could hear his father's soft yet strong voice echoing around the throne room. The prince was but a child, sat in the lap of his mother beside the Phoenix King, and Aenarion would occasionally pause in his conversation and look down upon his son. Always stern was that look; not unkind, yet not compassionate either, but full of pride. For years Malekith had gazed back at those strong, dark eyes and seen the fires that raged behind their quiet dignity. Malekith imagined that he alone knew the sinister spirit that hid within, clothed in the body of a noble monarch, masked against the eyes of the world lest it be recognised for what it truly was.

The soul of a destroyer, the wielder of the Godslayer.

And the sword! There across the Phoenix King's lap lay Widowmaker, Soulbiter, the Sword of Khaine. Even at a young age, Malekith had noticed that only he and his father ever looked upon its blood-red blade, for all other elves averted their gaze and would look anywhere else but directly at it. It was like a secret shared between them.

'Yet you did not pick up the Blade of Murder when it was offered to you,' said Morathi, dispelling the illusion that had so gripped her son.

Malekith shook his head, confused by the enchantment cunningly wrought upon him by his mother. Truly they were real memories she had stirred, but her spell had made them as tangible as life, if only for a moment.

'I did not,' replied Malekith, slowly, realising that Morathi had seen into his thoughts and learned of his episode on the Blighted Isle, of which he had spoken to nobody.

'That is good,' said Morathi. She was sat in stately pose, despite her near-nudity, and exuded regal poise. Not here the barbarous priestess who tore living hearts from the breasts of her victims; not the seductive, wily seeress who wove lies with every word and manipulated all around her into a tapestry to her liking. Here she was as queen of Nagarythe, full of quiet majesty and grandeur.

'The sword controlled your father,' the queen said, her tone hushed, reassuring. 'Since his death, it has yearned for you to seek it out. I was worried that you would be ensnared by its power as well, but I am proud that you resisted its bloodthirsty call. None can truly be its master, and if you are to rule, then you must be master of everything.'

'I would rather the world was devoured by daemons than unleash that fell creation upon it again,' Malekith said, sheathing Avanuir. 'As you say, once drawn it will consume its wielder until nothing but blood remains. No person can become a king with its power, only a slave.'

'Sit down,' Morathi said, waving a hand of invitation towards the grand throne.

'It is not yet my place to sit there,' replied Malekith.

'Oh?' said Morathi, surprised. 'And why is that?'

'If I am to rule Nagarythe, I shall rule it alone,' said Malekith. 'Without you. When you are slain, the army of Nagarythe will be mine again. I shall hold power over the pleasure cults and with them secure the Phoenix Throne.'

Morathi remained silent for a moment, looking at her son with ancient eyes, gauging his mood and motive. A sly smile then twisted her lips.

'You mean to slay me?' she whispered, feigning shock.

'While you live, always will your ambition be a shadow upon mine,' said Malekith, angry at his mother's charade. 'You cannot help but be my rival, for it is not in your nature to serve any but yourself. I cannot share Ulthuan with you, for you could never truly share it with me. Even my father was not your master. I would exile you, but you would rise up again in some forgotten corner, a contender for everything that I aspire to.'

'Cannot share power,' Morathi said, 'or will not?'

Malekith pondered for a moment, examining his feelings.

'Will not,' he replied, his eyes full of intent.

'And to what is it that you aspire, my son?' Morathi said, leaning forwards eagerly.

'To inherit my father's legacy and rule as Phoenix King,' Malekith replied, knowing the truth of the words even as he spoke them. Never before had he so openly admitted his desire, not even to himself. Glory, honour, renown; all but stepping stones towards his ascension to the Phoenix Throne. The circlet had revealed to him the true nature of the forces that now ruled the world, and he would not stand by while Ulthuan slowly succumbed to them.

'Yes, Chaos is strong,' Morathi told him.

'Stay out of my thoughts,' Malekith snarled, taking an angry step forwards, his hand straying to the hilt of Avanuir.

'I need no magic to know your mind, Malekith,' said Morathi, still gazing fixedly at her son. 'There is a bond between mother and son that does not need sorcery.'

'Do you submit yourself to your fate?' Malekith said, ignoring her obvious reminder of their relationship; an attempt to stay his hand.

'You should know better than ask such a pointless question,' Morathi replied, and now her voice was stern, harsh even. 'Have I not always told you that you were destined to be king? You cannot be king unless you are prince of your own realm, and I will not surrender it willingly. Prove to me that you are worthy of ruling Nagarythe. Prove to the other princes that the strength within you is greater than any other.'

At some silent command, four figures emerged from the shadows, two to Malekith's left and two to his right. They were sorcerers by their garb, two male and two female, swathed in black robes, tattooed with dark sigils.

Malekith struck out with a blast of magic, materialising as a thunderbolt from his fingertips. Instantly Morathi was surrounded by a shadowy sphere of energy, which pulsed as the bolt struck it. Her adepts unleashed spells of their own, fiery blasts that rushed in upon Malekith in the guise of howling wolf heads, and the prince cast his own shield of darkness to ward them away.

The sorcerers and sorceresses closed in, hurling fireballs and flares of dark power. Malekith protected himself, drawing in more and more magic from the energy seething around the throne room as the spells cascaded towards him.

Morathi sat contentedly upon her chair while her followers unleashed their hexes and curses, watching with interest as Malekith countered each. Churning and bubbling, magic flowed around the hall, growing in intensity as both Malekith and his foes reached their minds out further and further, drawing energy from the city outside.

'Enough,' barked Malekith, letting free the energy that he had pulled into himself, releasing a blast of raw magic not shaped by any spell.

The power blazed, surrounding each of the dark wizards, filling them with mystical energy; more than they could control. The first, a red-haired witch, began to quiver, and then spasmed so hard that Malekith heard her spine snapping as she flopped to the ground. The other sorceress screeched in agony as her blood turned to fire and exploded out of her veins, engulfing her in a tempest of lightning and flames. The third of them flew into the air as if struck, his nose, eyes and ears streaming with blood, his ragged body smashing against the distant wall. The last was consumed by the ravening magic and collapsed in upon himself, crumpled like a ball of paper until he disintegrated into a pile of dust.

'Your followers are weak,' said Malekith, rounding on Morathi.

The seeress remained unconcerned.

'There are always more minions,' she said with a dismissive wave of a beringed hand. 'That trinket upon your head gives you impressive power, but you lack subtlety and control.'

Quicker than Malekith's eye could follow, Morathi's hand snapped out, her staff pointed at his chest. He fell to one knee as his heart began to thunder inside his ribs, drowning him with pain. Through the haze of agony, Malekith could feel the slender tendrils of magic that extended from Morathi's staff, almost imperceptible in their delicacy.

Whispering a counterspell, Malekith chopped his hand through the intangible strands and forced himself back to his feet.

'You never taught me that,' said Malekith with mock admonition. 'How unmotherly to keep such secrets from your son.'

'You have not been here to learn from me,' Morathi said with a sad shake of her head. 'I have learned much these past thousand years. If you put aside this foolish jealousy that consumes you, then perhaps I can tutor you again.'

In reply, Malekith gathered up the coiling magic and hurled it at the queen, the spell materialising as a monstrous serpent. Morathi's staff intercepted it, a shimmering blade springing from its haft to slice the head from the immaterial snake.

'Crude,' she said with a wag of her finger. 'Perhaps you impressed the savages of Elthin Arvan and the wizardless dwarfs with these antics, but I am not so easily awed.'

Standing, the seeress-queen held her staff in both hands above her head and began to chant quickly. Blades crystallised out of the air around her, orbiting her body in ever-increasing numbers until she was all but obscured from view by a whirlwind of icy razors. With a contemptuous laugh, Malekith extended his will, looking to knock them aside.

His dispel met with failure, however, as Morathi's magic swayed and changed shape, slipping through the insubstantial grasp of his counterspell. A moment later and the shardstorm tore through the air towards him, forcing the prince to leap aside lest they rip the flesh from his bones.

'Slow and predictable, my child,' Morathi said, stepping forwards.

Malekith said nothing, but lashed out with his sorcery, a whip of fire appearing in his hands. Its twin tips flew across the room and coiled about Morathi's staff. With a flick of his wrist, Malekith wrested the rod from his mother, sending it skittering across the tiled floor. With another short hand motion Malekith dashed the staff against the wall, shattering it into pieces.

'I think you are too old for such toys,' said Malekith, drawing Avanuir.

'I am,' snarled Morathi, her face contorting with genuine anger.

Something invisible scythed through the air and connected with Malekith's legs. He felt his shins crack and his knees shatter and a howl of pain was wrenched from his lips as he crashed to the floor. Letting Avanuir fall from his grasp, he clutched at his broken legs, writhing and screaming.

'Stop making such a noise,' said Morathi irritably.

Making a fist, she wove a spell that clenched Malekith's throat in its grip, choking him. The pain befuddled his mind, and as he flailed and gasped he could not muster the concentration to counter the spell.

'Focus, boy, focus,' spat Morathi as she stalked forwards, her fist held out in front of her, twisting it left and right as

Malekith squirmed in her mystical grasp. 'You think you are fit to rule without me? I expect such ingratitude from the likes of Bel Shanaar, but not from my own kin.'

The mention of the Phoenix King's name acted as a lightning rod for Malekith's pain and anger, and he lashed out, a sheet of flame erupting from him to engulf the queen. She was unharmed, but had released her spell to protect herself. Malekith rolled to his side, coughing and spluttering.

The prince was then flipped to his back and he felt a great weight upon his chest. Numbness enveloped him as the weight pressed down harder and harder, and Malekith fought against losing consciousness. As black spots and bright lights flickered in his vision, he thought he glimpsed a shadowy, insubstantial creature crouched upon his chest: a slavering horned daemon with a wide, fang-filled maw and three eyes. Pushing aside the aching of his body, he tried to focus his mind, but his body would not move.

Morathi stood beside her son, looking down dispassionately. She reached down and grasped Malekith's helm in one hand and pulled it from his head. The queen regarded it closely for a moment, her eyes analysing every scratch and dint in its grey surface, her fingers lingering close to the circlet but never touching it. Gently, she crouched beside Malekith and placed the helm behind her, out of reach. Malekith fought back a surge of panic. He felt strangely naked and powerless without the circlet.

'If you do not know how to use it properly, you should not have it,' she said gently. She laid a hand upon his cheek, caressing him, and then placed her fingers upon his forehead as a mother soothing the brow of a fevered child. 'If you had but asked me, I would have helped you unlock its real power. Without it, your magic is weak and unrefined. You should have paid more attention to what your mother taught you.'

'Perhaps,' Malekith said. With a shout of pain, he swung his gauntleted fist at Morathi, punching her clean in her face and sending her slamming to her back. 'I learned that from my father!'

Stunned, Morathi lost her concentration and her spell evaporated. Malekith felt the invisible weight lifting from his body. With an effort, he drew magic down into his ruined legs, fusing bone back into place, knotting muscle and sinew together.

Whole again, the prince stood, looming over Morathi. With a flick of his hand, Avanuir jumped from the floor and landed in his grasp, its point a finger's breadth from Morathi's face, unwavering.

His face grimly set, he swung Avanuir over his left shoulder and brought it down in a backhand sweep towards Morathi's neck.

'Wait!' she shouted and Malekith's arm froze, the blade no more than a hand's span from the killing blow.

It was no spell that had stayed his hand, but the tone in her voice. It was not desperation or fear, but anger and frustration, as she had used so many times before when he was a child about to do something wrong.

'What?' he asked, confused by his own reaction.

'Use your mind, think about what is for the best,' said Morathi slowly. 'How will this truly aid you?'

'What do you mean?' Malekith said with narrowed eyes full of suspicion. He lowered Avanuir but kept the blade ready to strike the moment he detected the merest hint of a conjuration.

'Do you think that killing me will give you the throne of Nagarythe?' Morathi said, lying as still as a statue, her gaze never moving from her son's eyes. 'Do you think that my death will usher you to the rule of Ulthuan?'

'It cannot harm my cause,' Malekith said with a shrug.

'But it will not help it,' Morathi said. 'Slay me here, unseen by any other, and the truth of your victory will never really be known. "Malekith slew his mother," the chronicles will say, and then the deed will be forgotten, hidden away like a shameful secret.'

'And if I let you live?' Malekith asked warily.

'I will turn the cults to your bidding,' said Morathi. 'You cannot hope to control them, and without me they will splinter and either turn against you or simply vanish altogether.'

'If I let you live, you will use the cults of luxury against me,' said Malekith. 'You will undermine my power even as it grows until I am forced to treat with you. Do not think I will be so easily fooled. Better that you die here even if it means I must start afresh.'

'There is another way, Malekith,' Morathi told him. 'For the cults, you can imprison me as hostage against their loyalty. What better symbol of your new power than to see the sorceress-queen of Nagarythe bound in chains? Better yet, present me as your captive to Bel Shanaar. Your mercy will earn you great credit in the court of the Phoenix King and amongst the other realms. Would you be known to them as a merciless killer, or as a magnanimous victor? Which do you think they would choose as Bel Shanaar's successor? They have scorned your inheritance once already, naming you as a bloody slayer unfit to rule. Will the blood of your mother change their minds?'

'I care not concerning the opinions of lesser princes,' said Malekith, raising Avanuir again to strike.

'Then you are a fool!' spat Morathi. 'If you would wrest the crown of Ulthuan by force, then go now to the

Blighted Isle and take up the sword your father wielded, for you will need it. If you would perhaps take up your rightful inheritance and reign in glory, then you must make the other princes your followers. Already they look up to you; many would have you replace Bel Shanaar right at this moment. Woo them! Show them your kingly virtues, and the blood of Aenarion will prove its worth.'

For a second time, Malekith lowered his blade. He looked deep into his mother's eyes, seeking some deceit or falsehood, but saw only sincerity.

'You would be humbled before all of Ulthuan,' Malekith said. 'Your station, your rank would be worthless.'

'I care as little about such matters as you,' Morathi said. 'I am confident in you, and have much patience. When you become Phoenix King, I will be rightfully restored to my proper position. I have humbled myself before priests and gods to gain what I have. It is no hardship to masquerade for a while as prisoner to Bel Shanaar.'

Malekith sheathed Avanuir and lifted his mother to her feet. He laid a hand upon her shoulder and pulled her close.

'I will spare you,' he whispered to her. 'But if you wrong me, or play me false, I shall kill you without a second thought.'

Morathi clasped her son in a tight embrace, a hand on the back of his head, her lips close to his ear.

'You have proven that to me,' she sighed. 'That is why I am so proud of you.'

━◀ TWENTY-TWO ▶━

The Wheels of Power Turn

As MORATHI HAD predicted, there was much rejoicing when news of Malekith's victory spread across Ulthuan. Once Anlec was firmly under his control the prince rode to Galthyr to lift the siege there. The Naggarothi commanders threw themselves on Malekith's mercy and swore new oaths of loyalty to the prince. By secret command from Morathi, many of the cultists vanished into the wilds and their leaders hid themselves amongst the folk of Nagarythe. Prince Malekith sent word to the other rulers of Ulthuan that some measure of order had been restored, and feasts of celebration were held across the isle.

Malekith escorted Morathi south to Tor Anroc, accompanied by the three Sapherian mages Thyriol, Merneir and Eltreneth to guard against any sorcery from the seeress. With great show of humility, Malekith went incognito through the towns and villages, sparing his mother the spite of the elves she had all but enslaved.

Many days after leaving Anlec they came to the citadel of the Phoenix King, now an immense palace with a hundred halls and fifty spiralling towers. Swathed in black cloaks, they rode through the gate and were met by Palthrain. No words were said for all had been pre-arranged. The chamberlain ushered the small group through the long corridors and vaulted galleries to the heart of the palace, to the throne room of Bel Shanaar.

The floor was paved with white gold and the walls hung with six hundred tapestries picturing landscapes from the wide realm of the elves. Magical dwarf-forged lanterns bathed all in a pearlescent glow as Malekith pulled back his hood. The prince and his companions strode along the hall to stand before Bel Shanaar, who was sat upon his throne deep in thought. Imrik was there, as were Bathinair, Elodhir, Finudel and Charill.

'My king and princes,' said Malekith. 'Today is a portentous occasion, for as I vowed, I bring before you the witch-queen of Nagarythe, my mother, Morathi.'

Morathi cast off her cloak and stood before her judges. She was dressed in a flowing blue gown, her hair bound up with shining sapphires, her eyelids painted with azure powder. She appeared every inch the defeated queen, dejected but unrepentant.

'You stand before us accused of raising war against the office of the Phoenix King and the realms of the princes of Ulthuan,' Bel Shanaar said.

'It was not I that launched attacks against the border of Nagarythe,' Morathi replied calmly. Her gaze met the eyes of the princes in turn. 'It was not the Naggarothi who sought battle with the other kingdoms.'

'You would portray yourself as the victim?' laughed Finudel. 'To us?'

'No ruler of Nagarythe is a victim,' replied Morathi.

'Do you deny that the cults of excess and luxury that blight our realm owe their loyalty to you?' said Bel Shanaar.

'They owe their loyalty to the cytharai,' said Morathi. 'You can no more prosecute me for the existence of the cults than you can impeach yourself for assuming the mantle of Asuryan's chosen.'

'Will you at least admit to thoughts of treason?' said Elodhir. 'Did you not plot against my father and seek to undermine him?'

'I hold no position in higher regard than that of the Phoenix King,' Morathi said, her eyes fixed upon Bel Shanaar. 'I spoke my mind at the First Council and others chose to ignore my wisdom. My loyalty is to Ulthuan and the prosperity and strength of her people. I do not change my opinions at a whim and my reservations have not been allayed.'

'She is a viper,' snarled Imrik. 'She cannot be allowed to live.'

Morathi laughed, a scornful sound that reverberated menacingly around the hall.

'Who wishes to be known as the elf who slew Aenarion's queen?' the seeress said. 'Which of the mighty princes gathered here would claim that accolade?'

'I will,' said Imrik, his hand straying to the silver hilt of the sword at his waist.

'I cannot condone this,' said Malekith, stepping protectively in front of his mother.

'You swore to me in this very chamber that you would be ready for such an end,' said Bel Shanaar. 'Do you now renege on your oath?'

'No more than I renege on the oath that I would show mercy to all those who asked for it,' said Malekith. 'My mother need not die. Her blood would serve no purpose but to sate the Caledorian's vengeful thirst.'

'It is justice, not revenge,' said Imrik. 'Blood for blood.'

'If she lives, she is a threat,' said Finudel. 'She cannot be trusted.'

'I cannot decide this,' said Malekith, addressing the princes. He then turned his eyes upon the Phoenix King. 'I will not decide this. Let Bel Shanaar decide. The will of the Phoenix King is stronger than the oath of a prince. Is the word of the son of Aenarion to be as nothing, or is there yet nobility enough in the princes of Ulthuan to show compassion and forgiveness?'

Bel Shanaar gave Malekith a sour look, knowing that all that had passed here would be reported by means both open and secret to the people of Ulthuan. Malekith tested his judgement, and there was no course of action that would not damage his reputation with those who wanted to see weakness.

'Morathi cannot go unpunished for her crimes,' Bel Shanaar said slowly. 'There is no place to which I can exile her, for she would return more bitter and ambitious than before. As she enslaved others, so shall she forfeit her freedom. She shall stay in rooms within this palace, under guard night and day. None shall see her save with my permission.'

The Phoenix King stood and glared at the sorceress.

'Know this, Morathi,' said Bel Shanaar. 'The sentence of death is not wholly commuted. You live by my will. If ever you cross me or seek to harm my rule, you will be slain, without trial or representation. Your word is of no value and so I hold your life hostage to your good behaviour. Accept these terms or accept your death.'

Morathi looked at the gathered princes and saw nothing but hatred in their faces, save for Malekith's which was expressionless. They were like wolves that had cornered a wounded lion; knowing that they should slay their prey while they could, yet still fearful that there was fight left yet in their enemy.

'Your demands are not unreasonable, Bel Shanaar of Tiranoc,' she said eventually. 'I consent to be your prisoner.'

WITH MORATHI IN custody, Malekith returned to Anlec, to secure his lands against the cultists that still held sway over some parts of the kingdom. On the surface, a measure of order was restored, though in truth the agents of Anlec were now spread wider and further than ever before. Over the passing years a sense of security grew on Ulthuan once again; but it was a false sense, fostered by the machinations of Malekith.

In ones and twos the cultists began to gather again, now more careful than ever. Their leaders sent messages to each other by their secret ways, and the heads of the dark priesthoods emerged in new guises in Anlec. As councillors and advisors, Malekith masked these magisters within his court, holding over them the threat of exposure to ensure their loyalty to him.

For two decades relative peace prevailed. Often Malekith travelled to Tor Anroc to consult with Bel Shanaar, and ever the prince of Nagarythe would decry his own failure to capture all of those who had been henchmen to his mother. He offered what help he could to the other kingdoms, and spent as much time in the palaces of his fellow princes as he did in Anlec, fostering harmony and friendship.

On these travels he would also visit his mother, supposedly to check on her wellbeing and to accept a repentance that was never offered. On the twentieth anniversary of his mother's imprisonment, Malekith rode alone to Tor Anroc and was granted a private meeting with his mother by the Phoenix King. They were brought together in the majestic gardens at the centre of the palace of Tor Anroc. High hedges hid them from view as they walked across the plush green lawns, their soft words masked by the splashing of fifty fountains.

'How is the hospitality of Bel Shanaar?' asked Malekith as the pair walked arm-in-arm down an avenue of cherry trees laden with blossom.

'I endure what I must,' replied Morathi.

She led Malekith to a bench of ornately carved pale wood and they sat beside each other; the mother's hand on the son's knee, the son's hand on the mother's shoulder. They sat in silence for a while, both with their faces turned to the bright sky, the sun bathing their skin with her warmth. It was Malekith who first broke the peace.

'All is well in Anlec also,' he said. 'My mercy is now legendary. The cytharai worshippers captured by the princes demand that they receive the same opportunity for repentance as you were granted. They come to Anlec and I hear their confessions and apologies.'

'How many hide beneath your shadow?' asked Morathi.

'Many thousands, all utterly loyal to me,' said the prince with a smile.

'So you stand ready to move soon?' asked the seeress.

'Not yet,' said Malekith, his smile fading. 'Imrik yet resists me in the court of the Phoenix King.'

'Imrik will never be won over,' said Morathi. 'Not only is he jealous, he is shrewd. He guesses our intent, but cannot prove any wrongdoing.'

'Nagarythe also is not yet united,' said Malekith with a solemn shake of his head.

'How so?' asked Morathi.

'There are some princes and nobles who are still fearful of my power,' said Malekith. 'Eoloran of the Anars is chief amongst them. They wish to impose self-rule upon their lands in the mountains.'

'Then Eoloran must be killed,' said Morathi briskly.

'I cannot,' said Malekith. 'Since your fall, his influence has grown considerably. Not only do some Naggarothi nobles hold him in high esteem, some commanders of my armies are under his sway. His lands overseas are highly profitable. Before I can eliminate him, I need him to fall from grace.'

Morathi said nothing for a moment, her eyes narrowed in thought.

'Leave that to me,' she said. 'Word will come to you when you can act.'

'I will not ask what it is that you plan,' said Malekith. 'Yet, I do not understand how it is that you can do anything from here, right under the eyes and ears of Bel Shanaar.'

'Trust your mother,' said Morathi. 'I have my ways.'

The skies were greying and a cloud obscured the sun. Now in shade, the pair stood and walked back to the palace, each lost in thought.

As MORATHI HAD predicted, Imrik of Caledor remained steadfastly suspicious of Malekith's motives, and shunned the prince's overtures of alliance and comradeship. It mattered not though, for through subtle rumour and devious innuendo, Malekith spread the idea that Imrik was jealous of Malekith's popularity. The prince of Nagarythe never spoke out openly against his opponent, and was always ready to praise Imrik's deeds and the calibre of his lineage. He even went so far as to say that, but for the grace of fate, Imrik's father would have been Phoenix King instead of Bel Shanaar. While appearing to be a great compliment, this had the desired effect on the other princes, who had always harboured envy of Caledor's status. Such comments flamed the embers of rumour that Imrik felt wronged that his father had not been chosen by the First Council.

ONE THOUSAND, SIX hundred and sixty-eight years after first bowing his knee to Bel Shanaar, Malekith stood ready to make his claim to be Phoenix King. He needed a catalyst that would act as a spur to action on the princes. With a carefully orchestrated series of events, Malekith planned to plunge Ulthuan into brief turmoil once more, so that he could arise from the flames of conflict and claim his birthright.

It began innocently enough, with news that Malekith's warriors had arrested Eoloran Anar, when evidence had come to light that the lord of House Anar had been corrupted by worshippers of Atharti. Cultists rose up out of hiding all across Nagarythe and elsewhere in Ulthuan, supposedly in response to the persecution of a prominent leader. Those who disbelieved the charge against Eoloran were incensed and they too spoke out against Malekith.

Confusion reigned in Nagarythe, as claim and counter-claim spread from town to town, and violence soon followed. None could say for sure who started the killings, but soon there was bitter fighting between those loyal to the Anars and the cultists. The other princes looked on in disbelief as Nagarythe quickly descended into anarchy, where loyalties were so fractured that families were divided and brother fought against brother. Amidst the chaos, Malekith appeared to be doing what he could to restore order, but even his armies seemed fractured by the factions now contending for power.

The battles that had begun in Nagarythe rapidly spread to other parts of Ulthuan as the cults came out of the shadows and struck at the princes. Palaces burned and citizens were killed on the streets as Ulthuan erupted into bloody infighting. Malekith fought hard to restore his rule in his own kingdom, but the populace had turned against him, for one reason or another. He was forced to quit Anlec with a few thousand loyal troops, and he called upon Bel Shanaar to give him sanctuary.

So it came to pass that in the autumn of that year, Malekith dwelt in Tor Anroc, and came before Bel Shanaar with a plea. The two were alone in the Phoenix King's throne room, for the princes of the court had returned to their realms to restore what order they could.

'I would make right my mistake,' said Malekith, standing before the Phoenix King, head bowed.

'What mistake have you made?' asked Bel Shanaar.

'In my desire to seek accord with the worshippers of the forbidden gods, I have allowed them to spread unseen and unchecked,' Malekith replied. 'I have allowed myself to be lured into a web of deceit, and was fooled into believing that House Anar were my enemies. Nagarythe now burns with hatred, and I am cast out.'

'What would you have me do?' said the Phoenix King. 'I cannot command your subjects for you.'

'I would have peace restored, so that bitter enmities might be settled and wrongs put to right,' said Malekith, raising his gaze to meet the inquiring stare of Bel Shanaar.

'We all wish that, I am sure,' said Bel Shanaar. 'However, I cannot grant it by simply wishing it so. I ask again, what would you have me do?'

'We must be united in this,' said Malekith earnestly. 'The cults flourished before because we each acted alone. All of the princes must speak with one voice. All of the kingdoms must come together to defeat this dark menace.'

'How so?' said Bel Shanaar with a frown.

'The oaths sworn here many years ago to stand against the cults still hold true,' said Malekith. 'The princes of Ulthuan are still of one purpose on this matter.'

'I do not yet see what you ask of me,' said the Phoenix King.

'As one army we must fight, under one general,' said Malekith. He strode forwards and grasped Bel Shanaar's hand in both of his, falling to one knee. 'As did my father, the army of Ulthuan must be wielded as a single weapon. Each realm in turn shall be cleansed, and no traitor will go unpunished this time.'

'The armies of Ulthuan are not mine alone to command,' Bel Shanaar said slowly. 'I have already pledged the support of Tiranoc, and that has not changed.'

'All have pledged support and even now muster their forces for their own wars,' Malekith said. 'Though perhaps our need has grown greater, more princes than not swore in this chamber to lend their aid.'

'Yet, it is the very magnitude of the situation that will force them to have second thoughts,' Bel Shanaar said. 'It is one thing to ask them to send a few thousand troops to quell cultists and malcontents. To mobilise the militia, to gather their full armies now, on the cusp of winter, is a much greater undertaking. What they have promised and what you now ask is not the same thing.'

'We do not have time to stand idle,' Malekith growled. 'Within a season, civil war could engulf this island. I cannot go to each of the princes in turn and ask for their renewed pledges. You must call the rulers of the kingdoms to a council, so that the matter can be settled.'

'That is within my power, for sure,' said Bel Shanaar. 'For some, the journey to Tor Anroc will take some time, though.'

'Then call them to the Shrine of Asuryan upon the Isle of Flame,' suggested Malekith, standing. 'Thirty days hence, all princes will be able to attend, in the place where you were accepted by the king of gods to succeed my father. We shall consult the oracles there, and with their guidance choose the best course of action for all.'

Bel Shanaar considered this in silence, stroking his chin, as he was wont to do when deep in thought.

'So shall it be,' the Phoenix King said with a solemn nod. 'In thirty days we shall convene the council of princes in the Shrine of Asuryan to determine the destiny of our people.'

◄ TWENTY-THREE ►

A Council Convened

CARATHRIL STAYED IN Tor Anroc for several more days after Bel Shanaar's proclamation, while heralds were despatched to the princes of Ulthuan. In that time he spoke to Palthrain the chamberlain and others, gauging the mood of the folk of Tiranoc. They were resolute but afraid, was his conclusion. Beyond the Naganath now stood a terrible foe, who could sweep down over Tiranoc at any time. Acting on Malekith's advice, Bel Shanaar despatched an army of twenty thousand elves to the north, to patrol the border and guard the bridges across the Naganath. If the prince of Nagarythe was correct, the cults would not make their next move until spring, for only the desperate or the foolish started a campaign in winter. This was the hope of Bel Shanaar and his council: that the princes would agree to Malekith's mobilisation and send their forces to the west.

Just before Carathril was due to leave for Lothern to take word to Prince Haradrin, he was called to the audience chamber by Bel Shanaar. When he entered, he found himself alone with the Phoenix King, and the doors were closed behind him.

'Come here, Carathril,' the Phoenix King said, waving the captain forwards. 'You ride today for Eataine, yes?'

'This morning, your majesty,' said Carathril, stopping just before Bel Shanaar's throne. 'A ship awaits me at Atreal Anor once I have crossed the mountains, and it is less than a day by sail from Lothern to the Isle of Flame. I felt it better to ensure the other heralds were well prepared before leaving.'

'Yes, you have performed your duties with great dedication and precision, Carathril,' said Bel Shanaar. He opened his mouth to continue but then stopped. With a finger, he beckoned for Carathril to come closer, and when the Phoenix King spoke, his voice was but a whisper. 'I have one other duty for you to perform. We must gather our forces as Prince Malekith has said, but I am not convinced that it is he that should lead them. Though he seems determined enough to prosecute this war, it is by no means certain that he is entirely free from the influence of Morathi.'

'He resisted well enough at Ealith, I saw it with my own eyes,' said Carathril. 'Also, do we not cast away our greatest weapon if Malekith does not lead the army? If not under the command of the rightful prince of Nagarythe, do our forces not appear to be invaders rather than liberators?'

'I fear that is a poison already spread far by Morathi,' replied Bel Shanaar. 'The Naggarothi have been set against the other realms long before this day; ever have they been independent of thought and deed. Many in Nagarythe, not least Morathi, believe Malekith to be the true successor to Aenarion, and see me as usurper. By giving over command of our armies to the prince, it may be taken as a sign of weakness on my part. I will be seen as ineffective, unable to lead my own subjects. Another must command the army of Ulthuan, in my name alone. I will force Malekith to agree to this condition before I leave for the Isle of Flame.'

'I understand, your majesty,' said Carathril. 'Yet, I still do not know what duty it is that you ask of me.'

The Phoenix King pulled forth a parchment scroll from the folds of his robes and handed it to Carathril.

'Keep this safe, on your person at all times,' the Phoenix King said.

'What is it?' asked Carathril.

'It is better that you do not know,' said Bel Shanaar. 'You must pass it to Prince Imrik at the council.'

'That is all, your majesty?' said Carathril, wondering what message could deserve such secrecy.

'Let no other see it!' insisted Bel Shanaar, leaning forwards and grasping Carathril by the wrist. 'Let no other know that you bear it!'

Bel Shanaar sat back with a sigh, and then smiled.

'I trust you, Carathril,' he said.

BEFORE NOON, CARATHRIL had set out, the missive of the Phoenix King hidden in a leather canister under his robes, next to his heart. With him rode Prince Elodhir and a contingent of Tiranoc knights, to ensure the council was ready for the arrival of the Phoenix King. For Carathril, the journey was unremarkable; he had ridden back and forth across Eagle Pass dozens of times since becoming herald for Bel Shanaar. For six days they rode eastwards, crossing the mountains without incident, and met with Prince

Finudel on the eastward side of the pass, just south of his capital at Tor Elyr. The two companies joined for the two days of journeying to Atreal Anor, where they took separate ships. Carathril was bound for Lothern to meet with Prince Haradrin, while Finudel and Elodhir were to set course straight for the Isle of Flame, to prepare the Shrine of Asuryan for the council.

Both ships travelled south and east across the Sea of Dusk, westernmost of the two bodies of water that made up the Inner Sea, skirting the coast of Caledor. Their southerly route took them away from the Isle of the Dead at the centre of the Inner Sea, where the mage Caledor Dragontamer and his followers still stood, locked in eternal stasis within the centre of Ulthuan's magical vortex. Rather than pass by the ill-fated isle, the ships navigated the Strait of Cal Edras, between Anel Edras and Anel Khabyr, which formed the outermost pair of islands of a long archipelago that curved out from Caledor towards the Isle of the Dead. Once through the Cal Edras, the ships parted company.

There were many ships in the Bay of Whispers, plying trade between the coastal villages of Caledor and Saphery, passing in and out of the Straits of Lothern. Carathril spoke to a few of the other crews, and found them to be mostly unaware of the true extent of the tragedy that had happened in the north.

Word had spread of Malekith's expulsion and despite this setback many seemed confident of the prince's ability to reclaim Nagarythe. Carathril chose not to disavow the sailors of their current optimism, knowing that it would be upon ships that news of any disaster would spread fastest, setting panic like a fire in the heart of Ulthuan.

As they sailed onwards towards Lothern, Carathril wondered if his view of life had once been as blinkered as that of his fellow elves. They seemed to be preoccupied with their own dreams and ambitions, and did not give much thought to other forces outside of their immediate lives. He concluded that he had been the same; believing that the cults had been a problem but never once considering the extent to which they had infected the society of Ulthuan, never seeing the threat they truly posed.

The docks at Lothern were as busy as ever, packed with merchantmen returning from the burgeoning colonies or readying to depart with cargoes of goods from the realms of Ulthuan. In a way, it heartened Carathril to see the life of his home city bustling and progressing as if nothing had happened; yet deep inside he knew that this was all soon to change and that his people were utterly unprepared.

For over a thousand years since Bel Shanaar's election as Phoenix King, relative peace had reigned over Ulthuan. War and bloodshed was something brought back in stories from across the seas, and the elves had become complacent, perhaps even indulgent. Now Carathril could see that it was that very security and comfort, the social ennui of an entire people, which had allowed the pleasure cults to flourish so well.

There was no guard to greet Carathril at the Prince's Quay, for his arrival was to be kept secret lest cultists in Lothern learned of what Malekith and Bel Shanaar planned. He rode quickly through the city, allowing the chatter and crowds to flow around him unnoticed. So disturbed had Carathril become, so anxious of what the future held, that there was no joy in his homecoming. His thoughts were dark as he rode up the winding streets to the hilltops where the manses and palaces of the nobility were built.

The palace of Prince Haradrin was not a fortress like Tor Anroc or Anlec, but rather a wide spread of houses and villas set out in ornate gardens upon the mount of Annui Lotheil, which overlooked all of the city and the straits.

Carathril made directly for the Winter Palace, where he knew Prince Haradrin would be staying. The sentries at the gate recognised him as he approached and stepped aside without word to let him pass.

Prince Haradrin granted him audience immediately, in a great domed hall, its ceiling cunningly painted so that as light from the windows struck it at different times of the day it pictured the movement of the sun in a summer sky and then descended into a glowing twilight.

Before the assembled court Carathril relayed the recent news as concisely as he could, and the princes listened intently and without interruption.

'Bel Shanaar calls upon the princes of Eataine to remember their oaths to the Phoenix Throne,' the herald concluded.

'And what does Bel Shanaar expect from Eataine?' asked Prince Haradrin.

'The Sea Guard and Lothern Guard must stand ready to fight, highness,' said Carathril. 'He calls for Prince Haradrin to attend a council upon the Isle of Flame.'

'Who else shall be at this council?' asked Haradrin.

'All of the princes of Ulthuan are expected to attend, to pledge their support to the Phoenix King's cause,' said Carathril with a small bow of deference.

'Though now herald to Bel Shanaar, you were born of Lothern, Carathril,' Haradrin said, standing up from his throne and walking closer. 'Tell me truthfully, what is Bel Shanaar's intent?'

Carathril felt the letter to Imrik against his skin but kept his gaze steadily upon the prince.

'He would rid our people of the curse of the cults,' Carathril said evenly. 'War is coming, highness.'

Haradrin nodded without comment before turning to his courtiers gathered about the throne.

'Eataine will stand beside Tiranoc,' he declared. 'Send word to the Sea Guard that they should return to Lothern. They shall patrol the Bay of Whispers and bring word to me of all that passes on the ships of the Inner Sea. We shall not yet raise the call to arms, but upon my return be ready to do so. If war is to be our fate, Eataine shall not flinch from her duty.'

CARATHRIL WAS CONTENT to spend the following days wandering the city, safe in the knowledge that his part in these matters had been played. He would accompany Haradrin to the Isle of Flame, deliver the Phoenix King's letter to Imrik and then await the arrival of Malekith and Bel Shanaar. Carathril had resolved that he would ask the Phoenix King to absolve him of his duty as herald so that he could return to his rightful station as a captain of Lothern. While he had been content to march alongside Malekith on his expedition, if full-scale war was to come, Carathril wanted to fight with his own folk, in the army of Eataine.

As he walked the city, Carathril inquired after Aerenis, but of his friend he heard nothing. Wherever he asked, Carathril heard conflicting tales of his lieutenant's whereabouts. Shared acquaintances told Carathril that his friend had been seen little since returning from Tor Anroc those many years ago. Many thought he was on constant duty at the palace, attending the prince, others thought he had been despatched to one of the outlying towns to train young spearmen. Some claimed that he had resigned his commission and sailed over the sea to a new life.

Though disturbed by the lack of information concerning his friend, there was little Carathril could do further, for he was due to sail with Prince Haradrin to the Isle of Flame. The time came when the royal entourage was ready to depart, three days before the deadline set by Bel Shanaar. Carathril was given a berth upon Haradrin's elegant eagleship, although by rights he was not yet part of Lothern's guard again.

As the ship set sail and moved away from the wharf, Carathril looked back at Lothern, seeing it as if for the first time. He looked at the great statues of the gods surrounding the bay: Kurnous the Hunter, Isha the Mother, Vaul the Smith and Asuryan the Allfather. He had barely noticed them before, having grown up with them in sight. Now he looked again at their stern faces and wondered what part they would play in coming events. He also wondered if there were, out in the city somewhere, hidden cellars with images of the darker gods: shrines to the like of Nethu, Anath Raema, Khirkith, Elinill and the other cytharai.

The immense gold and ruby gate to the Inner Sea was open, and hawkships darted ahead of the prince's vessel to clear a path between the crowd of fishing boats, pleasure barges and cargo ships. Once out of the Straits of Lothern, the ship's captain set full sail and the eagleship danced across the waves, gliding across the water at full speed. The sun shone overhead and the blue waters glittered, and for a while at least Carathril was content to stand at the rail and marvel at the beauty of Ulthuan; happy to forget his woes as he lost himself in the sparkle of water and the blue sky.

They sailed overnight with reduced sail, and it was mid-morning when they came into view of the Isle of Flame. Though Carathril had passed it many times before on his way to Saphery, Cothique and Yvresse, the Shrine of Asuryan still amazed him. The white pyramid rose up from a marbled courtyard set within an open meadow.

The walls of the shrine blazed with reflected sunlight, bathing the grass and surrounding water with its majesty. The isle itself was surrounded by gently shoaling white beaches and long piers stretched out into the water. There were four vessels already moored as they hove into the dock: the ships of other princes already arrived on the isle.

◀ TWENTY-FOUR ▶

An Act of Infamy

It was the day before Bel Shanaar and Malekith were due to leave Tor Anroc for the council upon the Isle of Flame when the Phoenix King commanded the prince of Nagarythe to attend him in his throne room. Malekith walked quickly to the audience chamber, his instinct for intrigue curious as to what the Phoenix King had to say.

'I have been thinking deep upon your words,' Bel Shanaar proclaimed.

'I am pleased to hear that,' said Malekith. 'May I ask what the nature of your thoughts has been?'

'I will put your idea to the princes,' said Bel Shanaar. 'A single army drawn from all kingdoms will prosecute this war against the vile cults.'

'I am glad that you agree with my reasoning,' said Malekith, wondering why Bel Shanaar had brought him here to tell him what he already knew.

'I have also been giving much thought to who is best qualified to lead this army,' said Bel Shanaar, and Malekith's heart skipped a beat in anticipation.

'I would be honoured,' said the prince of Malekith.

Bel Shanaar opened his mouth to say something but then closed it again, a confused frown upon his brow.

'You misunderstand me,' the Phoenix King then said. 'I will nominate Imrik to be my chosen general.'

Malekith stood in stunned silence, left speechless by the Phoenix King's announcement.

'Imrik?' he said eventually.

'Why not?' said Bel Shanaar. 'He is a fine general, and Caledor is the most stable of all the realms at the current time. He is well respected amongst the other princes. Yes, he will make a good choice.'

'And why do you tell me this?' snapped Malekith. 'Perhaps you seek to mock me!'

'Mock you?' said Bel Shanaar, taken aback. 'I am telling you this so that you will speak in favour of my decision. I know that you have much influence and your word will lend great weight to Imrik's authority.'

'You would raise up the grandson of Caledor over the son of Aenarion?' said Malekith. 'Have I not forged new kingdoms across the world at the head of armies? If not my bloodline, than my achievements must qualify me above all others.'

'I am sorry that you feel this way, Malekith,' said Bel Shanaar, unabashed. 'The council will endorse my choice, you would do well to align yourself with me.'

At this, Malekith's frayed temper snapped utterly.

'Align myself to you?' he snarled. 'The hunter does not align himself to his hound! The master does not align himself to his servant!'

'Choose your next words carefully, Malekith!' warned the Phoenix King. 'Remember who it is that you address!'

The Naggarothi prince mastered his anger, biting back further retorts.

'I trust that my protest has been recognised,' he said with effort. 'I urge you to reconsider your decision.'

'You are free to speak your mind at the council,' said Bel Shanaar. 'It is your right to argue against Imrik, and to put forward yourself as candidate. We shall let the princes decide.'

Malekith said nothing more, but bowed stiffly and left, silently seething. He did not return to his chambers, but instead made for the wing of the palace where his mother was kept in captivity. Ignoring the guards at the door to her chambers, he knocked and then let himself in.

The chambers were well furnished, with exquisitely crafted furniture and splendid tapestries upon the walls. Though a prisoner, his mother had lost none of her aesthetic, and over the years had built up quite a collection of art and other ornaments. All of the finery however was somewhat overshadowed by the silvered runes carved upon the walls: mystical wards that kept the winds of magic at bay and thus denied Morathi her sorcerous power. They were a precaution Bel Shanaar had insisted upon.

There was no sign of her in the reception room, and Malekith strode through to the dining chamber beyond. There Morathi sat at a small table, a plate of fruit before her. She plucked a grape from the platter and looked up at him as he stormed in. She said nothing but simply raised an eyebrow inquisitively.

'Bel Shanaar will name Imrik as the general of the army,' growled Malekith.

Morathi dropped the grape back onto the plate and stood up.

'You think he will win the vote?' she asked.

'Of course he will,' snapped the prince. 'He is the Phoenix King, after all, and Imrik would be the best choice after me. If Imrik is made commander of the army, then Bel Shanaar has as good as named his successor. My chance will have passed and Ulthuan will be doomed to a slow dwindling under ever-lesser kings. My father's legacy will be cast upon the ashes of our history and his line will dwindle and die. I cannot allow that to happen.'

'Then Bel Shanaar must not be allowed to put forward his arguments,' said Morathi quietly. 'The time for plotting and patience has come to an end. It is time to act, and swiftly.'

'What do you mean?' asked Malekith. 'How will I prevent Bel Shanaar making his declaration?'

'You must kill him,' she said.

Malekith paused, surprised at himself for not immediately dismissing the idea. In fact, the thought appealed to him. He had waited sixteen centuries to become Phoenix King, a long time even for an elf. Why settle for becoming general of Ulthuan and waiting the gods only knew how long for Bel Shanaar to die of natural causes? Better to take the initiative and see the gambit out for good or ill.

'What must I do?' Malekith asked without hesitation.

'Palthrain is one of my creatures,' Morathi said. 'Long has he been my spy in Tor Anroc. He will hide certain objects in Bel Shanaar's chambers, as evidence of the Phoenix King's worship of Ereth Khial. These will be discovered by you, and you will go to Bel Shanaar's rooms to confront him with this proof. When you arrive, he will be dead, having poisoned himself rather than face the truth.'

'He leaves on the morrow for the Isle of Flame,' Malekith snarled in frustration. 'There is no time to fabricate such a plot!'

'Fabricate?' laughed Morathi. 'You are so short-sighted sometimes, my dear son. The evidence is already in place, and has been for years. Long have I mulled over how to rid us of this wretched swine, and now the time has come. See Palthrain and get the poison from him. Find some pretence to visit the usurper and give him the poisoned wine. Everything else will already be taken care of.'

Malekith paused, considering the implications of what he was about to do.

'If what you say is true, how is it that you have not acted before?' said Malekith. 'Why have you suffered embarrassment and captivity when you could have struck down he who vexes us both?'

Morathi stood and embraced her son.

'Because I am a loving mother,' she said quietly. Standing back, she smoothed the creases in her dress. 'If Bel Shanaar had been slain, Imrik would have stood ready to take his place, as he does now. There would be war between Nagarythe and Caledor. I could not hand you such a poisoned chalice. Now you are stronger and your claim will be agreed by the princes. Imrik's lone voice will not be an obstacle.'

'Surely Palthrain is more trusted than I am,' said Malekith, sitting down on an elegantly carved chair. 'It will be easier for him to administer the poison.'

Morathi shook her head in disappointment and crossed her arms.

'Palthrain will not become Phoenix King with this act,' she said sternly. 'Show me that you have the will to succeed your father. More than that, prove it to yourself. The throne is there for the taking. Only by your own hand can you take it and deserve to sit upon it. Bel Shanaar was given his rule by others. True kings seize it for themselves.'

Malekith nodded wordlessly, struck by the truth of his mother's words. If he could do this one simple thing there was nothing that would stand between him and his dream of ruling Ulthuan.

'Come on!' said Morathi, clapping her hands as if to chivvy along a wayward child. 'You will have plenty of time to practise your speech to the princes on the voyage to the Isle of Flame.'

'I will be Phoenix King,' murmured Malekith, savouring the thought.

Upon leaving his mother, the prince sought out the chamberlain. He took Palthrain to the gardens where they could speak in privacy, and informed him of his desire to enact his mother's plan for assassinating Bel Shanaar. Palthrain took this news without comment, merely telling Malekith that Bel Shanaar was wont to take his evening repast at sunset. He agreed to meet the prince by the Phoenix King's rooms just before then, and would provide him with the deadly wine.

For the remainder of the day, Malekith fretted in his chambers, pacing back and forth. Though he did not doubt that what he was doing would ultimately be for the benefit of all, he worried that the plan would somehow be forestalled. He wanted to speak to his mother again, but knew that to visit her so soon after their last meeting might arouse suspicion.

As the day wore on, doubts clawed at Malekith's nerves. Could Palthrain be trusted? Even now, was the chamberlain fulfilling his true loyalty and reporting the plot to the Phoenix King? Every footstep in the corridor beyond the door to his chambers set Malekith on edge, as he suspected the approach of Bel Shanaar's guards.

Pacing like a trapped animal, barely ready to believe that success was so close, Malekith prowled and brooded in his rooms, unable to settle. He constantly strode to the window to check the progress of the day, as if by his will alone he could bring the sunset more quickly.

After an eternity, the sun was finally upon the horizon and Malekith set out from his rooms to meet Palthrain. He kept his expression genial as he passed servants and guards in the corridors. He then realised that he was not normally so cordial and set his face in a determined frown instead; an expression with which all in Tor Anroc were now very familiar.

In the corridor around the corner from Bel Shaanar's main chambers Palthrain stood with a tray upon which stood a silver ewer and goblet, and a plate of cured meats and bread. Palthrain passed him the tray but Malekith's hands were shaking and the chamberlain quickly retrieved it.

Malekith took deep breaths, trying to calm himself as if summoning the power for a difficult spell. Ignoring the purposefully blank expression of Palthrain, the prince took the tray once more, now in control of his body.

'Are you sure this will work?' demanded Malekith. 'It must be final!'

'It is used in certain practices of the Khainites, to numb the senses,' Palthrain replied. 'In small doses it will render its victim incapable for several hours. With the amount I have put in the wine, it will be fatal. At first he will be paralysed. Then his breathing will become difficult as his lungs freeze, and then he will fall pass away.'

'No pain?' said Malekith.

'Not that I am aware of, highness,' said Palthrain.

'What a pity,' said Malekith.

THE NAGGAROTHI PRINCE walked down the passageway to Bel Shanaar's chambers, forcing himself to stride slowly so as not to garner attention. He knocked at the door and waited for Bel Shanaar's call for him to enter.

The Phoenix King was sat at a writing desk, no doubt penning corrections to his speech for the council.

'Malekith?' he said, startled.

'Forgive the intrusion, your majesty,' said Malekith with a low bow. He stepped across the room and placed the tray on the desk.

'Why are you here?' asked Bel Shanaar. 'Where's Palthrain?'

'I apologise for waylaying him, majesty,' said Malekith. 'I wished to bring you your wine as a peace offering.'

'Peace offering?'

'I wholeheartedly wish to offer my apologies,' replied Malekith, pouring the poisoned wine into the goblet. 'I spoke out of misplaced anger earlier, and I caused great offence. My anger is not with you, though it might have seemed that way. I have endeavoured to earn your trust and to be a loyal subject, and it is my failings not yours that have led you to choose Imrik. I will be happy to support your choice.'

The prince passed the cup to Bel Shanaar, his face a mask of politeness. The Phoenix King frowned and for a moment Malekith feared that he suspected something. The Phoenix King took the goblet however, and placed it on the desk.

'Your apology is accepted,' said Bel Shanaar. 'I do trust you, my friend, but you have personal concerns that far outweigh any duty to me. I choose Imrik not just on ability, but on the fact that I would have you address the problems of your kingdom without distraction. I would have you direct your energies solely to restoring your rule, not pandering to the whims of other kingdoms.'

The goblet remained on the desk.

'Your consideration heartens me greatly,' said Malekith, keeping his eyes fixed firmly upon the Phoenix King lest he dart a betraying glance towards the wine.

'You will offer your support in the council?' Bel Shanaar asked, finally lifting the cup to his lips and taking a mouthful of the wine.

It was not enough for the poison to work and the prince silently willed Bel Shanaar to drink more.

'When the debate rages, none will argue harder than I,' said Malekith with a smile.

Bel Shanaar nodded and took another sip of wine.

'If that is all, then I wish you a fair evening and look forward to sailing with you in the morning,' said Bel Shanaar with a polite nod.

Malekith stood there watching for some sign of the poison's effect.

'What are you staring at?' asked the Phoenix King.

'Is the wine not to your satisfaction?' said the prince, taking a step closer.

'I am not thirsty,' said Bel Shanaar, placing the goblet back on the desk.

Malekith twisted and picked up the goblet and sniffed it.

'It is very fine wine, majesty,' he said.

'I am sure it is, Malekith,' said Bel Shanaar, pursing his lips. His voice became more insistent. 'However, I feel a little sleepy all of a sudden. I shall retire for the night and see you in the morning.'

Stifling a frustrated shout, Malekith lunged forwards and seized Bel Shanaar by the throat. The Phoenix King's eyes widened with terror as Malekith forced open Bel Shanaar's mouth and emptied in the contents of the goblet. The goblet tumbled from the prince's fingertips and spilt a cascade of red droplets over the white boards of the floor.

Clamping one hand over the Phoenix King's nose and mouth and dragging his head back by his hair, Malekith choked the king until he swallowed the deadly draught. He then released his grip and stepped back to watch his future unfold.

'What have you–' panted Bel Shanaar, clawing at his throat and chest.

Malekith lifted the parchment from the desk. As he had suspected, it was a draft of the Phoenix King's speech for the council. Thinking it better that no evidence of Bel Shanaar's support for Imrik was found, he crossed the room and tossed it into the fire burning in the grate. Turning, he saw that there was still life in Bel Shanaar's bulging eyes.

Malekith padded forwards until he was very close, and bent towards the dying elf's ear.

'You brought this upon yourself,' the prince hissed.

With a last gurgle, Bel Shanaar died, his face purple, his tongue lolling from his mouth. Malekith stood for a moment, absent-mindedly looking at the contorted face, not quite believing that it was almost over.

'Well, I have to leave you now,' he said at last, affectionately patting the Phoenix King's head. 'I have a throne to claim.'

TWENTY-FIVE

The Wrath of Asuryan

PARTIES FROM YVRESSE, Cothique, Saphery and Ellyrion camped upon the meadows surrounding the shrine, in a pavilion town of bright reds, blues and whites. The banners of the princes flew from standard poles above the tents, and mailed sentries stood guard on the perimeter. A place had been set aside already for the prince of Eataine and his contingent, and while Haradrin's servants laboured at the dock to unload the wares and stores of the camp, Carathril went to the shrine itself.

The outer parts of the temple were open rows of columns decorated in relief with images of Asuryan in many guises: as a loving father, a swooping eagle, a rising phoenix and others. Between the colonnade and the shrine proper stood the Phoenix Guard, the sacred warriors of Asuryan, with glittering halberds and high-crested helms. Their white cloaks were embroidered with patterns of red and blue flames leaping up from their hems, and their scale armour shone with gilding.

All were silent, for they were avowed to never speak; each had passed into the Chamber of Days, where the history of Aenarion was recorded, and so too all the histories of the Phoenix Kings yet to come. Past, present and future were laid bare within that secret hall, and the Phoenix Guard were forbidden to speak of the knowledge they now guarded.

Two of the Phoenix Guards stepped forwards and lowered their halberds to stop Carathril as he walked under an arched entrance into the shrine. Carathril presented the seal of the Phoenix King and they let him pass. Inside, Carathril found himself in an antechamber, a small room unadorned but for a carving of a great phoenix over the closed door opposite. Stoops of clear water flanked the doorway, and Carathril paused to wash his hands and face.

He opened the door and moved further in, to find himself in a wide gallery that ran around the outside of the central chamber. Phoenix Guards barred any route to the left or right and Carathril walked ahead, passing through another archway into the holiest of shrines on Ulthuan.

His gaze was immediately drawn to the sacred flame. From nothing it sprang, hovering without fuel over the middle of the chamber, burning blue then green then red then golden, shifting colour every few moments. It gave off no heat that Carathril could feel, but he felt a wave of calmness wash over him as he approached. There was not a crackle or hiss of burning; the flames were as silent as their guardians.

'Do not approach too closely,' warned a voice beside Carathril, and he turned to see an ageing elf wrapped in a blue and yellow robe, leaning upon a staff tipped with a golden likeness of a phoenix. Carathril recognised him immediately as Mianderin, the high priest of the shrine, who had presided here for as long as Carathril could remember. His attention thus drawn from the flame, Carathril noticed that there was much activity in the central chamber, as priests and acolytes brought forth tables and chairs and arranged flame-patterned rugs upon the floor in readiness for the council.

'All will be ready for tomorrow,' said Mianderin. 'Is there something with which I might help you?'

'No,' said Carathril, shaking his head. 'No, there is nothing… except, perhaps, you might furnish me with some information.'

'What is it that you wish to know?' the high priest asked.

'Has there been any word from Prince Imrik?' said Carathril.

'A messenger arrived yesterday,' said Mianderin. 'Both he and Prince Koradrel are hunting in the mountains and could not be located. By choice, I would presume.'

Carathril's heart sank; how was he to present Bel Shanaar's message to Imrik now? He hoped that whatever the missive contained, it was not important to the business of the council.

'Thank you for your help,' he said distractedly.

'Peace be upon your life,' the old priest said as Carathril turned away. The captain paused and looked back.

'I most fervently hope so,' said Carathril before heading out of the shrine.

IT WAS GONE noon on the day appointed for the council to begin, and still there had been no sign of Bel Shanaar, nor Malekith, Imrik or Koradrel. In all there were nearly two dozen princes gathered, some leaders of realms, others powerful nobles in their own right, as holders of land or commanders of troops. As Carathril had seen before, they conspired and bickered in an almost casual fashion, directing vague slights against one another whilst making promises of cooperation and partnership. Though they had been sent word of the unfortunate events of Nagarythe, none knew fully why they had been asked to come, and as the day wore on without sign of the Phoenix King, tempers began to fray and arguments broke out.

Some of the princes, Bathinair chief amongst them, complained bitterly of the disrespect done to them by Bel Shanaar's tardiness. There were whispered threats of returning back to their lands, but they were persuaded to stay by courteous argument from the likes of Thyriol and Finudel. The presence of Elodhir did much to calm the situation, who spent every moment apologising for his father's delay and assuring that it would be worth the princes' while to remain and hear what he had to say.

It was late afternoon, and the autumn sky was just beginning to darken when the huge ship *Indraugnir* glided effortlessly to the quay, the flag of Nagarythe flying from her masthead. There were claps and cheers, some of them ironic, as Malekith strode down the ramp onto the wharf, followed by several dozen of his armoured knights.

Retainers of the prince swarmed over the gunwales, quickly unloading sacks and chests onto the pier. Malekith waved for the princes to predede him inside and they did so, leaving Carathril, the Phoenix Guards and a few other retainers outside with the knights of Anlec.

'Prince, what of the Phoenix King?' said Carathril, falling into step beside the swiftly striding Malekith. The prince did not reply but simply shooed Carathril away with a fluttered hand. Slighted, Carathril gave a snort and stormed away towards the quay.

* * *

INSIDE THE SHRINE, the princes and their aides had seated themselves around a horseshoe of tables that had been set up before the sacred flames, and in a chair directly in front of the flames sat Mianderin, his staff of office held across his lap. Other priests moved around the tables filling goblets with wine or water, and offering fruits and confectionaries.

The table nearest the entrance was empty, reserved for Bel Shanaar. Malekith stood behind it, earning himself frowns from Mianderin and a few of the princes. He was flanked by two knights who carried wrapped bundles in their hands. The prince of Nagarythe stood there, leaning onto the table with gauntleted fists, and stared balefully at the assembled council.

'Weakness prevails,' spat Malekith. 'Weakness grips this island like a child squeezing the juices from an over-ripened fruit. Selfishness has driven us to inaction, and now the time to act may have passed. Complacency rules where princes should lead. You have allowed the cults of depravity to flourish, and done nothing. You have looked to foreign shores and counted your gold, and allowed thieves to sneak into your towns and cities to steal away your children. And you have been content to allow a traitor to wear the Phoenix Crown!'

With this last declaration there were gasps and shouts of horror from the princes. Malekith's knights opened their bundles and tossed the contents upon the table: the crown and feathered cloak of Bel Shanaar.

Elodhir leapt to his feet, fist raised.

'Where is my father?' he demanded.

'What has happened to the Phoenix King?' cried Finudel.

'He is dead!' snarled Malekith. 'Killed by his weakness of spirit.'

'That cannot be so!' exclaimed Elodhir, his voice strangled and fraught with anger.

'It is,' said Malekith with a sigh, his demeanour suddenly one of sorrow. 'I promised to root out this vileness, and was shocked to find that my mother was one of its chief architects. From that moment on, I decided none would be above suspicion. If Nagarythe had become so polluted, so too perhaps had Tiranoc. My arrival here was delayed by investigations, when it was brought to my attention that those close to the Phoenix King might be under the sway of the hedonists. My inquiries were circumspect but thorough, and imagine my disappointment, nay disbelief, when I uncovered evidence that implicated the Phoenix King himself.'

'What evidence?' demanded Elodhir.

'Certain talismans and fetishes found in the Phoenix King's chambers,' said Malekith calmly. 'Believe me when I say that I felt as you did. I could not bring myself to think that Bel Shanaar, our wisest prince chosen to rule by members of this council, would be brought so low. Not one to act rashly, I decided to confront Bel Shanaar with this evidence, in the hope that there was some misunderstanding or trickery involved.'

'And he denied it of course?' asked Bathinair.

'He admitted guilt by his deeds,' explained Malekith. 'It seems that a few of my company were tainted by this affliction and in league with the usurpers of Nagarythe. Even as I confided in them, they warned Bel Shanaar of my discoveries. That night, no more than seven nights ago, I went to his chambers to make my accusations face-to-face. I found him dead, his lips stained with poison. He had taken the coward's way and ended his own life rather than suffer the shame of inquiry. By his own hand he denied us insight into the plans of the cults. Fearing that he would not keep their secrets to himself, he took them to his grave.'

'My father would do no such thing, he is loyal to Ulthuan and its people!' shouted Elodhir.

'I confess to having deep sympathy with you, Elodhir,' Malekith replied. 'Have I not been deceived by my own mother? Do I not feel the same betrayal and heartache that now wrenches at your spirit?'

'I must admit I also find this somewhat perturbing,' said Thyriol. 'It seems… convenient.'

'And so, in death, Bel Shanaar continues to divide us, as was his intent,' countered Malekith. 'Discord and anarchy will reign as we argue back and forth the rights and wrongs of what has occurred. While we debate endlessly, the cults will grow in power and seize your lands from under your noses, and we will have lost everything. They are united, while we are divided. There is no time for contemplation, or reflection, there is only time for action.'

'What would you have us do?' asked Chyllion, one of the princes of Cothique.

'We must choose a new Phoenix King!' declared Bathinair before Malekith could answer.

As HE APPROACHED the quay, Carathril watched the Naggarothi labouring on Malekith's ship. Amongst the throng, he spied a familiar face: Drutheira. Her hair was bleached white with a few blackened locks, but still the herald recognised her. Carathril pushed his way through the servants to where she stood on the dock, picking up a bale of cloth. She saw him approach and smiled.

'Carathril!' she gasped, grabbing his hand in both of hers. 'I thought perhaps never to see you again! Oh, this is joyous indeed!'

'Perhaps you can tell me what has happened to the Phoenix King?' said Carathril, and her smile faded.

'Why would you care about him?' she asked. 'Are you not happy to see me?'

'Of course,' said Carathril, uncertain. Seeing Drutheira had suddenly muddled his thoughts. Her eyes were glistening like mountain pools. Carathril struggled to concentrate.

'How is it that you come to be here?' he stammered. 'Why are you in the employ of Malekith?'

'He is a most noble prince,' she said, laying her hands upon Carathril's shoulders. A shiver of energy ran through him, setting his nerves alight at her touch. 'Glorious and magnanimous! When he is Phoenix King we shall all be well rewarded. You too, Carathril. He thinks very highly of you.'

'Malekith, the Phoenix King?' stammered Carathril. Something was wrong but he could think of nothing but Drutheira's pale flesh and the fragrance of her hair. 'Bel Shanaar is Phoenix–'

'Hush now,' said Drutheira, her voice a sighing breath. She stood on tiptoe so that her face was in front of his, her breath a breeze upon his cheek. 'Do not trouble yourself with the affairs of princes. Is it not marvellous that we can be together?'

'Together? What?' said Carathril, stepping away from her.

This attraction was not natural. Something thrashed inside Carathril's head, screaming for freedom. As soon as he broke her touch on him, his mind began to clear.

'You shall be his captain and herald, and I one of his handmaidens,' Drutheira said patiently, as if explaining herself to a child. 'We can live together in Anlec.'

'I am not going to Anlec,' said Carathril. Whatever Athartist enchantment she had woven was beginning to fade. Carathril's thoughts raced to catch up with what she had said. 'What has happened to the Phoenix King?'

She laughed, a sinister sound, and the gleam in her eye stirred fear in Carathril's heart.

'That fool Bel Shanaar is dead,' she said. 'Malekith will be Phoenix King, and he will reward well those that support him.'

Carathril stumbled back a few more paces, his mind reeling. In his confusion, he tripped over a coil of rope and sprawled to his back. Drutheira was over him in a moment, crouching close, her hand cupped to his face.

'Poor Carathril,' she purred. 'You cannot stop destiny, you must embrace it.'

Once again her touch dazzled Carathril before a moment of clarity engulfed him, as if a distant voice spoke to him: Bel Shanaar was dead and Malekith sought to become Phoenix King in his place. 'This cannot be allowed,' the voice said, 'Malekith is not fit to rule.' With a snarl, Carathril pushed Drutheira backwards and regained his feet. He stumbled into a run, heading back down the pier.

'Treachery!' he called. 'Beware!'

A few of Malekith's retainers tried to grab him, but he barged them aside and slapped away their grasping hands as he sprinted down onto the dock.

'To arms!' he shouted. 'Infamy is afoot!'

The Anlec knights drew their swords. Some turned towards Carathril, the rest advanced upon the shrine. Ahead of them the Phoenix Guards brought their halberds up to the ready.

'Is THAT YOUR intent?' asked Thyriol with a glance at the other princes.

'If the council wishes it,' Malekith said with a shrug.

'We cannot choose a new Phoenix King now,' said Elodhir. 'Such a matter cannot be resolved quickly, and even if such a thing were possible, we are not our full number.'

'Nagarythe will not wait,' said Malekith, slamming his fist onto the table. 'The cults are too strong and come spring they will control the army of Anlec. My lands will be lost and they will march upon yours!'

'You would have us choose you to lead us?' said Thyriol quietly.

'Yes,' Malekith replied without hesitation or embarrassment. 'There are none here who were willing to act until my return. I am the son of Aenarion, his chosen heir, and if the revelation of Bel Shanaar's treachery is not enough to convince you of the foolishness of choosing from another line, then look to my other achievements. Bel Shanaar chose me to act as his ambassador to the dwarfs for I was a close friend with their High King. Our future lies not solely upon these shores, but in the wider world. I have been to the colonies across the oceans, and fought to build and protect them. Though they come from the bloodstock of Lothern or Tor Elyr or Tor Anroc, they are a new people, and it is to me they first look now, not to you. None here are as experienced in war as am I. Bel Shanaar was a ruler steeped in wisdom and peace, for all that he has failed us at the last, but peace and wisdom will not prevail against darkness and zealotry.'

'What of Imrik?' suggested Finudel. 'He is every bit the general and fought out in the new world also.'

'Imrik?' said Malekith, his voice dripping with scorn. 'Where is Imrik now, in this time of our greatest need? He skulks in Chrace with his cousin, hunting monsters! Would you have Ulthuan ruled by an elf who hides in the mountains like a petulant, spoilt child? When Imrik called for an army to be gathered against Nagarythe, did you pay him heed? No! Only when I raised the banner did you fall over each other in your enthusiasm.'

'Be careful of what you say, your arrogance does you a disservice,' warned Haradrin.

'I say these things not as barbs to your pride,' explained Malekith, unclenching his fists and sitting down. 'I say them to show you what you already know; in your hearts you would gratefully follow where I lead.'

'I still say that this council cannot make such an important decision on a whim,' said Elodhir. 'My father lies dead, in circumstances yet to be fully explained, and you would have us hand over the Phoenix Crown to you?'

'He has a point, Malekith,' said Haradrin.

'A point?' screamed Malekith as he surged to his feet, knocking over the table and sending the cloak and crown upon it flying through the air. 'A point? Your dithering will see you all cast out, your families enslaved and your people burning upon ten thousand pyres! It has been more than a thousand years since I bent my knee to this council's first, wayward decision and saw Bel Shanaar take what Aenarion had promised to me. For a thousand years, I have been content to watch your families grow and prosper, and squabble amongst yourselves like children, while I and my kin bled on battlefields on the other side of the world. I trusted you all to remember the legacy of my father, and ignored the cries of anguish that rang in my blood; for it was in the interest of all that we were united. Now it is time to unite behind me! I do not lie to you, I shall be a harsh ruler at times, but I will reward those who serve me well, and when peace reigns again we shall all enjoy the spoils of our battles. Who here has more right to the throne than I do? Who here–'

'Malekith!' barked Mianderin, pointing towards the prince's waist. In his tirade, Malekith's waving arms had thrown his cloak back over his shoulder. 'Why do you wear your sword in this holy place? It is forbidden in the most ancient laws of this temple. Remove it at once.'

Malekith stood frozen in place, almost comic with his arms outstretched. He looked down at his belt and the sheathed sword that hung there. He gripped Avanuir's hilt in one hand and pulled it free, then looked up at the princes, his eyes narrowed, his face illuminated by magical blue fire.

'Enough words!' he spat.

CARATHRIL DUCKED BENEATH the sword of a Naggarothi knight and then rolled forwards, back onto his feet, before leaping aside to dodge another blade swung at his chest. He had no weapon of his own; why would he have come armed to such a council? It was a decision he was swiftly regretting.

Another knight thrust his sword at Carathril's throat and the captain swayed aside just in time and grabbed the knight's arm. With a twist, he broke the Naggarothi's elbow, the sword cascading from his enemy's grip to embed itself point first in the marble tiles of the shrine's surrounds.

He swung the knight around into the path of another blade, which lanced between his captive's shoulders and jutted from his chest just a hand's span from Carathril's face. Hurling the dead knight backwards, Carathril snatched up the fallen sword and parried another blow. Risking a look over his shoulder, Carathril saw that he was still more than a hundred paces from the shrine, and everywhere the Phoenix Guards fought against the knights. The only noise they made was the clash of their halberds upon sword and armour. With a grunt, Carathril shouldered aside another foe and made a break for the entrance.

* * *

'It is my right to be Phoenix King,' growled Malekith. 'It is not yours to give, so I will gladly take it.'

'Traitor!' screamed Elodhir, leaping across the table in front of him, scattering goblets and plates. There was uproar as princes and priests shouted and shrieked.

Elodhir dashed across the shrine, and was halfway upon Malekith when Bathinair intercepted him, sending both of them tumbling down in a welter of robes and rugs. Elodhir punched the Yvressian prince, who reeled back. With a snarl, Bathinair reached into his robes and pulled out a curved blade, no longer than a finger, and slashed at Elodhir. Its blade caught the prince's throat and his lifeblood fountained across the exposed flagstones.

As Bathinair crouched panting over the body of Elodhir, figures appeared at the archway behind Malekith: black-armoured knights of Anlec. The priests and princes who had been running for the arch slipped and collided with each other in their haste to stop their flight. The knights had blood-slicked blades in the hands and advanced with sinister purpose.

Malekith was serene; all trace of his earlier anger had disappeared. He walked slowly forwards as his knights cut and hacked at the princes around him, his eyes never leaving the sacred flame in the centre of the chamber. Screams and howls echoed from the walls but the prince was oblivious to all but the fire.

Out of the melee, Haradrin ran towards Malekith, a captured sword raised above his head. With a contemptuous sneer, the prince of Nagarythe stepped aside from Haradrin's wild swing and thrust his own sword into Haradrin's gut. He stood there a moment, the princes staring deep into each other's eyes, until a trickle of blood spilled from Haradrin's lips and he collapsed to the floor.

Malekith let the sword fall from his fingers with the body rather than wrench it free, and continued his pacing towards the sacred fire.

'Asuryan will not accept you!' cried Mianderin, falling to his knees in front of Malekith, his hands clasped in pleading. 'You have spilt blood in his sacred temple! We have not cast the proper enchantments to protect you from the flames. You cannot do this!'

'So?' spat the prince. 'I am Aenarion's heir. I do not need your witchery to protect me.'

Mianderin snatched at Malekith's hand but the prince tore his fingers from the haruspex's grasp.

'I no longer listen to the protestations of priests,' said Malekith and kicked Mianderin aside.

His hands held out, palms upwards in supplication, Malekith walked forwards and stepped into the flames.

CARATHRIL LEANED AGAINST a column, catching his breath. He had seen several knights enter the shrine, but the fighting outside was almost done. White-robed corpses littered the plaza alongside black-armoured bodies. Pushing himself upright, his heart hammering, Carathril took a step towards the shrine.

At that moment the ground lurched and flung Carathril from his feet.

The earth beneath him shook violently and columns toppled around him as the Isle of Flame was gripped by an earthquake. The isle heaved violently, tossing Carathril to the left and right before sending him hurtling into a falling pillar. He narrowly rolled aside as more masonry showered down from the cloister, crashing upon the cracking marble tiles.

Overhead dark clouds instantly gathered, swathing the island in gloom; lightning flickered upon their surface and a chill descended. Thunderous growling shook the earth underfoot as the herald forced himself back to his feet. Amongst the roaring and crashing, Carathril heard a terrifying shriek: a drawn-out wail of utter pain that pierced his soul.

WITHIN THE SHRINE, prince, priest and knight alike were tossed around by the great heaving. Chairs were flung across the floor and tables toppled. Plaster cracked upon the walls and fell in large slabs from the ceiling. Wide cracks tore through the tiles underfoot and a rift three paces wide opened up along the eastern wall, sending up a choking spume of dust and rock.

The flame of Asuryan burned paler and paler, moving from a deep blue to a brilliant white. At its heart could be seen the silhouette of Malekith, his arms still outstretched.

With a thunderous clap, the holy flame blazed, filling the room with white light. Within, Malekith collapsed to his knees and grabbed at his face.

He was burning.

He flung back his head and screamed as the flames consumed him; his howl of anguish reverberated around the shrine, echoing and growing in volume with every passing moment. The withering figure silhouetted within the flames pushed himself slowly to his feet and hurled himself from their depths.

Malekith's smoking and charred body crashed to the ground, igniting a rug and sending ashen dust billowing. Blackened flesh fell away in lumps amidst cooling droplets of molten armour. He reached outwards with a hand, and then collapsed. His clothes had been burned away and his flesh eaten down to the bone in places. His face was a mask of black and red, his dark eyes lidless and staring. Steam rose from burst veins as the prince of Nagarythe shuddered and then fell still, laid to ruin by the judgement of Asuryan.

Soon, all of Ulthuan would burn.

GLOSSARY

Aeltherin – Prince of Eataine who oversaw the construction of the first dragonships.

Aenarion – The first Phoenix King, saviour of the elves.

Aerenis – Lieutenant to Carathril of Lothern.

Aernuis – Prince of Eataine, one of the first to sail across the Great Ocean.

Alandrian – Lieutenant of Malekith.

Alith – Grandson of Eoloran of House Anar.

Anlec – Principal city of Nagarythe and location of Aenarion's palace.

Annulii Mountains – Chain of mountains separating the Inner and Outer Kingdoms of Ulthuan. Laced with magic, it is the home to many monstrous beasts.

Astarielle – Everqueen and first wife of Aenarion.

Asuryan – The Allfather, greatest of the elven gods.

Athel Toralien – Colony in Elthin Arvan.

Athielle – Princess of Ellyrion.

Avanuir – Magical sword carried by Malekith.

Avelorn – Oldest of the kingdoms of Ulthuan, ruled by the Everqueen. Its forests are home to many fey creatures.

Bathinair – Prince of Yvresse.

Bel Shanaar – The second Phoenix King, and ruler of Tiranoc.

Blighted Isle – Lifeless island to the north of Ulthuan, site of the Shrine of Khaine and resting place of the Widowmaker.

Caledor – Mountainous kingdom of Ulthuan, home to the dragons.

Caledor Dragontamer – Mighty mage, founder of the kingdom of Caledor and creator of the great vortex.

Carathril – Captain of the Lothern Guard.

Charill – Prince of Chrace.

Chrace – Wild kingdom in the north of Ulthuan, famed for its white lions.

Circlet of Iron – Ancient artefact of immense power, discovered by Malekith in the frozen northlands.

Cothique – Kingdom in the north of Ulthuan.

Cytharai – The twilight pantheon, gods embodying the darker aspects of the elven psyche.

Drutheira – Priestess of Atharti.

Durinne – Prince of Galthyr.

Ealith – Fortress in Nagarythe, south of Anlec.

Eataine – Kingdom of Ulthuan. Its riches come from the great city-port of Lothern.

Ellyrion – Kingdom of Ulthuan, famed for its horses.

Elodhir – Prince of Tiranoc and son to Bel Shanaar.

Elthin Arvan – Landmass across the Great Ocean, home to the dwarfs.

Elthuir Tarai – Site of the battle where Aenarion first wielded the Widowmaker in battle.

Elthyrior – One of the raven heralds of Nagarythe, agent of Malekith.

Eoloran – Prince of House Anar, a powerful faction in Nagarythe.

Everqueen – Title held by the chief priestess of Isha. Before Aenarion the Everqueen ruled all of Ulthuan.

Finudel – Ruler of Ellyrion, brother of Athielle.

Galthyr – Chief port of Nagarythe.

Great vortex, the – Magical siphon located on the Isle of the Dead at the centre of the Inner Sea, where the winds of magic drain from the world.

Grimnir – Dwarf Ancestor God who travelled north to close the gate of Chaos.

Grungni – Dwarf Ancestor God, who taught his people mining and smithing.

Haradrin – Prince of Eataine.

Imrik – Prince of Caledor and grandson of Caledor Dragontamer. A famed warrior, noted for his lack of diplomacy.

Indraugnir – Greatest of the race of dragons, and mount of Aenarion.

Indraugnir – First of the dragonships, a gift from Aeltherin.

Isha – Elven goddess of fertility.

Isle of Flame – Located in the Sea of Dreams, site of the Shrine of Asuryan.

Isle of the Dead – Located at the centre of the Inner Sea, the epicentre for the great vortex that drains magic from the world.

Ithilmar – Extremely rare metal found in the mountains of Caledor. It is used to make resilient yet light armour.

Karak Kadrin – Dwarf hold located at the head of Peak Pass in the north of the dwarf lands.

Karaz-a-Karak – Greatest city of the dwarfs and home to the High King.

Khaine – Elven god of murder, whose shrine lies on the Blighted Isle.

Kurgrik – Dwarf thane of Karaz-a-Karak.

Kurnous – Elven god of the hunt.

Lorhir – Captain of the city guard of Athel Toralien.

Lothern – City of Eataine, Ulthuan's greatest port.

Malekith – Prince of Nagarythe, son of Aenarion and Morathi.

Menieth – Prince of Caledor, son of Caledor Dragontamer and father of Imrik.

Mianderin – High priest of the Shrine of Asuryan.

Morathi – The seeress-queen of Nagarythe, Mother of Malekith and widow of Aenarion.

Morelion – Son of Aenarion and Astarielle, half-brother to Malekith.

Naganath – Border river in the south of Nagarythe.

Nagarythe – Kingdom of Ulthuan, founded by Aenarion and ruled by Malekith.

Oakheart – Treeman who rescued Morelion and Yvraine when Avelorn was invaded by daemons.

Palthrain – Chamberlain to Bel Shanaar.

Phoenix Guard – Guardians of the Shrine of Asuryan, who hold a vow of silence.

Phoenix King – Title held by the ruler of Ulthuan. Aenarion was the first Phoenix King.

Redclaw – Griffon ridden by Bathinair, prince of Yvresse.

Saphery – Kingdom of Ulthuan, famed for its mages.

Snorri Whitebeard – First High King of the dwarfs.

Sutherai – Lieutenant of Aernuis.

Sword of Khaine – The Widowmaker, the deadliest weapon of all time and said to bring ruin upon any who wield it.

Throndik – Son of Snorri Whitebeard.

Thyriol – Prince of Saphery and a mighty mage.

Tiranoc – Kingdom of Ulthuan, homeland of Bel Shanaar.

Tor Anroc – Principal city of Tiranoc, and home to Bel Shanaar.

Ungdrin Ankor – Extensive tunnel network connecting the dwarf empire.

Valaya – Dwarf Ancestor God, protector of the holds.

Vaul – Elven smith-god.

Yeasir – Lieutenant of Malekith.

Yvraine – Everqueen of Ulthuan, Daughter of Aenarion and Astarielle, and half-sister of Malekith.

Yvresse – Kingdom of Ulthuan.

ABOUT THE AUTHOR

Gav Thorpe has been rampaging across the worlds of Warhammer and Warhammer 40,000 for many years as both an author and games developer. He hails from the den of scurvy outlaws called Nottingham and makes regular sorties to unleash bloodshed and mayhem. He is aided and abetted by a mechanical hamster known only as Dennis, who will one day integrate with the nuclear defence systems of the world and hold us all to ransom.

HELDENHAMMER

The Legend of Sigmar

GRAHAM McNEILL

ISBN 978-1-84416-538-4

Wolfgart's horse pulled to a halt beside Sigmar, and his sword-brother put up his war horn to draw his great sword from the sheath across his back. Wolfgart's face was a mirror of his own, with a sheen of sweat and teeth bared in ferocious battle fury.

Pendrag rode alongside, his war axe unsheathed, and said, 'Time to get bloody!'

Sigmar raked back his heels and said, 'Remember, two blasts of the horn and we ride for the bridge!'

'It's not me you need worry about!' laughed Pendrag as Wolfgart urged his mount forward, his huge sword swinging around his head in wide decapitating arcs.

Sigmar and Pendrag thundered after their friend as the pursuing mob of orcs drew near. The re-formed Unberogen horsemen followed their leaders, charging with all the fury and power they were famed for, a howling war cry taken up by every warrior as they hurled their spears, before drawing swords or hefting axes.

More orcs fell, and Sigmar skewered a thick-bodied orc, who wore a great, antlered helmet, the spear punching down though the creature's breastplate and pinning it to the ground. Even as the spear quivered in the orc's chest, Sigmar reached down and swept up his hammer, Ghal-maraz, the mighty gift presented to him by Kurgan Ironbeard earlier that spring.

Then the two ancestral enemies slammed together in a thunderclap of iron and rage.

Buy this book or read a further extract at
www.blacklibrary.com